HEAVEN

Shi Po tamped down the elation that surged through her, focusing all her attention on riding the yin-yang tigress to her destination. The Heavenly portal was just ahead; she was sure of it. Indeed, she had already arrived at the antechamber: the Room of a Thousand Swinging Lanterns.

She had attained this level before, though many years ago. Indeed, the peace and joy of the space was tainted for her, the beauty of the swinging lights dimmed from her first experience. And yet, she still found great joy in the feeling of absolute rightness that pervaded the antechamber. Only here could she stand tall. Only here did she breathe without restriction and dance without pain. She'd forgotten how much she loved this place.

The darkness shifted, and the lights folded back. Shi Po strained forward, anxious to see what came next. What would be her future? What might ensure her status on Earth as an immortal? What...

Kui Yu? Her husband?

Other *Leisure* books by Jade Lee:

HUNGRY TIGRESS
WHITE TIGRESS
DEVIL'S BARGAIN

Desperate Tigress

JADE LEE

LEISURE BOOKS NEW YORK CITY

To my husband, David,
for always making me laugh.
Thank you, my love.

A LEISURE BOOK®

November 2005

Published by

Dorchester Publishing Co., Inc.
200 Madison Avenue
New York, NY 10016

ISBN 0-8439-5505-8

Printed in the United States of America.

Visit us on the web at www.dorchesterpub.com.

Desperate Tigress

A businessman was trying to teach his young son to talk flexibly—neither saying yes or no, but remaining ambiguous. "For example," he said, "if someone wanted to borrow food, you could answer, 'I don't know whether we have that or not. Let me have a look, and I will tell you later.'"

The boy kept his father's words in mind, so when a visitor asked if his father was in, the son replied:

"I'm sorry. Some are in, some are not. Let me have a look, and I will tell you later."

Chapter One

Shanghai, 1898

She knew!

The white woman knew the way to Heaven!

Shi Po pounded down the stairs to the front hallway, her bound feet protesting every stunned, angry, awed and gleeful step. She had no idea how she could feel all those things at once, especially since she had felt nothing for so many years. But she did. And her feet protested, pain forcing her to soften her steps.

In any case, it would be suicide to enter a general's presence appearing anything other than vapidly stupid, so Shi Po moderated her pace and pasted on her face an expression of ox-like placidity. She would appear as any wealthy woman in China: a useless thing of beauty. The servants handed her a tea tray, and she was soon pushing into the receiving room while struggling to quiet her spirit.

1

The General was an ugly man. That was her first thought. Not ugly in a physical sense, but in his fortune. His body was handsome enough, she supposed. His shoulders were broad and imposing, especially with his leather armor; his Manchu queue was dark and thick, the tight braid clubbed close to his head. But his face revealed the ugliness of bad fortune. His head was short and compact, depicting little luck, except for his chin which was long and pointed, suggesting a happier old age. His earlobes were also long and full, but Shi Po did not trust that. She guessed that his mother had tugged incessantly at his ears to counteract the fortune in his face.

The most damning evidence of all, though, was not in his body, but in the stench that pervaded the room. Horse and man and Shanghai mud produced a commonplace odor, a thick and sour stench that burned the back of one's nostrils. But all men in Shanghai carried that particular curse to some degree. It was the other smell that made Shi Po duck her head and wish for her perfumed oils. He carried the decay-like scent of fear covered by anger. And the smell of old blood.

This man was a killer. Not just a general of the Imperial Qin army, but a murderer of innocents. Of that she was certain.

"Tea, your honor," she said as she minced through the room. "To pass the time until my husband returns." She wished she'd had time to change out of her red skirt with the fashionable slits up to mid-thigh; she had no desire to display herself before this man. But perhaps the garb would help her appear completely useless.

One look at the General's thickly compressed eyebrows damped Shi Po's hopes. He saw through her feigned stupidity. And even if he didn't, this man disposed of useless, silly things. Of course, that did not stop the man from studying her face and body closely. Lust twisted his features as his gaze traveled from her high knot of black hair across features that she knew appeared extraordinarily young. Though she was nearing her fortieth year, her skin was milky white and her eyes and lips were expertly painted to appear lush. Her bones had always been fine, but her Tigress practice made her entire body lithe and willowy. Youth and beauty were a natural by-product of that practice. All her students drew the eye as they moved, Shi Po most of all. So she remained as still as she could, even though it hurt her tiny bound feet.

"You are Tan Shi Po?" he demanded in his northern Mandarin dialect.

She dipped in a respectful bow, answering in kind, though the language was difficult for her, Shanghai-born as she was. "Yes, your honor."

"When will your husband return?"

"He was sent for the moment you arrived." She folded her body onto a pillow near a low table.

All the cushions in Shi Po's home were scented with soothing, pleasant herbs, and the one she settled on was no different. So as she leaned forward to mix leaves and hot water in the General's cup, she should have inhaled the sweet scent of radish seed and cinnamon, ci shi and sandalwood. She didn't. Instead, she smelled the same vile mixture of fear and anger, rising like steam from her own skin.

She hated that women must serve as mirrors to men, reflecting their emotions. Women in the Empire had no voice of their own. They did as they were told, hiding their true selves or risking abuse and death. Even Shi Po as head Tigress—*especially* Shi Po—had to appear subservient. But there was power in submission, especially when one became a mirror. When one showed a man what he wanted to see most of all: himself. His emotions and desires. Shi Po had perfected that skill to the point of unconscious reaction. She reflected all around her whether she willed it or not. So when the General showed fear, she shared it with him. His anger sparked her rage. And no amount of tea or sweet herbs could cover the disgusting fumes that now rose from both of their bodies.

Shi Po poured the General's tea, her hands steady through an act of will. But all the while her thoughts writhed in her mind, searching for escape. Where was her husband? Surely he would be found soon. Kui Yu would not disregard an Imperial summons, especially when it came in the form of the most powerful general in China. He would be here soon, she reassured herself, and with his return, she could shift back, regain her calm. She would absorb her husband's quietness; her fear would fade, the rage dissipate, and she would be in balance again. As soon as Kui Yu returned.

"Might I know how to best serve your honor?" she simpered to the General, forcing herself into the aspect of total feminine subservience.

The man sipped his tea and grimaced before setting it aside. She had chosen tea leaves to purify and soothe, but he pushed his cup away. Clearly his spirit had no desire to moderate its temper. She bowed her head, softening her body in an attempt to distort the mirror she was; she did not want to increase her reflection of his foul aspect.

His harsh words interrupted her thoughts. "You are Tan Shi Po, sister to the traitor Abbot Tseng Rui Po."

She flinched, unable to keep a surge of blood from heating her face. Fortunately, she was able to shift her attitude to wounded confusion, as if he had just hurt a helpless animal.

"Why would you say such a thing?" she whispered.

"Because it is true." His tone was hard as hurled stone. "And he has paid for his crimes. He and all his so-called monks."

She Po already knew her brother was dead. The last of his students—a Manchurian—had brought the evil news some days ago. Along with a white girl. *The* white girl. The two had already managed to sow discord in her quiet little school. But Shi Po could not allow the General to know that, so she raised stricken eyes to him.

"Paid?" she gasped. "How . . . ?" She swallowed, making sure her voice remained breathy. "Please, sir, what were his crimes? And how . . . how did he pay?"

The General leaned forward, using his superior height to intimidate. In this, however, he failed, because the angle gave Shi Po a good view of the thin space between his upper lip and his nose. Indeed, this man was doomed by fortune, and that thought alone heartened her.

"Your brother trained rebels of the White Lotus Society. He and all his misguided followers have been executed for their foolishness." The General slowed his words for maximum effect, and Shi Po found her gaze pulled from his thin lip to his piercing eyes. "All are dead save one student. One man spared to pass the warning." He pushed loudly to his feet. "You know where this man is, Tan Shi Po. And you will take me to him. Now."

Such was the power of the General's spirit that Shi Po found herself rising. But she was a mirror; as his strength increased, so did her own.

"I know nothing of this," she lied. "Are you sure? Abbot Tseng of the Shiyu monastery?"

The General would have none of it. His hand was huge, the pressure intense where he gripped her arm, lifting Shi Po to her feet. His leg knocked the table, spilling his tea onto the ancient wood floor. He ignored it, focused on her.

"One monk. Carrying sacred scrolls. He came to you." Though he spoke it as fact, Shi Po felt a quiver of doubt through the General's hand. The man was guessing, hoping he was correct.

Which, of course, he was.

She shook her head, pretending to be stunned by her brother's death. "Rui Po!" she wailed, tears flowing like a river as would be expected from a woman at any relative's death. Indeed, over the years she had perfected the skill of crying on demand. But this time Shi Po's grief was real, the pain of her brother's death still fresh.

The General dismissed her with a grunt. "I will search your home now."

"But why?" she gasped through her tears. "I know nothing of your monk."

He turned, his eyes on fire, the stench of his fear keeping her on her knees. "Because he *is my* monk, Tigress Shi Po."

Shi Po barely registered the words. Her gaze, her mind—indeed, her entire spirit—was caught by the vision of the General's body in profile. A light reflected up from the polished floor, or maybe a similarity in gesture, revealed the secret. Both men were Manchu, after all. Both were warriors, for all that one was a monk. Whatever the cause, the truth burst into her mind:

"You are his *father*," she said.

And in that moment, all changed. Days before, Shi Po had accepted the truth-seeker into her home, the monk with political connections who needed time to recover from the massacre of his entire monastery. The monk, who had brought news of her brother. Now Shi Po knew she was keeping a father from his son—a sin punishable by death.

She rose to her feet, balancing precariously on her tiny heels as she wiped away her tears. The General was silent, his fury betrayed by clenched fists. "You know nothing about my son," he said with a growl. "Do not presume to understand your betters, Han sorceress."

Shi Po's gaze dropped to the floor, only now remembering he had called her by her title. *Tigress,* he had said. He knew who she was, what she was, and so cursed her as a sorceress. At least that was better than being called a whore.

"I merely guess, my lord." Her words grew softer, full of feminine modesty. "Only a father could claim a monk as his own."

"And only the unnatural leader of a twisted religion would dare deny me," he replied.

She had not denied him anything—yet. The insults to her calling she credited as noise from a monkey's mouth. And yet, her problem remained: She sheltered General Kang's son. Part of her longed to turn the boy over for bringing this trouble to her home.

"My house," she said, "is open to you. All except the women's quarters." She looked up, but kept herself blank, trying to stop reflecting his venom. "You are a powerful man in form and spirit. I cannot risk the chaos your presence would have on the delicate ladies of my household."

"You mean the misguided whores of your perverse religion."

She said nothing. Indeed, if he knew enough to call her a Tigress, then he knew enough to be enlightened if he chose. Obviously, he did not. She had no choice but to accept his condemnation, for such was the lot of all women in China, whether Manchurian or Han.

He continued to glare at her, his eyes narrowed in his pinched face. "I have no interest in your women. My son would not contaminate himself with the likes of you."

How she wished to tell the General the truth. Not only was his son contaminating himself with the Tigress "perversions," he did so with a white woman. But saying such a thing would be to hand the General a torch to burn her house to the ground—with herself and her followers all inside. So she remained silent, moving slowly forward and exaggerating the difficulty of walking on bound feet.

She led him through the main house, pausing only as the General motioned for six soldiers to accompany them. She remained gracious throughout, for that was a woman's duty. Even as the soldiers pushed aside large urns of rice or banged through the pots. They disturbed cats and servants, dragged aside tapestries and furniture. And they found nothing, of course, even though they dug their filthy hands deep into sacks of vegetables and piles of linens.

He was kind in that his men were careful. But Shi Po's sense of violation increased as the General's men pulled up floorboards looking for secret caches and poured water onto stone floors looking for hidden pits. Her entire home was disrupted, and she could do nothing but stand aside and watch.

Until she heard a scream. It came from the women's

quarters: the building where her students practiced; the place of many bedrooms, including the one that sheltered the General's son and his white partner.

Shi Po spun on her heel, grabbing the wall as she teetered, then rushed toward the sound. The General followed. She moved faster, knowing her home and the handholds needed to travel quickly to the inside garden. She guessed what had happened. Knew, in fact, from the very beginning that such a thing was coming. Still, she had thought her husband would return by now and find a way to prevent it. But Kui Yu was not here.

Shi Po scurried around the goldfish fountain and flowering lotus to see her best student—Little Pearl—struggling in the grip of a soldier. More of the General's men were throwing open doors, roughly dragging her Tigress cubs outside. Fortunately, none had partners with them. The servants had already seen to the gentlemen's escape.

All except one: the monk. No, she silently corrected herself. *The General's son.*

Shi Po slowed her pace, her mind working furiously. She could not afford a rash action here. The soldiers would soon work their way to the monk's room.

The General made his way over to her, and she rounded on him, allowing her fury to boil over. Tears and supplication had not worked with the man; she would try outrage.

"How can you be so cruel?" she screeched. "You swore to me you would not upset these ladies' delicate conditions!" Right on cue, her cubs descended into wails, not all of which were feigned. "Is the word of an Imperial general worth so little?"

"My gravest apologies, Lady Tan," Kang said as he took in every detail: her cubs' beauty, their fit figures, their easily removable clothing. "My men misunderstood my direction. Their actions were rash."

Shi Po sincerely doubted his men had misunderstood anything, but she held her tongue. Especially as the General ordered the soldiers to release the women. They did, but their lewd and hungry eyes continued to travel over the girls. At least none of her students seemed harmed.

Shi Po sent a speaking look to Little Pearl, who nodded her head and quickly shepherded the other cubs away. They would be given mundane clothing to wear, and each would disappear to their homes. Those who had nowhere to go would dress as deformed servants—scullery maids with dark red rashes or diseased beggars come inside for a crumb of bread. There would be no trace of the beauties that studied with her, and so they would be safe.

Not so with the monk and his white woman who were hiding on the upper floor, relying on Shi Po to keep them safe.

"General, call all your men back! I have sick women upstairs," she lied.

"Disease is a natural result of your unholy work," he replied in a bored tone. Then he spoke to his lieutenant: "Tell them to be wary of foulness."

"You said they would not disturb the women!" Shi Po cried again.

"Oh yes," General Kang drawled. "An error on my part. No harm done. My men will return in a moment."

What could she do? Nothing. Only scramble for an excuse for not having handed over the monk and his white woman earlier. And still there was no sign of Kui Yu. There was no rescue from her husband or the doom that awaited her.

She swallowed. "General Kang, surely this is not necessary. You can see—"

"Silence, sorceress. You have no voice here."

For emphasis, the nearest soldier drew his sword, the scrape of metal loud in the perfumed garden. All around Shi Po, the men tensed, ready to battle whatever mystical forces might appear between her ornamental bushes and sweet-smelling grasses. Their pose might have been funny if they weren't so earnest—if they didn't truly think she was some evil mystic they planned to kill if the wind so much as rustled in the trees.

"Very well," she murmured, her spirit struggling against the inevitable. There was nothing she could do to help the monk and his woman; she would do what she could to protect herself and her students. "I will see to my distraught women." She turned, intending to walk calmly and quickly out of the garden.

"You will wait upon my pleasure, Tigress." The General sneered her title, the sound so foul she would have preferred to be called a whore.

It was on the tip of her tongue to say that men waited upon *her* pleasure, not the other way around. Why else would she become a Tigress? But then there was a commotion from the building, and she managed—just barely—to keep her tongue.

"Anything?" the General called out to his men, his voice as tight as his face.

One soldier appeared. Two. Then two more exited the building. But no monk. And no white girl.

"We found empty bedrooms, General. Rumpled sheets. Water in the basins. But no people, diseased or otherwise."

The General stepped forward, the smell of his anger and fear multiplying. "No one?"

"No, sir."

"Were there signs of a man? Anything that would indicate—"

"Nothing, General. Just rumpled sheets and water."

Shi Po listened with a bowed head, her eyes carefully downcast. They had found nothing? No monk? No ghost woman? She lifted her gaze, narrowing her eyes as she tried to imagine where the two might be hiding. Where would the white woman go?

She cared nothing for the monk, except for the desire that he and his father quit her home immediately. That he had escaped meant nothing to her, as long as he left the girl behind. Shi Po had been most explicit. She had told the white woman to stay here, and the white woman had nodded in agreement.

Now, where was she?

Shi Po's anger got the best of her, and she pushed forward. "What of the sick girl? The one with no voice. She is not there?"

The soldier didn't look at her, answering her question as if the General had posed it. "No one, sir. No sick women. And no men at all. We searched most thoroughly."

General Kang spit out a curse that echoed through the garden. Shi Po would have blushed if she were not thinking the same thing. Where had the woman gone? She had to find her. Immortality depended upon it.

But first she had an angry general to deal with, and no husband to take the weight from her shoulders. "You see, do you not, that you were misinformed?" she said. "I do not know where your . . ." She would have said son, but the General's eyes narrowed to slits and she hastily changed her words. "Your monk is

12

not in my home. Please, you have disrupted everything. Will you not leave me in peace?"

The General stepped up to her. His body, his smell,
his very presence was poisonous. "If I find you
lie . . ." He did not complete his threat. He did not
need to. All knew what he meant.

She bowed her head. "He is not here. And I have no
way to find him." She spoke the truth, and it was her
doom. For the white girl was surely with the monk,
the pair fled to a place where neither general nor Tigress could discover them.

General Kang wasted no more time on her. Issuing
orders with a sharp tongue, he and his soldiers departed quickly, leaving noise and clutter and anxious
servants in their wake.

It was only after he was gone, after the last sound
of armor and horses faded from the street that Shi Po
allowed herself to move. Then, with heavy steps, she
moved through her building. It was empty; every
room open, every piece of furniture disturbed. She
did not need to walk to their room to know the truth;
she felt it in the still and suddenly sour air:

The white woman was gone.

And so Shi Po would die.

Kui Yu jumped from the rickshaw. His long, black
Manchurian queue bounced on his back as he ran
through the front gate. Fear churned in his belly as
his thoughts boiled. Why would an Imperial General
come to his home? On today of all days, when he was
with Lily and nowhere to be found?

He rushed through the receiving room and into the
back garden. What had Shi Po done now? He should
have paid more attention to her activities. A man was
responsible for his home, but what his wife did with

her women was of little interest to him. And what she did with the men left him cold and resentful. So he had looked the other way. And now an Imperial General had invaded his home.

His steps faltered. Vague impressions hit him— some from memory, some from what was directly in front of him. First he recalled the receiving room. Though he couldn't quite remember what, something had been amiss there. Something was skewed. And looking about, he felt the same strangeness in the garden but could not identify what he perceived. A branch was broken here. A stone was kicked into the pathway there. But what . . . ?

Silence.

There was total and absolute silence. Not from the birds or cats, not even from the wind in the trees or the clatter of wheels on the distant road; this was a different silence. A human silence. It was the absence of servant noise, of students in their rooms, of people anywhere.

Was his home deserted?

No. Here came a maid, sidling close. What was her name? He couldn't remember. His wife took in females from all over China: destitute girls, abandoned girls, girls of ill-repute. It seemed that all found their way to his home, were given a fresh start, then eventually went on their way.

So, what was this one's name?

"Master. Master, you are home." The maid probably meant to exclaim loudly, but her voice was too soft, her demeanor too quiet. Indeed, she was nearly on top of him before he realized she was speaking.

"What has happened?" he asked. The girl shied backwards and her eyes widened in alarm. He tried to soften his expression, but some of the maids were too delicate for his coarse features. He was a large man, strong and intense. His face was common and his hands were calloused with labor. But he was still master here and he required answers. "Where is Shi Po?"

"The mistress is in her meditation chamber."

Kui Yu nodded, knowing that was where Shi Po always sought refuge. At least she was not dead or arrested.

"What happened this afternoon? Are all the Imperial soldiers gone?"

She bowed and said again, "The mistress is in her meditation chamber."

"Yes, yes," he snapped. "But tell me—"

She grabbed his arm—a bold and shocking gesture for one so timid—and tugged him toward the private family quarters. "The mistress," she repeated.

Clearly he would get no more answers from her. So he pressed his lips together and lengthened his stride. All too soon the maid fell behind, and he maneuvered through the garden alone and into his disturbed home toward his wife's most private chamber.

The antechamber was in typical disarray. This was the room where Shi Po vented her spleen—on walls and furniture and clothing. It was always in chaos, and no cushion ever survived beyond a week. Kui Yu called it the Place of Ill Humors, for this was where Shi Po destroyed things as she released her frustrations. And when she was done, she would calmly and quietly walk into her meditation room. There she would sit in contemplation, her eyes half closed, her body completely still. Having just purged her ill humors, she was able to exist in absolute stillness.

That the room was completely destroyed did not surprise him; any visit by an Imperial general would likely produce a vehement response. So he stepped past the splinters of cheap wood and shredded cotton. He walked to the door of her meditation chamber, coming to stand beside it, his heart pounding until he feared it would jump from his throat. He opened the door.

His wife sat in the center of the room, her eyes fully open, her legs pushed out before her and not folded neatly in her meditative pose. To the side, Kui Yu saw rice cakes and wine, a mango and steamed dumplings. All these foods most tempted his wife, but she had not touched a single one. Nearby the statue of Kwan Yin, Goddess of Hope, stood in shadow. The altar candles had guttered into darkness. And set before Shi Po, arrayed in a line, were a hanging noose, a tea cup and vial of something unnamed, a cage of two scorpions, and lastly, a long, thin dagger.

Kui Yu stared, speechless. The Chinese were always aware of death, his wife much more than most. To see these things arrayed in front of her told him she had moved beyond thinking to planning.

"You are late." His wife's voice was flat. Dull.

He swallowed, his guilt overwhelming as he fought for balance. "I came as soon as the messenger found me."

"Then perhaps we should hire a new messenger."

Kui Yu nodded, though he knew it wasn't the boy's fault. He had worked hard to ensure he could not be found. He had not known an Imperial General would visit.

"Come in," his wife ordered.

He did as she bade him, easing the door shut before walking with steady, measured steps into the room. He sank to his knees before Shi Po, the long line of objects between them. They were all objects designed to kill.

"If you wish to die, a viper would be better than a pair of scorpions," he said. He did not know where the comment came from. Indeed, he had no wish to see his wife near any of the items. But that was his constant sin: speaking without thought, reaching for humor in situations that required extreme delicacy.

His wife looked at the small cage, a frown on her face. "You do not think two will suffice?"

He shook his head. "*You* would need a dozen at least."

She sighed, took the cage and carefully set it aside. "That is why I waited for you," she said. "You are wise."

He looked down at the remaining items, then picked up the vial. It was labeled, he now saw, but the words meant nothing to him. Given the other items, he expected it would be poison. A deadly one.

He set the vial back down and looked up at his wife. "Perhaps you should tell me exactly what occurred with General Kang. The messenger gave no details at all, and I have spoken to no one but you since returning home." It wasn't worth mentioning the taciturn maid.

His wife shrugged, the movement weary. "He came. He disliked my tea. He and his men searched the house, then left empty-handed."

"The monk? And the white woman?"

"Gone." She looked up at him, and for the first time that day, Kui Yu saw an emotion slip past Shi Po's control: anguish, deep and searing, and quickly masked. "They fled," she said. "Probably just in time." She swallowed, her gaze dropping back to the floor. "I told her to stay, but I could not prevent the soldiers from searching."

"But they found nothing, correct?" Kui Yu pressed. "There is nothing to prove we hid the woman or the—"

"General Kang's son."

He jerked back. "What?" He had heard her, of course, but it took time to imagine the implications. Shi Po understood, and waited in silence while his mind grappled with the possibilities. "General Kang is the most influential, most powerful man in China, with the exception of the Emperor and his mother," he said at last.

Shi Po nodded, encouraging him to voice his thoughts. This was the way they often spoke on important matters: She was silent, he wrestled aloud. In this she acted as a typical woman of China—silent and beautiful. He preferred it when she spoke.

"The monk," he continued. "The Manchurian. You are sure he is General Kang's son?"

She inclined her head, her shoulders swaying slightly with the movement.

"And we hid his son from him." It was not a question, so his wife said nothing. "We forced a white woman on him."

At this Shi Po looked up, her eyes flashing the fire that sometimes lit their dark depths. "*I* forced him. He wished to learn. I was the one to choose his partner."

He waved her comment away. "This is my house, Tan Shi Po. You may be the Tigress, but I am responsible for what happens here."

Her eyes burned with disobedience but then she lowered them, hiding their obsidian depths. Disobe-

18

dience was not all she hid, he knew, but he had no access to her thoughts. He never had. So he forced himself to continue his previous train of thought.

"The monk . . ." He pondered. "So, Kang's son is gone, running from his father for his own reasons. The white woman left with him." He saw his wife flinch at his words then still. Kui Yu waited, hoping she would speak, but she remained stubbornly silent. In the end, he continued: "They are gone. The general found nothing here to suspect."

"He needs no other reason," Shi Po snapped. "He knows of my faith, and accuses me of depravity with every breath."

"Then he is a fool," Kui Yu returned, both hating and admiring his wife for having chosen such a difficult path. "And powerful fools are always dangerous."

A moment later he frowned. "How did he know what you are?" he asked. The cult of the Tigress was virtually unknown in China. Few would accept a religion that embraced sex as a means to Enlightenment. Fewer still would learn from a woman. That the general knew of her practice and title suggested larger issues at work. And bigger danger.

Shi Po lifted her gaze to him, her pain obvious though she tried to hide it. "He murdered my brother."

Kui Yu sighed. He had suspected as much. There were few other ways the general could have learned the truth. "Because of a feud with his son?"

"It is a good guess," Shi Po agreed.

Kui Yu sighed again. "We are caught in a family struggle."

" 'When dragons fight, the rice field is destroyed,' " his wife quoted mournfully.

Kui Yu nodded, agreeing. Still, he was unable to explain the array of dangerous objects around her.

"Do you think to fight our way to safety?" he asked, ready to forbid such a rash action.

She frowned at him, obviously confused. "General Kang is gone. I do not fear his return."

"Then who will you poison? Or hang? Or stab?"

Suddenly, he knew the answer. A hanging cord was used for only one purpose. The poison as well, for it had a vile smell that could not be disguised. As for the dagger . . . He picked it up.

"Be careful!" she snapped, her hand jerking forward but stopping short of the blade. "It has been dipped in snake venom. The merest cut . . ."

He nodded. "So you did think of the viper." He looked at her face, trying to keep his expression open to encourage confession. "I am not dishonored by your life, wife. Why do you contemplate suicide?"

He watched her shoulders relax and knew that he had finally learned what she wanted to discuss. She said, "The ghost woman is gone." He blinked and waited for the full explanation, but Shi Po said nothing more. She sat, her eyes dull as old coal.

He played for time, repeating her words. "The white woman left. With Kang's son."

She nodded. Then, at his obvious confusion, she dropped another clue. "I told her to stay, but she left."

Kui Yu frowned. He still didn't understand. "She left despite your orders? She chose the Kang son over your tutelage?"

Shi Po nodded.

He shrugged. Many of Shi Po's students eventually chose a different path. Some left for husbands, some for the easier and wealthier life of prostitution. Therefore, the problem was less obvious than what she'd said.

"Why would you want the ghost woman to stay?" he asked. He purposely used the derogatory phrase for a white, knowing that Shi Po believed what the Emperor taught: The barbarians were insubstantial, ghostly, no more than animals. Indeed, she had once laughingly told him that one of her students kept a white woman as a pet—as his slave. So . . .

"Of what use was she?" he asked. "I thought her only purpose was to be a test of the Kang son."

His wife's eyes lowered, and her back slumped. She stared at her bound feet and tugged the edge of their binding. "Last night, the white girl practiced with the Kang son. It was her first time, and yet . . ."

As Shi Po's voice faded away, Kui Yu finally understood. "She touched heaven," he said. "On her first night of practice, she touched the divine." It was not a question. He could see the truth in his wife's posture.

Shi Po confirmed his guess with her anger, her every word torn from her like entrails. "She is a ghost person, too insubstantial to achieve even the smallest part of what I do!"

Kui Yu nodded, knowing that was what his wife believed.

"But Ru Shan's pet," Shi Po continued, her voice rising in outrage, "she also was a ghost woman, and she became an Immortal! He made me write her name on the tablet!" She gestured angrily at the sacred Tigress records arrayed along the walls of the meditation room.

Kui Yu tried to sum up. "You did not think whites could achieve Immortality. And now two of them—

the only two you have ever met—have achieved Immortality in a bare few months, whereas you—"

"The Kang boy's woman is not an Immortal!" she snapped.

No, she wasn't, realized Kui Yu silently. But she had obviously touched a part of Heaven that had come to Shi Po only after years of dedicated study.

"Why is it so easy for the whites?" he asked.

"I don't know," Shi Po answered, her voice breaking. "You know more of them than I. Do *you* know?"

He had no answer. He knew too little of the process of what she did. He should have paid more attention, but his time had been spent on his businesses. And she had never encouraged his curiosity.

"Is it because they are animals?" Shi Po wondered aloud. "Are they closer to their passions?"

Kui Yu remained silent, waiting to see where she went.

She sighed. "I think . . ." She swallowed. "I do not think the Emperor has been advised correctly. I think the white people are not fully barbarian."

Kui Yu nodded, but he was shocked. He remembered his own surprise the day he'd reached that conclusion, and now Shi Po had come to share his belief. He felt a glow of a pleasure. "You are wise, my wife, to see clearly what is so obscured to others." And she is strong, he thought to himself. Strong enough to admit when she is wrong, and to adjust her thoughts. Many men he knew would not do so much.

But why would such a revelation lead to his wife's suicide? He felt his chest tighten, frustration making him hasty, even though he knew he should speak with care. "I am sorry, Shi Po. I wish I could be more clever for you, but I am a humble man with a humble mind. Please tell me why you have gathered these things."

"I cannot do it, Kui Yu."

He flinched. She never used his proper name. Never unless her message was dire.

"I will never attain what a ghost pet did in a matter of days." Her distress was obvious not in her face, but in the aimless fluttering of her hands.

"But you study," he said. "You meditate." Indeed, the pursuit of immortality had driven her night and day for months. Which led to one preposterous conclusion: "You plan suicide out of dishonor? Because you failed to reach Immortality?" he asked. He shook his head in disbelief. "What would you say to a student who said such a thing?" he challenged. "You would tell her that only nine Immortals live in China."

"There are other buddhas. More than two hundred. And within the Tigresses—"

He continued without pause. "That not all attain Enlightenment at the same time. You would remind her of the tale of Li Bai and the lady with the iron rod."

Shi Po lifted her head, her eyes brightening with anger. They both knew the story of the old woman who day by day filed down an iron rod to make a needle, and how that had shamed young Li Bai into returning to his studies.

"'Great achievement takes great devotion,'" his wife recited, but she said the story's moral in anger.

Kui Yu ignored it. "Do you abandon your devotion now? After so many years?"

His wife straightened her spine, and he was pleased to see fire light her eyes, even if it was directed at him. "I have nothing *but* devotion!"

"Then why—"

"I *will* become an Immortal!"

Kui Yu stared at Shi Po, completely lost. "Dead women cannot become immortal," he said.

She shook her head. "Do you know why we work so hard, my husband? Why we Tigresses study and meditate and practice with such devotion? It is not so we can reach Heaven. I have had the right mixture of yin and yang since I was a young girl. Inside, I know the Immortal merely waits to be born."

He struggled to understand. She'd had the right ingredients for immortality when she was young? But she'd only begun her practice a decade ago, after their last child was born.

"We study, my husband, so that we can return to Earth after reaching Heaven. We discipline our minds and bodies so that we have the strength to rise there and then return to our bodies here in the Middle Kingdom."

"You believe you will be an Immortal no matter what?"

She nodded. "Yes. But one who cannot return."

His eyes widened as he began to comprehend.

"I am tired, Kui Yu. Tired of strengthening myself without testing my reward."

He shook his head, not understanding.

"I *will* be an Immortal, my husband. If I cannot go and return, then I will simply go." She took a deep breath, straightening her body and returning her gaze to the items before her. "All that remains is the method of my departure."

"Your death, you mean. The way you intend to die."

She glanced up at him, her eyes calm, her lips curved in a sad smile. "You are most wise, my husband. I was confident you would understand."

24

Desperate Tigress

❦

October 22, 1877

Lun Po—

Attached are my suggestions for your essay. Try to remember that Confucius and Lao Tzu had very different philosophies. Misattributing quotes from The Analects *as from* The Way *will be extremely damaging during the Imperial Examination.*

As for me, I have discovered that I can construct bamboo scaffolding in record time. Though I can barely hold a scholar's brush by sunset, the money I make far outweighs the aches. Indeed, the foreman tips me well for standing near the barbarian bosses and listening to their English words. I can speak the foreign tongue better than anyone, so I expect I will not be long on scaffolding construction. But even one day feels like a dynasty, and only a single image keeps my spirit from being completely ruined. You will laugh when you hear this, but understand that my life consists of unending tedium. I must think of something or go mad.

I think of a woman. A girl, really, one who embodies everything that is good and wholesome in China. Someone who is quiet with small feet and a sweet smile. Someone who has no need of painted flowers or wooden butterflies to adorn her hair. A girl who has skin the color of fresh milk and walks with the tiny steps and swaying hips of the greatest Empress.

You know of whom I speak. Pray do not be offended. Simply know that your sister Shi Po has accomplished the greatest thing a woman can. She is an inspiration.

Do not tell her of my foolish thoughts. It will upset her maidenly spirit, and she will think me a foolish, lunkhead coolie. I am those things, of course, while she is a vision of transcendent beauty. And yet without her pure image in my head, I could not survive my long, terrible days.

I must rest now. My writing has deteriorated, and you probably think me drunk. I am, perhaps, but only on endless days spent on bamboo poles and short nights of aches alleviated by memory. Yes, I remember our days studying together and our kind tutor. I still owe him money for all those years of teaching. Even more, now that he allows us to exchange letters through him. Could you not give him a small token for me? My pay will not come for weeks yet, so mother and I have nothing now.

In the meantime, study hard for both of us. One of us should pass the Imperial exam. I pray nightly that it is you. And by day, I remember the greatest beauty in China.

Your devoted friend,
Kui Yu

*A man planted many poplar trees and ordered a child
servant to watch them so none was stolen. Ten days
passed and no poplars were lost. The man, pleased
with this result, asked the child, "You've done a good
job. How did you do it?"*

*The child answered, "I pulled them out every night
and hid them in the house."*

Chapter Two

Shi Po felt her body relax. She knew a smile curved
her lips and softened her expression. Such was always the way when she spoke with Kui Yu; he was a
kind man, gentle and sweet, and so she reflected his
goodness.

She pitied the women of China who daily struggled with overbearing, brutal men. They did not understand that a woman was strongest when she
became mirror reflecting good to good, evil to evil,
even if they did not enjoy the tactic. But she could not
teach all women in China. Indeed, her time as an instructor had come to an end. She bowed her head in
thanks to Kwan Yin, Goddess of Hope, for gifting her
with a gentle husband. And for the knowledge that
her students would continue her work in her absence.

When her prayer was done, she lifted her head only
to be surprised by Kui Yu's expression. He was staring at her with horror, and she felt her body tighten in
reaction.

"Kui Yu," she began awkwardly. "You are angry?"

She didn't know how he felt, or why, and so had no clue what she would reflect. Uncertainty always bothered her.

Her husband shook his head. "I am merely thinking," he said, his words as hesitant as hers. "Tell me your thoughts on the . . . on these items."

She smiled, pleased he sought her opinion. Indeed, she knew of no other man who would ask questions rather than issue commands. Kui Yu sought truth, and in her reflection of him, Shi Po did the same.

She leaned forward, extending the motion into a kind of bow—a reward for his generosity of spirit. "The hanging rope," she began, lifting the cord, "is the traditional means of a wife ending her life. But I have not dishonored you, so I hesitate to use a method that might suggest I had."

He nodded, but did not interrupt. Indeed, his gaze was so unfocused that she wondered if he was listening at all. Eventually, she continued.

"The poison was my second thought, but that might be misconstrued in one of two ways: First, that I was in error with my herbs—"

"No one would believe such stupidity from you," he argued.

She glanced up in surprise, startled that he knew her reputation among women. "But few truly know my skill. There are those who would assume I was careless."

"Men, you mean."

She nodded.

"You said there was another possibility of mistake," he prompted after a silence.

She bit her lip and her voice dropped to a lower register. "Poison is also a traditional means of murder."

His expression remained bland. Obviously, he had

already thought of this possibility. "You don't want people to think I poisoned you."

She smiled sadly. "It might suggest you were too weak to force me to hang myself." She reached out, daring to touch his hand as she spoke. "And I could never stomach such a stupidity."

"My honor has always been safe in your hands," Kui Yu drawled, and Shi Po wondered at his tone. But when she would have protested, he waved her worry aside. Indeed, this was one of the things that most irritated her about her husband. He had no idea how difficult it was to maintain his reputation. Gossip was a daily enemy. But that was the toil of females, and she could not expect a man—even one as intelligent as Kui Yu—to understand.

"So, what of the poisoned dagger?" he asked.

"A single stab," she answered, "deep into my heart. That should be quick and effective, especially with the poison on it. But I expected you home earlier, so it could be done in the daytime." Annoyed, she flashed him a look of reproach. "Now that it is night, others may suspect a thief." Robberies were common, even in this wealthy area of Shanghai where homes were surrounded by walls and guards.

He sighed, his shoulders slumping. "I have already proffered my apology. I came as quickly as I could." He shifted awkwardly. "So now you think to wait until tomorrow? To make it clear that it was not done by a thief in the night."

She grimaced impatiently. "That depends upon you. No matter the method, there will always be gossip. I do not wish my death to be seen as . . . a failure. I require someone to speak of my dedication and purpose. Of the certainty that I have gone to immortality."

"You want your death to be known as an act of devotion and not cowardice." There was a strange note in his voice, which she had difficulty interpreting.

"That is exactly what I wish," she said cautiously. "Will you help me?"

He did not answer directly. Instead, he reached for the dagger, running his hands over the elaborately carved ivory handle. It was a dragon, designed to fit into a matching tigress cover. When sheathed, the two would form a seamless image of the two creatures wrestling.

As Kui Yu spoke, he idly rubbed his finger down the dragon's spine. "What of our children? You wish me to say this to them? Children do not understand acts of devotion. They will only see that you are not here to kiss them or tend to their needs."

Shi Po shook her head. "Our daughter is safely married and has no interest in me. She will have no concerns after I die. As for our two sons . . . they have passed beyond my influence." She had no words to express the emptiness that gripped her whenever she passed the boys' room, empty now these last seven months. Traditionally, now was the time for her to shut herself away, to wear dark colors and no longer be seen by the world. After all, her purpose was over. Her children were gone.

"But what of their love for you? Their—"

He stopped speaking at her snort of disgust. Chinese men were not raised to love. Her children were no different. Honor, respect, piety for one's ancestors— these things they understood. Love had no bearing on this discussion.

Her husband paused, his expression carefully blank. "The boys will return from their tutor in a few months. They are becoming men. Perhaps we should ask their opinion on this matter."

"They will return upon my death," she said. "And though they grow quickly, they have not the maturity to understand my decision."

"Your death will disrupt their studies," Kui Yu remarked.

Shi Po frowned. That *was* one of her worries. A classical Confucian education required long hours of tedious work. It had cut deeply at New Year's to send the boys to live with their tutor until they took the Imperial exam. She ached that she would never see them again. But such an education was crucial, and one could not have both immortality and motherhood. She had raised her children; now was time for her immortality and her sons' progress.

"The boys need not remain at home all forty-nine days of mourning," she said.

Kui Yu shook his head. "You do not understand my point. Even adult men take comfort in their mother's life," he said. "They honor her and remember her—"

"And so they still can," she interrupted. "Especially if she—if *I* achieve an honorable death."

He continued as if she hadn't spoken. "They are bound to care for her in her old age. Would you take that responsibility from them? Would you intentionally release them from a task that shapes and forms filial character?" He shook his head. "No, your death will disrupt their studies for more than forty-nine days."

She sighed. Even if what he said was true, should she delay her immortality until her sons were grown? Until they were established in Imperial careers? That could take years. Surely Kui Yu did not expect that.

But one look at his face told her he did. Their sons' education was of preeminent importance, their performance on the Imperial Exam of the gravest concern. No good mother would ever harm her sons' paths to success. And yet . . .

"I cannot wait so long," she said. Then she looked up, doing her best to read her husband's expression. "You exaggerate the impact."

"I assure you I do not," he replied.

"I would never harm my sons," she said, as much to herself as to him.

"I know this. That is why I mentioned it. You must understand all the consequences of your actions."

She looked at her hands as she fidgeted with the silk of her gown. "You have always shown me such things." She sighed. "I am glad that I waited until your return."

He did not answer at first, but waited until she looked up, surprised by his long silence. When he did speak, it was to say something completely unexpected.

"I think you misunderstand immortality."

Anger flared in Shi Po, hot and powerful. "Do not seek to instruct me in my faith."

"I seek nothing of the kind," he countered placidly. "I tell you what I believe. And one other thing . . ." His gaze narrowed on her face. "This story will take only a moment, but it will require you to listen carefully."

Shi Po straightened, insulted. "It is a wife's duty to listen to a husband. She must hear even the things he does not say."

"Of course."

"I have always been a dutiful wife to you. Obedient and respectful. I raised our children to honor you and have carefully managed the household. I—"

"I know you have," he interrupted in soothing tones. "I have never had cause to doubt your honor."

It was a lie, and they both knew it. The very fact that

she was a Tigress threw doubt upon her honor, and his by extension. But they never spoke of her practices or her lack of purity when they married. Like so many things in China, ugliness was simply ignored as if it did not exist. So she tried extra hard to see to his needs in all respects. In this way, she honored him for not constantly pointing out her mistakes.

"Will you listen now, Shi Po?" he asked. He waited until her gaze fixed upon his, then said, "Very well. Here is the story. . . ."

And he began a long, wandering tale filled with strange details about building materials and men she had never met. Shi Po did her best to understand, but the niceties of construction and Kui Yu's business were not easy to follow. She narrowed her eyes. Squinting at Kui Yu, she hoped that restricted view would focus her attention. Fewer distractions meant fewer mental wanderings. But still he continued. She opened her mouth to ask a question—anything to stop her thoughts from numbing.

"Please allow me to finish," he said harshly.

She settled back into silence.

He continued to the end of his tale, then:

"Do you understand, my wife?"

She blinked. Did she understand? "You . . . you had a building," she stammered. "The one that fell down." She remembered his fury at the incident; it had been early in their marriage. On the advice of a friend, Kui Yu had bought a building that needed repairs. The friend also recommended workers and had supervised the construction. But the friend was Shi Po's stupid brother Lun Po, who had never succeeded at anything. Within a year, the building had collapsed and their finances lay in ruins.

"So you understand?" her husband pressed.

She sighed, shaking her head. "I am sorry, Kui Yu. I am a woman and have no head for business."

His expression softened. "That is forgiven, my wife. The story means this: A building begun badly cannot be fixed, cannot achieve its full potential no matter how much devotion is given to it later. It must be stripped down to its foundations and begun again. Only then can it achieve greatness."

She frowned. Why had he not just said that in the first place?

"You have spoken little of the beginning of your practice. Are you so sure that your foundation is all that it should have been?"

She stared at him, her mind completely blank. His words formed and reformed in her mind, going nowhere.

"What was your initiation into the Tigress practice?" he asked.

"Of no moment," she snapped.

She was startled by her own harshness. He had approached her with nothing beyond simple curiosity, and so she consciously softened her anger, allowing her thoughts and body to reflect her husband. But he waited in silence.

"Your thoughts are wise, my husband," she said. But were they? "You believe I am like a poorly begun building." She was? "And that before I can go forward, I must return to the beginning. Test myself down to the foundation."

"I merely suggest it as a possibility."

"But you think it is so," she pushed.

He hesitated, his hands flat upon his knees, his fingers still. His fingers still. . . .

Shi Po's thoughts crystalized. Her husband's fingers were still now, but they hadn't been a moment before. Even when she narrowed her focus upon his face, she had seen his hands move. They always moved. They were always expressing or punctuating or emphasizing.

But now . . .

"Where is my vial of poison?" she asked. And the dagger? And the rope? They were all gone! The space between her and her husband was empty. Only the two pitiful scorpions remained in their cage. Her gaze flashed up to his. "Why did you take them?"

He blinked, as if he could not possibly understand what she was saying. "You asked my opinion. I require these things in order to judge their effectiveness."

"Give them back."

"You asked me to help."

"Where did you put them?" She studied his clothing. His robes were full enough that he could have hidden them on his person and no one would be able to tell.

"I have need of them," he said again.

She stared at him. "I can get others."

"But you will not."

She glared at him, furious with herself for allowing her attention to lapse. She needed her things! "Kui Yu, I believe your humors are out of balance. You are acting irrationally."

He huffed, folding his arms in a harsh show of intemperance. "My humors *are* sadly out of balance, wife, which is why I first came to you this evening."

She frowned. "It was not because of the summons?"

He ground his teeth. She heard it quite clearly. "Yes, it was because of General Kang. But it was also because his visit is just one of a myriad imbalances in an unbalanced month."

Shi Po tilted her head, trying to recall her husband's actions. It saddened her to realize that she had been so involved with her immortality and the Kang son that she had missed Kui Yu's difficulties. But then she daily failed her husband, despite all her efforts. If only she understood him better. Then she would know what kept his gaze somber and his laughter quiet.

Then he spoke, his voice and demeanor so firm as to make her straighten up in reflection. And after he spoke, after she reflected his thoughts back to him, she even understood what he had said. She repeated his words back, just to make sure she had them correct.

"You said, 'I wish to begin training.'" The words didn't make sense! She went on. "You want me to teach you from the beginning. The way of the Tigress, the way of the Dragon."

He blinked, but she detected a glint of joy in his eyes. "I wish to learn," he said clearly. "But it is an excellent and wise decision for you to begin again as well." He nodded, as if just now coming to the decision. "We will train together. As if we both were just beginning."

Her hands started to fidget, her thoughts spinning. "I . . ." *What?* "I cannot begin again! I cannot go back to when I was a child!"

"So, you were a child when you first learned the Tigress practice?" He sounded surprised.

"No, I . . ." She what? She *had* been a child. And yet, she had been so much older than that. "I cannot think." She sniffed at the air. "Your imbalance is affecting me."

He bowed his head. "I apologize. But that is exactly why I want to learn. So I can balance my energies."

"But . . . you cannot!"

"Is it too late for me? Should I resign myself to an early death?" Kui Yu's shoulders drooped. "How much time do I have? A year, do you think?"

"You cannot die!" Shi Po exclaimed. "Who then would care for the boys?"

Her husband shrugged. "I cannot change my fate." His gaze lifted to her face. "It appears you have many reasons to delay your immortality."

Shi Po pushed herself up, tottering a moment on her bound feet before finding her balance. "You are twisting my words and confusing me," she complained.

Kui Yu was silent, but Shi Po hardly cared, for she was busy thinking of her stillroom, of the herbs and possible poisons she had there. Then her spouse's words cut into her thoughts, even as his hands cupped her elbows and stilled her. She had not even realized he stood, but here he was holding her.

"I am not trying to harm you, Shi Po," he said. His voice was low and urgent. "I wish to give you an alternative."

She frowned, his words startling. "I don't understand."

"Instead of seeking immortality from an unstable foundation, and failing as you have, why not begin the practice again? From the beginning, with me. Then your progress will come from the best of all possible beginnings, and you will also balance my humors, thereby assuring that I live a long and healthy life when and if you choose to leave. Then I will be able to take care of our children."

She felt his yang flowing into her from the force of his passion. It slipped from his fingers into her arms, burning into her skin even through the barrier of her gown. Even worse, she felt her feminine yin respond.

Her resolve softened, making everything—her body and her mind—receptive to his penetration.

"I cannot believe this will be helpful," she murmured.

"Think of the benefits. Do you not understand them?"

He was battering her will as his dragon had once battered her cinnabar cave. What choice did she have but to allow it? It was her wifely duty to accept his attentions. And yet, she was not a simple receptacle, a receiver of his thoughts and his seed. She was a mirror. Had she not spent years in study so that she could be just that? So that she could reflect others, show them their true selves even as she herself used that ability to learn?

She was a mirror; and so she consciously hardened her thoughts to reflect his yang power and to strengthen her resolve. Her body straightened, and she bumped against the fabric of his pants. The long leg should have draped gently around his thigh, but it didn't.

Her dagger. In its sheath. Hidden in the long pocket of his pants.

She lifted her gaze to study her husband's face. How had he changed her? She had begun their conversation filled with resolve, and now she wavered. He had planted thoughts in her head, and now she felt like newly turned earth: soft and uncertain, but also fertile and rich.

He had given her such thoughts . . .

"Will you do this, Shi Po?" he asked, his voice and his touch urgent. "Will you teach me? Will you stay with me?"

At last seeing her path, she nodded. She was not just Kui Yu's receptacle, she was also his mirror. And that very contradiction was the reason she'd come as close as she had to immortality.

"I will partner you, Kui Yu, and in doing so, I will begin again—as if we were young cubs, just learning our power."

She felt him relax, his breath released in a puff like a summer breeze in the small, closed room. She waited until it was fully exhaled and his body was at its calmest. She waited until the last of that air had whispered past her brow, and then she struck: She reached inside his pocket and pulled out the dagger. And in a single swift move, she unsheathed it, holding the glittering blade before her.

Kui Yu reached for it, of course. He tried to take it, but she was too fast. She held the blade to her throat—to the notch in the neck of her gown—and waited until he stilled.

"What are you doing?" he gasped, his body poised to act.

"Do you know why I waited for you, Kui Yu?" she asked. "Do you know the true reason I did not use this dagger this afternoon, when my mind was prepared and the knife was within reach?"

He shook his head, his gaze trained on where the tip of the dagger rested against her throat.

"Because you always give me other options, husband. Where I see two possibilities, you see three. Where I see none, you see many. Such is your strength, and I value it greatly."

His gaze lifted to hers, somewhat confused. "So, you will stay?" His next question remained unspoken as his eyes returned to the dagger point. He wanted to ask why she held a dagger to her throat if she intended to remain alive.

"I wish to show you that I can and will do what I

39

have set out to. I have not replaced my choice with yours. I have merely chosen another option. For now." She blinked, startled to discover that her eyes were tearing and her heart ached. "I *will* become immortal, Kui Yu. Nothing can delay me for long."

"But what if—," he began.

She cut him off. "It will be my choice, Kui Yu. You merely supply options."

She sighed, seeing that he did not truly understand. What man could? She was an unnatural woman in this regard. It was the yang she had stored over the years, which gave her strength and resolve where other women were soft.

"This is ultimately my choice, Kui Yu. And I will not relinquish it." And with that, they both had to be content.

She watched Kui Yu's face contort with frustration. "All over China, people struggle to survive. To live. Why do you leap to death? Is your life so terrible? Do all our riches, your sons, and our home—does all that mean nothing?"

She stared at him, seeing that he understood so little of her. "They are nothing when compared to what I seek. It is what the most revered men in China seek: heaven and immortality."

"They do not put a dagger to their own throats."

"Some starve themselves. Some expose themselves to sickness so they wither. All seekers long for the last step into immortality. I am no different."

"You are very different, my wife. You always have been."

Kui Yu watched his wife sheathe her dagger, his heart still pounding in his chest. He could have taken the knife from her the moment the blade left her throat, but she always needed to feel in control. So he allowed her to keep it, though he clenched his fists to remain still.

She watched him, testing his resolve. He smiled blandly at her, but his patience was wearing thin. A wife's task was to keep her husband's home peaceful. He had already given Shi Po great latitude, especially since their sons left. But now . . . this had to end. He would not tolerate her moods much longer.

And yet, how often had he resolved to be firm with his wife, to bring her to heel in the most direct manner possible? All it took was one second, for when she smiled at him, her body softening with pleasure as she brought him tea or smoothed the sheets of his bed, then all his resolutions disappeared and his anger faded. What remained was a sweet longing and faded dreams of what might have been.

He looked in her eyes, expecting to see her soften. That was their usual pattern. Whatever the drama she enacted, whatever difficulties either of them encountered during the day, eventually those emotions passed. Eventually, his wife would take his arm and lead him to dinner or tea, or to his soft and lonely bed. Then his home would be peaceful once again. Quiet, if not loving.

But that did not happen this time. There was no return to normalcy, though she set the dagger aside. Instead, he saw only emptiness in his wife. Her eyes seemed like fissures into a deep cave. Shi Po was inside somewhere, but her spirit seemed lost, frightened, and alone.

"So . . . what of General Kang and his men?" he heard himself ask. "Did they hurt you?"

She shook her head, but her expression was angry. "There was little danger. The General was only interested in his son."

He detected no lie in her words, which allayed some of his tension. There was no way for a Han Chinese to fight the Manchurian invaders. The Manchurian Qins were firmly established as rulers in China, and any complaint would only bring more unwanted attention.

Fortunately, the General was gone, Shi Po appeared unharmed, and her students were safe. Yet, she now held a dagger in her hand and ached for death. It made no sense; but when had women ever been understood by men?

Kui Yu shifted his weight to rest on his heels. How should he proceed from here? He had no idea, and that realization shook him to the very core. So far he had been scrambling, saying anything, doing anything to delay his wife's decision for a moment longer. But now that she had taken his advice and chosen to wait, he was hard put to remember what he had said.

It took him less than a breath to recall. He had promised to start her religious practice from the beginning. With her.

The very thought nauseated him. Hers was a female religion. True, he had seen amazing transformations in her students—some even progressing from withered little nothings to beautiful, strong women—but he hardly needed to find confidence. Nor did he need education on how to forge his path in a difficult world.

But, he had promised. And the darkness in his wife's eyes told him that if he did not keep her busy, did not occupy her hands and mind with the business of life, then she would chose death. She would leave him and their children in her unnatural quest for immortality.

"Shall we begin?" he asked.

She blinked. Her focus had been on the dagger, but now she looked at him. "What?"

"Your practice. *The* practice." He shrugged. "Whatever your initiates do first."

She seemed to have sensed his reluctance. She said resignedly, "You need not bother yourself. It is for women, you realize."

He stiffened, feeling insulted. Which was absurd, for she echoed his own thoughts. "There are men who practice. Cheng Ru Shan, for one. He was your . . . your . . ."

"Jade dragon."

Heat suffused Kui Yu's face as he spoke. "You practiced with him."

She shook her head. "Not very well. And not for many years now."

"It was not so long ago," he countered. He remembered all too clearly the day she had come to him begging for money to help her jade dragon out of financial difficulties. That the man was also his nearest competitor had not bothered her. Instead, she had spoken about interest and collateral for the loan. Where she had learned such things, Kui Yu did not know, but she had certainly understood the possibilities for gain: The Cheng store would go to him should Ru Shan forfeit the loan. And if he repaid the debt—which he had—then the interest would provide a tidy profit.

So he had done the thing. He had given his wife's partner, his competitor, the means to survive through the year. And with that money, Ru Shan had saved his store, found a wife, and attained immortality.

Kui Yu, on the other hand, had stretched his own finances thin, and his wife had abruptly changed from a placid, sweet-tempered teacher to a moody woman obsessed with immortality. So he had little love for Cheng Ru Shan, even though his wife spoke with quiet vehemence.

"I have *not* practiced with Ru Shan for years," she said. "He gained his immortality with his white pet." She swallowed, obviously forcing herself to moderate her words. "With his English woman."

She was not lying. He could see the bitterness the words caused her. But Kui Yu knew Ru Shan had not discarded Shi Po in favor of the white woman. Indeed, if he had to guess, Ru Shan had been forced onto his path.

He frowned. "Who has been your partner if not Ru Shan?"

His wife shook her head, refusing to answer. He watched her, the truth dawning slowly on him. It was stunning.

"You have not practiced. Not for years."

Again came the flash of fire deep within her gaze. "I have practiced. Devotedly."

Obsessively, thought Kui Yu, but only after Ru Shan and his woman attained their status as Immortals. But she had had no partner. He knew this because he had been watching for the signs—flushed cheeks when he inquired about her day, creeping exhaustion that came from nights and days of practice riding the yin tide. And most especially, her absence from the house at strange hours. He knew her coming and goings; a man of wealth would be a fool not to watch his wife. But there had been no new partner for her. Only Ru Shan. Who had left China months ago.

Which meant: "You have been meditating alone. Stirring the yin and yang by yourself. But why?" If she was so determined to be immortal, why would she neglect this most obvious ingredient?

She drew herself up to her full, impressive height—a bare inch shorter than himself. And in that movement, he saw every wealthy, aristocratic ancestor of her parentage. She was indeed the granddaughter of those who had served the glorious Ming Emperors. When she spoke, her heritage and passion throbbed in her tones.

"Do you dare question my practice?"

He smiled. Indeed, he could hardly help himself, he so admired the power in her heart. "I do nothing of the kind," he said mildly, his good humor slowly returning. "I seek to understand what you do. After all, I have set myself to learn it, and how else does a student learn except by questioning his teacher?"

Shi Po's eyes narrowed, but it had been a long time since she intimidated him. Kui Yu straightened, rolled his shoulders back and down, and allowed his chest to expand with the humid Shanghai air. He resolved himself.

"It is time we began, wife. Teach me."

She gaped at him. Rarely had he ordered her to do one thing or another, and not for many years. He almost trembled to see if she would obey.

It was a struggle for her. He could see that. She stared at him, her eyes flickering with indecision. But in the end, her wifely modesty and training won out. She dipped her head in acknowledgment of his position.

"Very well, husband, it shall be as you desire. Please remove all your clothing and set your mind upon silent and peaceful contemplation." She paused, allowing her gaze to rise in challenge. "No matter what I do to your body."

November 30, 1877

Lun Po—

Your essay had excellent points, but I fear you made a critical error. The Qing dynasty stems from Manchurian invaders. They will not give you a high position in their government if you write your examination paper in praise of our Han ancestors. Neither would they appreciate unfavorable comparisons to the most excellent Ming Dynasty. In order to succeed, you must learn more of the Manchu culture. Discover what makes their nomadic, horse-riding race so powerful, and help them adapt it to the current, sedentary life of our Emperor. I have made some suggestions. I know there are many, but I am sure you will find at least a few of them worthy.

Meanwhile, I am most unhappy you told your sister that I often think of her. I do not believe you that she laughed uproariously at my expense. She is too modest and refined a girl for such a reaction. You are teasing me as you so often do. But beware, my old friend, do not bear false tales to your sister regarding me. If you do, Heaven will punish you by making me your brother-in-law! Yes, I believe that got your attention; and naturally I jest. But sometimes, Heaven makes the most unusual things happen, so school your unguarded tongue.

At least I do not have to break my back any more in construction. Especially since I learned that the foreman was corrupt and would not let me advance for fear I would take his place. He was right to be afraid, for you know of my ambitions. But it turns out that I should thank him. Because he kept me in the lowest position, because he forbade me to come to the attention of the foreign bosses, I made it my plan to do just that.

Can you guess what I did? I let the foreign bosses know I speak English. They were suspicious anyway. Why else would I always be assigned to work where they stood talking if not to spy on them? They would have discovered my skill eventually, but when have I ever waited for Heaven's blessing when I could grasp it with my two hands? Especially since I have been practicing the strange language. I have even visited the missionaries just so I could talk English.

My plans have succeeded, Lun Po! I am to be a white man's "boy." I will be playing servant to a ghost barbarian, but he is rich, rich, rich! Who knows what I can learn from him? Who knows what I can buy with his cast-offs?

I have already bought something, Lun Po, in anticipation of my new fortune. The New Year fast approaches, and I know you struggle to find a gift for your sister. Pray, allow me to select it for you. I know it is most improper of me, but it is her image that brought me through those most terrible nights when my back burned like fire and my arms could not lift to chase away the flies. Only she kept me alive. Only her beauty inspired me to rise for work again. So in this I beg, please allow me to select your New Year's gift for Shi Po.

> *Your devoted friend,*
> *Kui Yu*

A Taoist teacher told his students that mastering even one or two of Confucius's sayings was enough. A young man stepped forward and said, "I couldn't agree more. I've benefited quite a lot from mastering two sentences of Confucius."

"What sentences are those?" the teacher asked.

"He did not mind to have his rice finely prepared, nor to have his meat finely minced."

Chapter Three

Shi Po saw her husband's eyes widen with fear at her instruction, but she didn't care. For years she had scrupulously kept him out of her religion, away from her students, and blissfully ignorant of what she did. She had repeatedly dismissed the intimacy shared by partners as irrelevant, for according to the sacred texts, emotional intimacy was an earthly attachment that distracted from the heavenly goal.

He had accepted that. He had seen her students, paid for the large compound that served as both home and school, had even once walked in during a lesson. She had been explaining the various states of a man's dragon, using pictures. Kui Yu had blushed a fiery red and walked directly out again. He had no interest in seeing what she did, he'd told her. It only mattered that her students seemed happier after her training, and that she loved to teach.

Until today. Today she had abandoned all hope of happiness on Earth. She had accepted her Heavenly destination and the loss of all she held dear in the physical plane. And now Kui Yu wanted to join her, to practice with her, to learn what she did.

It was obviously a stalling tactic. He was not prepared to lose her. But as his wife, she had to honor his ridiculous request. And as a woman, she couldn't deny that he was still attractive to her in many different ways.

Very well. He would learn of the control a man in her religion must exercise, of the agonies they experienced in pursuit of immortality. He would learn; and when he abandoned it as too difficult, he would appreciate what she had achieved. He would value her great accomplishment in finally joining other Immortals in Heaven. This was her plan, so she stood back and watched as he slowly undressed.

The mandarin jacket came off first. It was the blue one she had given him upon the birth of their first son. Rich in color, exquisite in design, it covered him in the flying cranes of long life. She was pleased when he folded it carefully before setting it aside.

Next came his robe—a simple garment of cotton, oddly unstained by sweat on this hot, hot day. He unbuttoned it quickly, stripping it off with clear anger and embarrassment. She said nothing, but merely watched. Surprisingly, her mouth and throat moistened with desire at the sight of his broad, muscular chest.

How long had it been since she'd last seen her husband's lean form in the bright light of day? She remembered watching him labor as a poor coolie so many years ago. She was not supposed to be there— the rich protected daughter of a nobleman—but she had escaped to stand in the shade and watch Tan Kui Yu as he labored in the hot sun. How his muscles had bulged. She'd stared and stared at his broad shoulders and tight buttocks. But she'd also noticed how the other men deferred to him. Though he was nothing but a poor laborer, other men—older, more experienced men—looked to him for direction.

Now here he was, two decades later, still broad and muscular, still tight of body and lean of face. Good food had somewhat softened his harsh angles. And with fortune had come a wide smile on his features rather than coolie exhaustion. Except he wasn't smiling now. He was watching her, letting her fill her vision with his glorious form while his eyes dared her to demand more. After all, this meditation chamber had open windows no longer covered by paper over the elaborate latticework. Any servant or student could look in.

But a Tigress was often watched in her work. Dragons as well. So Shi Po would give him no relief. "Your chest has not diminished," she said, admiration in her tone. "But I said you must remove all your clothing—including your pants."

He arched a single dark eyebrow. His hands went to the tie at his waist, releasing it with quick jerks. His long black queue slid over his shoulder as he worked, and her fingers twitched with the desire to touch the dark braid. What a contrast it made to his beautiful skin. How she longed to run her fingers along it, to touch him as she once had so long ago.

His pants slid away to reveal his dragon. It was thick and heavy with arousal. There was no embarrassment in his eyes, merely a dark challenge, a question that asked how far she would go to humiliate him.

Shi Po paused. Panic shivered through her body as she looked at her husband. Or, more accurately, as she looked at his red and swelling dragon. He was pulling off his shoes, casting the last of his clothing aside, his gestures unusually short.

"Now what, my wife?" he demanded.

She softened. Despite her resolve, she did not want to poison what had been a peaceful and calming relationship. "Are you sure, Kui Yu?" she pressed, giving him a last chance to change their course. "You have never wanted to learn this before."

"You have never threatened to go to your immortality before." He looked up, and she saw a flash of hope in his eyes. "Would you now abandon that plan?"

She shook her head. "I cannot."

"Then I will understand what steals my wife from me and takes a mother from my children."

Shi Po swallowed, unable to speak. She could only stare at her gloriously naked husband, the fading sunlight touching his skin with rose and gold.

She held her breath as he dropped his hands to his hips, drawing her gaze to his jutting dragon. Her Tigress mind assessed his health with mechanical precision. The dragon head was full and pleasantly formed, the mushroom shape of lighter color, indicating a wholeness that came from years of healthy food and purifying teas—a course she had begun with him the first day of their marriage. The dragon's shaft curved only slightly to the right, a defect easily corrected within a few weeks of exercise. Beyond that she could not see, for hair shielded all from view.

"You must shave," she told him. "Every day."

He jerked slightly, making his dragon bob.

"It is for health reasons," she explained. "And be sure to maintain your regimen of bathing." Many Chinese women were plagued with men who passed on disease or vermin with every carnal act. That was why her students were required to bathe and shave their partners for even the briefest encounter.

But her husband was not like that, and so while these thoughts flashed through her head, they did little to distract her arousal. And Kui Yu's was growing. His dragon was of average length and girth, well-suited for her own rather modest cinnabar cave. But his dragon stretched up tall—straighter than normal for a man his age—and she was pleased with his vitality.

She lifted her gaze to his eyes. Surprised, she said, "Your qi flows strongly. You will have a long and healthy old age. You need not learn Dragon secrets to extend your life—"

"I think there is nothing to your practice but talk, wife," he interrupted. "Is this all a Tigress does with her partner? Stare? And comment?"

She lifted her chin, mirroring his challenge with a strength that surprised her. "I have spent decades learning my practice. Do not seek to insult it within your first moments of exposure."

"I am exposed," he growled at her. "What more is to come?"

"You are exposed so that you grow comfortable with your body and your dragon," she explained. "Perhaps you will discover pride in your form."

His expression lightened, and she caught a flash of a smile. "*Boys* are proud of their dragons," he said. "Men know that it is an organ—no more, no less. Not an indication of virility or power."

"That is where you are wrong, young cub," she returned, slipping into her teacher persona. It was strange, acting so before her husband, and yet it made some things easier. By ignoring their shared past—their movement from poverty to wealth, their three children, and a glorious future—she could look at him as just another man, another dragon, another soul in search of enlightenment.

"A dragon reveals a man's health. Your organ, as you put it, is the seat of your yang strength; and a more powerful substance cannot be found on this earth."

"My dragon," he repeated.

"Yes. Your penis—that which creates and delivers yang power in its emissions."

After a moment Kui Yu nodded, and she believed he understood. He could not have lived so long with her and not learned something of what she did.

"Your next exercise is meant to strengthen your yang, to heat the internal cauldron of creation so that you burn with yang power—"

"But do not release it," he interrupted.

She nodded, startled. He truly did know some of what she taught. And when she narrowed her eyes to study his expression, she watched his cheeks flush with embarrassment.

"I have read your sacred texts," he finally admitted. "Many years ago, when you first began to teach."

She said nothing, but her mind reeled. She had begun to teach in secret because they needed the money. Her aunt had a steady supply of new prostitutes in need of a basic education. She hadn't thought Kui Yu noticed what she did. After all, he was busy fixing their destroyed building and then selling it. And then doing it again with other buildings while the money poured in.

But he had read her texts? In secret? She wasn't sure what she thought of such a thing. "I will show you exercises, the handhold and stroke. You must do these things twice a day." She glared hard at him, emphasizing her next point. "And you must never release your dragon seed during the process."

"I understand," he said, his voice flat, giving no hint of his thoughts.

"And do you understand why you do this?"

"To gain immortality," he answered. "But I do not understand the full process."

"Female yin and male yang are like two strong horses. They must combine their strength together to carry you to heaven. The tigress . . ." She pointed to herself. "Or the dragon . . ." She pointed to him. "Must store these two essences until the time when they are excited."

"When we are about to have sex?" he asked.

She shook her head. "Sex is like two horses running wild. The tigress and the dragon learn to harness the horses. Yin and yang must be directed to heaven."

"And how does one direct yin and yang?"

"With the mind, my husband. There is a feeling when the horses begin to run. We call them two circles. You can think of them as two tracks, one for each horse."

"Your female yin and my male yang."

She smiled gently at him. "All people have both yin and yang. Male and female exist in everyone. It is merely a matter of degree."

"But you have a great deal of yang," he pushed. "You have stored it from other men."

She nodded. She would not lie to him. He pressed his lips together, and she eventually continued her lecture. "The yang horse runs on a larger track, the larger circle. The yin horse on the smaller one runs in the opposite direction. Once both horses are running at great speeds, the energy of the spirit is churned.

The spirit grows more excited, more powerful, more . . ."

"Immortal?"

She smiled. He did understand. "Yes. More immortal. And after a great deal of practice, the spirit is strengthened enough to reach Heaven."

"So the exercises you do are to strengthen the spirit?"

She widened her fingers across his still jutting dragon. "These exercises are to purify your yang. It will take practice with a partner for you to gather more yin. And even more practice to strengthen your spirit enough that it can touch the Immortal Realm."

He frowned. "But you have been practicing alone. How is this possible?"

"As you said, I have stored much yang. The circles can be established between partners or within a single person. It is merely harder when one works alone."

"I understand."

"Then I will begin. Remain still throughout."

He nodded, and she watched his muscles ripple in anxiety. It was a small reaction, completely normal, and nothing compared with her violent turmoil. Her stomach churned and her muscles quivered. She was glad to sink to her knees in front of him, because her legs would not support her.

What was happening? Why was she shaking? They had conceived three children together. Why should this simple act unbalance her so? She had no idea. She could only force herself to continue.

Reaching out, she touched her husband's dragon. It was thick and heavy. The color had darkened slightly, the dragon pushing far out of its sheath. "Grasp the dragon like so," she said, her hand going to the correct position, fingers curled around the stem, her thumb pulling the ridged foreskin down and away.

Kui Yu didn't move as she began the stroke, but Shi Po did. Her belly quivered and her cinnabar cave released its dew. She was more aroused than she'd been in a long time.

She tightened her grip. "You must stretch this side more than the other to straighten out your right-hand tilt."

He didn't answer, but a glance at his face showed he understood. One glance also brought a girlish yin flush to her cheeks. Completely illogical, given that she was no untried virgin.

"I will perform forty-nine strokes with my right hand. Some texts say seventy-two, but I can sense that your yang is already very pure." She swallowed. "Are you ready?"

"I have been ready for ten minutes, wife. It is you who seem hesitant." Was there a teasing note in his voice?

She glanced up. "I was checking for deformities."

He arched an eyebrow. "Are there any?"

She was caught by his bright eyes. "If there were, I would never have become your bride," she snapped.

He drew back in surprise. "But . . . but how would you know?"

She felt her lips curve in memory. "Do you recall when my brother begged you to go swimming? That he was most insistent?"

Her husband nodded. "You had him look?"

Her smile widened. "Of course." Then she pretended to go unconcernedly back to her task. "But even then I did not trust Lun Po's honesty. Certainly not on something so important." She delivered her final comment at the same time as she began to stroke his dragon. "And so I hid in the bushes to watch."

Kui Yu pulled back, but not far enough to jerk himself out of her hand. "You were there? The whole time?"

"I had to see all my suitors. This was the most efficient way." She gave a second stroke, and his body quivered in reaction.

"But we were boys. You watched while we spoke about women and compared our . . . assets?" His body was flushed all the way down to his toes.

"If you recall, that was my brother's idea." She spared a moment to give him a grin. "Yes, he claimed he was the most manly among you." Then she snorted in laughter, as she had so long ago. "As I said, I do not trust my brother to tell the truth in such an endeavor."

"But . . ." Again, her husband seemed to have lost his composure. "But if you were there, then you would know . . ." He reached down and stopped her hand from stroking him. "You knew I was not . . . I am not . . ."

"The longest or largest?" She laughed.

He nodded, his confusion apparent, and she shook her head.

"Only men think bigger is better. We women know a man's dragon must match his wife's cinnabar cave. Too long, and it is uncomfortable. Too short, and it is useless." She gently removed his hand from hers. "My husband, I knew even then that our fit was nearly perfect."

He frowned. "You knew this? Even then? But you were a child. We all were."

She bit her lip, the old tears feeling very close, but

she made sure no sign reached her face. "You knew I was not . . . typical, even before our wedding night." She slowed her stroking. "Does it bother you now?"

She did not look at him, shame keeping her gaze low. It was silly to be ashamed of something that had happened so long ago. An act that allowed them to marry, that had begun the life they now enjoyed. And yet, such was her irrational nature that shame was a constant companion.

He startled her with a single caress of her chin.

"I have always valued your uniqueness. I will not disparage you for it now or ever." There was no softness in his voice and he gave only a brief caress, and yet she felt comforted. His eyes surrounded her with happiness and his yang power enfolded her in strength.

Her insides quivered, and her yin cauldron bubbled over. Such was his power that he drew this most potent response. How had she forgotten he could do this to her? And how would she defend herself if he refined his yang? How would she keep herself safe when his every breath exuded awesome strength?

"I have lost count of the strokes," she murmured. Never in decades of practice had she lost count!

"Eight," he answered.

She scrambled to cool her yin. "Then I shall begin at nine."

But before she could begin the task, before she could fight the weakness in her fingers, he reached down, slowly uncurling her hand. "Perhaps I should finish."

She released his dragon in an unsteady jerk, mourning the loss of his heated flesh. She said nothing, pressing her lips together and trying to appear critical and instructive. But she had no idea if he held himself correctly, if his hand was firm and powerful, stoking the yang fire without causing it to blaze over. She saw only his eyes, for his gaze enfolded her. She knew nothing but him. Her body heated with his every movement. Her breath shortened until she matched his soft, tight panting. She moistened her lips, and her womanly juices flowed. His gaze leapt to her mouth, and his eyes grew hungry. She knew his yang churned hotly, but no more than her own yin. Truly, they were well matched as partners.

But he was her husband, not her true partner in her religion, and so she did her best to cool her ardor. As mates they had too many ties, too many earthly connections to attain immortality together. That was why she had chosen Ru Shan—her husband's competitor—to partner her so many years ago. There could be no tie to such a man, and therefore no impediment to leaving his side for Heaven.

With Kui Yu . . . She could already tell that the smallest act would multiply her earthly binds. All he did was stroke his dragon, and her body responded as if his hand were on her cinnabar cave.

Suddenly, he stopped. His hand stilled for two breaths before he finally opened his fingers and released his organ. She blinked, not comprehending.

"Forty-nine," he said, his voice thick and low.

She nodded. "Again," she whispered. "With the other hand."

She was watching his face, unable to break the connection of his gaze. Nevertheless, she saw him raise his other hand, bringing it not to his dragon but her cheek. She meant to pull away, but she could not force herself to move.

He extended his index finger, brushed it across her lips. Fire exploded there. Yin and yang combined to make an explosive heat. The alchemy was powerful, producing not actual flames, but a tingling current that flowed directly to Shi Po's womb. Kui Yu's dragon jerked, and emitted a single white pearl.

Shi Po's body continued to charge. She produced more and more yin to react with his yang. She felt the power draw up from her womb as a physical ache—a low and deep throb—that preluded the yin crest.

Without thought, she opened her mouth and extended her tongue to wet his finger. A streak of light shot through his eyes: the yang fire blazing unchecked. It would take very little to cause his yang release. All she needed to do was give in to her own desire, draw his finger into her mouth, caress it with her tongue . . .

"No!" she exploded, pushing away from him.

He staggered, but she fell, her bound feet numb from being tucked beneath her. She landed hard, her teeth rattling from the impact. Fortunately, the pain helped cool the fire in her mind.

"Shi Po!" her husband exclaimed, reaching for her. She pushed his hand away, scrambling backward in terror. Not from him, but from the reaction his touch would create in her.

"We cannot do this. We cannot be partners!" She gasped.

He stilled, his cheeks darkening. "You find me unworthy? Repulsive? Weak?"

She shook her head.

"Then are you saying it is you who are at fault? Are you a bad tutor? Do you renounce your Tigress name?"

Again she shook her head, but her misery joined with his reflected anger, both fighting for dominance in her mind.

Suddenly he was kneeling before her, his expression abruptly gentle. Even his voice became a caress. "Then perhaps we have exposed the root of your problem."

Her anger won out, breaking through her control with words that cut. "My problem? This was your exercise."

"But you are the one who faltered. Is it because your training has not the strength to sustain you?"

She shifted to her knees, then pushed up onto her aching feet. "You were the one who put his finger to my mouth. You were the one—"

"I am not the one who is afraid." His voice was quiet—a gentle summer breeze. And with the diminishment of his anger, her reflection of it faded as well, leaving her no defense against his sweetness.

"I am not afraid," she whispered. But as she spoke the words, she realized how much she lied. She was afraid. She was terrified. But not in the way he thought. She did not fear the alchemical reaction between the two of them.

"I fear the hold on you," she admitted, only half lying. "Attachments are inevitable between husband and wife, Tigress and Dragon. How will you feel when I go to Heaven without you?"

She watched her words penetrate his thoughts, saw him grimace then grow quieter. Sadder.

"Can you not stay, Shi Po? Put aside this quest for immortality, return to being the wife who was. I miss the woman who mothered my children and cared for my comfort." He straightened and extended a hand to draw her into the circle of his arms. "You could continue to teach, continue to help your girls—"

"Cubs," she corrected, as she stepped close to him.

He shrugged. "Whatever the name, they are your students and you should not abandon them."

"How can I teach what I have not myself done?"

"The same way you have taught for many years now. Why must that change?"

She closed her eyes and listened to the steady beat of his heart. In the early years of their marriage, the harsh days of little money and ceaseless toil, she would often lay her head on his chest and listen while he slept the deep quiet of total exhaustion.

She remembered that sound now, the beat like the distant bellows of a dragon's breath. That sound had comforted her in those early days. It was the pulse that had told her he still lived, whispering that she need never repeat what she had once done.

Until that pulse failed her, and she'd been forced to embrace what she hated, to accept what she had once reviled. His heartbeat, his dragon strength, could not save them from starvation. He was not at fault. Not for the building's collapse that nearly beggared them, nor for what she'd done to make money. And Fate had long ago decreed that she grow into a Tigress. But now she realized that she had always blamed him for not having the strength to accomplish everything on his own. For not being a god, but only a man. And that condemnation had been the first log on the yin fire that created who she was.

She pushed away from her husband, struggling with her thoughts. He released her, and she stumbled as she tried to stand. "My thoughts are twisted," she confessed. "Earlier you gave me another option. Now I cannot think for the questions and possibilities you throw at me."

"Shi Po—," he began, but she shook her head, unwilling to listen to more dragon logic, more words from a man.

"You tell me I must return to the beginning," she

said, "to tear away the foundation of my practice and begin again correctly. Very well. Because you ask it of me, I will do it. You are my husband and worthy of whatever obedience I can give you." She straightened to her full height. "But I will not take you as my partner. That work would bind us too tightly together, and then I would be unable to leave—even for the glories of Heaven."

She meant to leave then. She turned away and headed for the door. But bound feet were never meant to rush, and besides, without Kui Yu to reflect, she felt empty and cold. So she was slow to move, slow to leave, which gave him time to speak one last time.

"What if I sought to go to Heaven with you? What if I wanted to become an Immortal too? Would you then be my partner?"

She looked back over her shoulder. His face held shock, as if he didn't believe what he'd just said. "Do not reach for what is beyond you, Kui Yu. The scrolls say it takes a man many times more effort than a woman, a year of practice to do what she can accomplish in a day. You cannot achieve immortality in the time it would take me to climb the stairway from the very bottom. No man is that strong."

"I wish to try," he said firmly.

She sighed, forcing herself to speak the next words. "I will assign you a suitable partner in the morning."

A partner! Kui Yu glared at his wife's retreating back. A child, she meant. A girl who needed a husband to honor and guide her as a man ought. That's what her students required. Not her stupid religion. Just like he himself didn't need her religion; he needed a wife and a mother to his children. If he had wanted another pubescent child, he would have succumbed to pressure long ago and married more. Most men of means had four wives. He had contented himself with one. And now she sought to partner him with a lost and frightened little girl!

In a single, swift movement, he threw Shi Po's vial of poison against the wall. The tiny porcelain container shattered, hurling shards and liquid that flashed like lightning into the darkest cornerers of the room. But all too soon the pieces fell, and he was left with a pounding headache that filled him with dread.

Yet, he had won. She had promised to delay her immortality. She would begin again from the beginning, and he did not even have to go through this wretched quest with her. He did not have to delay his yang release until his balls burned and his dragon became a constant curse, flaring to life at the slightest accidental movement.

Yes, he had tried it once. After sneaking a peek at her sacred scrolls, after listening behind a tapestry as she taught her class, he had decided to see if he could accomplish what Ru Shan could, to see if he could be man enough for his wife to respect. But he had failed. He could not ignore his yang hunger. He could not delay and delay and delay his release with no hope of relief. Ever. So he had put her scrolls away; he had turned his back on his wife's profession, and he had left home searching for new ways to provide for his family. At least he'd learned he could do that, and do it well.

Until now. Until General Kang had burst into his home and he—the master of this household, the patriarch of the Tan family—had been nowhere to be found. Why? Because he had been with a white woman, taking his pleasure as he practiced his English and spread her milky-white thighs. That was what he had been doing while his wife and her cubs were threatened by soldiers; while his home was searched, their possessions violated, and his wife calmly decided on suicide to end her suffering.

His failures sapped his spirit and weakened him further. What did a man do when his wife sought only Heaven? When she disdained her husband and offspring? What could he do?

No, he would not take up with any child she pushed at him. He would not return to the forgetfulness that waited in the body of a whore. And he would not sit idly by while his wife found another lover to stimulate her yin.

No common man was strong enough to walk with her to Heaven? Perhaps not. But a husband could. And the father of her children must be. This he swore.

He would hold in his dragon fire, he would trap the yang roar inside until his balls burst and his eyes rolled back in his head. He would do these things while he stroked and petted her lotus petals, bringing Shi Po's yin to its crest. And then, together, she would finally see what kind of man he was.

And she would know he was too precious to leave behind.

❦

February 15, 1878

Dear Lun Po—

I am pleased your sister enjoyed the carved ivory. It was very difficult finding one with fifteen moveable balls, one inside the other. You are, of course, the most thoughtful of brothers. I was more startled to learn your father invited prospec-

tive bridegrooms to New Year's dinner. Shi Po is so young and pure in my mind I can hardly believe she is of marriageable age. But, of course, she is fifteen now.

Tell me everything. I confess to great curiosity as to who was invited and how they performed. Indeed, I can well imagine how your sister felt, trapped behind the women's screen, her tiny pearl teeth no doubt biting her lower lip in fear. Whom would her father choose?

I shall make a bargain with you, Lun Po. If you tell me all the details of your sister's courtships, I will share everything about my foreign boss's daughters. How strange these ghost women are, tittering behind their fans, baring their white bosoms while attaching huge wire contraptions to their hips and behind. Indeed, whenever they turn away from me, I cannot help but think of the hind end of a water buffalo.

What makes them think they look attractive like that? But then I see the white men panting after them, their eyes huge as they follow the large shift and sway of fabric. The women cannot move quickly, of course, and their every step is accomplished with short breaths because the wire contraptions are so tight. I suppose it is no different from the way our women bind their feet. But in this I think the whites have it worse. They can neither sit properly nor breathe. Our women are fortunate in being naturally small of shape. They have no need of such tight bindings to appear delicate.

Ah, how I long for the company of my own kind. Though I am learning a great deal about white business—counting with symbols instead of beads, lists of inventory and bills of lading—I ache for the quiet creak of our old tutor's bones, the feel of a scholar's brush, and the smell of freshly pressed rice paper. And, of course, the lively discussions we two once shared whenever we caught sight of a tiny foot or glimpsed a slender ankle.

Did you know the white foreigners speak exactly as we once did? They compare shapes and sizes, how white and how full. Apparently ghost people appreciate female beauty. And yet, I was shocked when I heard them discuss the huge, bulbous breasts of one woman. As if anything larger than a chrysanthemum bloom was desirable rather than grotesque! They are definitely barbarians. Me, I prefer petite and demure, with tiny feet and a sweet smile.

Write me soon and tell me more about your sister's prospects. I am vulgarly curious to know her future. Indeed, if you do not, I have half a mind to attend your next bridegroom dinner. With my new position, I am earning money like water. It drips into my hands as fast as I can catch it.

> Your soon-to-be-rich friend,
> Kui Yu

Zheng Guang, a pirate from Fujian Province, was made an officer after he gave himself up to the government. Known for his verse, his colleagues implored him to write a poem. He wrote this:
"Different from other officials and officers
On at least one point:
Your Excellencies became bandits after your promotions,
I got my promotion after being a bandit."

Chapter Four

Dinner was quiet and stilted, but Shi Po made sure it was accomplished as all their meals were: with Confucian decorum. She and her husband spoke of little things: the weather, his health, her clothing. And though Kui Yu tried to press for more intimacy, Shi Po refused to answer, her gaze shifting to point out the maids who served them. She would not talk in front of them. Eventually he understood and lapsed into silence.

Until her aunt arrived.

Sung Mei Ting did not wait for a servant to announce her. She burst into the room, her bound feet hitting the floor hard while the wood butterflies in her dyed hair slipped lower and lower. Shi Po rose immediately, startled by her aunt's rare display. Usually, Auntie Ting would never appear perturbed in front of any man, much less her niece's wealthy husband. Kui Yu also rose to his feet.

"What has happened?" he demanded.

"Oh!" cried Mei Ting, her gaze fluttering between the two. "So sorry, so sorry," she murmured. "I had not thought you home this early."

Kui Yu bowed. "Today has been most unusual."

"Yes," Mei Ting concurred. "I came immediately once I heard. I feared for your safety."

Whatever her aunt feared, it wasn't for Shi Po's safety. Shi Po said nothing, merely gestured for her aunt to join them at table. Meanwhile, Kui Yu pushed away from his food and said the expected words.

"I have business to attend." Then he turned his piercing gaze to Shi Po. "Unless you wish me to stay. I could—"

"Of course not," she interrupted. Her aunt would never reveal her true purpose with Kui Yu there. "I will send tea to your study."

Kui Yu nodded, his eyes troubled. But his expression was often troubled these days; today was no different. In the end, he acted as usual. He bowed and withdrew, leaving her to her business. That was his most endearing quality, and she valued it greatly. Even as a part of her perversely wished he was not so accommodating.

Auntie Ting wasted no time. The moment the door shut behind Kui Yu, she gripped Shi Po's arm. Her small fingers dug their extra-long nails into Shi Po's flesh. "Have you lost all sense of reason? What could you be thinking?"

Shi Po sighed. Her aunt always made her feel so weary, and the woman was in a rare state of fury. All Shi Po could do was wait for whatever imagined doom came next.

"Answer me, child! How could you allow this to happen? What other disasters are you brewing?" She tugged on Shi Po's arm. "Come. I will see your records. I wish to judge your idiocy myself!"

Those words woke Shi Po out of her stupor. She jerked her arm away and pasted on her calmest smile. "I have no records, aunt," she lied. "Like you, I have only such guidance as my husband can provide."

It was a most useful trick when any woman became too interested in what she did. Simply mention Kui Yu—or any man for that matter—and women were socially excluded from giving opinions.

Except, of course, her aunt. "Men! Bah," she said as she spat into Kui Yu's teacup. "What are they but pricks with legs? Yours at least is a golden one, blessed to make money. But what do they understand about anything important?"

Shi Po shrugged. While she found her husband more than capable, who was she to brag about her good fortune? So she nodded sagely as if agreeing, but kept her mouth shut while her aunt continued.

"Your uncle couldn't keep his pole in his pants long enough to think much less make money. Your brothers are no different. Shaolins look pretty but don't have a cent. And as for Lun Po . . ." She rolled her eyes. "Don't think his influence will save you. He'll sell you to prison for another opium pipe."

Again, Shi Po said nothing. Her aunt was completely right about their shared ancestors. Useless, all of them.

"That leaves me, stupid child, to save you from the fire. So, out with it. What disaster have you brought upon our heads?"

Shi Po blinked, finding it easy to appear confused. "I am in no danger at all, Auntie Ting."

"Oh!" the woman exclaimed, her butterflies bobbing even lower on her dyed black hair. "So you often entertain Imperial generals. You always send your girls fleeing for their lives to my establishment."

At last, Shi Po understood. Some of her girls must have gone to her aunt's brothel. What better place to practice their lessons, to harvest yang, than in a pleasure garden? "I expect you have made good money, Aunt, with all the new soldiers. Thankfully, my Tigress cubs are well trained."

"I would glory in the money," snapped Mei Ting, "if I were not in constant fear of being arrested! I *gave away* my women today. Gave them free in the hopes that they wouldn't come for me next. That is what you have done, you stupid girl, reduced me to penury because of your foolishness!"

Shi Po felt herself shrink. She knew it was ridiculous. She told herself that her aunt had no power over her, that what had happened in the past would never—could never—happen again. She had seen to that. But, her aunt's yin was strong and her yang stores made her presence powerful. It was difficult, even now, for Shi Po to keep her own power uneroded.

Choosing escape as the best course, Shi Po pushed to her feet. "But I am well, Aunt. General Kang is gone, and you can make much money off his soldiers. You need have no fear."

She barely made it to her feet before her aunt reached over and pinched her bottom, hard, making sure to twist her fingers to give the most pain. Shi Po remained standing, but only barely, while her aunt hissed in anger.

"You stupid, stupid girl. Do you really think it has ended? He will come back. In the middle of the night. He will take everything you have. You will be lucky if he kills you!"

Shi Po swallowed, feeling the fear that consumed her aunt, knowing that the woman's words could indeed be true. "But I do not have what he is searching for. I do not—"

"Then find it!" hissed her aunt. "That is the only way to survive. Feed them, please them, give such feral dogs what they want and you will be allowed to live."

Shi Po leaned forward, doing her best to intimidate in return the one person who frightened her most. "I do not have what he wants," she growled. "And I have no way to find it."

"The Manchurian monk." Her aunt spat, barely missing Shi Po's feet. "Why would you imprison him? Why would you force a white whore on him? What did you hope to gain?"

"I hoped to teach him!" Shi Po shot back, stung into defending herself. Why couldn't her aunt—older than she in the Tigress practice—understand the very basics of her supposed beliefs?

"Did you want him?" Her aunt pushed away from the table, gesturing wildly as she ranted. "Did you wish to taste Manchurian yang?" She grimaced in disgust, showing her tobacco-stained teeth. "That would be bad enough, but understandable. Why would you shackle him to a ghost pig?"

Shi Po had no answer. Some things she did with little logic; Shi Po did what her heart urged, and found justification for it afterward. Strategy was her aunt's province. Her aunt schemed and plotted and found success. But not immortality.

And with that thought, Shi Po found renewed strength. "Auntie Ting," she stated firmly, "you know I force no one. Those who come to me learn of their own free will, partner their own choices, and practice in their own ways." She narrowed her eyes at the older woman, daring to insult she who had once mentored her. "You of all people understand the choices that face a Tigress."

Her aunt straightened, no doubt feeling the implied criticism but too sure of herself to care. "You are a fool. Do you not remember your fortune? An earth person is what you are. Common dirt, ruled by your passions, moved only by extreme fire. It is only because of me that you married your golden husband. Without me, they would have shackled you to that other idiot. So all that you have, you owe to me."

"Auntie Ting—"

"Listen, foolish girl, leave Shanghai now. Tonight. Before disaster falls—"

"And crashes upon you as well?" Shi Po challenged. That was her aunt's true fear.

"Of course! Would you repay my kindness by visiting disaster on us both? Would you—"

"There is no danger!" Shi Po exclaimed. "General Kang—"

"There is always danger!" her aunt snapped. "Wherever there are Manchurians, the Han people suffer." She shook her head, her horror clear. "You have grown soft with your rich husband and your silly school. You believe you are safe when in truth you are more vulnerable than ever. You stupid, stupid child!"

She would have gone on. Indeed, Auntie Ting's face was red with yang fire, her spirit already caught up in the flow of the larger circle. She would not be able to stop herself now for many hours.

Or, she wouldn't stop unless Kui Yu interfered. Which he did. Right at that moment, he wandered in, his expression cheerful though his eyes were hard. And though he tried to hide it from her, Shi Po understood that he had been listening at the door. Kui Yu knew exactly what had been said, and his temper had reached its limits.

But no man would admit to eavesdropping, so he pretended to be simple, smiled with his teeth but not his eyes, and waved an empty teacup. "Ah, there you are, my wife. My tea does not taste right. Are you sure the maids gave me the right brew? It's not one of your womanly potions, is it? Will I wake tomorrow with breasts?"

Shi Po frowned at his crude remark. He was playing down to her aunt's expectations, pretending to be no better than a coolie. And true enough, Auntie Ting turned her venom on Kui Yu.

"You are your father's son," she said, the insult plain in her voice. After all, Kui Yu's ancestors were the most common of common in Shanghai. "How pleased I am that I was able to bring you two together in marriage."

Kui Yu's eyes narrowed, his fury growing. And yet, neither he nor Shi Po could deny Auntie Ting's part in their union.

So Kui Yu stepped closer to his wife and extended his teacup to her. "You spend so little time with your aunt," he drawled. "I grieve that I must interrupt." The lie was evident in his voice, but then he turned, and Shi Po watched his body shift and become more languid. Just as always happened before he went on the offensive.

"I never learned how it was that my wife came to live with you when she was so young. Her parents were always so protective of their children. How did you convince them to allow you to act as mother for even that year?"

Shi Po could barely contain her gasp. She shrank away from her husband and her gaze darted to her aunt. Did he know? What did he suspect? Every possibility left her spirit chilled to ice.

Not so her aunt. Auntie Ting had long since perfected the skill of creative half-truths. "Ah," she simpered, "without a son or daughter of my own, what could my sister do but share?"

"What a great boon my wife must have been to you then. A comfort when your husband died."

Auntie Ting grinned, her smile stretching wide in her powdered face. "I could not have managed without her."

Shi Po shuddered, and her knees weakened as memories crowded into her mind. She banished them, of course, but not without cost, and she soon found herself sitting, her hands too weak to even tremble. Meanwhile, Kui Yu stepped closer and dropped a single, large hand on her shoulder. "So you have much to be grateful for from my wife."

"Ah," returned her aunt, "but we are like mother and daughter, she and I. The one supports the other in times of need." She leaned forward, her small eyes gleaming with threat. "She has asked for my advice, Kui Yu, and I have given it. See how pale she is? She knows she has brought danger to your home. She knows you must leave Shanghai immediately. Visit your sons at their tutor's home, look for a new property to buy in Canton—anything you like, but you must leave now."

Kui Yu frowned and his gaze slid to Shi Po. "Do you fear General Kang?" he asked her quietly. "We can—"

"No," Shi Po answered quickly. She would not be

chased from her home by an old woman's fears. "The monk has fled. The General has searched our home. We are of no more use to him."

"The General does not believe it," her aunt pressed. "He will think you have hidden—"

"He searched everywhere," Shi Po interrupted. "But if you fear for yourself, then by all means, run. Perhaps we can help you with money—"

"Idiot girl!" her aunt snapped. "I have ten times the gold your husband—"

"Then you have no need for our help," interrupted Kui Yu. "Good fortune, Mrs. Sung. Please write us when you feel safe again, and let us know where you settle." He took hold of the older woman's arm, firmly escorting her from the room. "We will not keep you from your packing."

Then she was gone, and Kui Yu with her, no doubt escorting her all the way out the front gate. That left Shi Po alone, her hands shaking, her body in turmoil. Fear was her aunt's constant companion, but it leeched into Shi Po whenever the woman visited. Frustration, abuse, and twisted practice had made Auntie Ting the wealthy widow she now was. But did that make the woman wrong? Was there truly a reason to fear?

Shi Po didn't know, and so she sat in numb silence, her hands twisting her husband's abandoned teacup around and around. Until Kui Yu returned to the room.

"Why do you allow her to come here?" he demanded. "Why does she speak to you that way?"

Shi Po looked up and saw yang burning in his eyes. He had such power even in so small a thing as the way he stood: his legs spread, his fists planted on his hips. His power was obvious, and yet he stood before her and asked questions. How many times had her uncle stood just the same way, even when his legs shook with the effort? How many times had he ordered her aunt to perform? Ordered his niece to do his bidding? And to what end?

"I am most fortunate in my husband," she murmured. "I should be grateful." She was. And she wasn't.

Kui Yu grimaced, his lips pressing into a tight line as he settled across from her at the table. "What happened between you and her?"

"She is worried that General Kang will harm her out of spite toward me."

Kui Yu shook his head. "No, what happened when you were a child? Why do you allow her to bully you? You give her more respect than you ever gave Lun Po, and he is head of your family."

She felt her lips curve in a mocking smile. "My brother is an idiot. My aunt is not."

"Your aunt is bitter and afraid. She poisons your yin."

Shi Po reared back, startled by his understanding. Surprised too by his knowledge of yin and yang, of poison and purity. "How do you know these terms?"

He shook his head, refusing to be distracted. "Tell me truthfully, Shi Po. Do you fear General Kang? Will he come for us this night?"

She bit her lip. "The monk is gone. He and the white woman."

"We can leave. Now. I have gold hidden nearby."

She shook her head. "He has no reason to take us."

Kui Yu nodded, but did not look convinced.

Shi Po pushed to her feet. She walked around the table so she could touch her husband, stroke his brow, and send him yin to balance out the yang that

Auntie Ting always evoked in anyone she met.

"Do not fear, my husband. I will see that no harm comes to us from my actions."

He turned and grabbed her hand. "Do you not understand? It is a *man*'s job to protect his family. A man should see to your safety." He pressed his lips to her palm. "I am your husband. I will see to—"

"There is no danger," she stated firmly. "I know exactly what to do."

His hands tightened. "I can protect us. We can leave."

She jerked backward hard enough so that he was forced to release her or give her bruises. He chose to relax his fingers. And when she was free, she pulled herself to her full height. "This is women's business. It will be handled in a woman's way."

He didn't answer, but watched her with dark eyes and a rising flush. Shi Po stood before him, her back straight, her mind clamoring for escape. But this was her husband. She owed him respect. So she stood and waited for his answer, even though she had already chosen her course.

"Very well," he finally said, his voice heavy with hidden meaning. "You handle your women's business. I will handle a man's."

She frowned, wondering what he meant, but he did not elaborate. Instead, he strode out of the room. It bothered her that she knew so little of his business. He traded with the whites: Shanghai cotton for gold. Silks for . . . what? Once for medicine, but the other times? He was so secretive. But then, so was she.

She heard him call for a messenger. He meant to write letters, she guessed. He had his "man's plans and his man's goals."

Which was as it should be. Because he was the

man. But she had her own plans. And in this, the Tigress would jump higher than the Dragon.

⁂

December 3, 1878

Dear Lun Po—

I grieve to hear of your uncle's illness. How like your sister to give up her marriage plans to help your aunt care for him. Only the most wholesome of daughters would delay her future to tend to an old man. Truly, Shi Po will be lauded throughout China as a chaste and filial daughter. Indeed, I have written bad poetry to that effect. Fortunately, I have consigned my efforts to the fire. My offerings are much too coarse for one of your ancestry. And yet, I cannot seem to help myself. When I grow tired of endless rendering in ugly English, my brush begins to wander and I find myself composing as a means of escape. Shi Po has ever been my inspiration. It is only fitting that I write poetry to her when I tire of the English.

I have saved the best offering here. It is terrible, but all that I have. Please attach it to this year's New Year's gift. I have left space on the page for your red chop, though I think perhaps you should sign it with your own hand.

The gift is a bolt of the finest red silk. I realized after I purchased it that it is too expensive a present from you, but I have a ready excuse for you. Tell her that you have saved your food money, skipping your breakfast meal just to buy her a present. And if she will not believe that, then con-

fess with all embarrassment that you have been selling your poems.

I must return to evaluating silks for shipment to Europe. I am even gaining a moderate understanding of horses. In truth, the whites seem to long to become Manchurians, thinking ideal life can only be accomplished upon the backs of these large beasts. They even adore the same smelly cheeses!

I suppose it is our curse that they are drawn to our more refined culture. And yet, in the way of all barbarians, they seek to control everything—even what they do not understand. Given that, China will always be besieged. Fortunately, we Han Chinese have learned how to remain ourselves even when subjugated by other people. And perhaps we will one day learn warfare and business from them. Then, truly, we will rise to an exalted place among all men.

In sincerity,
Kui Yu

A flower blossoms among thousands.
A pearl lost beneath sea and shell and sand.
The sage sees the perfection of color.
The merchant prices the single pearl.
The poor man weeps as he labors.

Once there was a Grand Commander who spoiled his children. He came home one day to find his son without a coat on, kneeling on the snow-covered ground. When asked why, his son confessed he was being punished by his grandmother for wrongdoing. Upon hearing this, the General took off his coat and knelt in the snow beside his son.

His mother, hearing of her son's bizarre behavior, came out to ask why.

"You're making my son suffer and catch cold," the Grand Commander answered. "So I'm making your son suffer and catch cold, too!"

Chapter Five

Shi Po walked through the classroom, idly tracing her fingers over a blank wall. When she taught, a scroll hung there. She closed her eyes, remembering the text.

Whoever brings together movement, breath, and semen becomes indestructible.

It was hidden now, as it was after every class. Many thought Tigresses were deviant, evil creatures on the surest path to Buddha's displeasure. They believed it a virtue to revile one such as her. She didn't blame them for their ignorance. Once, she had thought exactly the same.

She turned away from the blank wall, wandering out into the larger room where she and her cubs exercised. It, too, was empty now, the walls stripped bare.

Looking around, she felt a kinship with this large,

81

hollow space. In this room, her students had become enlightened; they had learned about their bodies and men's bodies. They had expanded the narrow province of what women were allowed in China and found a way to provide for themselves and possibly attain immortality.

She had done great things here. Just as she herself had given birth to three children, managed a household, and been a good wife to her husband. But now, she felt a great, empty nothingness. Like this room, she had no ties, no decoration. And only one last task to perform.

She had that task in her hand. It had taken her a long time to decide, for choosing a new wife for one's husband was a strange but challenging task. Whoever replaced her would not only care for Kui Yu and his sons, but also take over her Tigress teaching. In that way, the new woman would fulfill both Shi Po's promise of sturdy sons to support Kui Yu in his old age, while also training warm and beautiful young women who were strong enough to hold their destiny in their own hands.

It was a large task; but when put so simply, there was only one choice, one woman whom Shi Po trusted: Little Pearl. And so she had written up the assignment, matching Little Pearl with Kui Yu.

She knew they would end up married. Little Pearl would know immediately what was expected, and Kui Yu was a man of easy passions. He would fall quickly into the trap of attachment to his new partner. She estimated two months at most before the wedding announcement.

She set the scroll on the slightly raised dias, right where she stood when leading her class's exercises. She set her dagger beside it and turned to her next task.

Now, where did she want to die? Where was best to stage her ascension? She asked the questions, but did not pursue the answers. Instead, she left the knife beside her instructions to Little Pearl and wandered across the large, dark room.

"I knew you would come here."

Shi Po spun around, startled by her husband's soft voice. He stood in the main doorway, his face shadowed, his evening clothing luminous in the moonlight.

Had she once again been waiting for him, wondering if he would come to give a final good-bye? Or was her dedication wavering? Did she wish him to talk her into another choice? She didn't know, and that bothered her. One could not ascend to Heaven with a cluttered soul. Which meant she could not ascend until she found peace with her husband.

"I have been waiting for you," she said with sudden illumination. "I wish for harmony between us."

The room was dark, but moonlight filtered in enough to show him the scroll and dagger, especially as he had excellent vision. "You are still determined, then. Despite your promise to start again," he said.

She shook her head. "I have no need to start again. Only to end well."

"Do not all people wish to redo what went wrong, to return to where they left the correct path?"

Shi Po felt herself smile, startled that he could evoke her humor even now. "But I have not left the correct path. And I have done all most excellently."

"Ah," he said, stepping fully into the room. "Sometimes I forget that you are indeed the most perfect wife a man could have."

She joined him where he stood. "I did not say I was an excellent wife. I said I have done all I intended.

And done those things well." She said the words, even meant them as she did, but inside a small part of her wondered. Had she truly done everything? Had she done all that could be done, accomplished all that she wanted in this life?

As she struggled with her thoughts, Kui Yu took her hands, his expression sober. "There is more, Shi Po. Truly there is much more for you."

She shook her head. "My children are grown, my tigress school thrives. There is nothing more but immortality." She turned away from him and crossed to her scroll of instructions. Picking it up, she spoke—but to the blank wall, not Kui Yu.

"I have assigned Little Pearl to you. She will instruct—aii!"

His arm wrapped around her throat, cutting off her breath as he dragged her backward. Her hands dug into his forearm to no avail. And all the while he spoke, his voice low in her ear.

"*You* are my partner, Shi Po. I will take no other."

She didn't answer, and after a moment's thought, she let her hands fall limp to her sides. She would not struggle. His hold was not intended to choke her, just to get her attention. He had it. But she had something else: a clear path. So she relaxed, and in time, so did he. But he continued to stand behind her, his arm wrapped loosely about her neck.

"Kui Yu—"

"You promised," he whispered, and his voice betrayed desperation more than anger. "You said you would wait."

"I have waited. Until I resolved those things you mentioned. But now all is settled—"

"Nothing is settled!" With a quick jerk, he spun her to face him. She tottered on her bound feet, but he held her safe. As he always had done. Looking into his eyes, she saw anguish.

"It will pass, Kui Yu," she said. "You will find—"

His mouth was suddenly on hers. She thought to struggle. She intended to fight him. This lovemaking would only bring him pain. But the yin tide was already rising, her body softening. And, she thought, perhaps this was meant to be; perhaps the Goddess Kwan Yin had sent him to be with her. He could bring her yin tide to its crest and aid her transition to immortality.

It was right and proper that a husband should ease his wife's transition from one life into the next, and so she allowed herself to relax into his arms, to arch her body against his, to open herself up as only a woman can with a man she trusts.

And in this way . . . "You will take me to Heaven," she murmured.

He stilled, his lips not leaving hers. Then he nodded, his words as much breathed into her skin as spoken aloud. "I will do this with you. I will take you to immortality. Here. And we will see what can be done."

She smiled, pleased he understood. "Start with—"

"I need no instruction in this, wife. I know how to love a woman."

"But this—"

His fingers stopped her words. He had drawn his face back, his body slowly separating from hers. "Trust me, Shi Po. I read your scrolls. I will bring your yin tide to such height that we will both drown in it."

She nodded, realizing that he had to express his good-bye in his own manner. So she relaxed and allowed herself to become all that was feminine, agreeable, and receptive. She would take what he offered and cherish the gift. It was the least she could do now that she understood how much he would suffer when she was gone.

So long as she kept the dagger nearby, so long as she had it when yin and yang flowed at their peaks, then she could ascend to immortality in the proper way. She had chosen a poison with just this plan in mind. It would provide that last bit of needed power to launch her to Heaven.

She reached up to the collar of her blouse and slipped the buttons free, opening the fine silk. She moved slowly out of habit, remembering that men loved to watch a woman undress. Indeed, her husband's eyes followed the slow slide of fabric to her undergarment—a diamond-shaped thin gauze that hinted at the shapes and colors beneath. She dropped the silk on the floor, then began untying her skirt at the waist. The binding clung to her hips until she shimmied. Then it slipped down.

She stood before her husband, her only covering the bindings on her feet and the undergarment that covered from her breasts to her navel. Knowing the effect it would have on her husband, she stepped out of her skirt and into a wash of moonlight, allowing the ghostly light to illuminate her skin.

His eyes followed her, slowly traveling from her face down past the two embroidered butterflies spiraled together on her undergarment. His gaze hovered at the tasseled bottom of the diamond, where the gathered threads swayed. Then he stopped, his vision transfixed by the tattooed tigress just beneath that silk fringe. The tattoo continued down between her thighs and up her back to where the tigress's tail coiled at the base of her spine. Without conscious thought, she began to move, making the tigress dance.

She quickly stopped, choosing not to tease him in

this manner. Now was not the time for such artifice. They would have honesty instead.

Kui Yu reached out, stroking his fingers across the tiger's eye ridge, across the flesh above her shaved sex. Then he pushed onward, sliding his long middle finger down and across the tigress's belly. In and in he went. Deeper. Lower. With excruciating patience. While Shi Po's legs trembled.

She stood there, watching him watch her. And below, she felt his middle finger wiggle and caress, his other fingers fanning out to graze all of her pleasure grotto. It was as if he were holding not only her, but everything she ever was or would be. She wanted to speak, but her throat was dry. She wanted to whisper endearments, but such words had never come to her lips. Never in honesty, at least; and she would not lie to Kui Yu now.

So she stood silent, and her breath hitched with every shifting of his fingers, until he was nearly inside her.

Her cave was moist, but the opening remained virginally narrow. Shi Po had spent many long hours making sure it was so. But so plentiful was her yin rain that his longest finger easily slid around and to her opening. It poised there, her husband waiting and watching while she said nothing.

She understood his thoughts. It had been years since she had allowed anyone, even Kui Yu, to penetrate her cave. No dragon had stretched her entrance. No finger or even Tigress ball had strengthened the muscles. Nothing beyond her own hand for bathing had been allowed. Would she accept his intrusion? Would she . . .

She tensed, years of training instinctively tightening her muscles against him. And feeling her reaction, he slowed. She grabbed hold of his arm.

"Let me control my breath," she whispered. With

control of her air, she could control her body.

He stood absolutely still while she breathed through her nose and recited Tigress poetry in her head. She would allow the lotus to open. She would let the dew coat its petals. And she would feel the bee as it . . .

He was inside her.

She gasped at the intrusion, tightening her hold on his arm to steady herself. Deeper and deeper he delved. His finger twisted, shifting and adjusting while she felt his every firm inch against her petals.

His other fingers were not idle. They fanned open, and now they adjusted, pressing against places that were not in the scrolls, areas that many a tutored hand would not find. But her husband was not instructed in any technique, so he simply touched all, teased every part of her. And now, his thumb joined its brothers, burrowing cleverly in a manner that sent bursts of yin heat across Shi Po's skin.

Shi Po wanted to lie down. She wanted to spread her legs and allow Kui Yu an open field in which to explore. Her yin was strong, but she knew how much more could be done, how white hot the blaze could grow. But she had no focus to form the words, no desire to interrupt his explorations merely to ease the strain on her feet. So she stood as still as her trembling legs would allow, her breath coming in tiny pants.

And still he pushed deeper. She had not thought his finger so long, so large, and yet it was. She felt it to the top of her womb as he continued to twist, to slide, and to probe. Until he was done. Until he withdrew his hand in one abrupt pull.

Shi Po cried out, tightening her thighs against his escape, trying desperately to slow it. But he'd been too strong for her, too quick.

"Terrible, isn't it? To suddenly lose that which has grown comfortable?" he asked. She knew he referred to her imminent departure. He was trying to give her a small taste of the pain he would experience on her death.

She shook her head. "You were never fully comfortable, my husband. And even if you were, why would you want it to continue? 'He who is not satisfied with his life will grow,'" she quoted. "'A comfortable man becomes lazy and stagnant.'"

Anger flashed cold and hard in his eyes. "I am done wasting words on you, wife. I would forbid your suicide if I thought you would listen. I would lock you in your room and tie your hands, but that would only harden your determination. Therefore, I will take my last enjoyment of your body. I will bring your yin tide to its peak, my yang to its fullness, and then we shall see who enters Heaven first. Will it be you, with your training and your discipline, or me, drenched in your yin rain?"

"It will be me," she whispered. "You know it will."

He shrugged, his eyes glittering with feverish zeal. "Do not be so sure," he growled. "I have as much yang as you have purified yin. Tonight, I intend to take what I want and leave tomorrow to fortune."

Shi Po nodded, accepting the challenge. She was startled to find her breath quickening with excitement. So much of the Tigress path echoed with sameness, repetition, and boredom. This, at least, would be different.

"Then it shall be," she answered, knowing she reflected his determination back at him.

As she reached behind her neck, intending to release the upper tie to her undergarment, he stopped her, his hands firm as he gripped her wrists. He said, "I will undress you, wife. In my time and in the manner of my choosing."

He released her hands, which dropped slowly down her sides. She frowned in thought. Something was different about Kui Yu. Something dark and powerful possessed him. Something blacker even than the moon-drenched night. For a moment she paused, her thoughts slipping to the outside world, to the question of what exactly her husband did in Shanghai during his days. What tasks could have brought such darkness to his usually bright spirit?

"Kui Yu . . . ," she began, but she had no time. He reached behind her to the dais. Grabbing her dagger, he unsheathed the blade with the ringing sound of metal against metal.

"Kui Yu!" she cried as he placed the naked blade in his palm. It glittered there, cold and deadly. "It is coated with poison," she warned. One tiny cut and he would die.

"I know," he said, continuing to stare at the blade. Then his gaze flicked to her for a brief moment. "Arrange yourself, wife. On your back."

She glanced around the empty room, to the cold wooden floor. "We should retire to our bedchamber," she suggested.

He glanced at the floor, then with long strides stepped to the hidden compartment in the wall. He knew the cache well, and exactly what was hidden there. In no time at all, he pulled out the silk hanging that adorned the wall when she taught. With a mighty heave, he unrolled it on the floor.

"Lie on that," he snarled.

She did not argue. She knelt on the soft white fabric, then, as he glared at her, shifted position. Her bottom hit the pristine silk, her legs slowly extended before her, astride the word "semen." Kui Yu stood above her, his eyes blackened pits in a shadowy face.

"Array yourself!" he commanded again.

She shivered. Though she had wanted just this situation a few moments ago, now it made her quail with apprehension. She knew her yin rain had dried, yet she would not disobey. She couldn't, for she sat directly upon the character "bring together," her feet extending toward the word "indestructible."

"Lie down."

She did, her stomach quivering beneath the tiny tassel of her undergarment, her neck straining to keep her head upright to watch the dark and unbalanced stranger above her. He was stripping off his clothing with hard and angry jerks. Perhaps she could reach him now in his distraction, find again the man she knew, the one who would hate to see her uncomfortable, who would leap to reassure her.

But her words died in her throat the moment he turned back, roughly pushing her legs apart. He was completely naked as he dropped to his knees between her spread thighs, the hair on his legs brushing a tingling heat along her sensitive skin.

"Do not speak," he ordered. "Do not even breathe deeply."

She swallowed, feeling as weak as her tattooed tigress, who now lay with its naked belly exposed. Then he brought out her knife, extending the tip toward her as he lay it lengthwise on her belly. The point aimed toward her neck, the carved hilt dragon extended down to where her husband's own organ bobbed in hungry desire.

"I would see your breasts, my wife. I would have all your secrets exposed tonight." And so saying, he slid the blade upward, easily slicing the silk tassel. Then, stitch by tiny stitch, he cut her undergarment away.

She could kill herself now. All she needed to do was take a deep breath, one sharp inhalation, and the dagger tip would pierce her skin. With a quick tightening of her belly, a slight lift to her chest—part of her daily Tigress exercises—she could ensure the point went deep enough. The poison would flow into her blood. She would die.

But she wasn't ready. Her yin fluids were rapidly cooling in her prone state. Death now would be fruitless, a certain descent into a cold grave rather than the ascent to Heaven that she'd planned.

No, she would not impale herself now. And looking at Kui Yu's hardened expression, she knew he'd been certain of that. Despite all the imbalance between them, he understood her better than anyone.

So it continued: the cold blade sliding against her shrinking flesh, the steady tug then release as thread after thread strained against its sharp edge, then lost the battle and fell away, split neatly in two. Shi Po didn't speak. And she didn't close her eyes. She wanted to watch this new man who lived inside her husband's skin. She wanted to read his thoughts and learn what he intended next.

At last, the coarse brush of gauze slipped across her breasts and fell away. Shi Po's nipples tightened in the cool air and thrust toward her husband. Her only covering remained at the top of her garment, where the double-stitched hem stopped her blade. Kui Yu settled the dagger there in the notch at the center of her collarbone.

"Arch, my wife," he ordered, his voice a thick

growl. "Lift your breasts to me, show me the white of your throat."

She did as he bade her. How could she not? She dared not risk a nick on her chin. But she acted in her own way, moving of her own choosing. She was a Tigress after all, with a set of skills well learned from years of practice.

Pressing her bound feet down against the floor, she lifted her hips, then her back. As she moved, she felt the knife slide downward, back between her breasts. But she didn't stop there. She continued her undulation, forcing her belly upward, rolling her chest high so that her breasts trembled just below his mouth. And then, at the very last, her head fell back, exposing her neck.

She froze there, in arched display before him.

"Is this what you meant?" she asked, her voice overly sweet, because she knew it was not at all what he intended; it had been so much more. In this manner, she planned to regain some command over the situation. A man overcome with lust could be easily controlled.

Her husband, however, was not overcome. Instead, he leaned farther and farther forward. Shi Po's nipples tightened as his hot breath skated across them. He was kneeling on all fours over her, the blade inching higher and higher on her body. Surely it was against her throat now. She could feel the death energy tingling against her chin.

"Yes," he whispered, his voice coarse and low. "You are exactly what I want."

Then he lifted the blade, clipping the last of the fabric away. Then he tossed the blade across the room.

Her back was beginning to strain, her arch too heavy to hold. But she felt Kui Yu's yang heat like a hot breeze against her chilled body. It drew her upward, no matter that her muscles protested the strain. Despite the strangeness of this encounter, despite the anger that still hardened his features, Shi Po's body recognized the roiling yang within her husband. She wanted to touch him, she wanted to merge with him. She simply *wanted*. But he would not lower himself to her. And she could not sustain her position for long.

Eventually her back gave out, and she sank back to the floor. Only then did he follow. Only then did he touch her. And only then did she close her eyes, the exquisiteness of his tongue's caress bringing a sigh of delight from her lips.

He sucked on her left nipple. Without touching any other part of her body, he drew the peak into his mouth and rubbed his tongue across it. Up. Down. Up. Down. Suction at every stroke.

Shi Po's yin tide surged higher with each caress. Her yin rain flowed freely again. What had closed up in fear, now opened with joy. Even the belly of her tattooed tigress quivered with hunger. And still Kui Yu continued his rhythmic assault.

Up. Down. Up. Down.

Then he stopped. Tightening his lips, he pulled himself—and her breast—higher and higher. Her body once again arched, her hands pushed down on the floor so that she might remain with him for a moment longer.

Then he moved away, and she fell backward with a crash. She landed hard on the floor. Her eyes were open now, and she searched for clues as to his next action. She found him grinning, the evening shadow unable to obscure the pearly whiteness of his teeth. Indeed, for a moment, she thought he appeared more beast than man, more dragon than husband.

Reaching out with his left hand, he casually kneaded her right breast.

"You liked that, didn't you, wife?" His voice was calm, almost bland, except for the low purr of satisfaction that trembled just beneath. On any other man, she would not have noticed, but this was her husband whom she had known since they were children. She recognized gloating satisfaction in him, even though he thought he hid it.

Oddly enough, she wasn't displeased. Let him have his joy. She was his wife, after all. He should enjoy their last time together. So she smiled, a lazy expression that startled him. "Yes, Kui Yu," she purred, "I do like that. Very much."

He watched her a moment and his hand stilled on her breast. "We have never talked this way before," he said slowly. "I have always done what I enjoyed and you allowed." Then he began to mold and shape her breast again, slowly narrowing his fingers to her nipple which he squeezed in short tiny pulses.

"Do you like this as well?"

His hand was large. She had forgotten how engulfed it could make her feel.

"I enjoy knowing the hard textures of you, Kui Yu," she said. She reached up and touched his face. "The rough scratch of your beard." She tightened her legs, drawing her calves up along the sides of his legs. "The coarse brush of the hair on your thighs." Then she reached out and pulled his other hand to her so that he held both her breasts. "And most especially, your hands."

He squeezed. He touched. He played. While she

95

closed her eyes and savored the yin rise. She knew that what he did was against practice. He was too rough. His motions would eventually make her breasts loose and flabby. She didn't care. She liked his too-hard touch. Especially when he tweaked her nipples.

"Your skin is rough," she murmured aloud, speaking as much to herself as to him. "Thickened from hard labor."

He stilled. "I'm sorry—" But she shook her head.

"You don't understand." She drew his hand to her lips. She spread his fingers and gently kissed each ridge. "I have always loved your hands. It is the soft, perfumed hands of my brother that sicken me."

She could see that he was watching her, thinking hard about her words, so she set about proving them. She tongued his hand, exploring in short strokes the crevices between his fingers. Then she shifted to long lines down his palm before finally sucking his fingers one by one into her mouth.

She took a long time at this, releasing his one hand to raise his other to her mouth. He allowed her. But as she began her ministrations to his left hand, his right slid down her side. He paused only briefly at her breast before flowing down her belly, across the tigress face, and then between her legs to stroke the tigress's belly.

Once there, he followed her lead. When she dipped between his fingers, he slipped between her petals. When she licked long strokes across his palm, he pulled his thumb from her cave opening up to roll across her tigress pearl. And when she pulled his finger inside her mouth, he pushed himself deep inside her.

The small circle of yin established itself in her body, flowing from her breasts, through her womb, then up to her brain before returning to her breasts. She gloried in that wonderful current, which lifted her belly and heated her thoughts. With each stroke of his hand, the quivering deepened, became more intense and more holy.

She rolled her tongue across the side of his hand. Taking the meaty part between her teeth, she bit lightly. He growled low in his throat and spread her lotus petals wide, sliding his thumb and forefinger up to her pearl. Her jaw quivered, and she nibbled. So too did his fingers pinch and roll. Her yin flowed fast and hard, her internal bellows tightening in preparation.

But she had no larger circle, no yang river to complement and mix with her yin. She would not reach Heaven this way. She had to create the yang circle. She had to touch and stroke and bring her husband to fullness in order to create the dual rivers. So she pushed away his hand, struggling to sit up.

"No," she gasped. "The yang circle . . . It's not—"

"I know," answered her husband, his voice harsh enough to sound cruel. Then he pressed her back to the floor with his free hand. The other hand continued mercilessly. "There will be no yang circle tonight, wife." He held her down, while between her thighs he continued to pinch and roll and rub.

If she were alone, she would meditate her stored yang into a circling flow. Now there was no time. She had to end this. She knew that the yin river took a huge amount of energy. Too soon, and she would exhaust herself before she established the yang circle. Too late, and she would be frustrated with no power at all.

But he would not let her escape. The yin tide surged. It crested. It engulfed her. Too soon! Too soon!

He knew what he was doing: That was the last thought filtering through her mind as she began to ride the yin tigress. Her body clenched and writhed, her breath came in gasping bursts. And still Kui Yu continued, smiling at her while he held her frozen, his free arm pressed across her hips, his other hand alternating between thrusting deep into her womb before pulling all the way out to stroke a hardened thumb over and around her yin pearl.

It was wonderful. It was the yin tigress in her full, explosive ride. And it was also totally useless. Without the yang circle, Shi Po would not go to Heaven. So she sobbed at her husband, pleaded as best as she could for him to release her, to stop the torment.

He did not, and her heart trembled even as her mind and body exploded with ecstasy.

Then there was no thought, no practice, only the sweet enjoyment of pleasure, the deep breath of expansiveness, with no mind whatsoever.

What?

The yin tide receded. Shi Po's body began to still and her breath began to recover. But her mind was still trembling.

What had . . . ?

Her legs rolled open as her muscles gave out. Her lungs steadied, though their pattern remained quick. And her tattooed tigress tilted upward as her back muscles finally gave way, dropping her body unceremoniously flat onto the floor.

What had he . . . ?

Her breathing returned to normal; the yin tide receded to a pleasant warmth, but no more. Her eyes opened, and in the darkness, she saw little beyond Kui Yu's moonlit outline and his ivory-white smile.

At that moment, she realized something was different. Something vast and huge and fundamental had shifted in her. But she couldn't quite identify the shift, much less give it a name.

What had her husband done?

❧❧❧

July 9, 1879

(Sent to the Tseng patriarch upon the return of Shi Po from her aunt's home, forty-nine days after her uncle's funeral.)

    Dear honorable Mr. Tseng—

    Please accept this humble gift, a pale reflection of the joy and double happiness that must fill your home at the return of your chaste and filial daughter.

                With great respect,
                Tan Kui Yu

(Attached was a scepter of Imperial jade, exquisitely carved in three oval segments: the first, a three-toed dragon; the last a phoenix, her sharp talons extended. Between them, on the center segment, danced a magical pearl trailing celestial ribbons of power.)

    September 10, 1879

(Sent to the Tseng patriarch upon the occasion of his son's departure for the Imperial examination.)

Great sir—

Please accept this most modest gift. It is but a small reflection of the benefits I have received from your most learned son, Lun Po. We studied together, and I have ever felt inspired by his intellect.

> *In humble gratitude,*
> *Tan Kui Yu*

(Attached was a rare copy of the Confucian Analects.*)*

January 24, 1880

(Sent to the Tseng patriarch on the occasion of his fiftieth birthday.)

Double Happiness on the glorious anniversary of your birth.

The Heavens celebrate with birdsong.
The Earth brings forth its beauty.
And your children reflect your eminence.

(Attached was a Mandarin jacket made of red silk shot through with gold and silver threads. The style modern, the design elaborate, the fasteners made of carved ivory.)

A man asked a craftsman if he could make a table with less timber than usual so as to save money. "I can make a table with only two legs," the craftsman suggested, "and by leaning it up against a pillar, it will work fine."

One night, the moonlight was bright and the man tried to set his table out in the yard, but of course it wouldn't stand up. Then he sent for the craftsman and complained.

"It's no problem cutting costs at home," said the craftsman, "but how can you expect to economize when you go out?"

Chapter Six

Kui Yu watched fear slip into his wife's expression. Her joy was a thing of beauty, something to immortalize in poetry or opera. In happiness, Shi Po had a glow that expanded outward from her center and encompassed all.

He had only seen her happy four other times. Three occasions were on the births of their children, in that incredible moment after the baby emerges. The children themselves were angry, scrunched, wailing balls covered in fluids. But when they finally quieted and settled against Shi Po's breast to nurse away their fears, Kui Yu had seen Heaven. In that moment, he had looked into his wife's eyes and felt that threefold happiness wished to all new parents. Except Shi Po's joy at those times was not threefold. It was a hundredfold, a thousandfold. And it touched not only the child, but him as well. Her joy was so expansive, she encompassed the whole world in welcoming their new child.

Those three moments were etched upon his spirit as indelibly as the day he had lifted the veil from his new wife's face and known, without doubt, that he had wed Shi Po. He did not know if the joy he'd felt that day had been only his or hers too, but he remembered the same welling of life that could only be divine. Such had been his happiness to wed this woman.

And now was the fifth time, a moment begun in frustration which had led to a beauty that humbled him. He saw contentment and awe in her face and writhing body. He felt an overwhelming honor that his delicate woman could find such fulfillment from his large, work-roughened hands. And most of all, he felt his own worries scatter, his emptiness ease when her joy touched him.

But then it faded. Fear stole into her eyes. That too was quickly hidden, covered by the hardened facade she so often adopted.

"Why do you hide from me, Shi Po?" he asked. He spoke the words without thought, knowing it was a foolish question. One could not confront fear so abruptly. It only made terror grab hold, and brought a response of sharp, angry words and a quick withdrawal. He knew this, and yet he could not stop himself.

She straightened onto her elbows and pulled away from him. "I hide nothing!" she snapped. "I am laid open before you!"

He remained silent, feeling her defenses harden. What did men do to find softness in the world? How did a man create comfort in a spirit that was only

sharp edges and glittering pain? For that was what
Shi Po's fear made her: sharp and painful. No wonder
she sought to escape this world into immortality. She
longed for the safety of Heaven.

The thought came to him on a breeze that deposited its wisdom before blowing past. Most days he
would have missed it, too busy with making his fortune. But he was quiet just then, and his gaze rested
on the moon-washed form of his beautiful wife even
as she scooted backward on the silk tapestry.

His wife needed to feel safe. The thought rocked
him to the core. Despite her position as lead Tigress,
despite all his fortune and their many things, she was
nearly paralyzed by fear. And that fear brought out
all that was terrible inside her. That was why she was
so angry now. That was why she hated that he had
given her pleasure without practice. Because she did
not feel safe unless she controlled her experience. Unless she managed everything to the tiniest detail.

Kui Yu straightened, fighting his new understanding. He did not want to believe that all his work to
make money meant nothing. That all this time, his
goal had been the wrong one.

What did a man do to make his family safe?

"I am weary, Shi Po," he said. He did not want her
to retreat completely from him, so he placed his hand
on that part of her he could reach: her still-quivering
thigh. And she obliged him by not pulling completely
away.

He stroked his hand down, liking the touch of her
skin, the smooth slide down her elegant leg and
strong calf. Until he came to her foot bindings. They
interrupted the flow of his hand and the length of her
leg. Without even thinking, he began to unwind
them.

"What are you doing?" she cried, clearly alarmed.

He stilled and frowned first at her then down at his hand. He hadn't fully realized what he was doing, but now that he had, he would not be denied. "It is my right as your husband to see your feet." His voice was cold. Why did he sound angry with her?

"Of course it is your right, Kui Yu," she soothed, "but surely you don't wish—"

"Surely I do," he snapped in frustration. He shut his mouth and tried to keep his venom inside. But his anger came out in his motions as he roughly unwound the cloth.

She squirmed, clearly unhappy.

"Does this hurt?" he asked. If it did, he would stop.

He saw something flash in her eyes, a deviousness that came from fear, but in the end, her gaze dropped to her lap.

"No," she said, her voice barely audible. "It doesn't hurt."

"Then why . . . ?"

"Because they are not washed. Because they are not my best asset. Because no woman wishes to be exposed in all her ugliness."

He did not understand. "Your feet are beautiful." Then to emphasize the statement, he pulled away the last wrap around her left foot. He lifted it, the scent unpleasant, the golden lotus shape as beautiful as it was grotesque.

"Stop, Kui Yu," she begged. "Leave them alone. They smell."

He nodded because it was true. So he set her foot down and stood. "Stay there," he ordered as he moved quickly into a side room. It was a room for practice, available at all hours for the students. It would be empty now because of General Kang's visit, but there would be fresh water and cleaning cloths.

He grabbed those things, also finding more binding strips and a basin, and he returned as quickly as possible, releasing his breath only when he saw his wife still on the tapestry. She had not fled. She sat with her foot bindings in her hand.

"Put those cloths away," he said. "I have brought fresh."

She didn't respond, except to watch him with wary eyes. As he settled at her feet, she finally spoke with a tart tone. "You cannot go about the house naked. It is unseemly," she complained.

He nodded to acknowledge it. In truth, he had forgotten he was naked. His entire focus had been on his wife. "Very well," he replied. "I will restrict such behavior to the kitchens."

She gasped at his audacity. Still, the fear in her eyes lessened. It did not disappear, however, especially as he lifted her right foot and quickly released the bonds.

The bindings were as smelly as the others, so he quickly tossed them across the room. Shi Po leaned forward to bathe her feet herself. She poured water into the basin and began to arrange herself, but Kui Yu stopped her.

It had been well over a decade since he had seen her naked feet. He had looked his fill as a new bridegroom, of course, but he had not touched them, too interested in his wife's other assets. Later, he had seen and even occasionally touched, but his wife was well skilled in methods to distract him.

Not this time, he vowed. Tonight, he would look and touch his fill. And tell her what he thought, for she was obviously embarrassed by their size.

He lifted her feet, carefully setting them both in the

105

basin of water. She tried to fight him, but he needed no words to show his determination. His touch was firm, his expression hard, and in time, she gave in to his strength with an irritated huff.

"You need not do this," she protested.

"Yes, I do," he replied. Then he moderated his hot tone. Tonight was for honesty, so he spoke with unaccustomed frankness as he stroked a bathing cloth over her nearly five-inch feet.

"How can you think these are large?" he marveled as he held a foot in his hand. It barely covered half his palm.

She drew back at his question, but he had hold of her ankle and would not release her. "Don't be a fool," she snapped. "You know it was done too late and with great ignorance."

He nodded. He knew the story, probably in more detail than she thought, for he had heard her tell the tale to their daughter. So he began speaking with awe as he caressed her tiny golden lotuses. "Your four toes were curled under first," he said as he lifted and washed beneath the tiny pads of her smaller toes. She gasped as he worked, and he looked quickly at her face, trying to read her expression.

"Go slowly, Kui Yu. They are very sensitive."

He nodded, knowing this was true. Nothing so hidden away could be exposed and not feel every brush of air, every whisper of water and cloth.

"Your big toe came second," he continued, "curled over the smaller ones." He took his time with the large digit, circling its base all the way out to the tip as one would cup a beautiful flower bud. "Then broken pottery was pressed into your sole to bring on infection and to soften the flesh."

He pulled back her toes and applied himself to the

moist, hot center of her foot. He washed as gently as he could, letting the tepid liquid flow along her flesh, easing the remembered pain. She remained silent, frozen in stillness until he applied the cloth. Then she began to pant with tiny puffs of breath that indicated great sensitivity.

"All this mass is pulled tighter and tighter until the bones break, the flesh softens, and the child stops crying," he said.

"We never stop crying, Kui Yu," she answered in a whisper. "Not until it is all done."

He knew that was true. "Eventually, the flesh is putrid. Then the foot is opened, the shards removed, the infection cleansed, and the tightest bindings are applied. That is when the foot is molded into this most perfect lotus shape."

He thought she had lost her anger, and so it surprised him when she abruptly pulled her foot away. Her bitterness was a palpable thing. "How do you know all this?" she asked.

He blinked. "We have a daughter. I was there for—"

"You were not!" she snapped. Then she swallowed, her eyes dropping to her lap. "That was women's work."

He nodded. It was. But he had listened to their daughter's sobbing, heard every scream, even watched his beautiful child totter and fall as she relearned how to walk. He had heard it, seen it, even felt it . . . for as long as he could stand.

Then, in the way of all Chinese men, he had fled the house, immersing himself in his work, his money, his dreams of building a safe and happy home out of the sweat of his body.

He had succeeded. And so had Shi Po. Their

daughter had married excellently. Her three-inch golden lotuses had passed the mother-in-law inspection, garnering her a wealthy, prestigious future.

His own mother, of course, had not known to inspect her future daughter-in-law. And so she had not know Shi Po's lotuses were too large and poorly shaped. Kui Yu hadn't cared, but Shi Po did. Shi Po knew. And so she had perpetually hidden her feet from him.

He grasped her other foot and pulled it toward him. He was firm, and as always her womanliness gave way to his strength. But she gave in with ill grace, growling, "My mother was a fool. To go through that agony and do it wrong . . ." She closed her eyes, her bitterness clear.

"It shows strength, Shi Po," he said without thought. "Your feet are a symbol to me of your strength and determination. I see this, and I marvel that you would do this to yourself. That your sex would endure such agony for men's pleasure." He shook his head, still confounded.

"It is not our choice, Kui Yu. It is done to us when we are too small to understand."

He nodded, nonplussed. "I could not have done it, Shi Po. Not to our daughter. Not to any child. You have the strength I do not." He shrugged even as he continued to cup her tiny feet. "I know that a woman with large feet will never marry well. That she often starves to death on the street if she cannot or will not prostitute herself to survive. That her husband, if one is bought for her, is an object of pity and scorn. I know these things, and yet I do not have your strength. I ran when I should have added my voice to yours. I made money for her dowry when you were ensuring that there would be suitors."

"That is your task," Shi Po said. "It is what a father does."

Kui Yu shook his head, knowing she would never understand. He looked at his wife and saw strength in her tiny feet, power in her swaying carriage, and a stunning resilience in her determination to survive anything that life demanded. He saw her, and he was amazed. He held her feet and was ashamed of his own weakness.

And yet, as he looked at her, he knew she understood none of that, could not comprehend his thoughts, and most of all, did not even believe that a man—any man—would think these things. So he remained silent in the face of her bitterness, unable to express that two inches or ten inches of feet made no difference to him. Well-shaped or grotesquely altered, her feet were a reflection of her spirit, and that he admired.

He said none of these things. He had no words for them. So he applied himself to her feet, letting his thoughts translate into his touch. His fingers dallied in each tiny crevice, gave attention to each softened curve or hardened callous. He gave to all parts of her feet, and in time, he heard her soft, barely stifled moans of pleasure.

The sole of a bound foot was the most sensitive part of a woman's body, save her yin pearl. A man educated in the ways of a dragon knew just how to touch a woman's feet in order to arouse. Kui Yu had read the dragon texts, knew just what to do, though he had never attempted the techniques before now. So he was pleased when his actions produced the very result promised in the manual. His wife began to pant, her hips shifting with rising yin. The scent of her desire rose in the humid air, mixing with the yang in his body to confound his thoughts and harden his dragon.

He loved to watch her lost in the yin embrace, and so he turned, facing her as he thrust his thumbs deep into the recesses of her two golden lotuses. She was watching him, her eyes still clear even as her yin tide made her thighs tremble and the belly of her tattooed tigress glisten with dew.

"The yin runs hot," she gasped. "But what of the yang?"

He shook his head. She could not attain Heaven without the greater yang circle. If he gave her no yang, she would remain here on Earth. With him. That was his plan, and it had succeeded well only moments ago. But he had not reckoned on Shi Po's determination. Or her skill.

One of her feet escaped his grasp. It lifted away from him only to wend its way to his dragon. The merest brush, and his yang fire surged high enough to singe his mind.

He gasped, startled by his reaction. Was he not a man? A thinking creature who had vowed to walk the dragon's path? He would not succumb to the yang hunger. He would not thrust into a woman's hot, tight opening like a beast driven mad by lust.

He would not, and yet before he realized what had occurred, his dragon was surrounded. Her feet cupped his organ, her twin lotuses slid up and down in blatant invitation.

"No!" he exclaimed. Or he thought he did. But he heard only the guttural moan of a man in pleasure.

Her tattooed tigress danced before him. Her cinnabar cave perfumed the air.

He could not . . . And yet, as the thought filtered through his fogged mind, he already knew it was too late. He felt the yang circle establish. From his dragon to his mind, his blood burned with desire. But that was not the worst of it. Another circle established hard and fast. It flowed male yang into Shi Po and returned sweet yin back to him. Even inexperienced as he was, he recognized the energy, knew the arc for what it was.

She had his yang. And the more she rubbed her sensitive lotuses against his dragon, the higher her yin rose.

Already she was near the peak. He heard her gasping breath as it matched his own. But her eyes were clear, her focus intent, and he knew she was preparing. With his yang and her yin, she would find Heaven.

To his horror, he watched as she extended her hand. He had thought the dagger far, far away, but she must have retrieved it when he left the room. She must have placed it next to her, and—fool that he was—he hadn't noticed.

He knew what she intended. When yin and yang reached their peak, she would cut herself. It didn't matter where. All that mattered was that the poison enter her blood. That moment of death would provide the last boost she needed to attain immortality. It would launch her to Heaven, leaving him abandoned on Earth.

Heedless of the cost, he threw himself forward, stretching his hand to pin her wrist.

He caught her, his greater weight holding her hand down, the dagger away from her tender skin. It was over then; he had stopped her. Or so he believed.

But again, he had not counted on her determination or skill.

Hissing in anger, she glared at him. "I will not be denied," she said.

Then she applied herself to his pleasure. If he thought her feet skillful before, it was nothing compared to what she did now. She stroked his dragon. With her feet, she pushed down his sheath to expose its full and hungry head. A yang pearl escaped, and she rolled it around with the curved center of her lotus. Her toes wiggled along the dragon ridge, just behind its head. Her heel rotated along the opposite axis, a rough counterpoint to the pulsing movements of her toes. In this way, she stimulated her own yin and set his yang to throbbing against her sensitive sole.

She was stealing his yang, using it to leave him, and there was nothing he could do to prevent it; nothing except bring her tide to its fullest height. Now, before she gained enough to attain heaven. Before he lost control enough to release her wrist. Before his dragon commanded all his attention.

He had the means directly before him. Indeed, he had been fighting the scent of her yin perfume since this began. Given his position, she was open directly before him. He needed only to dip his head to raise her yin too quickly to match his yang.

He did just that. He had no hand to help him; his left supported his weight and his right held her wrist pinned. Fortunately, he needed no tools beyond his mouth and tongue.

He pressed his lips to her pearl and extended his tongue to skate and swirl around whatever he could find. Her reaction was immediate. Her body arched, and she screamed. She had not expected this sudden surge in yin, and so he continued his motions, redoubling his efforts to bring her too quickly to her peak. Meanwhile, she used all her skill against him, and the feel of her writhing beneath his tongue was as much a weapon as anything else.

112

Another circle established. Yin entered Kui Yu's body and mind through his mouth, aided by his wife's scent. It flowed into him, drawing a matching surge of yang in his blood which flowed straight back to Shi Po.

Did she have enough yet? She couldn't. And yet, he was thrusting hard against her feet, nearing completion despite his every effort to stop. It was coming. The yang surge would be more than enough for her. He had to take her beyond her ability to ride the yin tide before that moment. He *had* to.

So he began to suck, and nip and stroke. He did everything his limited control could manage while she bucked and surged beneath him.

He heard her scream. He felt her body tense beneath his lips, and felt rhythmic contractions convulse her flesh on the yin tide. She was lost. He heard it in her scream. And in that moment, he lost his own battle. He exploded against her feet, yang fire erupting through him and into her.

But then there was more. . . .

❦

April 9, 1880

Dearest Lun Po—

I am in despair. Your father still will not receive me. I have nearly beggared myself sending him gifts, thinking up poetry. I even found Imperial jade and bribed the merchant to sell it to me. As if the price alone weren't enough! I want to quit this English master. I want to open a store of my own. But how can I save money when it all goes into

113

gifts to your father who will not even open the door to me?

Lun Po, you must get me to the next bridegroom dinner. You must. Or I will come anyway and you will have to throw me out. Imagine the scene I would cause then.

Do not fail me, my old friend. Help me in this small way, and I shall be forever in your debt.

> Your most desperate friend,
> Kui Yu

April 13, 1880

Dear Kui Yu—

Be reasonable, my old friend. Your family name was born yesterday, and your hands are rough from labor. You work for the white barbarians and have less education than I. You cannot expect us to hand the flower of our generation into hands that daily commerce with devils.

> With great sadness,
> Lun Po

There was once a man who had great faith in geomantic omens. He consulted the geomancer before every action, always searching for beneficial or unfortunate signs. One day while he was sitting at the foot of a wall, the bricks collapsed on top of him.

"Help!" he cried.

His servants rushed over, then ran away. Only one remained to explain.

"Be patient," the servant said, "while we consult the geomancer to see if it's a good omen to break ground today."

Chapter Seven

She was ascending to Heaven! All thanks to her husband. Kui Yu was amazingly capable at helping her create the small yin circle. She had not thought him so experienced in the sexual arts. Indeed, her ignorance of him disturbed her, but she had no time to examine it carefully; the yin tide engulfed her and her focus became riding the wave to Heaven.

Thankfully, she had forced Kui Yu's yang into the appropriate large circle despite his resistance. It mixed with her female yin, and now provided enough energy to take her to Heaven. And without the addition of poison to her blood! Which meant . . . Was she . . . ? Could she . . . ? Would she become an Immortal now?

Shi Po tamped down the elation that surged through her, focusing all her attention on riding the yin-yang tigress to her destination. The Heavenly portal was just ahead; she was sure of it. Indeed, she had already arrived at the antechamber: the Room of a Thousand Swinging Lanterns.

She had attained this level before, though many years ago. Indeed, the peace and joy of the space was tainted for her, the beauty of the swinging lights dimmed from her first experience. And yet, she still found great joy in the feeling of absolute rightness that pervaded the antechamber. Only here could she stand tall. Only here did she breathe without restriction and dance without pain.

She'd forgotten how much she loved this place. If only she could remain here forever, spinning in circles of delight. Indeed, she would have if Kui Yu had allowed her to use the dagger. If she could have poisoned herself, she would even now be settling here—or someplace even better, someplace beyond this antechamber.

But she had not. Because Kui Yu had stopped her.

The darkness shifted, and the lights folded back. Shi Po strained forward, anxious to see what came next. What would be her future? What might ensure her status on Earth as an Immortal? What . . .

Kui Yu?

Kui Yu! Her husband was there, standing on the steps to Heaven. He was talking with a celestial creature, a woman of great ethereal beauty and power. Was it Kwan Yin, Goddess of Hope?

He was here! He had come with her, joined Shi Po as she entered Heaven. They'd entered together. Except, it hadn't been together she now realized. He'd been here before her. And he was in conversation with a goddess without her.

Emotions tumbled through Shi Po. Confusion warred with envy and anger. But awe and joy held equal parts. It made no sense. She was thrilled that gentle Kui Yu had joined her. And yet, how could a novice precede her? Especially on his first night of practice? And what was he saying to that heavenly woman?

She strained toward him, but at the same time wanted to turn her back. He had already usurped her in everything else; how could he take Heaven from her as well? And yet, how could she not be gloriously happy for his success?

She wasn't! And yet, she was. One could not be in the antechamber to Heaven and not feel a generosity of spirit. But how had this happened?

Her emotions would not resolve themselves; her thoughts would not remain clear. And with her confusion, she lost her focus. She fell off the tigress.

The plummet was horrifying. But then again, it always was. And after three times now at the antechamber, she recognized the experience. It was cold, and dark, and worst of all, she felt heavy. After the lightness of immortality, even experienced for a single moment, the return to Earth was ugly. In the space of one heartbeat, she went from glorious to mundane, from stunning to coarse, from all that was most holy to all that was unimportant. Shi Po's chest and back folded in on one another until she could barely breathe. The cold dulled her thoughts, and the darkness made her long for death.

Yet, this time was even worse than usual. This time she knew she was leaving Kui Yu behind. This time, he would walk into Heaven while she—once again—fell into despair.

She wished she had it in her to be happy for him. He had attained perfection of spirit. But her goodness was not so pure. She was not happy; she was abandoned. And the pain of that made her think of her dagger even without the promise of Heaven to come. Just so long as she found an end, she would be content.

Or so she thought as the last of her spirit plummeted into her body, gasping and angry.

Air filled her lungs and her heart lurched, then steadied in her chest. If Kui Yu's body had not restrained her wrist, she might have immediately plunged the dagger into her heart. But she could not move, and in time, life and strength returned to her. No matter how cold or dark the Earth was, she was alive, and with life came possibilities.

Perhaps she would try again later. After all, she had made it farther tonight than she had in a very long time.

Moaning slightly, Shi Po tried to move, though her eyes remained closed. She was naked, lying on the silk banner, Kui Yu's body heavy on her lower body. Little aches seeped into her consciousness. Her thighs felt open too wide. Her ankles ached where they were pinned beneath her husband. And Kui Yu still gripped her wrist with surprising strength.

"Kui Yu," she croaked, her voice thick and heavy. She meant to push him off of her, forgetting that he would be as still as the dead until he returned from Heaven. Assuming, of course, that he did return.

She frowned and forced that thought from her mind. He would return to her; he would come back from Heaven. He was not poisoned, so the cord that bound him to his Earthly body remained strong. She would simply have to wait for him. She would remain still no matter how long it took, no matter how painful her position. She would not disturb his ascent. She would not rob him of that.

So she sighed, willing her body to relax, trying to regain a Tigress's discipline of mind. She brought her attention to her breath. Steady. In. Out. She became aware of the ache in her feet, pressed awkwardly against his belly. She acknowledged the pain, then moved her awareness on. Her lower back. Her shoulders, her arms, then her face. Her cheeks were cold and wet.

Tears? She was crying? She hadn't even realized it, and yet her sadness had been flowing out of her in a steady stream. She felt herself frown as she lifted her free hand and wiped away the yin that saturated a woman's tears.

A giggle sounded, and then a rustle of movement. All about her came the noises.

Shi Po opened her eyes, narrowing them immediately as they were stabbed with light from at least three different lanterns.

Men!

She blinked, focused, then gasped in horror.

Imperial soldiers! General Kang's men! Surrounding her! The youngest of whom stood on the blade of her dagger while he struggled to contain his embarrassed giggles. While she lay naked, trapped beneath her unconscious husband.

Shi Po bit her lip, fighting the urgent need to cover herself, to throw these crass intruders out of her home. But she couldn't. Kui Yu could not be disturbed. Even though jealousy still seethed within her, she would not take away his time in Heaven. Which meant she needed to deal with this herself, quietly, without changing her position or jostling her husband.

She swallowed, pitching her voice as low as possible and yet still trying to maintain authority. "How

119

dare you enter our bedchamber?" she hissed. "Get out!"

The oldest of the soldiers stepped forward. A boy in his twenties, he smirked, his bow mocking.

"My apologies," he said, and she winced at the grating noise of his voice. "But this is not a bedchamber."

She glared at him, wishing she could reach the slightest covering. At least her feet were hidden by Kui Yu, but the rest of her was hideously exposed. "This is my home," she said, keeping her voice as low as possible. "Get out before you disturb my husband!"

More titters came from the other soldiers as again their leader spoke. "Mister Tan appears—"

"He's dead!" interrupted the titterer. The others openly guffawed.

"Stop it!" Shi Po cried, her voice rising in panic. Kui Yu was not dead. He couldn't be. Still, she twisted slowly to a sitting position, bringing what she could of the silk hanging with her. Kui Yu would not release his grip on her dagger arm, so she could only move partway, but it was enough to wave her free hand before his face.

The soldiers fell thankfully silent, and Shi Po could guess their thoughts. Was Mr. Tan truly dead? Had they just mocked a man while his ghost was nearby? Such an action could curse a man and his family for generations.

Her own worries were mounting, despite the warmth she felt beneath her husband. But she could not calm herself enough to feel his breath. To know . . .

A hot caress of air crossed her fingertips. Kui Yu had exhaled. He was still alive. And his slow, shallow breath told her better than anything that he remained in Heaven. That at all costs, he must not be disturbed.

"You must leave," she said hoarsely to the soldiers. "My husband is . . ." What to say? They would laugh if she said he was becoming an Immortal. Most believed that such a thing could be done only through ascetic meditation, not from a position between a woman's thighs. "He is ill," she finally managed.

"I'm ill, too," joked a soldier. His friends' laughter echoed in the large chamber.

Shi Po didn't know if it was their laughter or the way she flinched away, but either way, Kui Yu woke. His first reaction was to gasp, and his grip on her wrist tightened painfully. For an Immortal, the descent from Heaven was a slow, gentle process; but when interrupted like this, the result could be violent.

"Kui Yu," she said. She tried to keep her voice soothing, though her wrist throbbed. "Kui Yu, you are on Earth. You have returned."

All around her, the soldiers made crass comments, but Shi Po ignored them. Her entire focus was on her husband, on gentling his descent. Legend spoke of interrupted Immortals returning insane, and fear made her hands tremble as she stroked his brow.

"Kui Yu," she said again. "Try to breathe normally. Think of nothing else."

She didn't know if he heard or not, but eventually, his harsh gasps settled to a steadier rhythm. Soon after, his grip on her arm eased and she felt his other hand stir against her inner thigh.

"Don't try to speak," she said. "You've been ill."

"No . . ." He mumbled against her thigh. "No—"

121

Naturally he would protest. He hadn't been ill; he'd been in Heaven. But she couldn't risk him saying so aloud before these soldiers. Who knew how they would react or what they would say to General Kang?

"You've been ill," she said firmly, though she could see the bright glow of glory surrounding him. It brightened his skin and illuminated his eyes when they finally opened.

"I am not ill," he croaked, his voice steadying as he returned to her. "I—"

"There are people here," she interrupted. "Soldiers. From General Kang."

She did not glance at the men around them, but was excruciatingly aware of their presence. Fortunately, Kui Yu was quick to reorient himself. A blink. Then another. Then his eyes shot wide as he took it all in: his position on his wife's spread thighs, their nakedness, and the men surrounding them.

He stood. Or at least he tried. She knew his body was stiff; hers was painfully so. Still, he got upright quickly enough, taking the low edge of the tapestry with him to cover Shi Po even as he stood. He made no attempt to shield himself. He gained his feet with no apparent embarrassment, though he was naked and still wet where he had expended his seed.

"Why do you disturb us?" he demanded, doing his best to shield her from view. The soldiers turned to face him. Though they probably could not see the vestiges of Heaven that clung to him, they certainly responded to his tone of authority.

"General Kang wishes to speak with you," responded the lead soldier.

Shi Po did not flinch. She had guessed as much.

Still, her hands trembled where she was working beneath the banner, quickly cleaning herself and rebinding her feet. Unfortunately, her clothes were far out of reach.

"Have you no manners?" snapped Kui Yu. "To barge in on a husband and wife? Out! Wait in the reception hall. We will attend you in due time."

There was an abrupt rustle of movement from the entire circle of military men, but not because they departed. If anything, they closed in tighter, their hands on their swords, their manner threatening.

"With respect," the lead soldier sneered, "I understand you are ill. We will remain here to assist you."

They would remain to keep watch, was what he meant.

Shi Po quickly wrapped the last of her bindings around her feet, wondering what the General could possibly want. He had searched the grounds. If this was revenge, then she and Kui Yu would have been slaughtered as they lay vulnerable on the ground. Clearly the men had orders to capture them, but why? What could General Kang possibly gain from such a thing? She didn't know. But when dragons played, the crops were destroyed.

"My wife has no need of assistance. Turn your heads so that she may leave."

Shi Po glanced at her husband, touched that he would try to take her place. He surely knew that whatever ills fell on them came from her hand. He was all that was moral and upright in China, whereas the Shanghai Tigress was liable to all sorts of punishments. So she stood, using the silk to cover herself even as she passed her husband his pants.

"All I require is a moment to dress," she said

smoothly to the soldiers. "Then I will accompany you. My husband must tend to our son," she lied. "He has been traveling, and the boy misses him."

Kui Yu jerked his head up at her lie, but he did not delay in drawing on his pants.

Meanwhile, the lead soldier curled his lip. "Leave the boy to the servants. General Kang requires both of you."

"Not until—," Kui Yu began.

"We must—," Shi Po tried.

"Now!" the soldier exploded, and his face purpled with vehemence.

Kui Yu was not cowed. His pants rode low on his hips, his belt still lost somewhere on the floor. He looked like the lowest coolie laborer, and yet he squared off with the soldiers as if he were the Son of Heaven himself.

"You will not parade Viceroy Tseng's granddaughter naked through the streets," he snapped. "You will give her the courtesy appropriate to one of China's most beautiful flowers!"

Her grandfather was long dead, her family far from its former glory, but such was the force with which Kui Yu spoke that many of the men drew back a half step. Their hands even slipped away from their swords.

Not so their leader, whose gaze slid long and slow down her wrapped body. "The Manchu Qing rule China, Mr. Tan," he drawled. "We have no need for dead viceroys or their granddaughters." And as he turned his head back to Kui Yu, she saw the Manchurian cast to his features.

Kui Yu, apparently, did not. Or he did not care, for faster than she could see, he had his hand upon the man's swordarm. The muscles of his forearm rippled as he held the Manchurian lieutenant still. "No one gains from parading Shanghai's leading women naked through the streets. Especially where foreign eyes watch everything. Manchu or Han, we are all Chinese. Such a thing weakens us before the barbarians." He paused, leaning forward for emphasis. "Only a fool ignores such things, and General Kang has no love of fools."

The implied threat hung in the air, and all awaited the outcome. Especially as General Kang was famous for his loathing of foreign things. Still, the lieutenant was young enough to be nervous, and so with a quick flick of his eyes, he despatched the giggling soldier to retrieve her clothes.

The giggler did so quickly, handing them to her as if they were soiled.

"Turn your backs," ordered Kui Yu.

The soldiers ignored him until the leader nodded in agreement. Then, one by one, all but Kui Yu and the lieutenant presented her their backs. She dropped the silk banner, all too aware that they had seen this much and more of her already. Speed, not embarrassment, would serve her now. Especially as she watched her husband tense.

His gaze flickered over the soldiers. He measured the distance between himself and each of the six. He had little hope of overpowering them all, but still, he was clearly considering it. His fists bunched and his weight pushed to the balls of his feet. But then he glanced at her, his gaze hopping between herself and the two who stood closest. He could not kill them all. Not before at least one got to her. And so Shi Po watched his shoulders slump in defeat. He would not fight them now.

She was wrapping her silk skirt about her, tying the

ribbons as quickly as she could. But she murmured to him, letting him know with words that she agreed with his choice. "More would come," she said, and saw him nod in acknowledgment.

These six would not be the only men here. Likely another half dozen waited just outside the door. So she continued to dress while he watched the men around her.

Try as she might, she could think of no escape. It was the middle of the night. What servants they had were probably already subdued. If some had escaped, where would they go for help? No authority in Shanghai would challenge General Kang. So they were doomed to arrest. Or at least she was. And Kui Yu too, she supposed, for he would not leave her now; she saw that in his tense muscles while he glared at the lieutenant. For good or ill, he would remain at her side. She could only pray that it did not cost him.

If they both died, who then would care for their sons?

She finished dressing. There was little she could do about the terrible mess in her hair, so she concentrated on grabbing Kui Yu's clothes. She was near enough to his shirt, which she lifted in a single smooth motion. Unfortunately, the lieutenant was watching her. While he had allowed her to dress, he was not so nice to Kui Yu. The moment she reached for his jacket, the man began barking orders.

The soldiers all spun, tightening their circle before heading outside. Shi Po was only able to toss Kui Yu his shirt before they were both grabbed and herded away.

"But he has no shoes!" Shi Po exclaimed. She was close to them. If only they let her reach . . . But they

didn't. And soon she and her husband were march-
ing through the garden, and then the outer courtyard, where more men on horses waited.

There was no opportunity to struggle. None even
to call for help, for she saw only General Kang's men.
Someone lifted her roughly, and she was deposited in
front of another man on a horse. To her shame, she
squeaked in alarm. As the granddaughter of a
viceroy, she had been carried in palanquins or sedan
chairs, but she'd never ridden a horse. The soldier
wrapped a thick, smelly arm across her middle, then
roughly ordered her to remain still or fall off and die.

She thought he was exaggerating the danger. After
all, didn't children ride these beasts? But as soon as
Kui Yu was secured—his hands tied and his body
tossed across a saddle—they all rushed off like the
wind. Or at least half of them did, since half remained at her home. She had no time to figure out
why as the narrow streets of Shanghai flew past. The
noise was deafening, and she shrank back in terror. If
only she could find the courage to jump. She was
bouncing all over the saddle. How much harder
would it be to add a twist or a push? She would neatly
escape her captor, then fall in a heap on the ground
because of her bound feet.

Then she would surely be trampled to death by the
other horses. She clenched her teeth, forced to accept
the truth: There would be no escape.

In time, they made it to their destination—a dark,
gray stone building that was part of the wall that surrounded old Shanghai. Other men came up to meet
them, and she wondered how so many men and
beasts could be in such a tight space with no injuries.
She was roughly prodded off her perch. Fortunately,

someone was waiting to catch her as she tumbled forward.

She caught a glimpse of Kui Yu, hauled off his horse like a sack of rice. He collapsed on the ground in an ungainly heap. She was prodded from behind and stumbled, but a soldier held her up, his grip bruising but at least stable. No one helped her husband. He struggled to his feet and then was shoved toward a door. She would have gone to him then, if only to stand beside him as a wife should. But she had no choice. She was dragged away to a different door, a different hallway. And finally, she was shoved inside a small, dark cell with a hard, iron-reinforced door.

No one spoke to her. No one answered her questions. And in the end, she could do nothing but sit and regret.

Kui Yu struggled. Not physically; it would be better if his captors thought him docile and accepting of the situation. At the moment, he had little hope of escape, especially as he had no idea where they had taken Shi Po. So he sat quietly in the small room, staring at the empty table and chair across from him while trying to get a mental hold on what was happening.

The plummet from Heaven to Earth had been hideous. Ripped from that place of glory by his own indecision, he had felt the plummet as a donning of a heavy, dulling cloak. It had weighed down his body, his spirit, and worst of all, his thoughts. Indeed, though he knew logically what had happened, he still struggled to believe that this nightmare was real and Heaven had been only a fantasy.

Even the aches in his body did little to ground him. Only Shi Po seemed real. He saw her in his mind's eye, standing pale but resolute before their captors. He held on to that image and used it to ground himself in the world. She was his anchor here, and the goal. Her safety was paramount. So he aimed steadily for that end, despite the confusion that still reigned in his mind.

The door opened behind him. Kui Yu didn't move. In time, he saw General Kang step into his field of vision. The man was shorter than expected. Or perhaps it was the armor that thickened and broadened the General's form, which made him appear so stout. His face was unremarkable in the way of many older men. Facial hair, thick bones, wide nose—all were Manchurian features. But this man was no courtier. Even the muscles in his face were hardened, and worry was etched in every sun-roughened crease.

"Tan Kui Yu!" the man boomed with hearty good cheer. "What? They bound your hands? Stupid, stupid boys," he muttered as he pulled a dagger from his boot and quickly sliced the rope. "They are so anxious to please, they do too much."

Kui Yu didn't respond, recognizing the man's friendship as a ruse. He kept silent and used the time to rub feeling back into his hands. Meanwhile, General Kang settled heavily into the other chair, his dark eyes keen despite his genial attitude.

"Bah, it's late," he said, then smacked his lips. "Are you thirsty? I'm thirsty. Ling! Some burnt wine for our guest." The General frowned at the bloody marks left by the rope. "And some *hanshisan* for his injuries."

Kui Yu shook his head, recognizing the drug from discussions with Shi Po. The General's "cold-eating powder" would fuzz his mind. "I have a weak stomach," he lied. "Any opium, and I am ill for days." He

129

sighed in mock regret. "It has made some of my negotiations most difficult."

The General frowned at him. "How unfortunate for you." He glanced up at the soldier who brought wine, the drug, and two cups. "Are you quite sure you wouldn't like to try a little? Our herbalist swears it is most effective."

Kui Yu shrugged. "I would not insult your honor by becoming ill in your presence."

The General nodded and ignored the small vial of powder in favor of pouring the wine. Then he pressed a metal cup into Kui Yu's hands.

"Drink. Drink. Then we will talk."

The General took a long pull at his wine. Kui Yu pretended to do the same, but did not even wet his lips. He had no wish for even mild alcohol, so strong burnt wine did not appeal at all.

Meanwhile, the General leaned back and smiled, stretching his short legs out in front of him. "You have a beautiful wife, Mr. Tan," he commented in a casual voice. "Most beautiful indeed. All of my men noticed."

Kui Yu nodded. To deny the obvious would be stupid.

"It must be quite a challenge keeping control of your wife. Beautiful women know their power over us men. They take advantage when they should not."

The General paused, staring hard at Kui Yu, obviously hoping he would expound on Shi Po's eccentricities. But Kui Yu only shrugged and quoted a proverb: " 'Beauty is a quality much to be desired.' "

The General nodded. "To be sure. To be sure. But sometimes these women—ah, such a plague sometimes—these women do things we know nothing about. They have their secrets, their little lies."

Kui Yu did his best to remain impassive, but his thoughts struggled through a fog. "I am most pleased with my wife, General. And her secrets are only those of all women: lotions for ageless skin, exercises to keep the body young, paints to appear respectable."

"And what of men?" the General snapped, clearly growing tired of the friendly approach. "What of the men she brings into your home? What does she do with them?"

Kui Yu adopted the facade of an idiot husband, besotted and ignorant of all that went on before him. "My wife has occasionally taken in lost people, confused or hurt spirits. She has skills with herbs and tea. They heal and move on." He straightened, blinking stupidly at his captor. "Charity is a great virtue among women."

The General's hand slammed down on the table. The cups clattered in their tray, sloshing the wine and filling the room with the acrid stench of strong liquor.

"A monk!" he bellowed. "An acolyte of her brother. He stayed in your home under guard. Him and a white barbarian woman." He spat on the floor in disgust. "Where is he?" He pushed to his feet to tower over Kui Yu. "I could kill you now for imprisoning him."

Kui Yu let his pretend stupidity fall. The General had not been fooled, so Kui Yu lifted his gaze and spoke as calmly as possible. "You could kill us now for no reason at all. You need no excuse beyond your name, so let us speak plainly as we are both weary. What is it that you wish to know about this monk?"

"So . . . he *was* at your home?" the General demanded, a sudden urgency in his tone.

Kui Yu shrugged. "I have no idea," he lied. "Men

131

do occasionally come to my home. My wife aids them and lets them go on their way."

"There was a guard at his door!" the General barked. "One of your own servants told the tale: a monk and a white woman, guarded and forced together in perversion."

Kui Yu released a snort of disdain. "No man would be forced by us into perversion with a white barbarian. That would be suicide here in Shanghai, with the ghost people so protective of their virgins. As for a guard, would you not protect your family as well when strangers ask for hospitality?"

"I do not open my home to the cursed ghost people."

Kui Yu nodded. He appreciated the man's attitude. The white foreigners brought a great many evils with them. Still, that hardly mattered. The white foreigners had not dragged him from his home in the dark of night. "If my wife brought a monk and a white woman into our home, then she would have done so with an open heart and a chaste manner—"

The General snorted. "Your wife—"

"Is as chaste as yours," snapped Kui Yu. "And if she is not, then I shall deal with her in my own time and manner."

The General narrowed his eyes, staring at Kui Yu as a mongoose would a snake. He said nothing, but merely stared. His expression hardened with every second of silence.

In the end, Kui Yu sighed, appearing to give in to the General's intimidation. "What is it that you wish to know?"

"Where is the monk now?"

"Is he at my house?" Kui Yu asked.

"He is not."

Kui Yu remembered the soldiers that remained at

his home. It was likely being torn apart brick by brick in a search for the missing monk. "Then, if he even was at my home, he is long gone. Neither I nor my wife will know any more than that."

The General's eyebrows drew together and down. His eyes lost some of their keen focus, but only for a moment. He abruptly stared at Kui Yu. "A beautiful wife is a nuisance," he said with forced casualness. "You married well with her. The connection to her family must have helped you build your fortune."

Kui Yu didn't answer. They both knew it was true.

"But your fortune is made," continued the man. "Perhaps you would prefer to find another wife. A younger one. One who would not be harassed by a spoiled first wife."

Kui Yu pressed his lips together. He was well aware that most people assumed he had only one wife because Shi Po would plague any younger woman brought into his home.

"I could rid you of the nuisance," the General offered. "Shi Po would simply disappear. Arrested. Discredited. You may pick the crime." He leaned forward and dropped his voice to a low whisper. "I tell you the truth—as one man to another—I have been watching your wife. She is not as chaste as you believe."

Kui Yu swallowed, hating that such words had the power to hurt, to make him doubt. He shook his head. "I shall handle my wife alone."

The General growled, low and in the back of his throat. "You do not see what I do. Other men laugh behind your back. Your wife takes lovers, and you do not see. Can you honestly claim you know everything your wife does? How she occupies her time while you work?"

Kui Yu swallowed, knowing his mask slipped despite his best efforts. Truthfully, he had often asked himself those very same questions. What *did* Shi Po do every day with such dedication? Exactly how far had she gone in pursuit of immortality? And what had she done with the monk and the white woman?

The General must have seen the doubt flitting through Kui Yu's mind. He must have known, because he sighed and leaned back, folding his arms with an expression of deep sadness. "Those women's secrets you spoke of earlier? One of them is how to fake virginity on a wedding night."

Kui Yu shot out of his chair, furious. But also, fear darkened his thoughts. How much did the man know about Shi Po? What had he learned?

He swallowed his questions, and also put away his hot defense of his wife, which would be half lies. Instead, he forced himself to speak in a cold, calculating manner. As if he had just come to a dark and merciless conclusion, as if he intended to beat Shi Po senseless.

"Release me, General Kang. Give me the time and freedom to see to my wife." He nearly spat the last word.

But the General was not convinced. "You accept your wife's perfidy?"

Kui Yu did not answer. He did not trust his acting skills.

"You suspect, at least, because that is the nature of beautiful women." The General narrowed his eyes. "But I think you are easily bewitched by her beauty. I think your hand would be too light in this matter." He stood and headed for the door. "I will handle her for you. This will be my gift to you."

Desperate Tigress

❧

May 5, 1880

Lun Po—

I am afraid I cannot assist you with your studies. I know the Imperial examination looms before you. I understand that your future rests upon the outcome. I discount the rumors that your family coffers are empty, for I know such a distinguished name has unlimited money despite disdaining commerce. So do not lie: only your family's honor—not their survival—rests upon your performance.

Unfortunately, my mind is completely filled with languishing thoughts of your sister. Who will she marry if not me? Who will clothe her, feed her, see to her health if not a man of wealth and means?

I must stop writing now. It seems my ghost boss is pleased with my work. He wishes to gift me with more gold.

In great sorrow,
Kui Yu

Chen Zhi was a censor-in-chief with an explosive personality. He beat his servants every day. No matter how small his dissatisfaction might be, Zhi's massive fists would strike. Someone who knew Zhi well tried to help him control his temper by giving him a wood stick on which three words were carved: "Hold Your Temper."

From then on, Zhi struck his victims with this stick.

Chapter Eight

"So I am once again in the presence of the whore of Shanghai."

Shi Po kept her head down, her hands neatly folded as she stood before General Kang. She understood what the man wanted. He was the kind of man who liked a slightly disobedient wife—one with a flash of spirit that he would systematically crush. His daughters would be silent, terrified little things. His sons would by necessity excel either in mimicry, becoming ten times worse their father; or, if they were very strong, they would completely reject their early training to become the exact opposite. General Kang's wife was to be congratulated for rearing the Buddhist monk Kang Zou Tun. A month ago, Shi Po had wondered what the young man was running from. Now she knew.

And knowing, she lifted her head to gaze directly into General Kang's eyes. After all, he would only be happy if she showed enough spirit for him to crush. She smiled as she spoke. "If I am a whore, then what

136

are you, twice barging into my home, twice demanding my presence? You are insatiable, and you have already been refused."

As expected, he did not pull back at her insult, but let his expression widen into a smirk. "Your husband has given you to me. For punishment."

She flinched, knowing that was what he wanted. But the reaction was not entirely faked. Kui Yu would not give her over; she knew that. But that wouldn't stop this man from punishing her anyway.

She smiled wanly. "Men's games are beyond one as simple as I," she said. "Let my husband say so to my face, and I will do as he bids."

General Kang did not answer. He walked around her, and she stood statue still. When he was behind her, he leaned in close, sniffing loudly. "Perfume. And sex. You smell like a nail-shack whore." He reached around to paw her breasts.

She broke off his groping with a quick jerk of her shoulder. He drew back and raised his arm to strike her, but she spoke quickly, praying he wasn't the beast he appeared. "Would you piss in a Ming vase?" she asked.

"You are no great work of art," he sneered.

She shrugged. "I am only the granddaughter of Viceroy Tseng, and the humble wife of Tan Kui Yu." She raised her eyes to match his gaze. "Now, what do you wish of me?"

His arm slowly lowered and he stared at her. "Your family is nothing compared to mine. The Qin rule now. And I am a Manchurian."

"Of course, your eminence," she said with a slight bow. "How may I serve my country?"

He moved in front of her, his eyes hard. He accused, "A monk came to your home. You imprisoned him there with a ghost woman." The venom in his voice intensified as he leaned forward. "I could kill you for that."

If he meant to scare her more, he failed. He could kill her now for whatever reason he chose. She had long since accepted that situation. So she bowed her head with calm acquiescence. "Whatever you say, your honor."

Gripping her chin, he hauled her face upward. "Shall we rut here on the floor like dogs? Shall I give you to my men to use as they want? Or should I give you to the ghost people and laugh as they perform evil magic on you? Is your magic stronger than theirs, I wonder?"

Fear trembled through her frame, but she said nothing. She did not trust her voice.

He threw her from him, then watched with grim amusement as she stumbled on her bound feet. Tripping over the chair, she fell gracelessly to the floor. Her head banged against the wall, and though she tried, she could not slide farther away. The room was too small.

"What do you want of me?" she rasped again.

"Where is my son?"

She shook her head. "I do not know."

"He was with you! You imprisoned him! Where did he go?" the General roared.

She shook her head. "I do not know."

The General stomped forward, his boots barely missing her hands. "Where is he?"

"I don't know!"

He grabbed her by the collar of her blouse, using it to lift her off the floor. "A monk came to your house!" he repeated.

Disgusted, Shi Po twisted away from his foul yang breath. "I do not ask who anyone is," she lied.

"You imprisoned him with a ghost bitch," he screamed.

"They choose their own partners!" she returned.

With one swift move, the General ripped the neck of her blouse. It split easily, baring her breasts to his gaze. He let her fall heavily to the floor, though his eyes never left her chest. "Lie to me again," he softly dared her.

She refused to cover herself, though the urge burned inside her. Let him see what he could not have except by force—that was the way to deal with men like this.

"What did my son say to you?"

She swallowed. "A man came to the house seeking refuge. That is all. He brought an injured woman. I gave them a place to rest. Herbs for healing. Then they left."

"When?"

"Two days ago," she lied.

He cursed and stomped his boot like a distempered horse. "What do you know of your husband's business?" he snapped.

She blinked, startled by the sudden change in topic. "I am a simple woman. What would I know of men's work?"

"Whore!" he bellowed; then he buried his hands in the band of her skirt. This too, he tore apart, so she was completely bared to him. His eyes fixed on her tigress tattoo, while his body slowly turned red with rising yang fire.

"Lie to me again," he whispered, stepping between her legs and kicking them wide.

She blinked back her tears. She would give him no yin, not even the little that saturated her sorrow. "I know nothing of where your son is," she repeated in absolute truth.

The General dropped to his knees between her legs. She tried to scoot backwards, but was blocked by the wall. She could do nothing but lie there and dread what was to come.

He put his hands on her thighs and dragged her fully open. "Lie to me again," he whispered. "What business does your husband have with the whites?"

Fear thickened the air in her lungs. How exactly did her husband make so much money? As far as she knew, Kui Yu's business was to take the barbarians' money in exchange for cheap fabric. He sold clothing and built houses. But was that all? The possibilities were endless and ugly. Would he betray China to the whites? In exchange for what? Medicines for their children? Or something worse?

General Kang was watching her closely. She had no idea what he saw on her face, but apparently it disgusted him. Curling his lips, he roughly shoved away from her.

"Your smell nauseates me." Then he stomped out the door.

Shi Po's feet were unsteady, her balance precarious as she tried to both walk down the dark corridor and clutch her skirt closed. The guards who escorted her knew, of course. They could see the state she was in, and their comments would have made another woman blush. But Shi Po's aunt ran a brothel. There was nothing they could say that would upset her further.

What they succeeded in, on the other hand, was making her skin crawl and her stomach heave. They touched her. Not overtly; they clearly thought she was reserved for General Kang, so they didn't grab her harshly. They certainly didn't leave bruises that their commander would see.

No, they were subtler than that. A grip here, a poke there, all punctuated by crude comments. She could do nothing to defend herself. She wanted to release her clothing. She wanted to stand tall on her unsteady feet and let the damned soldiers look their fill. Let them see what they couldn't have.

Except, they could have it. And they very well might before this ordeal was over. And she wasn't strong enough to face that right now. She was afraid. And tired. And wished desperately that she had listened to her aunt and run.

But she hadn't.

She swallowed, fighting the tears. Where was Kui Yu? What had happened to him? Was he even still alive?

The guards stopped before a dark room. She recognized it as the place she had sat before. The tiny cell had bars at the door and likely peepholes along the side. She didn't care. So long as these men stayed on the other side and left her alone, they could look all they wanted. How she could want to be inside, she didn't know, but she would do almost anything to escape these soldiers. Even return to that dark, lonely cell.

Two guards were with her. Another five stood in a room a few steps away. While one unlocked her cell, the other held her, his hand sliding up and down her arm and his long extended fingers brushing her breast. She tried to pull away, but to do so would back her into his body, and she had no wish to touch more of him. So she closed her eyes and held back her nausea with an act of will. Her Tigress calm was nowhere to be found.

With her eyes closed, she focused on the sounds: the clatter of the keys and the groan of the door hinges. Soon she would be inside. Alone. Soon . . .

There came a sudden surprised grunt. Thuds and a bellow. Shi Po's eyes sprang open, but she could not make sense of the shifting shadows in the dark corridor. The only light came from lanterns hung in the guardroom many feet away.

Fighting. The men were fighting. She saw a flash of pale, golden skin. She watched it impact with studded leather armor and win. Bare feet. A naked upper body. Against two soldiers in armor?

Kui Yu! It had to be him. Who else would be so fierce and silent?

The man who held her bellowed to his fellows before he was ripped away from her. She stumbled and pressed herself against the damp wall. She could not help her husband if she fell down right in the middle of things, so she clung to the wall and searched for their best escape route.

She saw nothing but more soldiers rushing from the guardroom. She teetered forward into their path. Anything to delay them. But such a ruse was useless. She had no purchase on her bound feet; she weighed next to nothing compared with their bulk. She was slammed against the wall hard enough that her head bounced on the stone. She whimpered in pain.

"Shi Po!"

She focused on Kui Yu's bellow, finally separating form from shadow enough to understand. Two soldiers lay on the ground behind him. His face was matted with grime, but his fists were large, his shoulders broad as he met the newest attackers.

He fought like a demon. No, he fought like a street boy, all fists and kicks and raining fury. He was too fast for her to see, but she heard. Grunts. Growls. Bestial sounds of men at war. The smack of fist against flesh. The thud of body against leather.

The ring of many swords being unsheathed.

She screamed. Kui Yu was unarmed, and he would die here. Seven against one? He had no chance. "No," she sobbed. "Stop. Please, stop!"

They did. But not because of her. They stilled because they won. Because Kui Yu was on his knees, one sword at his neck, others pricking his side and back. Even in the dim light, she could see blood dripping from his face and sides.

"Stop," she whispered. Tears obscured her vision.

"Are you all right?" rasped Kui Yu. Then he grunted as one of the soldiers kicked him in the side. He fell over with a moan, and Shi Po lurched forward, falling to her knees before her husband. Her skirt widened, fluttering around her, but she curled herself around Kui Yu, twisting to glare at their captors.

She said nothing. No words came to her mind. But she reached up to push a sword point aside. The soldier let her do it, though he laughed at her stupidity. She could only push one sword away at time, and though they allowed her to move whichever she touched, their weapons returned a bare second later. They returned and cut tiny nicks into her husband's body no matter what she did to stop them.

In the end, she saw it was futile, so she looked to her husband. He was holding her clothing closed for her and his eyes burned with a fury she had never seen.

"We'll go inside the cell now," she said to the guards. To Kui Yu: "We'll go," she repeated, but she couldn't move her husband as long as the blades prevented it. So she waited, her chest tight, her every breath shallow with fear.

Then Kui Yu spoke in hard, cold warning. "She is

General Kang's woman. He'll kill anyone who touches her."

Shi Po's breath thickened in her throat. Was it true? Had he given her over to General Kang? It was possible. Life was everything to Kui Yu. He would indeed hand her over to the general rather than watch her hang. She wiped away her tears at those words, struggling to regain some composure. Meanwhile, one of the soldiers nodded, and another pushed the door to the cell wide. Then the swords lifted, but not very high.

They were forced to crawl into the cell. Shi Po kept her one arm around her husband. She could feel the bunching and release of his muscles. She knew the tension he restrained. He still wanted to fight, so she tightened her hold on him. He had no protection except her body; the soldiers had weapons and armor. She would not let him do anything so foolish.

Apparently, he understood, because his head dipped on a low growl. Together they crawled across the threshold into their cell.

Kui Yu was on his feet the moment the last sword left his leg. He jumped up with a speed that surprised Shi Po almost as much as it startled the guards. They jumped back and slammed the door as hard as they could. Seconds later, she heard the jingling of the keys as the cell was locked tight. Kui Yu was at the door, his hands wrapped around the bars, but he said nothing. He merely watched the soldiers retreat, his body tensed, his breath harsh and short.

He pushed once on the door, a furious shove that achieved nothing except expending his yang fire. And then, to her surprise, he moved quickly to her side. She had not shifted from the floor. She had dropped to her bottom as he sprang up, and she had remained there, her thoughts heavy, her body too weary to do more than wrap her arms around herself.

She watched him approach, and surprised herself by flinching when he touched her shoulder.

"Shi Po?" he asked in a whisper. "Shi Po, where are you hurt?"

She shook her head, stunned that she had no voice. In her mind, she spoke clearly to him. She reassured him that she was unharmed, while she assessed his wounds. She knew he had been hurt in the fight. She ought to be cleaning his cuts, seeing to his pain. But she simply sat.

"Why did you give me to him?" she whispered.

He glanced over his shoulder to the door, and then along the wall. He was trying to tell her something, but her mind was too fogged to understand.

"I had to. He wants you. He might even marry you." He spoke loudly, but as he did, he reached out and stroked a character on the back of her hand.

She knew it was a word, but she couldn't decipher it. The lines were too hurried.

"Stand up, Shi Po. Come sit on the bed."

He reached around, drawing her upright. She shrank away from him, not wanting anyone's touch, but he was insistent. He guided her to sit on the dirty straw pallet. Then he shook out their single, thin blanket and sat beside her. When he put the covering on her shoulders, his arms remained—he held her despite the way she shrank from him.

"He cares for you," Kui Yu continued. "He knows of you, of your skills. He wants you for his own." He reached forward and gently brushed aside the remains of her skirt to touch her bare thigh. "He will pay well for you," he said.

But on her thigh, he wrote one character: *Lies*.

145

He wrote it over and over as he expounded on a pretend reason for their capture.

"He's arrested us to intimidate me. To make me sell you to him."

Lies, he wrote again and again.

"I have agreed, but we must settle upon a price."

Lies.

"You must keep yourself pretty. You are very important to him."

Lies.

She grabbed his hand, stilling his frantic writing. He looked at her firmly, sliding his gaze to the door. His message was clear: The soldiers were to listen to what was said. Why else would this cell be so close to the guardroom?

She nodded in understanding. "I'm so tired," she said out loud.

Hurt? he wrote on her leg.

She shook her head, but could see that he didn't believe her. So she reached out and touched his jaw. He flinched when she found a bloody cut.

He grabbed her hand and pressed it to his lips. "I'm fine," he whispered.

She didn't believe him, either. Abruptly her fears overwhelmed her, and she shuddered. He tightened his hold and pressed his forehead to hers, his lips against her cheek.

What do we do? She wrote quickly on his chest.

He shook his head, and she struggled to hold back tears.

Sorry. Sorry. Sorry. She stroked the word repeatedly on his chest. This was all her fault. She had thought her aunt imagined spies in every corner. She had thought General Kang would not seize them out of spite. She had thought she could ascend to Heaven, and that with her death, any threat to Kui Yu would disappear.

But she had been wrong, and now everything was lost. Her children would be orphaned, her students abandoned. All she had ever done would be wiped away; everything Kui Yu had accomplished would be destroyed.

Sorry. Sorry. Sorry.

He gripped her hand to stop her furious strokes. Leaning back against the wall, he tucked her tightly to him. She went easily; she had no strength to fight him. And as she settled against him, he turned her hand over and wrote an answer in her palm.

Hope. Message. Brother. Hope.

She sighed. If he had sent a message to Lun Po, they were well and truly doomed. She stroked her answer onto his chest.

My brother. Idiot.

Kui Yu chuckled, tightening his hold on her. He returned his fingers to her arm, stroking this time on the inside of her wrist: *Hope,* he repeated. Then: *Sleep.*

Shi Po raised her eyes, making sure her disbelief was clear. Her husband simply shrugged and tucked her close again, even as he continued to write his message on her skin:

Hope.

They slept.

Shi Po laughed. The sound bubbled out of her, slipped free of her lips, and flew high above her into a beautiful blue sky. She was seven years old again, her hair in pigtails that flopped about her shoulders whenever she turned. She hated them because her brothers would always grab them and hold her still with a single fist. Her aunt also delighted in such tricks.

But not today. Today, her relatives reached for her but she was too fast. She could run. Like a bird, like the wind—she was that fast and that happy.

She felt each heavy thump as her heel hit dirt, each impact quickly lost as she pushed forward. Her toes spread, and her foot pressed into the ground. Shi Po loved the way the dust burst up around it. She giggled at the feel.

Where was she going? she wondered. Where would a child run to with such gleeful abandon, especially when her family waited behind, their hands stretched out to grab her? She didn't know, but then again, she truly didn't care. She knew this was a dream, and saw her conscious mind as yet another hand stretching to hold her back.

Where are you going, little dream girl? she asked herself. Then she laughed as she shook her pigtails and pushed herself to greater speeds.

Then she saw it: her destination stretching far off in the distance. First she saw the black carpet of glittering lights. Her toes tingled as she ran through. She pushed down on the black fabric and felt the stars sway and hop as they squished through her toes. So beautiful. And so far behind her now, for she ran faster. The gateway was ahead. Heaven. Blindingly bright and just out of reach. But she was nearly there.

The gate was barred! She could see that from here, but it didn't bother her. She was fast enough now to leap over it. One mighty jump, and she would vault inside. It was coming now. It was time.

She bent her knees, scrunching her tiny body as small as it would go. Then, one last deep breath and she exploded upward. She thrust with her spine, pushed with her knees, vaulted with her ankles, and then the final touch: She rolled through her arches to push with her toes.

She could do that in her dream. Because here, her feet were large and healthy and so very, very strong.

Except, they weren't. Or she wasn't. Because she stopped. She grabbed the gate, high up, just before the top but not quite there. She hung there like a fly stuck to honey strips. Her arms trembled. She would not be able to hold on much longer, much less climb. But she would try. She would haul and grab and bite, anything to gain another inch and reach the top.

She knew she wouldn't make it. She realized she'd had this dream many times. And yet, each time, she tried again. Every dream, she struggled with all her will to go a little farther, to at last reach that glorious other side. Heaven, even a dream Heaven, was worth any sacrifice.

But always her struggles toppled her backward. No matter how careful she was, no matter how she clung to the wall with fingers and toes, the urge to climb higher always ended with her tumbling backward into the dirt.

This time, she did something different. This time, she looked through the bars and into Heaven. Always before she had looked up and focused on her goal: the very top. This time, she looked through the bars to see what was on the other side.

Not just a bright, beautiful light. That's what Heaven had always been in her dreams: beautiful, bright, and very, very indistinct. But this time she saw a person. Two people. They were vague and indistinct, but grew clearer with every moment.

She shifted her energies. She stopped struggling for the top of the gate, but instead clung to the barrier while trying to sort form and meaning from what she saw.

Two people. She knew them. Kui Yu. And the Goddess Kwan Yin, the female angel of hope.

"Kui Yu!" she screamed. "Kui Yu!"

He heard her. Both husband and goddess turned to see her, flattened like an insect against the gate. She saw Kui Yu's eyes narrow as he made out her distant shape. Then she saw him grin, his eyes lighting with delight.

She laughed, thrilled that he had seen her. He would help her.

He waved. She didn't dare wave back; she would fall off the wall. She watched his face fall. He continued to wave, but with more desperation, more determination.

"Kui Yu!" she called. "Kui Yu!"

But he was growing disappointed with her lack of response. His arm lowered, his face grew grim.

"I can't wave!" she screamed. "I'll fall!"

He didn't understand. In the end, he shrugged and turned away from her, his attention once more on the goddess.

"Kui Yu!" she bellowed, but he was gone. He'd walked deeper into Heaven with the goddess, leaving her alone on the wall. So she risked it. She chanced it even though she knew what would happen.

She released one hand and pulled herself tight against the bars. Then she waved and waved and waved. "Kui Yu! Look now! Kui Yu!"

He didn't come back for her, and she tumbled off the wall. She landed with jarring force on her feet, which broke, crushed beneath her weight. And soon her entire body collapsed into the cloying stench of muddy earth.

She tried to get out. She pushed with her broken feet, but only slipped and fell deeper in. She pulled with her slender feminine arms, but her hands had nothing to grasp and she sank further. She fought and gasped and pulled and struggled, but every effort pushed her deeper in, further encased in mud, buried well above her head.

And then everything collapsed down upon her.

She woke with a scream.

Arms tightened around Shi Po, holding her down. She screamed again, but this time with fury. Somewhere in her mind she knew it was Kui Yu holding her. Her husband restrained her. But that only made her fight harder.

Gathering all her strength, she shoved, throwing herself away from him. She tumbled to the floor. A rat squealed as it fled.

"Shi Po!" her husband called. "It's a dream."

She shook her head. Her body trembled, her breath coming in harsh gasps.

"It's a dream," he repeated. "You're safe."

She laughed. Safe? Here in a stinking cell at the mercy of a spiteful general? Or safe here on Earth where she was so encased that she curled into herself, barely daring to breathe for fear of what she would inhale?

She stared about her. She was out of control, her mind spinning in hysterics. And yet, she couldn't stop the horror. She knew that whatever she did, however she struggled, she would fail. No one would help her, not even Kui Yu. He might try. He might even see her and reach out for her. But in the end, he would turn away because he didn't understand.

Shi Po burst into tears.

151

July 9, 1880

Kui Yu—

My father will not change his mind, and will beat me if I bring up the topic again. My gravest apologies, old friend, but there is nothing I can do. But in the name of our long friendship, I beg you to help me with the examination essay. I have received the topic question, but I cannot form the words.

I have saved some money. I could pay you for your time.

In great fear,
Lun Po

July 12, 1880

Lun Po—

I have no need of your money. My English boss gives me more gold than I have time to spend. Unless, of course, I had a woman on whom to shower my wealth. A wife of noble ancestry. A woman to father my children and bring light to my dreary life. My joy would be such that, of course I would be happy to share my time and skills with you. I would offer any assistance I could as you prepare for your examination.

Anxiously,
Kui Yu

A ferry boat was once crossing a river when it struck a rock and water began pouring into the cabin. All the passengers were terrified except for one man who laughed at the others' fear.

"Don't worry. It's not our problem," he said. "This isn't our boat."

Chapter Nine

Kui Yu stared at his wife, saw her tears, and felt fury rage through him. His wife never cried; her strength defied tears. General Kang would die for the pain he'd caused her. Yet, as much as a vow of vengeance eased his spirit, it did nothing for his wife. And so Kui Yu slowly slid to the floor, feeling every bruise as he knelt before her on the cold stone.

"It was just a dream, Shi Po," he said. "It's over now."

She shook her head, and he saw that she trembled. He reached out to touch her, but she flinched away.

"The bastard hurt you." He hadn't meant to speak aloud, but the words came out on a low growl.

"No!" Her word was a soft hiss, but he heard it anyway. Then she repeated herself, her voice growing stronger. "I am to be Kang's concubine. You're going to sell me. Why would he hurt that which he intends to buy?" she asked angrily.

Kui Yu frowned. She understood, didn't she? She knew he had made up that story to keep the guards away. She knew that, didn't she? But with one look at her rapidly drying eyes, he wasn't so sure. There was anger there, and a hatred that glittered in her gaze. And most of all, he saw pain and fear.

"We will be all right," he whispered. "There is hope."

She swallowed, her face pale as she slowly pushed to her feet. "What did she say, Kui Yu? What did the goddess say to you?"

He, too, pushed to his feet, wincing as he did. His ribs burned with every breath and his back ached, making it difficult to focus. "There is no goddess here."

"There was last night," she hissed. "You were there. I saw you. You were there before me in Heaven." Her voice broke. "What did Kwan Yin say to you?"

He sighed. Now he knew why she was so angry. Still, it was hard to answer, so he took a moment, filling it with the agonies of sitting down, of trying to find a soft spot on the moldy straw, of trying to sit and breathe without pain.

"Kui Yu!" Shi Po snapped, and he heard her desperation.

"Sit beside me, wife," he said wearily. "It is not an easy thing to explain."

She nodded. Moving carefully, she settled beside him, careful that they did not touch. She faced him, her dark eyes wide and somber, her blouse open and revealing her breasts swaying before him.

His body stirred, his yang rising even as he fought the reaction. Now was not the time; and yet, as he looked at her, he could not forget the feel of last night. Her touch. Her caress . . .

"Let me touch you," he whispered.

She shook her head.

"I see you, Shi Po, and I think of other things. I am your husband. It is my duty to protect and honor you, and yet we are here in a prison cell. I cannot spring us free. I cannot banish your evil dreams. I cannot even control my hunger when I see you like this before me." He sighed and wondered what he was trying to say. "Have pity on me, wife. I will tell you everything you want to know, but at least gift me with your warmth in this frigid cell."

She blushed and ducked her head, but not before he'd seen a lightening of expression. He knew she would come to him, even as she shook her head. She said, "I have never understood your mind, Kui Yu. The cell is not cold, and your body aches. My touch will only increase your pain."

"Never," he whispered. Then he opened his arms.

She came to him shyly, but he felt the slide of her arms across his chest, the press of her breasts against his skin. She was warm and giving, and her heat did ease his pain. But it also woke his dragon.

He leaned his head down and brushed a kiss across her temple. "When I remember last night, I do not think of my time in Heaven."

She didn't speak, stroking a single word on his chest: *Liar.*

Truth, he countered. Then: *You—miracle. Heaven—strange.* He had wanted to say those words to her for a long time. He had wanted to tell her how much she meant to him. How bizarre, that he could only express himself in silent writing in the dark of a prison cell.

"Tell me everything," she commanded.

He sighed. He knew she didn't believe him, did not comprehend the depth of his feelings. She was a beautiful woman. Men of all types gave her compliments. They meant little to her, and he admired such a lack of vanity. And yet, how could she not know that he meant what he said?

155

She was getting impatient, her body stiffening against him. So he began to answer, caressing the words slowly on her skin as a way to buy time to think.

I was angry, he wrote. *Brutal with you.*

She laughed, her chuckle reverberating through his body. "You do not understand brutal," she murmured. "Last night was what I wanted. I went to Heaven, too."

He jerked and pulled back enough to see her face. *Immortal?* he stroked on her palm.

Her gaze dropped; her body shrank. But he didn't release her. Instead, he pulled her tighter against him, even if the motion made his ribs burn. He held her in silence and wondered how to salve her pain. He understood her unspoken message. She was not an Immortal yet, and the knowledge cut at her.

Then she touched him, with frustration that made her strokes hurt. *You? Immortal?*

"No. But I understand, I think, why you work so hard to go there. The place . . . The room of lights . . ."

"The antechamber. The Chamber of a Thousand Swinging Lanterns," she said with awe.

He nodded. That was where he had gone. "It is like the light shines through you. Even in the darkness, it is bright and holy. And you are beautiful, too." He shook his head. How to describe the indescribable? "It's like . . . It feels . . ."

Good. That was the character she stroked on his chest. *Heaven feels like all is good.*

"Yes," he murmured. "I felt like I was good."

"What did she say, Kui Yu?"

Kui Yu took his wife's hand, turning it palm-side up as he stroked his words into her palm. He didn't know if the guards were listening, didn't know if they could hear. But this was too personal to be overheard. So he took the time to write it slowly to only Shi Po.

Goddess asked question.

She lifted her head up when he stopped, her face taut with interest. He forced himself to continue. *She asked what I would give up.*

Shi Po didn't move. She didn't react, except to stroke another word.

Again. Then she held up her wrist, telling him to write it on the smooth flesh there.

Goddess asked, What would I give up? he wrote.

He felt her shiver in his arms, and he wondered at its cause. Did she tremble from his touch? Or because the question meant more than he knew? He waited, but her only response was another question.

For what? she asked. *What would you get?*

He sighed, choosing to speak aloud. "Whatever I most want." He didn't even have to look at her to know her question. What *did* he most want? "I don't know," he lied. "I didn't answer. And then I fell back to Earth."

She stroked her comment onto his chest. *Soldiers interrupted.*

No, he returned. *I was cast out. No answer.*

She lifted her head, her expression puzzled. He acted on impulse, moving swiftly before he changed his mind. Before she could ask another question, he kissed her. He pressed his mouth to hers while simultaneously gripping her tight. He would not let her run from him.

She reared back, as he had expected. It was such an unusual thing for them, for most Chinese. Kisses were for sex, a precursor to creating children. And they had not worked thusly in a very, very long time.

But he persisted. He liked the taste of her, the scent

that was only her. Her mouth was closed, but he stroked his tongue along the seam. He felt her shudder again, a more violent trembling than before, one that made her gasp and give him entrance. He took her then. He plunged his tongue into her mouth, wanting to own her, needing to feel her respond.

She didn't. She shifted and planted her hands on his chest. Then she shoved him backward with a surprising amount of strength.

He fell back, his head nearly cracking on the wall, his ribs fiery with pain. She scrambled away from him. Her breath came in harsh pants; her hands clutched her tattered skirt closed.

"Why?" she rasped.

He frowned. "Why what?"

"Why do you kiss me?" Her eyes narrowed, and she hissed, "Do you seek to return to her? To Heaven?"

He scrambled to answer. He could only voice the truth, though his tone came out colder than he intended. "I am a man. You are a woman and my wife. Why should I not kiss you?"

"Do you now have an answer?" she asked. "Do you know what you want?"

He wanted only her. That was all he knew just then—her taste, her body, their passion. But she didn't comprehend his need to simply touch and be touched by her. For Shi Po, sex had a purpose, a goal. Either for children or to gain Heaven; there could be no other reason.

Rather than explain, he simply shrugged and gave the answer she expected. "Yes, I wish to talk more with the goddess."

She grimaced, but she relaxed a little. "You cannot think to do this here."

He glanced around the dark, smelly room. He knew

the guards waited just beyond the walls, probably watching them right now, listening to their every word and hoping to take something of importance to their commander. He knew this, and yet he didn't care.

"Why wait? All depends upon the General's pleasure." And the prayer that Lun Po wasn't as much of an idiot as he appeared.

His wife took a moment to internalize his words, and he could see when she finally understood. They waited upon the General's pleasure. If the man chose, they could be locked up for a very, very long time. Days. Weeks. Years. The Qing were known to forget their prisoners. Or kill them.

She abruptly ran to the door and bellowed out the barred window. "Guards! Guards! I demand to speak to General Kang immediately! Guards!"

There came no answer.

"Guards!"

Kui Yu joined her at the door. His wife clutched her skirt closed about her hips, but it barely hid anything. So he wrapped their blanket about her shoulders, then stood beside her, one hand pressed to her lower back, while they both waited for a response.

"Guards!" she cried again.

Nothing. Kui Yu didn't know if she had a plan or just wanted to escape. Either way, it didn't matter. He was ready to try bargaining again.

"Guards!" Kui Yu bellowed.

Finally, then came a response: a creak of armor and heavy booted footfalls. A face appeared. A soldier, but one older than any of those Kui Yu had encountered before.

"We must speak to General Kang," he said firmly. "We have a bargain to make."

The man's grizzled face split into a lewd grin. "I bet

159

you do," he chortled as his eyes went to Shi Po's chest.

His wife shrank backward, deeper into the shadows, while Kui Yu stepped forward. "That's not your concern," he snapped. "Deliver the message." In truth he had no idea what bargain he would strike. General Kang had not seemed like a bribable man— at least not with gold or property. All the General wanted was news of his son, and they had none to offer. Still, this was worth a try, especially as they had few other options.

But the aged guard didn't move. Instead, he stood there chortling, as if they were some great joke.

Shi Po spoke up. Though Kui Yu tried to block the cur's view of her, she pushed him aside and spoke in a voice that was soft and gentle, and so very feminine. "Please, sir, why do you laugh at us?"

The man continued to chuckle, but the sound faded, his embarrassment mounting as she gazed at him with wide, limpid eyes. The laughter stopped. Where intimidation hadn't worked, softness had. The guard finally explained. "The General left for Peking this morning. Got some urgent news."

"He's gone?" Kui Yu snapped. "So, we are to be released!" The man hadn't said anything of the kind, but perhaps they could bluster to such as outcome.

"You're to be held until further notice," the guard answered coldly.

Shi Po stepped forward. "But sir, surely you can see this won't do. I have children."

"And gold," added Kui Yu. "I could—"

"Save your breath. Any man who helps you escape will be flogged then hanged. Kang's watching for bribes."

Kui Yu leaned in. "He needn't know. You can hide the gold until—"

"The General said he'd kill me on principle, bribe or no. You have to be here when he returns or I'm dead. My family, too."

"The Qing go too far," Kui Yu muttered, hoping to spark a patriotic response from a fellow Han.

But the man only chortled. "He pays us well for obedience and punishes us for dereliction. I got no complaints with the Qing." And with that, the guard turned and walked away, going back to the guard-room. Or just out of sight so that he could listen. Either way, it didn't matter; the man would not help them escape. And without the General to free them, there would be no release either.

They were stuck. Possibly for a long, long time.

Kui Yu stroked his wife's back, afraid of what he felt. Her body was unnaturally still, her muscles clenched tighter than rock. She was terrified.

Hope, he stroked against her back. *Hope.*

She didn't answer, either with body or voice. She simply stood, looking out their barred window, her expression bleak.

"Shi Po . . . ," he began, not knowing what to say.

"Kill me," she begged.

He flinched, and she abruptly spun around.

"Kill me. We're only being held because of me. Because he thinks I know about his son."

"Shi Po—" Her name came out as a warning growl, but she didn't seem to notice.

"You must be released. To take care of our children. If I am dead—"

"Stop!" He held up his hand and shut his eyes, trying to think. Thankfully she understood, and he took his time, fitting pieces together.

161

"You knew this was a risk," he said slowly, and as he opened his eyes, he saw her nod. "Your plan was to die last night. Then there would be no reason for General Kang to hold me. I would have my ignorance, and you would be dead."

"You can still—"

"Enough," he said, but this time he spoke more softly, allowing his weariness to show. He felt every ache, every injury as he walked to their straw pallet and dropped down. "There will be no more talk of death," he commanded.

She stepped toward him. "I am not seeking immortality this time, Kui Yu. I am trying to think of our children, of our—"

"The boys are fine at their tutor's. At least for another month."

"But you—"

"General Kang is gone!" He took a deep breath to calm his raging temper, which took some time. She stood before him, her head bowed, her body still. "General Kang has gone to Peking," he said slowly. "It matters not what we do now. If we live or die makes no difference to him." He raised his gaze to show the anger that boiled inside him. "But I care, Shi Po. And I will have no more talk of death."

She didn't say anything. Indeed, for a moment he wondered if she'd even heard. But in time, she shuddered. The movement shook her entire body, and she dropped to her knees before him.

He winced at the sight. Yet she was always at her strongest when she appeared weak. Over the years, he had learned to be wary when she dropped to her knees. So he waited in tense silence until she finally spoke, her voice a breathy whisper that cut him to the core.

"It makes no difference because General Kang has

162

left? Or because I am not the reason we are imprisoned?"

"Do not be stupid, woman!" he snapped. And then, in the deafening silence that followed, he closed his eyes and let his head fall back against the wall. Of all the times to be too tired to mind his tongue. Of all the times . . . He sighed. Shi Po settled beside him on the pallet.

They knew each other so well. How many times had he ever called her "woman"? How many times had he snapped at her without cause? Only once, and it had been because he felt guilty. Only once, and it was when he'd been at fault.

He opened his eyes. She was seated beside him, her eyes wide in the darkness, her body so still she might have been meditating. But she wasn't; she was simply waiting. Listening. Acting the feminine aspect of yielding acceptance, and he hated it.

"Do not be a Tigress now," he muttered. "Not around me."

"Then what should I be?" she asked, her voice casual as if he were a stranger.

My wife, he wanted to howl. But that was not true. She had always been his wife. And he had always wanted more.

"Give me your hand," he said.

She complied without hesitation, and that simple act reassured him. He cradled her hand in his palm, stroking his thumb along her fingers and allowing memory to take hold.

"Do you remember the first time I held your hand?" he asked. He pulled her closer and extended her arm so that he could write messages on her wrist.

I sell merchandise to whites.

She answered the question he'd spoken aloud.

"You have held my hand many times, my husband. I do not recall the first." Meanwhile, she stretched out her other hand to write her own question. But she was not close enough, so he helped her scramble nearer. She settled facing him, her knees pressed against his waist, her hip pulled tight against his thigh. Her tiny hand brushed open his torn shirt to write upon his chest.

Illegal?

He shrugged. *To some*, he answered. Meanwhile, his thoughts traveled back to her hand in his, her face so nearby.

"It was the day we wed, Shi Po." He lifted up her fingers to play with them, to trace the shape of her tiny, fragile bones. "During the wedding feast."

"You held my hand." He heard her tone soften. "My family was scandalized. Auntie said it showed your low class that you would seek to touch me before retiring to the bedchamber." *The General accuses you of worse.*

He stilled. *Worse?* Meanwhile, he continued their other conversation. "I didn't know if it was you. I didn't believe I was actually marrying you."

"So you held my hand?" *He didn't say. He implied.*

"I touched whatever I could of you. I didn't know if it was you or someone else." *He was fishing for information.*

"Who?" she asked. "If not me, who?"

"Your aunt," he pronounced.

He felt the jerk of her body, the sudden withdrawal of focus from what they'd been writing.

"My aunt? You thought my father would try to marry you to Auntie Ting?"

He nodded. "She was an impoverished widow. I was a poor wedding candidate."

"And so you held my hand."

"I was trying to see if your hand was young or old. If the skin—"

"Sagged or felt fresh?" she interrupted.

"Yes."

She shook her head, laughter in her voice. "But Auntie Ting is a beautiful woman. You could not have told by her hand."

He didn't answer. Truthfully, her aunt was a vicious witch. But yes, many would believe her beautiful.

Is she a Tigress? he asked. *Is that how she stays young?*

His wife paused before she answered. When she did, her strokes were slow and careful. *She spends much money on youthfulness potions. And she harvests yang when needed.*

Kui Yu acknowledged Shi Po's words with only part of his mind. He had known the truth, but there was yet a more pressing question to ask. A more important answer he needed. And yet, it took a great deal of courage for him to press the question into her wrist.

Do you regret our marriage?

She frowned. Even in the dim light he could see her body tense. Then she shook her head. *Never.* There was a pause. *Do you?*

No.

They had both answered firmly, both with little hesitation, and yet he knew they both lied. How could she not wonder? He certainly did. How could she not have regrets? He had a thousand.

What do we do now? she asked.

He was so distracted, he had trouble understanding her question. In the end, she had to write it twice, and still he had no answer.

"I cannot think clearly," he finally confessed. *I don't know*, he wrote into her wrist.

"The air here is unhealthy," she said. "It poisons the body and the energy."

And there was his answer. A way to pass the time. Perhaps even a way to bridge the gap that still separated them. *We must practice*, he wrote. *To purify yin and yang.*

He felt the refusal in her body, felt her stiffen. *The Manchurians call practice immoral. We could be killed*, she wrote.

He almost laughed. *Sex is normal for a husband and wife. No need to show another purpose.*

She hesitated, and he knew she wavered. Though he knew observing others was a normal part of the Tigress practice, he didn't think Shi Po had ever allowed herself to be watched. To do such intimate things here—with a bored guard perhaps watching every act through a peephole—would naturally revolt her.

But how else would he understand her passion if not to learn it himself? And how else would he ever return to Heaven to answer the Goddess Kwan Yin if not with her aid? She had to agree, and so he continued to push his thoughts on her.

Is there another way to keep our energies pure?

She shook her head. There was no other way.

So he looked at her, slowly moving his hand. Her blouse was ripped down the front, exposing her breasts. He knew what to do. He'd studied the texts carefully, and even secretly watched as she performed this daily exercise. But would she let him do it? He could tell by her stillness that she hadn't decided.

Up and up his hand moved, brushing her upper arm, across her shoulder. It took little for him to brush open the fabric, but she was curved away from him, her shoulders hunched forward.

He didn't yet move toward her breasts. Instead, he

lifted his hand, caressing her neck as he touched under her chin to draw her taller. And to stroke her lips.

You want to go to Heaven, she wrote on his chest. Her face was both awed and jealous. *You want my yin*.

He didn't deny it, though she was completely wrong. He wanted her, not the fulfillment of her religion. But what was the point of arguing?

These exercises will not give yin, she continued. *Only—*

He used his free hand to catch hers. The touch of her fingers on his body was clouding his thoughts. His yang was already surging, his dragon thrusting forward in eagerness. If he wanted to pursue her religion, if he wanted to return to Heaven to speak again with Kwan Yin, as his wife believed, then he would have to contain his yang. He would have to learn control, beginning with touching her and not descending to mindless rutting. Which meant, for now, that she would have to stop stimulating him.

"I know what to do," he whispered. "Will you allow it?"

She actually smiled. How long had it been since she'd turned such radiant beauty his way? How long since her face had shown simple joy without restraint? Too long. And it was too strange that it would come now—here—when she had never been so kind in their luxurious home.

"I know my duty," she answered as she straightened. But as she did, his hand slipped lower to rest at the top swell of her right breast.

He paused, then stroked a question high on her chest. *Duty?*

Practice, she answered. He paused. He knew better than to ask his next question, but such was the disquiet in his mind that he pressed the point against all logic. "What of love?" he asked.

They sat close enough together that he felt her entire body flinch. "What?" she gasped.

"Love," he pressed. "Is not sex a part of love?"

"We do not speak of such things!" she said in her most aristocratic tones.

He nodded. He knew that to be true. The elite did not sully themselves with petty emotions. "But I am a commoner, and I wish to know."

She shook her head, her body still withdrawn from him. "There is no love in practice," she said firmly. "Love is an earthly attachment. One that keeps us from Heaven." She leaned forward and cupped his hands. "That is why husbands and wives do not practice together. A tigress's partner is a convenience. It is easier to focus when a partner stimulates. It has nothing to do with feelings."

He could see that she believed it, that she spoke with complete honesty. All these years, her sexual partners had been simple convenience? "There is no attachment?"

She grimaced. "Of course not! It is an earthly tie. We strive for Heaven."

He wanted to ask about the two of them; if there was love between them. But he hadn't the courage. After all these years, he couldn't risk finding out that she had never loved him.

"Shi Po . . . ," he began as she shaped his hands into the correct position. Then she pressed his fingertips to each of her puckered nipples.

"Begin," she whispered.

But he didn't move. Instead, he straightened his spine. He would be a man in this. He would face his fears. "What of us, Shi Po? What of our love?"

She smiled. "We will strive to overcome it."

So there was his answer. If there ever had been love

between them, her tigress practice had destroyed it. Now he understood why she could embrace death. She had daily fought to distance herself from himself and their children, from every tie that bound her to earth. "And what if I do not wish to overcome it? What if I wish to love you with my every breath, the very essence of my being?"

She pulled away from him, and her tone was that of an instructor who gave a failing grade. "There is no halfway in this, Kui Yu. Either you wish for heaven or earth. You cannot have both."

"And love is of the earth?"

"Yes." Then she sat in absolute stillness as she waited for his decision. Obviously, she had already chosen. Years ago, she had decided to abandon him, to discard their love—if they'd ever had it—and to walk without earthly ties into Heaven. He could try to dissuade her. He could woo her with soft words and tender kisses, but his wife had always been steadfast. Once her mind was set upon a task, nothing would sway her.

So she was already lost to him. His only hope was to understand what had stolen her from him.

He swallowed, feeling his spirit tremble. Last night's practice had begun in anger and desperation, but today was different. It had nothing to do with their location or situation. Nothing to do with the guard outside or the fear that still lingered in the room, poisoning everything they did. Today, he chose this for himself. Today, he began to work with conscious intention. He would learn this religion. He would return to Heaven. He would understand what his wife so desperately sought at the cost of their love and life together. And, he would have an answer for Kwan Yin.

With that thought firmly in place, he banished all doubt. He pushed aside all tender feelings and set his mind on Heaven. Then he began the worship of his wife's breasts.

❦

July 20, 1880

Kui Yu—

My aunt has many women for you—great, small, expensive, or cheap. You could shower your wealth upon them, and they would leap to do all that you ask.

Come Thursday evening to the Garden of Blushing Flowers. I will introduce you.

Your dearest friend,
Lun Po

July 26, 1880

Lun Po—

I have more blushing flowers than I can handle. They throw their petals at men of wealth. They use their twisting, creeping vines to trap men of influence.

I wish for the sweet innocence of a Chinese blossom untainted by cloying perfumes.

Kui Yu

Once there was as lazy fellow looking for an easy job. A friend told him to work at the graveyard. "There's no easier work around."

So the fellow took the job but soon quit. When asked why, he loudly exclaimed, "It's too unfair! They're all lying down while I have to stand there all by myself!"

Chapter Ten

Shi Po closed her eyes, doing her best to relax into her daily ritual. She had already shifted her legs to pull her left heel hard against her cinnabar cave. Her back was straight, her breath steady, and her breasts pressed forward into her husband's hands.

And right there, her mind faltered. She had always performed these exercises herself. Never—even at the very beginning—had she allowed another soul to do this most important purification task for her. And yet today, she had not even suggested that she do this herself.

She had no idea why suddenly she wanted Kui Yu's touch so desperately. Why her breasts were already heavy; her nipples long and hard in anticipation. But they were, and her belly trembled even as she tried to steady her heart and mind.

He began. He performed the dispersal strokes first, starting on the inside of her nipples, circling ever wider as he cleansed all negative energies from her

171

yin. Small tight circles first. Then the spiral expanded, opened, flowed.

He had large fingers and thick hands. Yet they were a man's hands, strong and calloused from labor, and she found she liked the texture. The rough slide against her skin reminded her that he could lift heavy bales of cotton as easily as he smoothed tiny ripples in silk. She had seen him do both, and yet he seemed to be treating her as something finer even than his fabrics, something more delicate than the thinnest silk.

She closed her eyes, liking the image, enjoying even more the touch of his fingers on her yin center. His yang heat left a tingling wake along her skin, and she wanted to push deeper into his hands, more fully into his energy. But that wasn't part of the exercise, and so she maintained her discipline and contented herself with deep breaths that drew his power into her lungs.

"Forty-nine," he said.

She opened her eyes, startled to realize she hadn't kept count. When was the last time she had lost the mental click that marked the passage of time? And when was the last time her heel came away from her cave slick with yin dew?

"I'm sorry," she murmured. "I lost track. There must be a great many pollutants in my yin."

She watched his smile grow, pure male satisfaction lighting his eyes. "I like it when you lose track," he said. "Your face flushes—"

"That's the yang heat—"

"And your lips turn celebration red."

"When yang combines with yin, there is a heat—"

"And you begin to babble, especially when you become self-conscious."

"It brings . . ." She blinked. "I do not babble."

"Of course not," he laughed, his grin huge. "I must be mistaken."

She arched her eyebrows at him, and tried to reflect injured dignity. But her husband had never cared much for such dignity, and so she lost the image of it and reflected his amusement instead. "You are a very strange man to say such things to me," she remarked with a smile.

"And you are a beautiful woman, too tender-hearted to be offended by my coarseness."

Her lips curved into a deeper smile and—strangely—the motion made the rest of Shi Po tingle even more. "I suppose I have a weakness for coarse things."

"Truly?" he asked, surprised.

"You did not know?"

He shook his head, and his hands hovered slightly above his lap. He opened his mouth to speak, but no sound came out, and his expression remained confused. Until it became wary.

"Kui Yu?"

He did not reveal his thoughts, except to look down at his hands. "Do you wish to continue?"

Yes, of course she did. But she didn't say so. Instead, she reached out and enfolded his hands in hers. Except, her hands were so much smaller. She could only cup him, not restrain him. "If we are to be partners, we must remain honest with one another," she lied. In truth, the practice only required the exchange of yin and yang; honesty was rarely part of the deal.

Fortunately, he didn't know that, and so he answered, his voice low and hesitant. "I am coarse and lowborn." He twisted his hands, turning so that he grabbed her left wrist to press her fingers against his palm.

"Extend your fingers," he said.

She did, and her largest finger barely reached his second knuckle. "A woman is supposed to be small where her husband is large," she remarked. "We are flowers as compared to—"

"A lumbering ox?" He laughed, and she pulled back.

"You are no dumb beast."

He sighed. "I am large—"

"And I am small. Yes. Male. Female—"

"Laborer. Scholar."

She nodded, knowing his background. But still, he continued.

"I am poor and ill-bred, while you are rich and refined."

She sighed. "Opposites, Kui Yu. That is all to the good."

Finally, he raised his gaze to her, and she saw a darkness in his eyes. "Is that why you chose me? Because we are opposites?"

She shook her head, the denial automatic even if it was prevarication. "My father chose you. I had little to do—"

His hand shot out, covering her lips with his fingers. He didn't hurt her. Indeed, his skin barely touched her. But he surprised her enough to silence her casual lies.

"Honesty, remember?"

She didn't respond. Indeed, there were some falsehoods so ingrained that when taken away, they left her feeling bereft. But she had forced him to be honest with her. As his mirror, she had no choice but to reflect his own goodness back. She reached up and pulled his hand from her mouth.

"You are strong. Strong body, strong mind, strong

yang. When one is surrounded by weakness, such power shines like a beacon."

He looked at her, their hands poised in the air between them. She could not tell what he was thinking, and so she became emptiness: a blank reflection that slowly changed to quietness.

They did not speak more. She wasn't surprised; such was his way: absorbed in silence, speaking only when necessary. If she was a mirror, he was the wind, hearing without comment, knowing without unbalancing. Until it was time. Then the furious winds would blow and whole cities could be laid low.

Which made it all the more exquisite when he at last used his fingers to caress her breasts. Hot wind would warm her coldness; strong yang stimulated her yin. And his wonderful hands started in the center point of her chest and circled. But this time, he narrowed his spirals until he touched her nipples.

She actually purred at the thought.

She was pleased when he flattened his hands, using four fingers to flow over the tops of her breasts and skating around her sides, then raising up from below. Years of this kind of exercise had kept her skin tight, her breasts high despite age and nursing three children. And yet, some deterioration was inevitable. Her nipples pushed downward as if reaching for his hands. Her muscles grew lax with pleasure, making her breasts droop even more.

Kui Yu did not seem to mind. When she looked at his face, she saw rapt attention. When she let her gaze slip lower, she saw dragon hunger. And still his hands narrowed in their spiral. They drew higher on her breasts, closer to their tips.

Higher. Tighter.

She breathed in with his downstroke, then exhaled

fully as he traveled upward. Waiting. Wanting. When would he finish?

Now.

His fingers were beside her nipples, and her cinnabar cave tightened in anticipation. But then he stopped. He lifted his hands and reset them on the center of her breastbone.

"What are you doing?" she demanded, frustration making her curt.

He frowned. "The exercise—"

"Finish the stroke!" she ordered.

"I did," he responded, equally firm.

She shook her head, forcibly moving his hands back to their places next to her nipples. "You are to squeeze the plum flower."

He did not move. "That was not in the sacred text I read."

She frowned and pretended to think. She knew it wasn't in the text, but it was how she had been taught. She gave her students the choice. But for her, she always ended the stroke with pain.

"It is how it is done," she said.

"But—"

"It is how I have always done it."

He didn't move at first, and she feared he would be difficult. But in the end, he nodded even as he pulled his hands back to her breastbone.

"At the end of this stroke," he said.

She nodded and used her Tigress discipline to quiet her disappointment. She knew how to wait for pleasure.

He began again: the long stroke from center to top, around and down before narrowing slightly. His hands rode higher on her breasts and lifted closer to her peaks. She breathed with his movement, the tingle in her skin expanding, growing hotter with each breath.

He was close. So close. And then . . .

She felt a soft touch, the lightest of presses. It shot like lightning through her body, saturating her womb with yin fire. But it was not enough. It seemed weak and insubstantial, despite her reaction.

"What are you doing?" she snapped. The pulse had left her unsettled.

"That's what you wanted," he returned.

"No! You must do it harder. Firmer." She cupped his hands and forced him to surround her breasts. Then she made him squeeze. Hard.

He resisted, and the confusion made her hips squirm against her heel.

"Harder!" she ordered.

This time he pinched her with some force, but so quickly as to make her tremble but not flinch.

"No," she muttered, annoyed with her own lack of clarity. What did she want?

Abruptly, she brushed away his hands and performed the exercise herself, as she had for so many years. Her hands moved by rote, and her thoughts quickly settled into the familiar pattern. Her hands narrowed, her breath increased. Then she reached the end.

She not only squeezed long and hard, but she also twisted. The pain made her muscles tighten and her breath clench. There was no lightning stroke of excitement. Only the welcome bite of pain.

"*That* is how it is done," she said to herself.

"But that must hurt."

She opened her eyes and read confusion on his face. "That is how I was taught."

"But it hurts. It must."

She looked down to watch herself as she performed the circles again. Pinch. Twist. Hold. Yes, her nipples were flushed, their dusky peaks raw.

She looked up at her husband, the memory only now coming back to her. "It is to remind us that nothing happens without pain. Conceiving a child, birthing a new life, even the most casual of practice must be accompanied by pain. Because that is life."

"That is not in the texts, Shi Po." He frowned. "Who taught you that?"

She hesitated, knowing what his reaction would be.

"Honesty, Shi Po. Remember, we look for the cause of your problems. The reason you have not made it into Heaven." He lifted his chin, his expression one of simple interest, not interrogation.

She had to answer. But when she spoke, different words came out. "This is why we cannot practice together, Kui Yu. You question too much. You—"

"And you have too long followed the same path to the same failure. When will you change?"

He was right. Slowly, she let her hands drop to her lap. "Auntie Ting," she finally said.

"Auntie Ting—the woman who owns a brothel?"

Shi Po nodded.

"You took your early training from that bitter old toad?"

She felt her back straighten as she lashed out. "She knows more about pleasure than any man or woman I know."

He grimaced. "She also knows about perversion and sickness." He leaned forward, his words harsh. "I will not cause you pain. There is enough agony in life; why would one deliberately inflict it?"

"Because . . . because . . ." She had no reason for her actions. None beyond what she had already said.

Auntie Ting had taught her the practice and the reason when she was still a young girl, barely fifteen. She had not looked further than that.

Kui Yu continued to press her, delving into things she had never questioned. Things that no one had ever questioned. "Is there no sensation when I squeeze lightly?" he asked.

She shook her head. "There is . . ." How to explain? "There is no pain. No dulling of the experience. Only an excitement that builds."

His lips curved. "Isn't that good?"

"Without pain, how will I have the distance to control the experience?"

He arched a single questioning eyebrow. "Do you need to control it?"

"I have to ride the Tigress. How else can I get to Heaven?"

"Perhaps the Tigress dislikes the pain."

"Perhaps the Tigress will not obey otherwise," she challenged. "Have you ever seen a horse ridden without a crop? An ox led without a nose ring? Or a goose without a stick?"

He shook his head. "You are not a dumb beast, Shi Po. And pain was never a good motivator for one of intelligence."

She almost laughed at that. Imagine the stupidity of one who would discipline without pain. Except, of course, he had never beaten their children. He'd rarely even raised his voice. And they responded to him nonetheless. True, their children also leapt to obey her, but the greater respect went to her husband.

"You have always been gentle," she realized in a murmur. And revered because of it.

"Pain will not take you to Heaven," he said. He reached out and stroked the top of her breasts in a

179

manner not dictated by the texts. "Let us try it my way and see what happens."

She knew what would happen. She knew the power of painless caresses. Had she not conceived three children with him? Had she not lost herself in his yang just last night? But there was nowhere for her to run, and no way to dissuade him. So with a trembling that began low in her belly, she took a deep breath and lifted her chin.

"Without the pain, how will I control myself?"

"I will hold you," he answered. "I will keep you safe."

Then he began. He pressed his fingers to the center of her chest, and she felt his heat quicken the beat of her heart. His hands stroked over the tops of her breasts, down their sides and then beneath, always spiraling in, always firm enough to heat her body, but not hard enough to hurt. All too soon she gave up comparing his spirals to her usual stroke. Kui Yu was ever his own person.

She tried to fight his seductive touch. The yin needed to be controlled in order to be ridden. But not this time. Not when his hands widened, touching more and more of her breasts. He surrounded her. He heated her. And he drew her purified yin to a boil.

Or so she named it. In truth, there was no burning, only heat. There was no crushing weight, only pleasure. Her breath began to rasp in her throat, not because he frightened her, but because she suppressed moans of pleasure.

Then he touched her nipples. No pinch, no twist; he gave a gentle tug, as if he were pulling on the yin river itself. He widened its boundaries and drew it up to meet his yang.

Shi Po felt her mouth go slack on a gasp. She could

Desperate Tigress

not breathe without his touch. She could not feel anything but him. And she could not think at all.

"Release to me," he murmured, even as he began
his spiral again. Wider, then narrowing. Gentle, only
to make her sob.

Why was this so hard? Why did she fight this escape? She wanted to open herself up, to simply enjoy
without control, to ride without restraint. But still her
muscles clenched and trembled. She fought what he
did to her. She was facing him, her fists resting on her
thighs. But now she extended her hands, needing to
hold him, needing to ground herself.

She stroked a character on his leg without thought,
an answer to her questions:

Fear.

He stopped his movements. Her breasts were full
and hungry, and the yin river pounded in her heart
and mind. Her husband lifted his hand and touched
her cheek, wiping away the tears she hadn't known
were there. Then he leaned forward and pressed his
lips to hers, murmuring nonsense words against her
mouth. She had no idea what he said, and no mind to
interpret if she had. All she knew was his touch and
his gentleness.

And her fears eased.

"Take it," she whispered. "The yin is too strong.
Take it."

He drew back to search her face, but she grabbed
his wrists and pulled him closer.

"More," she said, as she placed his hands fully on
her breasts. "Now."

Then she guided him, not in the spirals he had
been making, but in the way of a man massaging an
aching muscle or stretching a twisted cord. Part of
her still wanted the pain, but she ruthlessly sup-

181

pressed that. And as Kui Yu lifted and shaped her breasts, she leaned back on the pallet. He followed, stretching over her.

"Take it," she said again. "I cannot hold it all." The yin tide was too full, the surging ocean too overwhelming. Soon she would drown in it if he did not help her.

He did. Fortunately, he didn't require explanation, because she had no breath to tell him, only the arch of her back and the frantic plea of her hands on his face, his neck, and broad shoulders.

"Please," she murmured, as he lowered his head.

He expanded his grip to use his entire hand to hold each breast. Then, slowly, he pressed his fingers in just hard enough to make her moan, and drew his stroke up. He narrowed his fingers and pulled inevitably to a nipple.

Then he took that nipple into his mouth.

Her womb convulsed, and the yin tide surged. She bucked on the pallet. It was a harsh, abrupt movement that dislodged Kui Yu, and she cried out at the loss.

He came back to her, but not quickly enough. She tightened her hold on his shoulders and maneuvered him to lie on top of her. Then she wrapped her legs around his waist and pressed her cinnabar cave into his hips.

Again and again she ground her pelvis against him, and the yin pulsed with every push.

"Now," she gasped. "Take it now."

He did. He put his lips to her left nipple and began to suck. On the right breast, his hand pulled and kneaded in time with his mouth. And both joined in the rhythmic push and pull of her hips.

The yin began to flow in earnest. The deepest cavern and fastest rush of such a river came from the center of her womb. It flowed upward in a straight line to where Kui Yu's tongue lapped and circled her nipple. His lips kept the suction strong and the nipple distended in his mouth, but it was the yin river that joined them together and made them one body, one flow of power. Shi Po's inner muscles contracted, lifting and pushing as a pump, and she thrust toward him to disgorge her power into his mouth, his body, and therefore his spirit.

Shi Po did not mourn the loss of yin. She had too much, and he too little. This was her gift to him even as the fullness of her river was his gift to her. There was no riding this yin Tigress, no controlling the flow, only an overwhelming thrusting into her husband. She was subsumed in the yin river, and she poured herself into him. Easily. Beautifully. And with such an ecstasy of energy that for a moment she became her own yin. She was no longer Shi Po, no longer his wife or General Kang's prisoner. She was simply an eternal female power, pulsing with life as she emptied into him.

Many times she thought she finished. A woman could only have so much yin; a body could only contain so much. But there was always more. As Kui Yu shifted to her other breast, there was more. And again and again.

At last, her body faltered. The river did not end, but her limbs could no longer pull, her womb could no longer writhe. And yet, still the energy moved, the river remained. It flowed endlessly as she floated upon it, borne away and reborn.

Kui Yu kissed her breasts, her shoulders, her chin, and her mouth. His body was heavy upon her, his eyes dazed when he took in her features. He knew they were still connected. She could see the wonder shimmering in his eyes.

Then the strangest thing happened. Never before had she heard of such a thing, and yet it was right. Her yin searched for another outlet, another means of expression. It found it in her mouth and her heart:

She laughed.

Kui Yu looked down at his wife's serene face, still stunningly beautiful even slack-jawed in sleep. She had laughed. Shi Po had laughed, and not in the suppressed titter typical of Chinese women, not even the giggle of a young girl, but in a deep belly laugh that had filled the room. The sound was rich and expressive and still echoed in his mind. Joy—pure and overflowing.

It was a wonder. And a miracle. And he had no idea what it meant.

Had she become an Immortal? He hadn't thought so, but then he was only two days into this bizarre practice.

He sat back and dropped his head against the cold, stone wall. Damn, he was stiff. His shoulders ached from supporting his weight while his wife writhed beneath him. His mouth and jaw felt tight, but mostly his dragon was rock-hard and hungry. His body didn't care that Shi Po had dropped into an exhausted sleep; it smelled her in the air and knew she was wet and soft, and a bare handsbreadth away. He wanted her, and in a most painfully insistent way.

And he was supposed to withhold release forever? Yes, because that's what dragons did. He had read it quite clearly in the sacred texts: He was to keep his fluids inside at all times or risk losing a year of his life.

Frankly, a year of life in this state wasn't worth keeping.

His gaze drifted back to his wife. What would he

give to feel such joy as she pursued, even for a moment? What would he do to return to Heaven once again?

He shook his head. Hers was a bizarre religion, one he had secretly scorned for years. He hadn't cared, so long as she was happy. Who would have thought that these women had found the pathway to Heaven through sex? Ridiculous! And yet he could not deny his experiences or his wife's serenity.

He sighed, his breath temporarily clearing the fetid air. But then the stale prison scents returned, only partially masked by what he and Shi Po had done. His gaze traveled to the door and the narrow view of the hallway beyond the barred window. He needed to get out of here. He had business ventures that needed his attention. He had sons to care for and a son-in-law to watch. And he had a wife who was changing before his eyes—one day threatening suicide, the next overwhelming him with her happiness.

But how to escape? Protests would not serve. Their guard would not break General Kang's order, not even with the promise of an exorbitant bribe. What recourse did a Han merchant have against a Manchurian general? None.

Which meant he and his wife were stuck here, with nothing but the certainty that they were being watched and the faint hope that Shi Po's brother would forsake his drinking and whoring long enough to render some aid. Kui Yu almost laughed out loud at that thought. Instead, he released a frustrated grunt and lay down beside Shi Po.

Settling himself around her, he tucked her close, her back to his chest, her bottom heating and torturing his throbbing dragon.

Odd, he realized as he closed his eyes, he didn't

mind so much. His discomfort was a small price to pay to have his wife in his arms again, to have joy spill from her spirit into him. Even this incarceration was an acceptable price.

Assuming, of course, it didn't go on much longer. Assuming, as well, that Shi Po remained full of joy, and did not succumb to the crushing depression of their situation.

Assuming, as well, that controlling his yang did not kill him.

❦

August 2, 1880

Friend Kui Yu—

My sister is not the untouched bud you imagine. She is a poisoned creature with a vile tongue and large, ugly feet. Whoever is cursed with her as a bride will suffer eternal poverty and daily recriminations.

> *In honesty,*
> *Lun Po*

August 3, 1880

Lun Po—

I will meet this termagant. Or I will find and beat you for your slander. Thursday afternoon in the park where we used to play.

> *Kui Yu*

One day, a teacher fell asleep during class. After waking up, he said to his students, "I dreamt of Prince Zhou."

The next day, one of his students fell asleep in class. The teacher woke him with a whack of his wooden stick, saying, "How dare you fall asleep in class!"

The student said, "I dreamt of Prince Zhou, too!"

"What did he say to you?"

"He said that he didn't meet you yesterday."

Chapter Eleven

Kui Yu was awake when the guards changed. Indeed, he was awake most of the time now. One day's lying about had more than made up for the interrupted night's sleep, and by the eighth day, he was out of his mind with irritation at his lack of activity.

He and Shi Po's only source of information was when the guards greeted each other and gossiped about the world. He knew more than he wanted about one soldier's corns and the other's aching tooth; the men discussed their bodily functions with the frankness of age and long acquaintance.

But neither guard had the slightest idea when the General would return, or what was happening in Peking, or any news that would ease the growing panic in Kui Yu's heart. So Kui Yu and Shi Po sat in the darkness and listened to nothing.

They spoke little but practiced much. There was nothing else to do. And that made Kui Yu even more irritable. One day with a rock-hard dragon was uncomfortable; four were excruciatingly painful. After a week, the slightest twitch set his yang fire to pulsing. He didn't dare walk. Indeed, he wondered if he could stand, so intense was his need.

Shi Po understood his condition. At home, she had herbs to ease his pain, special teas to soothe the yang fire. And he would have had privacy to break training and ease his torment. (Indeed, he was convinced that most young dragons did exactly that.) But he was trapped in a cell with his wife, a woman growing more beautiful, more lighthearted, with every passing day.

He hadn't a clue how she managed it. She cared nothing for their miserable conditions, the hideous food, or even the vermin that nightly visited their cell. Her only thought was for practice, and when not spent with him, she meditated in a joyful stillness. If anything, their incarceration was an aid to her, because it had ended all the distractions of teaching and household management that frittered away her time.

In short, he was amazed by her even as he was eaten by jealousy.

How dare she find joy in this deplorable situation? How could she embrace captivity with such grace? And why was she allowed to find her yin release with every touch while he had to hold his dragon back, feeling it swell with frustration and pain?

She had offered once to relieve his ache. She knew how difficult was his path, but it was the path of the Jade Dragon, and Kui Yu had decided he would not abandon it. Not because it would take him to Heaven, and not even because there was nothing else to do in this devil pit; but because, for the first time in his life, his wife seemed proud. And she looked truly happy.

And he would do nothing to upset that, not even release his seed and end his agony.

He sighed, and his wife stirred from her meditation. She was sitting on the pallet, her legs folded beneath her, her body still as a statue. Even as she opened her eyes, the rest of her remained frozen, not softening even for speech.

He turned away, his bitter gaze fixed on the door. "They ought to give you clothes," he growled.

It was his most frequent complaint: that his wife remained garbed in her ripped blouse and torn skirt. No matter what she did, both gaped open, revealing her flesh. She only wore the rags for warmth.

He had demanded new clothing for them, of course, but the guards ignored him. He daily offered her his own pants and shirt, but she claimed complete ease with her nakedness. Indeed, she said, it made some aspects of practice easier.

But it also meant his wife's charms were constantly before him. Her breasts bobbed a hand's-breadth away, her tattooed tigress too. He smelled her musky scent with every breath, saw her high-pointed breasts with every glance, and could touch her cinnabar cave whenever his dragon madness seized him. And he did, foolishly trusting his strength of will.

But he did not have faith in his will today. Today, the yang fire burned with white-hot power. So he turned his head to stare at the door and grumbled nonsense, while his wife watched him with an aggravating stillness.

He banged his head backward against the stone wall. It felt so good, he did it again. Then again. And again. He had no understanding of why, he just did it. And with every impact, he released a small measure of frustration.

"Stop, Kui Yu." His wife's voice was gentle, filled with peace.

It made him slam his head against the wall even harder.

"Kui Yu, enough!"

He flinched, embarrassed, but his dragon was riding him hard and he could not stop himself. Pain in the head was infinitely preferable to what tortured him every other moment of this incarceration.

"Kui Yu!" Her hand interfered, pushing between his skull and the wall. He had to stop or risk smashing her fingers.

"Leave me be, wife," he warned. "I am in an ill mood."

"Your yang has built up to the level of insanity, husband," she replied. "You must abandon this foolishness."

He whipped around and glared at her. "This is what your religion teaches, is it not? This is what all young dragons go through, is it not? To contain their power? To grow greater with every breath?"

She grimaced. "Yes—but with the aid of herbs and time."

"I am as strong as your Ru Shan!" he growled.

She sighed, and his eyes fell to her breasts.

"Ru Shan was never mine—"

"Enough!" He shoved to his feet despite pain that nearly crippled him. He would stand on his own two legs like a man, though he nearly broke his teeth as he clenched his jaw.

His wife remained silent. He felt her gaze upon his back. It was a tangible presence that spread in his mind as he imagined her hands elsewhere, her lush mouth—

With a howl, he threw himself at the door, gripping the bars as he bellowed. He had no words. His mind had completely deserted him. He simply screamed. But it was all to no avail; the guard didn't even respond.

He slumped against the bars, his sanity shattered. Who knew that his wife's religion could be so difficult?

"Come back to bed," said Shi Po, her voice a gentle caress.

He knew what she intended: She would seduce him, force him to release his seed, and thereby end his pursuit of Heaven.

And he almost allowed it. Almost. But then he stopped himself for her. Well, not for Shi Po specifically, but for an image of her. He recalled the moment she had laughed, her body flushed with a joy that went beyond physical. According to the sacred texts, she could only achieve such felicity with the aid of a pure and capable partner. Which meant him. And with such a duty, he could not allow her to touch him. Not until he regained some measure of control.

"Leave me alone," he muttered wearily.

Shi Po shifted on the pallet but did not stand. He couldn't see her, but he had become attuned to her slightest sound, her smallest change. He knew what she did by the shift in the air, and so he knew she accepted his ill temper in the way of all good Tigresses— with meek acceptance, even as she quietly plotted his undoing.

"Do you remember the last time we paced a room together?" Her words drifted past, and he struggled to make sense of them.

"I only remember this room," he said. Each word was spat like a curse.

"I remember a different one. In our house many years ago." His wife paused, and Kui Yu narrowed his eyes while trying to read her expression in the halflight. She smiled, her eyes distant with memory.

"Our daughter was ill. She had the gasping cough."

He flinched, the memory all too clear. But his wife continued.

"My herbs did nothing. The balancing of her qi— nothing. I was sure—"

"Stop!" he interrupted. "It was not your fault. We have been most fortunate to have three children, all grown healthy and strong. What other family can say they have lost no one? We cannot expect they would never have grown ill, either."

She nodded, but he knew she was unconvinced.

"She survived," he reminded her. "That is all that matters."

Shi Po's eyes were unfocused. She looked at the wall, around the cell. And then she spoke, her words distant, as if they came from the bottom of a deep, dark hole.

"You joined me in our daughter's bedroom. What Chinese father goes to his daughter's bedside? None. Auntie Ting thought it a perversion, but I knew it was that you cared for her. You valued your daughter."

"No child is worthless," he snapped. "No woman either." But he knew his was a rare opinion. Fathers often ignored their daughters. Some didn't even remember their names.

His wife shrugged. "You visited all our children; Li Shi no less than our sons. Then she became ill."

Kui Yu crossed the room and settled beside Shi Po, despite the way her nearness fogged his mind. "Our daughter is strong, like you. She fought the illness and is whole."

Shi Po shook her head. "I remember, Kui Yu. I remember the way you paced that night. You and I walked around her bed, praying, pleading—"

"Crying. I remember your tears most of all."

"You held her. You wiped her face and shuddered whenever she coughed."

He reached out and held Shi Po's hand, wishing to be rid of this conversation. "She recovered. She is strong," he repeated.

Again she nodded, but this time Shi Po turned to him, her eyes dark echoes of the emptiness in her voice. She didn't speak. Instead, she drew words on his arm.

I know what you did, she wrote.

He felt his breath stop in his chest. She couldn't know. She had been sleeping.

He shook his head. "I prayed. As you did."

"Of course," she said aloud. But on his arm, she wrote something different: *You bought medicine from the barbarians*.

He had no answer. She was right. And still Shi Po wrote, her scrawl cutting into his spirit.

You took our sons, too.

"I was desperate. She was dying."

She smiled. "I know," she whispered. "You were desperate. For our *daughter*."

He sighed, at last understanding. He had broken the law, ignored the policies against interaction with Barbarians, and risked his reputation on a secret mission for white medicine. And it had been all for a female child that most other fathers would consider worthless.

"Your potions cured her," he said aloud. "And the ancestors."

The white medicine cured her, she wrote on his arm.

He shook his head. They didn't know that for sure; it had still taken many days. But the possibility was there. As was his fear, for he had taken his boys to the whites as well. He had stolen them away from their studies for an afternoon's play, or so he had claimed.

Secretly, they had gone to the whites for "inoculation."

He had no idea if there was any power in the injections, but his desperation had been enough to convince him to try, in the hope that he would never pace at one of his children's bedside again. And Shi Po had known all along.

Is that why they hold us here? she wrote on his arm. *Because we took the white medicines?*

He frowned at the thought. Was it possible? Could General Kang know?

How did you pay for it? she pressed into his flesh. *What did you give them?*

He stared at her, nonplussed. *Money,* he answered.

Shi Po shook her head, disbelieving. *Li Shi lived,* she wrote on his arm. *No men—not even whites—give away such magic for simple gold.*

He straightened in horror, the air thick in his chest. She thought he had betrayed his country. She thought he had done something immoral to save their daughter's life. She thought he was capable of such a thing?

"Just money," he said aloud. "Only money." Then he pushed away from her, pain squeezing the breath from his lungs.

She followed, and when he turned from her, she stroked new words on his back. *I understand. I agree there are sacrifices worth making. But I must know what you did.*

"Nothing!" He whirled around. He grabbed her arms and raised her off the ground in his fury. He was careful not to bruise her, but he would make her listen.

"The ghost people only care for money," he stated loudly. Firmly. "I have no other dealings with them, except in the taking of that." It was a lie. In truth, he had many conversations with the whites, and there were many business possibilities. There were so many thoughts about improving China.

But he'd never betray his country! Unfortunately, there was no way to prove his innocence to anyone. So he paced the tiny cell, stomping in frustration from one corner to another. His wife's eyes followed him, her doubts plaguing his every breath.

"I have done nothing wrong," he moaned half to her, half to himself. He dropped back onto their pallet. "Nothing."

"I know," she soothed. And she seemed to mean it.

He let his head roll back against the wall, questions clouding his mind. Did General Kang know the extent of his dealings with the foreigners? Were he and his wife imprisoned because Shi Po had dared to keep the General's son, or because Kui Yu's fortune was based on commerce with the whites? Who was to blame? And how could they escape?

He banged his head back against the wall, wishing he could knock away his confusion. If he were free, he would have ways to discover the truth. He had resources and friends. But in here he had nothing but questions, a half-naked wife and a starving dragon.

A brilliant sun, a crystal-clear sky, birds, trees and the crisp bite of autumn in the air. The scent of newly harvested fields. The sound of children laughing in a game of tag. The fullness of peace and great joy. Kui Yu inhaled deeply. He let the air of the open field fill his lungs, even though he knew this was a dream. Especially because it was a dream. How else could he be here? And with Shi Po.

She came to him from a dark cavern. Even in his dreams, she wasn't completely free. But she was happy and open and robed in clothing fit for a goddess: a silver gown shot through with gold thread, trailing ribbons of glory.

But he barely even noticed. His eyes were on her face. Never before had she seemed so relaxed. Her skin was smooth, her smile so warm that it brought tears to his eyes. And her gestures were as wide and expansive as her gaze, which seemed to encompass the entire world, welcoming it all. Accepting. Loving.

She looked at him. What had been accepting in her, now shifted to something more. What had been a general focus, narrowed to encompass only him. She saw only him. Even the radiance that expanded from her heart, the light of love that overflowed from her center, it too contracted, drawing into her, focusing like a beam on Kui Yu. It curled even tighter into his wife, slipped away from him, drew down and in. He could see it compress. Indeed, as the light curled into itself, its brilliance increased. It became whiter, brighter, folding into a blaze that should have blinded him. It remained there inside her, a tiny gem of the most amazing beauty, secreted deep within her. He could see it, but barely. Mostly, he remembered and felt and knew.

As for Shi Po herself, her celestial clothing folded away. It became one with the light, absorbed into a part of her as integral as the jewel. Which left her standing before him in her all her earthly glory. Her naked skin gleamed pearly white. Her lush red mouth glistened. Her firm, rounded breasts bobbed. And her sexuality called to him. She tilted her head back, and her dark black hair, pinned high, slipped free of its restraints and slid down her back like an onyx river.

She looked at him and smiled. There was no artifice in her face, no fear or even any understanding of the world in all its ugliness. She was completely innocent, and she held out her hand for him. He took it.

How could he not? As they touched, his own clothing slipped away. Such was the magic of his dream and the glory of her caress.

She did not know what to do. She trailed her fingers along his chest, not out of coyness, but from curiosity. She smiled like a child when his muscles quivered, and she giggled at his gasp when she spun a tiny circle with her finger around his nipple.

He didn't move. He let her explore at her own pace. She traced his chest, the width of his shoulders, then slid her hands upward. She grinned at the slight roughness of his jaw, then poked at the tip of his nose, making them both laugh like toddlers. Then she stepped forward and pushed her fingers into his hair, letting it slide through her hands while her sweet breath heated the underside of his jaw and set his mouth to tingling.

She was so close, and he could not resist. He reached up, spanned her tiny waist, then drew his hands to her breasts. She stilled, her eyes wide with surprise. But he caught curiosity in her expression, too, especially when she looked down to watch his hands lift her breasts and thumb her nipples.

She shivered, and that made her breasts dance. Then she lifted her arms. He had no idea why she would do such a thing, but it was an elegant motion nonetheless. One which made her body long and sleek, and showed off her youthful grace. She was stretching, her spine arching, her head tilting backward, and he ached at the sweetness of it all.

He lowered his lips as though worshipping at an altar. But this wasn't an altar, it was his wife's sweet skin, her trembling heart, her full breast. He drew that into his mouth, rolled his tongue around it and suckled at wonder and joy.

She moaned in honest delight, her breath already coming in gasps. Kui Yu wrapped his arms around her and supported her weight as she lifted her breasts to him. Soon, he laid her down on the grass. They were in the pathway between fields. On the one side, lotuses grew rich and full, spreading wide green leaves to the bright sun. On the other, rice grew in emerald abundance, its spring scent lingering even now.

But in the center of his vision lay his wife, her eyes open in trusting innocence. Her legs slipped wide as well, and the smell of her arousal mixed with the heady perfume of life all around.

She looked at him, her hand extended in interest as she compared their two forms. His dragon was thick and eager, and it quivered in delight as she stroked its head and fondled its long underbelly. Kui Yu's muscles quivered, and he panted, but he remained still. He would do nothing to interrupt her exploration. This caress was completely untutored, and it aroused him to a pounding hunger.

Don't move. Not yet. Not yet.

His silent orders to himself were nearly impossible to obey, but somehow he managed. Until Shi Po leaned down, her tiny nose twitching as she sniffed at his chest.

Don't move, he told himself as she slid down his abdomen.

She tilted her head and flashed a happy smile. Then she extended her pink tongue to lap at his dragon as a kitten might a plate of cream.

Don't move. Don't—

He couldn't stop himself. He threw her backward and spread her thighs with his knees. She went willingly, her expression trusting, her lips curved in a smile that was equal parts wonder and delight.

"This might hurt," he said, hating to bring truth into even this dream.

"You could never hurt me."

He winced. She was so young, so untouched. And yet, he gloried in that as well, taking solace in her faith. "I won't mean to—," he began, but she stopped him with her fingers against his lips.

"There will be no pain," she said firmly. Then she arched into him, pressing her yielding flesh against his dragon.

There was no stopping now. Not when he was surrounded by heat, his dragon reveling in her body's wet caress. He had no restraint, especially as he felt her heels slide up the backs of his legs. She drew him to her and gripped his hips with all the strength of her young thighs.

Kui Yu thrust. He buried himself as completely as he could, and if he could have climbed inside her sweetness, he would have. As it was, he could only shudder at the exquisiteness that was Shi Po.

She surrounded him in her warmth, her beauty, and her absolute purity. Even as she gazed at him with wide-eyed surprise.

"Did it hurt?" he whispered.

She smiled. Drawing his mouth down for a lingering kiss, she whispered into his ear, "You could never hurt me. You're too good."

And when she said it, he could believe.

She arched her hips into him, and he knew true happiness. Not because this felt amazing. Not even because her body was his most luscious and willing pillow. But because he was buried deep inside of something wonderful, a sweetness that rubbed off on him. Shi Po's goodness became his, her strength infused him.

Her strength . . . ?

Since when had innocence implied strength? Even in a dream, he struggled with that truth, unable to accept its illogic. There was no strength in innocence. Only cruel experience gave strength.

And since he struggled, the dream dissolved. He tried to pull back, wanting to keep this young Shi Po, this untouched virgin, but he couldn't. She was gone, dissolved into the mists that had created her.

He woke, finding himself between his real wife's thighs, thrusting deep inside her cinnabar cave. And his stunned gaze met hers, which was open and vulnerable.

"No!" he gasped, and tried to pull away. He would not abandon his work. He would not—

But Heaven itself could not feel as sweet as what he now experienced. Even if he had possessed the strength to break her grip on his legs, he did not have control of his dragon. It was inside her, reveling in her rhythmic grip and release. His yang bellows began to pump, his breath caught and held as his dragon prepared to roar.

He had enough focus to hold back one moment, no more. Enough time to ask a single question.

"Why?" he gasped.

"Because this matters," she answered.

He had no time to demand explanation, and she had no interest in giving one. Instead, she pulled his head down to hers and kissed him with a hunger that startled him.

She wanted him. She wanted *this*. Even though she had refused him for the last twelve years, since they had conceived their last child.

It made no sense that she would change here, in this situation. But he had no more time to think, only the steady increase of his yang fire and the hard pounding of his dragon's demands.

Not yet. Not yet, he begged himself.

He needed to know that her contractions were not false, that her pleasure was not faked. So with an unsteady hand, he slid a finger between their bodies. He pushed and stroked and fumbled in his need. But then he knew the moment of her true release. Her eyes shot wide, her body stretched and she screamed in shock and joy.

Now! he told himself.

The yang roar rolled through his system, tearing out every measure of his body and spirit while pouring from him. His release was all-consuming, a flash fire that burst free of him, and into her.

Always and forever, her.

And then the fire was gone, his dragon spent. With nothing to support it, his body collapsed. Kui Yu barely managed to roll to the side so as to not crush his wife. He was boneless. Mindless. Soulless.

He knew true bliss.

Then he began to cough. It wasn't bad, just a rumble in his chest and a little tightness. He had felt it coming for the last few days, was as familiar with the onset of the illness as he was with judging a bolt of fabric or pretending to drink with a white ship captain. He'd been free of it for a decade now, but had always known it would return when the situation was ripe. When he was imprisoned in a dank cell and served food that vermin refused. Indeed, given the situation, he was surprised it had taken so long.

He thought nothing of it, until he looked into his wife's face. She had gone pale, her jaw slack with horror. Even her skin had turned cold.

She had heard the cough, though he'd tried to hide

it. Indeed, pressed so intimately to him, she had probably felt the hitch in his breath as he fought the restriction in his lungs.

She knew. She remembered.

And in that moment, all his hopes died.

Love in the Moonlight
Chang Chiu-ling (678–740)

A golden moon rises
over the waters; the dark blue
curtain of night covers the sky,
which I share with my beloved
though she be so far away, and I
impatient with the length of the night;
a night with a moon that makes
me think only of her;
rather than waste the moonlight,
I put out the candle, get up and pace
fretfully outside, the dew
wetting my face; I would clutch
a handful of moonbeams, sending them
to her, but as I cannot, so
at long last return to bed to sleep
and dream of the day
when we shall be wed.

❧

August 4, 1880

Dearest Shi Po—

I write this to you in a fit of anxiety before our
first meeting. I have known you for so long, spo-

ken with you nightly, risen to your sweet smile by day. Yours is the face that I have worshiped since the day I first saw you deliver lunch to your brother, all pigtails and innocent blushes.

I am not easy with words. I know when we meet I will stammer and blush, and my tongue will not obey the dictates of my heart. So I write this to you now, so you will understand what I offer. Your father will not see me, will not consider me as your bridegroom. But this I tell you honestly: The men he considers are fools. One wastes his time on drink and women, the other on opium. Their houses have not the wealth they appear to, nor will their family connections support them when they are proven to be idiots.

You, I think, understand the difficulties of a great family brought low by the rise of the Manchurians. And also, you know the fear of having one's survival depend on a young son who cannot live up to his promise. This I tell you: Your other bridegrooms are cut from the same cloth as your brother.

I have no great family name. And in truth, my wealth also is not as it appears. Shi Po, you are doomed to wed a man of stringent economies. Therefore, you must look to your future.

I have spent many hours dreaming of what I will do in the years to come. This too, your brother and your prospective bridegrooms have done. The difference is, I have a plan and the means to accomplish my goals, whereas they have only great words.

I only lack two things, Shi Po. Your beauty beside me to inspire me, and your name to finalize the last of my business transactions. I wish to open a clothing store. I have saved money to buy fabric and to hire the tailors. I have even designed the look of the shop, the arrangement of goods that will bring foreign gold like rain. But I cannot buy the building or get the acceptance from the local authorities. That requires a great family connection—yours. And a great deal more money.

I must work for many years yet for my English boss to gain so much money. But I have been carefully planning. I also bribe where I can and pray where I cannot. But in the end, it will take five more years to open my store. Five years of privation while I struggle.

But after five years, Shi Po, this I promise you: My store will make profit. My time among the foreign devils has taught me well. I know I can move their gold into my pocket. I can give you a wealthy old age. I can provide a heritage for our sons and great dowries for our daughters. And I swear that from the first day, your rice bowl will always be filled.

I do not waste time with women or drink. I despise the evil stench of opium. And I will work until my back breaks and my fingers gnarl with pain to make sure your tiny feet never need walk anywhere. I swear to build a great fortune, if only I can wake each morning to your smile and receive my tea each evening from your hand.

My future rests upon you.

With great hope and love,
Tang Kui Yu

One night a thief sneaked into the house of Mr.
Woodhead, only to be surprised when the owner
returned. Horrified, the thief escaped, leaving behind
his fur coat. Mr. Woodhead was pleased about getting
something for nothing. Since then, whenever he
returned home to find his house safe and sound, he
frowned and said, "Darn, no thief tonight."

Chapter Twelve

A Tigress never felt guilt. She did not betray, and she
did not steal; she simply harvested the yang that men
willingly offered, giving up her attention and yin in
return. It was an equitable exchange that should
never involve guilt.

Or so she had been taught from the beginning, because men willingly ejaculated those years off their
lives. Indeed, many were most eager to do so, over
and over and over until they inevitably died.

So she had been taught.

But now, the man throwing away his life was her
husband. And even worse, she had created the very situation that was causing his death. She'd seduced him
while he slept, and now he was on the path to dying.

"It's just a cough," he snapped. "I'm not going to
die."

She didn't answer, except to grimace as he withdrew his rapidly shrinking dragon from her body.

"I've been feeling it for a while," he continued, his
voice curt. "It's because of this damned cell."

She narrowed her eyes and examined his body. "You have been ill for days? And you didn't say—"

"I am fine!" he interrupted. Then he slowly twisted to look at her. "But you . . ." He took a deep breath to control his temper. "Why would you do that? Why would you . . ." His words trailed off as he looked down at her body.

She drew her legs together and covered herself as best as she could. But that did not lessen the fury in his eyes, or her own guilt at what might end up as Kui Yu's death.

His eyes focused on her thigh, and his hand shot out. She would have pulled away, but there was nowhere to move, trapped as she was between her husband and the wall. So she could do little as he wiped dark fluid off her leg and examined it in the murky light.

"This is blood," he said, his voice so low he might have been speaking to himself. His gaze cut to her. "Are you in pain?"

She shook her head, drawing herself into a sitting position with head bowed and legs curled beneath her.

He looked again at the blood on his hand. "But . . . but . . . How is this possible?" He looked back at her legs. "You have had three children."

She swallowed, then found her voice. "It has been twelve years, my husband. And all my practice is aimed at restoring youthfulness." When he did not understand, she rephrased: "At restoring . . . smallness."

His eyes widened, and she shrugged to dismiss the burning pain his large dragon had inflicted.

"But . . . you are bleeding."

"It is not uncommon."

He had no response, and so they stared at each

other, the air thick with their unspoken thoughts. Until he coughed.

She winced at the sound, even as he tried to mask it. If they were at home, she would ply him with healing teas and send him directly to bed. Such had been her prescription twelve years ago when the strain of begetting another son had taken its toll on his body. But here, in prison, what could she do but watch him expire, and feel the guilt because she had seduced him into expelling the last of his strength?

He groaned, and her gaze jumped to his face. She had been staring at his withdrawn dragon.

"That too is perfectly normal," he growled, indicating his shrunken size.

"I know," she answered.

"I'm not dying."

"Of course not," she soothed.

He cursed, then pushed up from the pallet to pace in angry strides back and forth across their cell. She wanted to tell him to sit down, to conserve his strength, but she knew it would only push him to foolish displays of manliness. So she simply watched him though her head was tilted down in apology.

He stopped directly in front of her, his hands on his hips, still naked. "Why would you do that? Why would you force such an . . . an encounter, if you think it would kill me?"

She swallowed and forced herself to meet his gaze. "You were irritable. Angry. It was yang poisoning," she confessed. She blinked away her tears, as they would only infuriate him more. "I did not know you were already weak."

"I am not weak!" he bellowed. But the statement was undermined by the bout of gasping coughs that followed.

Shi Po leapt to her feet, but she didn't dare touch him for fear of his reaction. So she stood beside Kui Yu and tried not to hover. At least it was a dry cough, high in his chest. The malady had not yet spread through his lungs. With careful management—even here in prison—they might be able to stave off disaster.

He pushed her arm away. She tried to hold him, to wrap him in her warmth, but he threw her off. So she stepped away and pressed her lips together. She would not say something stupid, something that would only inflame the situation. Perhaps if she occupied the center of the cell, he would sit down just to escape her.

He accepted none of it. He straightened to his full height and glared at her.

Then came the change. Shi Po watched in horror as his power faded, his shoulders slumped, and he did indeed take the two steps he needed before dropping wearily back on the pallet. She once again rushed forward, but he lifted his head and glared her back. When he spoke, it was with fatalistic weariness.

"I cannot win, Shi Po. I embrace your religion only to have you subvert it. Once that is accomplished, you flutter about me, terrified I am going to die." He lifted his head, and his eyes locked onto hers. "What do you want, Shi Po?"

She swallowed, her mind completely blank. And in that silence, her husband continued to speak, his voice a recitation of despair.

"For years I left you to your practice—to your yang harvesting and your yin purification—only to find you plotting your own death. So I gave myself to your cause, only to have you stop me. But now that I am stopped, you are still unhappy." He leaned his head back against the wall and sighed, his shoulders hunched. "What would you have me do?"

She stared at him, quiet. How could he know her so well and yet not understand anything?

"Why do you believe you can fix my unhappiness?" she asked.

He blinked, clearly confused. "If a man cannot find peace in his own home—"

"If you wanted peace, Kui Yu, then why did you marry me? Surely you knew—even then—that I was the wrong choice."

"You aren't the wrong choice," he snapped, and she pulled back in surprise. His words reflexive, as if he had said them many times.

"You have been criticized for our marriage?" she gently probed. Could her status have fallen so drastically?

"No," he muttered, and she knew he lied.

Her strength gave way, and she slowly sank to her knees. "Of all the things I have done, never did I wish to harm you," she said.

He watched her there, on her knees, and in time his stiff posture softened and he leaned toward her. "I have not been harmed," he said. Then his tone turned dry. "Indeed, a man of my delicate condition would surely have died without your daily potions and tender care."

Shi Po lifted her chin, using anger to ease her guilt. "You mock me," she said, "and yet you want to embrace my religion? You understand nothing of what I daily try to do for you: how I have made a study of your health, how I have prepared your food and your teas and your bed! But here"—she waved angrily at their cell—"I can do nothing, and already your cough has begun. Heaven's curse, my husband, you are not immortal! Everything else you do may be beyond the skill of mortal men, but not in this!"

Her tirade ended on a gasp, and her body shook with fury. How could he not understand the simplest workings of Heaven? She lowered her voice, speaking slower and more calmly to him, as if he were the youngest cub she'd ever instructed. Men were always taught they could defy fate.

"You have power in your body well beyond what others of your age exhibit," she agreed, elaborating on his great fortune. "Your every business endeavor rains gold down upon our heads. Even your first attempt at immortality . . ." She swallowed her own bitterness and forced herself to speak plainly. "You reached the antechamber of Heaven ahead of me and spoke with Kwan Yin." She sat beside him on the pallet. "Yet . . . you know you cannot be successful at everything. Somewhere, Heaven will make you weak and vulnerable. How else will the gods maintain their superiority?"

He reached out and grasped her hands. "My body is firm because I continue to work. While other bosses rest fat and happy in their beds, I labor alongside the lowest coolie to be sure what I want done is done correctly. I pay for that in aches when I rest, and injuries when I fall."

She nodded. She'd long since lost count of the nights she'd spent rubbing salve into his muscles.

"My ventures do not always succeed, my wife. Many fail utterly. Those that succeed do so modestly, and only because of constant vigilance. The cost of our life was paid by you, Shi Po, for you gave me the money to begin my first business. And then, later, after your brother's friend . . ." He shook his head. "After that first building collapsed, and we had nothing. You brought the money in then, not I."

She winced at these words they never spoke. They never discussed the first money given to him on their wedding night, or what she'd later been forced to do.

"As for your religion . . ." His voice trailed away and he shrugged. "Kwan Yin visits fools and failures as well as successes. If I attained the gateway to Heaven, it was because of the purity of your yin." He drew her hands to his lips and pressed a kiss into her palms. "My greatest blessing is that you chose me as your husband."

She stared at him, numb with shock. He could not truly believe that! But one look at his face and she knew it was true. He actually believed his success was all due to her.

"Kui Yu, you are a fool."

"Then let me be a happy one," he countered. "Tell me what it is you need."

She laughed. She actually laughed, and her pain and joy tumbled together into the sound. It was neither happy nor sad; it was simply a sound, an overflow of excess emotion. And all the while, her husband stared at her as if she were a puzzle, as if she were a problem with inventory or a mistake in carpentry.

"My happiness cannot be solved by your labors Kui Yu," she said. "Surely you understand that." But of course he did not. It was the most basic of philosophies, not just for Tigresses, but universal to all Buddhists, and yet he did not understand. "Each man, each woman must look to her own salvation. You cannot find the answers for me."

He opened his mouth to speak, but she rushed on.

"Kui Yu, *I do not want you to.*"

He frowned, and tilted his head in confusion. "But you asked for my help. At the very beginning, when

211

you were choosing which method . . . between the poison and dagger and . . ."

She sighed. "I asked for your counsel. You are wise in so many ways." She paused. How to explain what was unclear even to herself? "You are a leader among men. You speak and they jump to obey."

His bark of laughter stopped her cold. "Men follow gold, Shi Po. As long as I have that—"

"Not true," she interrupted. "They followed you even when you were a boy. Even my brother listened to your schemes. You were the one to drag him to school. You were the one who made all the boys study."

He shook his head. "I could not pay our tutor, so I had to help in other ways. He let me remain so long as I drilled and forced the other boys to learn."

Shi Po nodded. This was no surprise to her. "And so you learned to lead."

He shook his head. "Shi Po—"

"Listen to me!" She grabbed his hand and wished she could guide his intellect as easily. "Your successes circle you like a god's mantle. Your strengths are many, your happiness assured. But I am cut differently, husband. I am a woman with grown children. What can I still do to find purpose and honor?"

"Your children bring you honor. And your goodness brings honor to your home, and to your husband." It was the traditional Confucian answer, and it gave her no solace.

"Kui Yu, do not try to take away the thing I pursue," she said. When he frowned at her, she tried again to explain. "You cannot hand me what I most want, Kui Yu. Otherwise, I will not want it."

He dropped his head back against the wall and gazed at the dark ceiling. "Women's logic," he groaned.

She did not deny it. "You have your work, Kui Yu. Will you take away mine?"

He gazed at her sadly. "Your work does not bring you joy."

"Does yours? Every day? Every moment?"

"Of course not. No man has so much."

"And yet *you* do not stop. Even after days or months of frustration."

He shook his head. "Your discontent has grown, Shi Po. Over the years, it has become larger and darker. You hide your tears, but I see them. You struggle for sweetness when it came naturally so many years ago."

She frowned, wondering if what he said was true. "Perhaps you did not see me clearly when we were younger."

He shrugged. "Perhaps. But can you say that you have grown happier over the years? That your joy—"

"No," she interrupted. "I cannot say that. Can you?"

He nodded. "I have a full, rich life. My discontent comes from your misery. And this wretched cell."

"Which is my fault as well."

This time he growled in displeasure, though the sound rapidly fell into a cough. "I do not assign blame, Shi Po! I search for a solution."

She ground her teeth. All this talk, and he still looked to solve her problems for her. So rather than argue further, she curled up next to him. She would give him her body heat while she searched for peace in the circle of his arms.

They sat for a long while. Finally, he dropped a kiss upon her forehead. "We have solved nothing here."

"Sometimes there is no solution," she replied.

He did not respond, and so they settled back again. Shi Po's eyes began to droop with sleep.

"It is a joy to hold you like this," her husband said.

Shi Po nearly laughed. "In prison?" she mocked. "While spies listen at the door to everything we say? To everything we do?"

He pressed his lips to her forehead. "To have you in my arms, held close to my heart."

She lifted her face, startled by the feeling in his voice. He sounded like a young man, or the new bridegroom he had once been with her. And as she looked up, he lowered his mouth to hers. His kiss was earnest; and she realized that, until prison, they had not shared such a thing in many years: a sweet and loving caress of tongues and lips.

She felt his arms tighten around her even as she stretched up to him. She felt the silky touch of his hair against her hands as she pulled him close. But most of all, she felt his mouth, full and alive as he moved with her. He teased her lips open by stroking his tongue across their seam. It was an easy thing to yield to him, and yet it had been so long, she went slowly, and her jaw actually popped with the effort.

She took control, for that was her practice and her habit. She was the one who stimulated, the one who stirred and stroked and enflamed. But not this time. In this kiss, he was master. His tongue dueled with hers and conquered.

But she was his mirror, and accustomed to taking control. She reflected his desire, and she too began to fight. Their tongues clashed—touching, stroking, pushing, even sucking. And it all brought Shi Po to a state of yin excitement beyond any previous experience.

How could a single kiss begin such yin dew? And how could this struggle between husband and wife make her smile? Kui Yu did too, for she felt his grin pull at his lips even as he continued his assault.

But then he coughed again. It would have been a

small thing, barely heard, but he tried to hide it. And from hiding it, his body rebelled. His chest heaved in its attempts to expel the infection.

Kui Yu broke away, gasping for breath. Shi Po's hand slid to his back so she could feel every contraction of muscle and spine as he breathed. She also felt the tension that built within him, not because of his cough but because she witnessed it.

Finally, his breath eased. She said nothing as he straightened. Merely watched as his eyes searched her face.

"I have been with a prostitute," he said.

She blinked, sure she had not heard him correctly. He, too, appeared stunned by his confession, especially as he frowned and quickly grabbed her hand, drawing it to his side.

"I . . ." He swallowed. "Since Shen Zan's birth twelve years ago, you have not . . ." He grimaced. "You have not harvested any of my yang."

She thought back. "You had this cough then. I would not weaken you."

He shook his head. "Making love doesn't weaken me, Shi Po. I have . . ." He let his gaze drop away from her. "I waited for you. But with the new child, you were occupied."

She frowned, her body still cold, her thoughts sluggish. "You accuse me of neglecting my responsibilities to you?" Such would be unsurprising from most men, but Kui Yu had never been like most men.

"No. But I seek to understand. You would not come to me, even when . . ." His words trailed off, but she remembered.

"I refused you." She had found every excuse, every reason to avoid him. She had been involved with the children, stricken with an imaginary illness, even simply weary. Anything to forestall his attentions. Not because she hadn't wanted them, but because she'd feared for his strength. His cough had been a terrible thing.

"I went to your aunt," he said, his voice low, his eyes still canted away. "I pretended to be searching for you."

Shi Po felt bile rise in her throat. She knew what her aunt would do, what—obviously—her aunt *had* done.

"She introduced me to . . ." He took a deep breath and his voice became more commanding. "The yang release has not weakened me. It never has."

"How often?" She didn't know from where the words came, but they rasped out of her throat nonetheless.

He shrugged. "A few times a month." His gaze dropped to his hands. "That was why the messenger couldn't find me when General Kang came."

"You were at my aunt's garden? With . . . ?"

"Not there, but . . . yes."

She felt cold invade every part of her body. It grew into the freezing burn of true horror. "Why tell me this? Why now? Why here?"

He struggled to answer. "So you would know. The yang release—"

"I know your opinion," she snapped, but there was more; she was sure of it. He wanted to tell her more.

He stroked a single character on her thigh: *White.*

She stared at him. She did not understand. So he tried again.

Ghost woman.

"Prostitute?" she gasped. The prostitute was a white woman?

He took a long time, stroking characters onto her arm despite the trembling of her limbs: *Practiced speaking English. Learned much of value for business with whites.*

She stared at him. "You *talked* with her? Or you released your yang?" She could hardly believe her voice was so calm, so deliberate.

"Both," he answered.

Both. But if she was white . . .

"Is that why?" she asked. Is that why General Kang had arrested them: Because Kui Yu had been with a white prostitute? Men had been killed for such things, she knew.

Kui Yu could only shrug. He had no idea.

They stared at each other, the silence stretching thin. Outside, the guard muttered to himself and shuffled past. Neither Shi Po nor Kui Yu looked at him. He often passed by their door to tease them by jangling his keys or speaking vile insults, and Shi Po had long since learned to ignore it.

Until now. This time the keys jangled because he was opening the cell door.

"Get up, you filthy vermin," the guard spat. "You're to go to execution now."

❧

August 14, 1880

Kui Yu—

My father will never accept a son-in-law who works with whites. We take the barbarians' gold, but never their instruction. I have no influence in this matter.

Shi Po

A very greedy official had extorted a lot of ill-gotten wealth. Having finished his term of office, he returned home and saw a strange old man among his relatives. "Who are you?" he asked.

"I am the Earth God of the county you used to rule."

"Have you come to honor me?" the official asked.

"There is no green place left for me in my county. What could I do but come live with you?"

Chapter Thirteen

Kui Yu didn't waste any time. Though he had been sitting on the pallet, he was more than capable of dropping his head and ramming the guard. The only thing that had prevented him up to this point was the hope of a peaceful solution. With that hope gone, he was prepared to devastate his foe by any means possible. He exploded forward the moment the door opened.

His head impacted the guard's chest hard enough to crack ribs. He kept going, driving forward until he rammed the guard against the wall. His foe dropped to the floor unconscious. Shi Po ducked forward and quickly removed the guard's sword and passed it to him.

He suppressed his surprise. He had expected maidenly horror at the violence; instead, his wife had acted with impressive practicality. He would have kissed her right then if they didn't have to run.

They rushed down the hall. They knew the only escape was to the left, through the guardroom and out into the main building. With luck, those places would be nearly empty.

No luck. Nearly a dozen soldiers crammed into the tiny guardroom, and the nearest were already advancing. Kui Yu pushed his wife behind him, despite her resistance.

"You can't fight," she said. "They'll kill you."

He didn't have time to argue that they were already marked for execution. At least this way, he would die fighting. He focused on his task. Their only hope lay in the narrow hallway: only two soldiers could attack at a time. But they were younger men, trained for battle and protected by armor.

He did the best he could. Shi Po as well, for she grabbed the weapon off the first man he felled; but he was doomed from the beginning. He hadn't the strength or skill to fight these men. And all too soon, he was knocked to the floor, his head ringing with pain, his breath slammed from his body by well-placed fists.

Then he was held by three soldiers while he watched them casually bat Shi Po's sword away. On her bound feet, she couldn't even run. They were faster, stronger, and merciless, and they shoved her to the ground and ripped off the last of her tattered clothing.

Kui Yu bellowed. With a surge of strength, he pushed to his feet. But then his knees were kicked out from behind. His arms were wrenched backward, and he was slammed sideways and down. As his face hit the floor, his left shoulder wrenched and he screamed. But the sound was cut off by the heavy impact of a knee against his back and a booted foot on his neck.

Still, he fought the pain. If only he could get free, if only he could fight . . . But there was nothing he could do. Even his view was blocked by the soldiers converging on Shi Po. He heard her scream. He heard—

A growl of a Manchu command. He understood nothing of what was said, only the tone.

The soldiers separated. Was it . . . ?

Not General Kang. It was an older man with a sour expression that pulled at his battle scars, a captain by his uniform. The man's gaze barely flickered as he sized up Kui Yu. Then he turned to Shi Po.

Kui Yu tensed. He hadn't a clue what to do. He could barely hold on to consciousness. But he would do something. He would not let any Manchurian dog have his wife.

Another command echoed in the narrow hallway. A soldier jumped forward and pushed a wad of fabric at his commander, who didn't even touch it. Instead, his gaze cut to Shi Po. Coolie pants and a shirt landed with a soft whoosh on top of her bound feet. Shi Po snatched at the clothing and held it tight to her chest.

"Dress!" the soldier ordered in Shanghai dialect.

She did: pulling on the shirt first, then rushing to don the pants. They even allowed her to stand to do so. The guards pulled back to give her room as the captain watched with flat black eyes.

Kui Yu released his breath, feeling a small measure of relief. They wouldn't bother to dress her if they intended on rape.

Which meant . . . what? They were to be appropriately dressed for execution? But the Manchurians didn't have formal killings; prisoners just disappeared. Unless the executioners planned for Shi Po to be decently attired as they walked her to the killing pit. But why would they bother? Why dress a soon-to-be-dead woman?

Unless the guard had lied. Unless they weren't about to be killed, but presented to someone. Unless . . .

There were no more "unlesses," for the captain barked another order. The soldiers were quick to obey, and hands flipped Kui Yu onto his back. The boot that had been on his neck now shifted to his chest, while a sword point pressed into his cheek below his eye.

He stilled, despite the shoulder pain that burned through his body. He barely breathed as the captain came to stand over him. Kui Yu couldn't seem to focus clearly on the man's flat expression, because of the blinding sheen of sharp metal extended upward from his cheek.

The captain flicked his wrist, and the boot lifted off Kui Yu. Kui Yu still didn't breathe deeply, though, because the swords remained very close.

The captain stepped forward. Another wrist flick, and Kui Yu was shifted onto his good side, the sword point hovering just above his face.

"Leave him alone!" Shi Po cried, and was roughly cuffed for her pains.

Kui Yu might have said something to reassure her. He had an idea what was coming, though he could hardly believe it possible, but he had no breath to explain as the captain shoved a boot hard into his hurt armpit. Then, before he could draw breath, the man grabbed his damaged arm and yanked.

Kui Yu's shoulder popped again. He felt it, but couldn't hear it. He was too busy screaming.

Pain. Pain.

He was on a horse, belly down, strung across its back like a sack of rice. His head bounced like a upside-down chicken's, and he had just vomited. Agony came in rhythmic waves matching the horse's gait.

He tried to move, but he was bound tight. The ground rushed past.

Pain. Pain. Pain.

Ground—cold and hard. Near a campfire. No more pounding. Not on a horse. Soft hands dripped water onto his face. And there came the clink of metal. Chains?

Shi Po.

He tried to move, to reach for her. His arm was bound tightly by strips of cloth. The rest of his body barely twitched.

"Shhhh," she whispered. "Sleep."

He fought waves of darkness. He needed to know something. He had to do something. Protect her?

He took a breath to speak, only to have his words lost in a hacking cough.

The pain overwhelmed him.

Pain.

The horse again. No food to vomit up. Fuzzy head. Hacking cough.

Would it never end?

Pain.

Fever.

She said it. He heard it. The Goddess Kwan Yin, smiling, bathing his face:

What would you give up to get your heart's desire?

Pain.

Cough.

Shi Po.

Cough. Burned through his chest, bringing awareness.

Pain.

Not on a horse. In a bed. A soft bed with sweet-smelling sheets.

Home?

Not home. Where?

A woman cried great wracking sobs. Kui Yu frowned. Not a woman. A child. A girl-child? Who?

He was sick, his mind fogged. He remembered sex. Prison? A horse?

How long had he been ill? Days?

Tea. Bitter. Cool. It wet his lips, filled his mouth. He swallowed out of reflex. Then pain swamped his consciousness again.

No more darkness! Use the agony. Focus.

Where was he?

"Drink," the voice said.

Kwan Yin? Shi Po?

He swallowed again. This time the pain was manageable. The liquid tasted terrible, but then his wife's potions often did. Bitter taste, good healing. Or so she claimed.

When would that child stop crying?

He swallowed again. And again.

"Good," she said, and she set his head back down.

He tried to speak, but no sound came out. His mouth opened, but only on a sigh.

She smiled. It was his beautiful wife. "Get well, my husband," she said. "I have need of you."

He nodded and pushed himself upright to help her. He rose to whatever task she needed. Or so he thought. A moment later he realized he had only imagined the action. Against his will, his eyelids drooped down and he slept.

Shi Po pressed her fingers to Kui Yu's face, pleased that his fever had finally broken. She still worried about his cough, but all in all, he seemed much better. He slept easier now, and praise Buddha, they no longer traveled on those cursed beasts. Horses were a Manchu's first playground. She had heard they ate, slept, even copulated on their horses. Not so the men who had escorted them here. They had simply roped their beasts nearby, right next to their chained prisoners.

She rubbed at the raw marks on her wrists. The chains had been removed the moment they arrived, so ordered in curt tones by General Kang's wife. Shi Po had not understood the words, her Mandarin rusty from little use, but the meaning had been clear. The captain had abruptly ordered their manacles released, then had carried Kui Yu to this bedchamber.

Shi Po had stayed by her husband's side, of course. She had even managed to obtain the appropriate tea to ease his pain. But she had learned nothing new. She'd done nothing but sit by his side and sponge his brow for the last few hours.

That, and listen to a young girl sob as if her heart or her feet were breaking.

Shi Po stood. This was ridiculous. She would not sit imprisoned in this room just because she was too timid to learn more. She needed a bath and fresh clothing, Kui Yu needed a strengthening broth, and someone needed to see to that bawling child.

She took one last look at her husband. He was resting peacefully, his fever a thing of the past. He would sleep for many hours yet; she had no fear on that matter. And yet, she was strangely reluctant to leave his side. How many days had they lived in the same household and barely seen each other except to know that the other still breathed? How many mornings had he left before she woke? How many evenings had she been deep in class while he ate his dinner alone?

If it weren't for Kui Yu's frequent visits to the nursery to chat with their children, he and Shi Po might have never seen one another. He was a capable man, well on the mend. She was an intelligent woman who needed to learn more about their situation. Indeed, their very survival might depend on what she could figure out now.

Yes, she had to go. And yet, she had not left her husband's side for over two weeks. Not even for the barest second. She found it excruciatingly difficult to walk away now, no matter the reason. What if she could not return to him? What if he began to cough and she was not there to . . . what? Hold him and worry? There was little she could do but watch.

And yet . . .

Shi Po forced herself to stand, and to stop mirroring her husband's illness. He slept; she had to find the strength to act. So she turned away from him and willed herself to walk out the door. Once started, she found herself moving quickly, desperate to accomplish her task.

The Kang estate was built in a traditional Chinese design, with living quarters arranged around a central courtyard, situated behind a gate, settled behind another garden and another gate and guardhouse; that much she had seen when they first arrived. They were in the country, some distance from Peking—or so she guessed from the Mandarin she heard. Their bedroom was on a side wing designed for guests, which is why the child's sobs were so unusual. Would not the girl be in the children's area; in her own bedroom?

Shi Po wandered the narrow hallway in search of the sobbing child. She found her quickly enough, despite the fact that the girl was tucked away underneath a table. Her face was buried against a tapestry, her black pigtails askew, her tiny body shaking with the force of her grief.

Shi Po had not necessarily meant to talk with the girl, especially since she doubted the tiny thing spoke Shanghai dialect. Her plan had been to assure herself that the child was safe, and then leave her to whatever adult eventually found her. But when she saw the little girl—likely no more than four years old—Shi Po could not turn away. Those miniature shoulders shook with grief as she lay on her side, her tiny hands wrapped around her knees. And as Shi Po advanced, the girl wiggled tighter against a tapestry, probably trying to hide beneath it.

How many times had Shi Po wanted to do just that: to shrink into the smallest of dots until she just disappeared? She knew of only one pain that could so destroy the child of wealthy, powerful parents, only one reason for a girl to want to disappear.

But why would a Manchu bind his daughter's feet? The Qing Emperor had long since declared the practice anathema.

The mystery was enough to push Shi Po into action. She wanted to crouch, but knew better. Even in coolie pants that allowed such a position, Shi Po's feet would not have supported her. So she dropped onto her bottom and tucked her feet demurely beneath her. Reaching out, ignoring the girl's suddenly fierce struggles, she picked up the child and pulled her into her lap.

It took some time, but Shi Po was familiar with how to comfort a child in this stage of foot binding. One glance at the poor girl's feet showed that the child was in the worst stage—for the mother: her tiny bones were not yet broken, her feet simply restricted. She was small yet, and it was the way of some mothers to slowly introduce their daughters to the horrors to come.

Yet for now, there was full awareness and rebellion. Naturally, a child used to running free would despise her bindings. She would scream and sob, refuse to walk, and rip off the strips of cloth whenever possible. Indeed, this child showed bruises on her hands and arms—evidence of disciplinary actions.

Apparently, they worked, for the girl's feet were still wrapped.

Shi Po sighed and smoothed the girl's forehead. She had more than once wished for a different world, one where daughters were not so deformed. But wishing did not bring excellent marriages, and only a woman with correctly shaped feet under five inches in length could marry into wealth. And only women with wealthy husbands could ensure that their children grew strong and prospered.

It was an ugly cycle, and one against which the Qing empire struggled. It was said that even the Emperor thought bound feet hideous. But China had been thus for countless dynasties. One man—even an Emperor—could do little against tradition. And one woman could do even less.

So Shi Po held the young girl and rocked her tiny, shaking body, while murmuring Confucian dictates on appropriate female behavior. The words meant nothing, of course. Not to the child or to herself, remembering binding her daughter's feet and her grandmother's botched creation of Shi Po's own misshapen lumps.

At last the girl quieted. Shi Po still held her, though her back ached from her hunched position. And when the girl reached up and brushed away Shi Po's tears, she knew they'd reached an understanding.

"Your mother is Han Chinese," Shi Po said as she inspected the child's facial features. Obviously, the mother was Han, for only they bound their daughters' feet. But the father was clearly Manchurian. Probably General Kang himself.

The girl didn't understand, so Shi Po switched to halting Mandarin. This close to Peking, the girl probably spoke the official language.

"My name is Madame Tan," she said.

The girl's eyes widened. "I am named Wen Ai," she responded formally. Then she blinked, and—in the way of the young—discarded all ritual in favor of simple directness. "Why are you in my home?"

"I don't know," Shi Po answered honestly. "Do you think you could help me find out?"

Tears flooded the girl's expression, and she shook her head. "I can't walk," she whispered. "I can't walk or jump or run or . . . or . . . or . . ." Her words ended on a hiccoughing sob, and Shi Po clutched her even closer.

"You will again," she murmured, repeating the lie told to all young Chinese girls. "You just have to practice." Then she extended her own tiny feet. "These are huge compared to yours. They are wide and ugly and badly done. Your mother is very wise to bind your feet now. You will have many wealthy men vying for your hand. You will have a big home and fat children and your husband will value you above all others because of your tiny, perfect feet." She lifted the girl's chin and said, "Is that not worth a few tears?"

No, it isn't, said the girl's mutinous eyes. But she was trained well enough not to speak the words aloud. That would be too disrespectful. And in that moment, Shi Po felt the crushing weight of despair. In that moment, she experienced shock and disgust and fear, all because of one simple realization:

Life wasn't fair.

That was it. Or, more specifically, life for females wasn't fair.

And wasn't that a ridiculous realization? After all, even the youngest girls knew that life did not treat women equitably. Her father doted on her idiot brother. His only attention to Shi Po had been to order her feet bound.

Yes, she'd known from the first that life was not fair for girls. And yet now, with the added maturity of years, she could see that it was not just girl-children who were bound, but all Chinese women. What decree said that a widow should be locked away, never to venture out from her home, as if a woman without a husband was a shame to be hidden away? Who ordered that women could not be educated, could not learn anything beyond beauty and gossip? That girls should have no choices in their lives beyond what their fathers, brothers, and husbands ordered? And who said that a girl's only value was in her beauty and her obedience to those very men?

No one. No one had decreed it, and yet all Chinese women followed these rules. It was insanity. They obeyed, and they taught their daughters, and any soul who dared step outside of their rigid lines was roundly condemned. Usually by fellow women.

Which was why Shi Po's life was hampered and fettered and bound as tightly as her feet. Except, it wasn't. She had the freedom to explore her Tigress teachings, to instruct other women in this form of liberation, to stretch out her hand and reach for immortality. She alone was allowed such freedom, and by her husband, Kui Yu. He let her do as she willed, even to the point of supporting her choices against the condemnation of society.

Which was why she loved him.

And *there* was the true enlightenment. Shock echoed through her system, cracking open her mind like an egg crushed beneath a mountain. She loved her husband. And that love bound her more tightly to him than any rope or chain. Which meant that he was the real reason that she had not reached immortality. Because she was too Earth-bound. Because she loved her husband.

So, Kui Yu was the real reason she'd failed at her goal. He was the anchor that held down her spirit, and all she needed to do in order to finally attain Heaven was quickly and simply sever her tie to him. She had to end her love for him, or his for her, for no true tie could occur unless the attachment was mutual.

Yes, she realized, they loved each other. And unless she wanted her life's work to end in failure, she had to end that love completely and irrevocably. In short, she had to choose: Kui Yu or immortality. Which did she want? Because she couldn't have both.

She burst into tears.

The child had no idea, of course, what to do with a suddenly sobbing adult. In fact, the situation was so bizarre that she immediately scrambled away, pushing to her feet and crying out in pain even as she bellowed for her mother.

The mother must have been nearby, for she came quickly, too soon for Shi Po to control her sobs. Then mother and child stood nearby, their eyes dark, their demeanors somber. They watched as if neither had ever seen a woman cry before.

Shi Po bit her lip. She took deep breaths. In time,

she even managed to think of something other than her husband or immortality. Only then did her tears subside. Eventually she was able to look at the other two with an equal measure of silence. Until the mother finally stepped forward.

"You are the witch Shi Po of Shanghai," she said.

Shi Po shook her head, tears still perilously close. "I am nothing but a stupid woman." She took another breath. "I am Mrs. Tan. And you?"

"Wu He Yun. And my daughter, Wen Ai."

"Wu? But are you not . . ." Shi Po cut off her words, but it was too late. Obviously this woman was General Kung's servant, not even having the status of a third or fourth wife. She and her child had the run of the Kang estate and dressed richly, but with a surname of Wu and a Han Chinese face, she was clearly not a wife. It had only been stupidity—and extreme distress—that had made Shi Po so careless with her tongue.

The woman hunched over her child, clearly expecting scorn.

"My deepest apologies," Shi Po hurried to say. "I am not thinking clearly. My husband is ill and I . . ." How to explain her situation? "I am so lost in this place." She pushed to her feet, tottering slightly before steadying herself. Then she touched He Yun's hand. "Please, can you tell me what is happening here?" The woman already knew her name and title; surely she would know something of what General Kang planned.

"You are to be his new concubine," He Yun said, her voice barely above a whisper.

"But I cannot marry him. I have a husband." And General Kang had gone to some expense to bring Kui Yu here alive.

The woman nodded. "That is his pattern. He finds a woman he desires and brings both husband and wife here. Then he forces the husband to watch."

Shi Po felt her breath stop hard in her chest.

"The shame is so great," He Yun continued. "My husband . . ."

"No . . . ," Shi Po whispered, not wanting to hear.

"A weapon is made available. But there are too many soldiers to fight and no escape."

Shi Po understood. Kang toyed with his prisoners, just as he had toyed with her in Shanghai. He offered the illusion of escape, but in the end the only choice was in the manner of death. Kui Yu would be allowed to die fighting or in an honorable suicide. "What did your husband choose?" If there was to be any hope for her and Kui Yu, she had to know what had happened before.

"He attacked the soldiers. He took the sword and fought, but they were ready for him. He . . ." Her words ended on a sob.

Shi Po touched the woman's hand, offering comfort. She didn't want to press, but she had to know. "What of you? What will become of you? And of me?"

"If you are entertaining, then you will be allowed to live." He Yun's gaze hardened. "I am to learn your Tigress secrets."

Shi Po shook her head. "I will die first before I pleasure that man."

The woman tucked her daughter tight to her chest. "Then do so quickly. He holds the children as ransom." Tears shimmered in He Yun's eyes. "I have a son. He prospers, or so I am told."

Shi Po didn't think the constriction of her chest could grow any tighter, but it did. Fear for her two sons nearly bent her in two. "How many times?" she managed to gasp out. "How often does he do this?"

He Yun dropped her head against her daughter's, her sorrow a palpable force. "There were two before me and one since."

"How have you survived?"

He Yun lifted her chin, her expression growing defiant. "I spy on the new women for him. I tell him their secrets."

Shi Po reared back. She had already suspected as much, but to have the woman say it out loud surprised her.

"I will make a bargain with you," He Yun continued. "You tell me your secrets, and I will tell you the general's."

"Why would I hand my power to you? My only value is in my Tigress secrets."

He Yun shrugged. "Because without me, you will know nothing of what he intends. He tells me secrets, and I can tell you. But only if I have something of value to give him." Then her eyes abruptly hardened. "What choice do you have? No one else offers you friendship."

What she offered wasn't friendship, but He Yun was right in one thing: she knew more of what went on in this household than Shi Po did. Which mean Shi Po would have to at least pretend to agree. So she nodded slowly as she looked at little Wei An, the only true innocent in this household.

"Do you hope for a better life for her? Is that why you bind her feet?"

He Yun shrugged. "The General commanded it. He likes tiny feet. And he thinks girls run too fast otherwise."

Shi Po understood. Of course a cruel man would insist on a cruel tradition. Very well. If nothing else, it gave Shi Po something to offer this woman. "I know of a tea," she said. "One that numbs pain, especially mixed for daughters with tiny feet. It helps quiet their crying."

He Yun looked up, excited. "Tell me how to make it," she whispered. "Please. The General does not like noisy children."

"No man does," agreed Shi Po, but as she stepped forward, she too winced. Bound feet were not made for riding horses. Nor were they intended to pass day after day without a change of cloths. She herself needed the tea.

He Yun noticed immediately. After all, her own feet were shod in lovely curved four-inch shoes; she would recognize a fellow sufferer. The woman straightened, though her shoulders retained some stoop. "We will bathe Wen Ai's feet and mix her tea together."

Night Vigil
Chen Yu-Yi (1090–1138)

Our boats we anchored by Hua Jung County
and over the lake spread the brightness
of a moonlit night; too cold to sleep
I stood pondering, listening to the sound
of reeds rustling around us; thinking
of all the disappointments of my life
which make even this beautiful scene
one of foreboding; and now in the third watch
watching fireflies over the gravemounds,
looking up into the heavens at the Milky Way
hiding the great unknown behind it, and

remembering that here it was that Tsao Tsao,
King of Wei, was brought to bay, with now only
the quiet majesty of hills and rivers as a
memorial; so does one ponder over rise and
decline thinking that it is in vain for a poor
scholar like me to feel so anxious for a better
world; yet what can we do about all the wars?
No clear solution can I find, though my hair has
turned so gray.

August 16, 1880

Fairest Shi Po—

I cannot leave my position right now. I will never
have enough money to open a shop. The only
other choice is to become an opium trader, and I
will not do that. Can you not delay your marriage
for a few years? Perhaps a womanly complaint?
Or deep grief over your uncle's death?
    I pray nightly to Buddha for a miracle.

                              Yours in deepest love,
                                    Kui Yu

A Parting Song
Tu Mu (803–856)

So young and
your lovely figure
supple as a vine
in early spring; now
coming to Yangchow,
a warm breeze has removed

screens from doors
down all the streets, but
of beauties seen, none
are such as you.

How can a real love
be lightly disguised?
How may we smile so lightly
through our parting meal?
Even the candles share
our emotion, weeping tears
as we do, until the
morning breaks.

August 20, 1880

Kui Yu—

My uncle was a good and excellent man. I could
never, ever use his death to my own ends, even to
delay my marriage. That would be despicable.
What must you think of me to suggest such a
thing?

In grief,
Shi Po

236

A scholar prepared to take the civil examinations. His wife was very puzzled by his constant worrying.

"Look at you, you worthless wretch," she said. "You probably think that it's more difficult for a man to write an essay than for a woman to give birth to a child."

"It's easy for you women," the scholar sighed. "You carry the child in your stomach, but I have nothing in my head, so how do you expect me to think of something to write?"

Chapter Fourteen

Kui Yu heard his wife return. She tried to be quiet, but he had been waiting, dozing lightly, trying not to give in to the fear that she wouldn't come back. If only he weren't so damned weak, maybe he could do something. But at the moment, he found it difficult even to use the chamber pot without passing out. Though his fever was gone, his shoulder burned with a dull agony. Until, of course, he moved his arm. Then lightning-like explosions of pain cut off his breath and darkened his vision to black.

What a great figure of manhood he was. Now that he finally had an opportunity to shine before his wife, he was brought low by a fever.

Shi Po's tiny hand brushed across his cheek and slid down his neck. She was checking for fever, especially the hot skin around his swollen shoulder, and yet he felt her touch like the sparkle of a bright jewel: ephemeral, barely noticed, but so brilliant as to be blinding.

He would have laughed at his own ridiculous thoughts—he was often driven to bad poetry when thinking of his wife—but he was busy capturing her tiny fingers and drawing them to his lips.

"You are awake!" she murmured in surprise. "I thought . . ." Her voice trailed away as he pressed tiny kisses along her palm and used his tongue to stroke tiny whorls along her flesh. "Kui Yu . . . I . . . ," she murmured, her voice catching on a sob. Confused, he opened his eyes and peered through the darkness. He couldn't read his wife's face not because it was dark, but because she was tugging away from him, her eyes downcast.

He did not release her but used her struggles to help him sit upright. "What has happened?" he demanded, alarmed.

"Nothing," she answered.

"Don't be ridiculous." His wife did not cry. Even when contemplating her death, she had approached it with cold logic. And though she sometimes appeared femininely soft to him, or sweetly maternal, he had never ever seen her cry. Until now.

"What has happened?" he repeated, subduing his anger.

She raised her gaze, apparently startled. Even in the dim twilight, he could see her eyes were red and puffy from tears.

"Have they hurt you?" he demanded. He quickly perused her body. She wore a simple silk gown, clean and a little too large. She looked pale, but the loose garment could hide a great deal.

"Light a lantern," he ordered.

She shook her head. "There are none."

He wanted to demand she get one, but he had no wish to be separated from her again. Not if this was the result. Instead, he tugged at her wrist and pulled her closer.

"Come to bed, wife." Then he stroked a single character on her wrist:

Talk.

He felt her hesitation, but he insisted. He wrote the character again. He had to hold her, had to feel in the most basic of ways that she was fine.

"How do you feel, Kui Yu?" she asked, her voice gaining strength. "There was a tray outside the door—"

"Dinner. I ate, and am doing much better." In truth it had been a hell of a struggle to maneuver the chopsticks with his hurt shoulder, but he had managed.

"I did not mean to be away so long," she confessed. "I met a woman—a servant here. She gave me this gown. I helped her with her daughter. She lives in the building behind us. She is a servant, you know. This gown is one she doesn't wear anymore. She is binding her daughter's feet. I helped her do it right. You know how little girls can struggle. A servant woman. With her own house. And a daughter."

She was babbling, her sentences disjointed and her movements anxious. Kui Yu mulled over her words and searched for their underlying message. A servant woman with a cast-off silk gown and a Chinese daughter in a Manchurian household? Kang's Chinese mistress! Shi Po had befriended her!

He softened his hold on her wrist and wrote on her arm: *You learned much.* Then he added, *Be careful.*

"Kang toys with us. He will kill us after he watches us suffer."

Kui Yu nodded. He had suspected so much. *Hurt?* he wrote on her arm.

Tired, she answered on the back of his hand. Then she tugged free of his grasp.

He waited. He watched her undress, loving her dark silhouette against the dim moonlight. Sweet heaven, she was a beautiful woman. Even more so now that he could see she moved without difficulty. The shift of shoulder, slender back, and graceful arm flowed without hitch or excessive protection, which left him room to admire the swell of her breasts, the willowy flow of her waist and hips, and the tapering length of her legs.

His dragon stirred with renewed vigor. But though his illness had passed, his thoughts were still clouded. Had Shi Po really been crying? He hadn't imagined that. Even in the darkness, he had seen it. And he had heard the catch in her voice.

Did she cry because of him? She knew he wasn't dying. Perhaps it was something else he had said or done?

One possibility was obvious. He remembered their earlier conversation with excruciating clarity, the one interrupted by the soldiers. The one where he'd confessed to seeing Lily. That he had discharged his yang with her on a regular basis. What devil had possessed him to make that particular confession? And how would he ever explain his actions?

He supposed as her husband and the master of his household, he didn't need to explain his actions. After all, many Chinese men visited prostitutes with no ill humors from their wives. Some even married their favorite whores and gave the poor women a small amount of status in their limited lives.

But Shi Po had never been like other wives. Nor had they ever had a typical marriage. He had always felt a gnawing guilt whenever he visited Lily, and a deep shame afterward. And yet, he had never stopped.

He sighed, echoing the creak of the mattress as Shi Po climbed in beside him. Only now, as she slipped naked beneath the blanket, did she seem awkward. And he understood why. She was angry with him. Angry and unsure about Lily, angry about how to act given their situation. And hurt. She was hurt that he had expended his yang elsewhere.

She shouldn't be, he thought irritably. He wouldn't have gone elsewhere if she had allowed him to release his yang at home. He sighed. It sounded perfectly reasonable to him, but he was a man. When had women ever thought like men?

She was lying down now. Her eyes stared at the ceiling, and her body felt stiff as a board. Somehow he had to reestablish a partnership with her. Quiet anger like this was difficult enough under normal circumstances in a marriage, but it would be deadly now.

Making a swift decision, he rolled over. Gritting his teeth against the pain, he wrapped an arm around his wife and tugged her against his body. He moved more than her, but that didn't really matter. All he cared about was that she pressed her soft naked body against him and he hardened. If nothing else, their bodies knew one another. He planned to start there.

Incredibly, his ploy worked. Instead of turning away, Shi Po twisted her face to his, her mouth to his, her tongue to his. His breath caught in his throat, and his mind was seized by shock at his wife's sudden attention. She was kissing him! And he . . . He was going to take advantage of this unexpected development without searching for explanation.

He deepened the kiss. Where her tongue dueled with his, he matched her thrusts, dominated her. Soon he was between her lips, stroking between her teeth, pushing his tongue deep into the recesses of her open mouth.

He heard her breath catch; then she released a soft moan. Never had he heard such sounds from his wife—even in the current of the strongest yin tide. They were of both surrender and pleasure, desperate hunger and sweet joy. And they fired his blood as nothing else.

She wanted him. She clung to him. She was shifting her hips in invitation. He adjusted his weight to climb on top even as he continued to explore whatever he could of her mouth. They needed to breathe, so she broke away. But he did not stop, trailing kisses down her neck and between her breasts.

He needed a better position. He rolled on top of her, bracing himself equally on both arms. Pain cut through his thoughts and made him gasp. He shifted immediately, but the damage was done. His eyes temporarily rolled back in his head as he fought radiating bolts of agony. And when they finally faded, when he gained control of his breath, he opened his eyes and saw Shi Po, her face blanched white.

"I'm fine," he said, but she shook her head and scrambled out from under him. He would have argued, but all his attention was taken with not jostling his arm again.

"Shi Po. Truly, I—," he began, but she cut him off.

"No. You have been ill. You must not expend more energy," she commanded.

"I will remain very still. You can do most of the work."

She cast him a look that said she was not amused. Indeed, she was profoundly angry. Moments before she had clung to him as if he were her very life; now, with a short huff, she spun on her side and showed him her back. "It is late. You should rest," she said.

"I've been resting all day," he muttered, his anger rising like his stiff and hungry dragon. What did a man do with such a woman? Hot one moment, icy the next? He would not force her. And yet . . .

He collapsed on his good shoulder and contemplated his bizarre wife. He often did not understand her, but never before had she been inconsistent. Always her decisions were well thought out. Even her moods—good or ill—lasted for days or weeks.

"What has happened, Shi Po?" he asked her.

"Nothing," she snapped. But he knew she lied. "I am tired. I have been caring for you all this time without rest."

He knew that was true. He trailed his fingertips across her shoulder, down her side, then slowly up the curve of her hip. How smooth her skin was. How soft her body. His dragon stretched toward her, leaking a yang pearl in its hunger.

He began to trail his hand in the other direction. It slid gently up her hip, then dipped toward her waist to linger on her ribs. If he pushed the tiniest bit forward, he would stroke the outside edge of her breast. But even as the thought occurred to him, she curled away and tucked the blanket tightly around her.

He sighed and let his hand drop. He knew what had to come. His wife had never done anything halfway, nor would she tolerate half a confession from him. He would have to tell her all. Not just that he had been with Lily, but the whens and the whys. Most especially the whys.

He closed his eyes. He did not want to look at the unyielding expanse of her back while he spoke.

"When I visited your aunt . . ." he said out loud. She would know what he meant. She would know he was referring to their earlier conversation. "Ten years ago, I paid back the loan. The one that sustained us after the building collapsed. After everything went bad."

He felt Shi Po stiffen beneath his touch. Her shoulder jerked and her back tightened, and her entire body became like stone.

"Your aunt was very pleased. There was a woman there . . ." *Lily*, he wrote on her back. "A friend of your aunt's."

How to explain the rest? Especially with no response from his wife, no clue as how to continue. He stroked into her back:

White. Practiced English. For negotiations with Captain Jonas.

That had been his original intent when he'd met with the lost, white woman: to practice English, to find someone who was loyal to him and could help negotiate the difficult path of selling goods to white sea captains. It had not taken long for him to learn her story. Fate and debt had forced Lily and her husband to hop aboard the first ship available. Leaving behind thousands in unpaid bills, they headed for China and a hoped-for new life. But her husband had died on the passage, and with no money and no skills, she'd ended up in the nail-shack district. A year later Auntie Ting had received her as a apology gift from her usual supplier, who had sold her a virgin who wasn't remotely virginal. Auntie Ting knew the novelty value of a white woman; she invested money in cleaning Lily up only to discover afterward that the woman was pregnant with a half-breed bastard.

It was Kui Yu who that day convinced Auntie Ting not to dump her back onto the streets. And Kui Yu had also eventually saved enough money to buy her out of the life and apprentice her child as a cabin boy to Captain Jonas.

"I don't remember exactly when it first began . . ."

He stopped himself. He did remember. Perfectly. *Ru Shan*, he wrote on his wife's back. *It started when he became your partner.* Despite his intention, his calligraphy was harsh against her back, his movements quick and angry.

That was when I first saw Lily.

Her baby had been nearly four months old, and Auntie Ting uninterested in keeping the boy around. Babies interfered with business.

I helped her escape, he wrote. *Catholic mission.* "Now she cares for orphans with the priests," he whispered.

He got no response from his wife. He let his hand drop away. He didn't want to touch her while he said the rest.

"Do you know what it is to live without hope?" he asked. "She had nothing when I met her. Now she cares for children who would die without her." He stopped. This was not what he had meant to say, but he couldn't find the right words. Finally, they came.

"She talks so much. Words, feelings, hopes, fears— all flow like water. She says what she did one day, what she wants to do the next. What one child may do or not do, what the priests say. What the plants do! All moments are shared without restraint." How could he explain? It felt so wonderful to hear, to know the tiniest details of Lily's spirit, because Lily shared everything. Unlike his wife.

"She talked to me," he said. And when she'd talked, his dragon had become hard and eventually found its way between her thighs.

His wife's whisper drifted to him over the smooth wall of her back. "What did you say to her?"

He shook his head. "Nothing much. We talked of my sales. Bad shipments. Good days. Nothing important." And yet, it had seemed like so much.

"All men of wealth have concubines and lovers. As your fortune grew, I knew there would be other women."

He knew it was true. One wife for one man was a barbarian concept. And yet, he could not forgive himself. "I wanted only you. But when you refused me, I became lonely. I should have insisted. I should not have gone to someone else."

"I should not have refused you." She sighed, the sound echoing in the dark chamber. "I love you," said his wife.

Kui Yu was lost in regret. It took some time for his wife's words to slip into his thoughts, to sear like a brand into his consciousness.

She loved him?

Shi Po rolled toward him onto her back, her face hard and cold. She spoke to the ceiling. "That is the damage done today. I realized you are a good man, and that I love you." He detected anger, bitterness, even horror in her words. And her eyes were wet, leaking tears down her cheeks. So shocked was he by the sight, he had to reach out and touch her face, to feel the moisture to be sure it was real. And still her words burned through his mind. She *loved* him?

She looked at him, her eyes tragic. "I thought I could not leave because you were too attached to me. That you were not ready to release me. It turns out . . ." Her voice caught and she could not finish. She gave a self-deprecating laugh.

But he could finish, stunned by his new understanding of this woman who had been a stranger for the last ten years. "It turns out that *you* are attached to *me* and

246

cannot attain Heaven because of it." He knew the truth even before she dipped her chin in acknowledgment.

"Do you love me?" she asked, her voice high and frightened.

He stared at her. The Chinese did not speak of these things. Certainly not mature adults. Love was the fantasy of children, of young boys and girls in the first flush of adolescence. Did he love her? He intended to say yes. His devotion to her had been a constant in his life. But the words would not form. So many cold years lay between them, so much emptiness stretched between his youthful adoration and now.

"No," he said, stunned by the revelation. "No," he said again, shocked by the cold hole within him where her image had once resided. "And yet . . ." He stroked her tears. He rubbed them between his fingers while his mind whirled.

"And yet?" she echoed.

"And yet I have no wish for you to die. Indeed, I would do—I *have done*—a great deal to keep you alive, my wife." He caught her gaze and held it. That firmness became his anchor. "You will not kill yourself because of this," he ordered. "I have need of you." He did not explain his need; he had little understanding of it.

"Now I understand why you reached Heaven ahead of me. Your tie to me is already broken."

He frowned, still struggling with his thoughts. A boy who lost his love usually became bitter and angry. But what did a man do when he realized his heart had deadened? Kui Yu did not know. And so he reached for the one thing he did.

He was atop her in the space of a heartbeat, inside her the next. His thrust was brutal, filled with all the conflicting, churning emotions that cluttered his thoughts. It was cruel and almost animalistic. And yet he could not stop himself. Neither, apparently, could she.

Her body had been ready for him, somehow, but it had not been ready for their combined animosity. How could it? As harsh as he was, she was harsher. His thrusts were like hammer blows, their force tripled by the clutching of her calves. She jerked him against her, writhing fast. He could not put pressure on his shoulder, and was quickly unbalanced. He collapsed atop her, and she grunted with his sudden weight. He might have thought to spare her, then: the force of his drop was enough to jar the breath from his lungs. But she was not so affected. Her hands wrapped around him, her nails cut his back. He could not have pulled away without long rivers of blood.

She arched into him. She growled words and sobbed into his ear, though what she said was unintelligible. And yet the sounds blazed in his mind and blood, driving him to a madness unlike anything he had ever experienced.

He knew the moment the yang circle became established, it burned like a white-hot river through his body. It began in his groin, disgorging yang energy in prelude to his seed. It flowed into Shi Po. It expanded and grew in her until he could taste it on her skin. He licked it off her neck, felt it pulse through her and into his mouth. He inhaled it with every breath until it flowed downward to his dragon and completed the circle like a chain forged of lava.

Shi Po's body began to contract around his dragon. It pumped him in a steady push-pull of yin that flowed in a smaller circle. At the point of joining, where her yin pearl pushed repeatedly against his *dantien*, the hard bone at the base of his dragon, he felt the boiling fires begin. Never before had the flames blazed so quickly. The yin rose like steam through his body, only to be drawn back to her. It radiated from his chest into hers and the yin circle was forged.

Only one thing remained: one last burst of power.

His rational mind scrambled to gain control. Everything was happening too fast. He had to hold back. *Don't*—

Too late.

His dragon disgorged its white fire. The explosion blew through Kui Yu's body and mind. There was no controlling it, no hiding from the roar. All he knew was fire and power, yin and yang, and the climb to heaven.

He had traveled this path before. He knew the darkness that was not cold, the inferno that brought peace. But this time he fought. He had no wish to see the goddess Kwan Yin again. He still had no answer to her question.

But there was no fighting his ascent. Even before his vision dimmed, he knew he would open his spiritual eyes to see the Chamber of a Thousand Swinging Lanterns. Even as his dragon continued to erupt with yang fire, he knew his spirit would walk to Heaven's gate to meet . . .

No one?

He was alone. He watched the swinging lights and breathed in the joy that was Heaven. But where was the Goddess Kwan Yin?

The answer came like a thunderbolt. The velvety darkness parted and there, far ahead of him, stood the goddess. He smiled, and his spirit winged forward before he saw Kwan Yin was not alone.

It was Shi Po who stood with her! And what an odd sight that was. The Goddess shone pure and bright, the glory of Heaven surrounding her in what should have been trailers of blinding light, but was in fact pure beauty. Yes, it was so wondrous it could have been painful, but wasn't. Beside Kwan Yin stood his wife, the image of her there before him. But something else shone through: her true self, perhaps, beneath the body and so much larger, so much more.

Shadow and light played with Kui Yu's senses, making Shi Po both a brilliant woman of beauty and a darker, richer, more Earthly wonder than the ethereal Kwan Yin. Shi Po was like a brilliant jewel, drawn from the ground in its crystalline glory. Light shone from inside her, splintered through her, became a prism of wonder.

Beside his wife, Kwan Yin seemed insubstantial, and yet such a thing could not be possible. How could a goddess be less than a woman?

The answer came from the background vibration suffusing the antechamber: Shi Po was neither more nor less than the Goddess. They were equal in their glory, their only difference in the way they chose to display their light.

He had married a woman comparable to a goddess? The thought stunned him. It slowed his ascent, and he stared and stared at the woman who was his wife. But he came to only one conclusion, only one truth. Shi Po was the equal of a goddess. He'd married a goddess.

Kui Yu stopped completely, and his knees buckled as he instinctively dropped on his knees before these beings so above him. Indeed, he continued to drop. He pressed his head to the floor in a traditional kowtow. Only then did he think, only then did he wonder: What exactly was his wife saying to Kwan Yin? What did these two goddesses discuss?

He knew the answer. After all, he had just told his wife that he didn't love her. How appalling was that thought now? How could he not love a goddess?

His mind scrambled, and he felt himself begin to fall back to Earth. He lifted his head instinctively, searching for a handhold, an anchor, anything that would keep him in Heaven for just a few moments longer. He found it in Shi Po. Without thought, his gaze sought hers, his heart reached out to her, and in the moment when their eyes locked, his descent halted.

He froze in the antechamber, held by the will of his goddess wife.

But for how long? He knew that doubt made his hold even more tenuous, but he could not keep the fear from his mind. How long would she keep him with her? How long would he have her on Earth?

That was what the goddesses were discussing, wasn't it? It made sense. Goddesses belonged in Heaven. If his wife was a goddess, then she would naturally come here. No wonder she'd been obsessed with reaching to Heaven. No wonder she had spent every waking moment working toward this end, even considering poison, hanging, and knives just to get here. This was her natural milieu. This was where she belonged. Without him.

He was just a visitor here, brought by the force of her yin and his relationship with her. He knew that in his bones. That without her, he would not, could not be here.

"Don't stay," he pleaded with her. He didn't think she could hear him, but he saw her head jerk, her eyes widen in surprise.

Then he was sinking again. He had barely a moment left to speak to his wife, but he had no words, no true thought. Only anguish and fear—the two emotions that would drop him back to Earth faster than an arrow plunging to the ground.

He had lost his chance.

JADE LEE

The Son
Ku Kuang (725–814)

A son was born in Fukien
and when he grew, the official there
bought him to be made a eunuch; and
thenceforth, though he brought great wealth
to his master, his life was but
one long record of crude punishment;
used just as if he was some gross
material thing; surely Heaven
could not have known he suffered so,
surely the gods could not have understood
that his bitterness should be
but for the amusement of others!

When his father in desperation had
to sell him, he said it were better
had he taken the advice
of neighbors, and not reared him,
for now the sadness of parting
was worse than death; and the son
told his father how his heart bled
knowing well this parting was final,
that never in this world would they
meet again—never!

September 4, 1880

Fairest Shi Po—

Pray do not listen to my ignorant words. I should
never have thought you capable of deceit, much

252

less suggested it. I know you already grieve deeply over your uncle's death. To suggest you use such an event for ulterior reasons was crass and despicable. I am the lowliest worm in your sight. But I am also a most desperate man.

I fear my ability to find an excellent resolution to this matter. Though I nightly pray for a miracle, I cannot see a way out. I even went to an opium den today. There is money to be had for one with the correct connections, and my English boss will agree if I can show him a good plan. But I could stand no more than ten minutes in that place. The despair in those people's eyes, those hopeless dead people who still breathe!

No, I could not do it, Shi Po. I would not be a whole man if I helped spread that most evil drug. I damn the foreigners for bringing their contamination to our country where so many have no defense against this horror. It is despicable how so many otherwise excellent Chinese men, women, and yes, even children, daily slip into opium stupor. I cannot work there even if it means I will fail you.

If only you were of less value to your family. If only your name were not so exalted. Then I would have hope. But you are a night star, and I am a mere man hopelessly stretching to your light, only to have it slip through his fingers.

> In utter despair,
> Kui Yu

There was a woman who had never seen a mirror before. One day, her husband bought one for her. While looking in the mirror she was surprised and hurriedly ran to tell her mother-in-law.

"Your son has brought a new wife home!"

"Really?" the old woman asked. "Let me have a look." Stepping behind her daughter-in-law, she became very startled. "What are we to do? The bride's mother has come too!"

Chapter Fifteen

Shi Po came back to herself slowly. She groaned at the heavy weight that was Earth, her thick body, and the dense air that clogged her lungs and numbed her mind. She was back. And the thought depressed her.

Or perhaps it was not her return to Earth, so much as being sent back with more questions. Weren't goddesses supposed to answer questions? Not raise more?

She forced herself to inhale as she struggled to remember why she had worked so hard at living. Wouldn't it be better to just die and end the ceaseless search for meaning? Even if no Heaven waited at the end, even if she went to simple oblivion, wouldn't that be easier than all this ceaseless thinking?

Easier, she supposed. But not truly better. And at that moment, she heard her husband. He must have been talking for a long time. His words were disjointed and confused. He spoke and held her hand.

And he pressed his lips to her face, her neck, her mouth as he cried.

He was crying? She distinctly felt moisture on his cheek where he pressed against her. She heard the telltale catch in his voice as he tried to speak and sobbed at the same time.

"I did not understand," he was saying. "A goddess. I did not know you could be born on Earth and we would not know. That I had married you, and that you . . . But you cannot go back. Not yet. Not now that I finally understand. Please, sweet wife, be merciful. Remain here a little longer. So that I can worship you as you deserve. So that I . . . that we . . . that our children and your students . . . All of us must learn from you. I did not know. Forgive my stupidity. Please, Shi Po, you cannot leave us now. Don't leave me—"

Usually Shi Po struggled to open her eyes after such a descent. Usually it took an act of will to breathe and to move and to reenter the world of the living. But not this time. This time, her eyes flew open, her body shifted, and her grip tightened on her husband.

"What are—," she began, but he did not let her speak.

"Shi Po!" He rained kisses on her face and gasped in relief. "Thank you! Thank you for blessing us. Thank you!"

She wanted to stop him. She needed to find out what he was talking about. But truthfully, she liked the feel of his lips feathering across her body, enjoyed hearing his disjointed whispers of devotion. Especially as his words and lips warmed her all the way to her toes.

Then she frowned, her thoughts confused. Why

was her body so cold? She knew about the weight. Everything about life on Earth was slow and heavy. But when had it become cold? When had she become frozen? And when had the smallest touch from her husband brought such heat?

It wasn't a sensual heat. She had felt the yin rise in all its various forms, and this was different. This was hot tea on a cold morning. This was wrapping yourself in your mother's fur coat, or the impulsive hug of a small child.

And yet this was her husband, expressing complete joy and relief that she still breathed.

She smiled, reveling in the feeling, even if she didn't understand. He was pleased, and that made her reflect his pleasure. She would think no more than that. Except, he was pulling back, still touching her face and neck as if he could not stop himself. But his lips separated from hers.

"I did not understand, Shi Po. I am so sorry. How could I not know?"

"What are you talking about?" Her voice came out as a thick croak, but he understood nonetheless.

"I didn't know you were a goddess. I am so sorry. I was a fool—"

She pushed up slightly, and rolled to her side so she could face him more fully. He pulled back to give her room, but would not completely separate from her. His hand slid from her cheek, down her neck and shoulder, to rest gently on her upper arm. And the warmth that accumulated beneath his palm befuddled her thoughts.

"Why do you call me a goddess?" she asked.

He flushed, his gaze dropping to the ground in shame. "I saw you. With Kwan Yin." He took a deep breath and lifted his eyes in worshipful awe. "I saw you," he repeated.

She nodded as understanding slowly dawned. After all, this was her fifth visit to the heavenly antechamber. Though she had never spoken with Kwan Yin before, she had seen others—most especially Kui Yu—in their heavenly garb. But he had not seen anyone. And therefore, his confusion was understandable.

Still, she felt a selfish melancholy that she would have to disillusion her husband. "I am not a goddess, Kui Yu. You simply saw me as a spirit."

He nodded, but the movement was sluggish. He clearly was trying to understand her words. "I saw you. You had a holy light inside you. You infused everything with glory."

She nodded, pleased by his description despite the fact that everyone appeared so in the antechamber. "Let me tell you what *I* saw of *you*," she said. But then she paused, wondering if she dared express how he had been surrounded by power, how he was so much greater than he believed. It never ended well to inflate a man's ego.

Kui Yu pulled back, his expression wary. "You saw me? When you were with Kwan Yin?"

She nodded. "You saw me. Why would I not see you?"

He had no answer, so she pushed herself to continue, despite her fears. "You are a being of light, my husband, of blue skies and the sweet caresses of the spring wind. When I looked at you, I saw a thousand sunbeams that warmed whatever you touched. You are a bringer of life, Kui Yu. And in that, you are as much a god as I am a goddess."

Perhaps more, she realized silently. For on Earth, as a wife and Tigress, she only reflected his light.

He stared at her as he tried to absorb her words, but she could see he struggled. So she finally confessed. "What you saw of me, my husband, was a reflection of you."

He shook his head, but she had already begun her explanation. She would not stop now. "That is what Kwan Yin told me," she said.

"That you reflect me? But that is . . . It is . . . It is . . ."

"What women do, my husband. And what I have become is the extreme example of all that is feminine. We are submissive, we are giving, and at our most powerful, we simply reflect back what is presented to us."

She watched him think. His eyebrows twitched, furrowed and smoothed open again. But he said nothing.

She went on: "Kwan Yin asked me the same thing she asked you. She asked what I would give up to have what I most desire."

He nodded. He clearly recognized the question.

"But there was more," she said. She had to tell him everything. She had need of his wisdom. "I knew my choice, Kui Yu. I knew it. . . ." She blinked away the tears that flowed so easily today. "I have to choose. I cannot go to Heaven still . . . attached to you. I cannot." She would not say she loved him again. She was not ready to re-feel the humiliation.

Her husband's expression shifted, but she could not read it. He seemed both happy and sad, both confused and content. And how could he be all those things and yet silent as a windless afternoon?

She leaned forward. "Do you understand, Kui Yu?"

He shook his head. "Tell me everything," he whispered. "Was that all Kwan Yin asked?"

He knew. He knew what she'd learned. She did not know how he could, and yet, in some things, her husband understood what years of training had not taught her. "I told her I had not chosen. That I did not know. But . . ." She swallowed. How could she explain?

"But?" he prompted.

"But then she said I could have both." She looked up, and her gaze pinned his. She tried to make him understand—or perhaps she tried to draw understanding from him.

"How? How can you have both?" His voice was urgent. And sensing his strength, she was able to finish.

"She asked me if I would stop," she said.

"Stop?" He frowned. "Stop being a Tigress? Stop trying to become immortal? Stop what?"

"Stop reflecting." She took a deep breath. "Stop being a mirror."

He stared. Clearly he had no idea what she meant. He had no understanding of this fundamental part of her character; it was as if he had never even seen it.

"It is the image I use," she explained, "when I teach. How can a woman be so gentle, so giving to a man, and yet still protect herself?"

"But—," he began. She cut him off.

"Men wish a submissive woman. Men want a woman who gives them what they want. That is the ultimate in femininity—an entity to absorb, receive, and accept all in humility and subservience."

"You are speaking of a dog, not a woman!" Kui Yu said.

She couldn't stop her shrug. "To men, there is little difference."

He stiffened, but did not argue further. So she continued.

"A woman who takes all is doomed to an early grave. One cannot absorb the evils of the world without being poisoned. So I teach that a Tigress must go one step beyond. She must find a way to accomplish all." Shi Po straightened and sat upright before him. "I become a mirror, Kui Yu. I reflect back whatever is presented to me. If you give me violence, I will become your violence. If you give me gentleness, I will become that kindness. And I will return either to you."

"You strive to be a mirror?" he repeated. He was clearly stunned.

She straightened her shoulders and stared at him. "How else can one be feminine and still protect herself?"

He had no answer to that, only a dumb look. But then he slowly sat straight and matched her pose. "Kwan Yin asked you to give that up? To stop . . . reflecting?"

She nodded, misery welling up inside her. "But how can I do that? I cannot absorb the evils of the world. I will go mad!" She gestured wildly about the room. "General Kang will return. What will I do when I meet him?" Panic began to choke her, but still questions tumbled out. "What will I absorb from him? What will—"

"Absorb? But that is being a sponge," he said. "That is not . . . It can't be . . ." He shook his head. "You are a mirror?" he repeated incredulously.

She nodded, miserable. How could she give up the very attitude that had made her who she was? And yet, how could she give up either Kui Yu or her quest for immortality?

Kui Yu continued to stare until abruptly his face crumpled. "Women's religions!" he practically spat. "Mirrors! Sponges! And now I am talking like an idiot, too!" He pushed off of the bed to pace in irritation. He rounded on Shi Po, opened his mouth to speak, then abruptly shut it again before stomping about the room.

She knew better than to stop him. She had seen him agitated before; he often paced away bad humors. But this went beyond ill temper. This was fury, boiling before her like a thundercloud, and she knew better than to brave this storm.

Finally, he stopped before her, his hands planted on his hips. "Why can you not simply be you, Shi Po? Why must you be a mirror or an Immortal or a Tigress or even a mother or a wife? Why can you not simply be *you*?"

He waited for her answer, but what did one say to a question like that? She was all of those things. And yet . . .

"Shi Po," he began, his voice the low rumble of distant thunder. "Do not run from this question."

She flinched. How had he known she was thinking of ways to distract him? Of things she could do to delay giving an answer. She shook her head and felt cold air on her wet face. Tears, again! she thought in disgust.

"I have no answer," she said, wiping the moisture away. "Perhaps I am nothing." She had not meant to say the words aloud. She had not even dared think them to herself before. And yet, once again, when she was with her husband, she reflected his intelligence. She was forced to see herself clearly.

He snorted in disgust. "You are many things, wife. 'Nothing' is not one of them."

She lifted her chin, challenging him. "How do you know?"

"I did not marry nothing. I have not been plagued night and day by a vision of nothing, by a life with nothing. I have not been incarcerated or gone to Heaven with nothing! What are you thinking?"

She stared at him, completely silent.

He stared back, his clenched hands slowly relaxing, his trembling shoulders dropping. In the end, he climbed back into bed. She had no idea what he intended as he knelt before her, so she sat without moving and waited to learn.

Nothing, apparently. He reached out and stroked her cheek. She closed her eyes to better appreciate the sensation. It was wonderful, all things good. Warmth. Hot tea. Mother's arms. A child's hug. A man's kiss.

A man's kiss?

She opened her eyes as his lips moved over hers. She melted into him, and opened her mouth to allow him entry. But he did not push further. Instead, he pulled back.

"If I had wanted 'nothing,' Shi Po, I would have married anyone but you."

She had no response to that. She could only hear his words and feel his touch. With a sigh, he pulled away and lay down on the bed, his movements careful because of his shoulder. Then, when he was flat on his back, he looked at her and spread his arms.

She went to him without thought. She slipped beneath the covers and molded herself tightly to his side. She closed her eyes to savor his heat, and in time, she slept.

The bedroom door burst open, but Shi Po didn't flinch. Not because she had been expecting the noise;

in truth, she'd been deeply asleep for maybe the first time in years.

The bang of the door against the wall yanked her out of oblivion into the harsh light of day, but her body was still tucked tightly against her husband, and his cocoon of warmth kept her calm despite the appearance of two large servants.

"Why do you disturb us in this rude manner?" Kui Yu asked, his voice a low rumble near her ear. Carefully hiding her face from view, Shi Po smiled at the power in his tone. Only Kui Yu could sound threatening while lying naked and injured beside a woman.

"Apologies, sir," the servant said, not apologizing at all. "General Kang invites you to morning meal with him."

Kui Yu nodded, and his beard stubble scratched her forehead. "Tell him we will be there in . . ." He glanced down at her, silently asking how much time she would need.

"An hour," she answered. That would be long enough to maintain the illusion that they were guests without pushing the bounds of propriety. "We will need water and soap to bathe," she added. "Fresh clothing as well."

Kui Yu understood, and he immediately commanded the servants, "Bring water, soap, and a razor. And see if our clothing has arrived." It wouldn't have, of course, because they had none. But perhaps General Kang would provide.

Then Kui Yu paused, and she knew his expression without looking. He was arching a single brow, looking imperial and very irritated. "Immediately!" he snapped.

It worked. The two intimidating brutes scrambled to obey.

Shi Po pushed upright before the door closed, but Kui Yu held her fast. She didn't struggle, but adjusted to look at him and tried not to reveal just how loath she was to leave his arms.

The morning light slanted across his angular face in an unflattering manner. In truth, her husband's body was not as young as it once was. The planes of his face had softened from good food, and knew the beginnings of wrinkles. His beard, haphazardly shaved yesterday, now dotted his skin like dirt, and his hair pushed every which way upon his head.

And yet, Shi Po stared at him like a lovestruck young girl. She remembered his body suffused with all that was heavenly, and she remembered every kind word, gentle caress and frustrated grunt he had ever made. They all added up to Kui Yu, the man she loved, and she would always see that when she looked at him. So she smiled when he drew her back down into his arms.

"Do not be so quick to abandon me, Shi Po," he murmured into her hair, and she wondered if he invested extra meaning into his words.

"Kui Yu," she began.

He waited, but she faltered and fell silent. He filled the silence. "I wish to exact a promise from you, my wife."

She tensed, wondering at his tone, but she did not argue.

"Promise me you will think on what we said last night."

She swallowed. She didn't want to remember. *Do you love me?* she had asked. *No,* he'd answered, clearly surprised to admit it.

"The Goddess Kwan Yin has offered you everything," Kui Yu continued.

264

Shi Po blinked and consciously shifted her thoughts. "I do not always understand what the Goddess means," she admitted. Then she paused as her mind returned to her husband. "But what of you, Kui Yu? Do you have an answer yet for the Goddess? What will you give up to have what you most want?"

He shook his head. "I no longer even know what I have left."

"You—"

She was interrupted by a knock on the door, and by the entrance of more servants. Water, simple clothing, and a large gentleman with a razor waited to shave to Kui Yu's face. Apparently no one was going to trust them with a sharp knife.

So their discussion ended, and dressing began—silent, efficient, and with a mounting tension regarding what was to come. When they were done, they were escorted into the family dining area.

Shi Po had been trained from birth to evaluate a person in a moment, a home in the most casual of glances. Although raised in Shanghai, far from imperial Peking, she still knew enough to evaluate a Manchurian home and a Manchurian wife. She could see from the moment they arrived that General Kang had great wealth and that his servants feared him. She saw his home was built to impress, not to welcome, and concluded that he was the type of man who required his wife to serve with total obedience.

Thus, it was with great surprise that, when she and Kui Yu entered the Kang dining area, she found a wife serving her husband breakfast not in submissive obedience but love. Affection shone in the woman's eyes, and it lingered in her minute attention to his every comfort—even to the placement of his cushion and the exact number of tea leaves in his cup. Most especially it radiated through the room when he casually dismissed her and turned his attention to Kui Yu and the draping folds of Shi Po's gown—the gown that was, in fact, his Han mistress's cast-off.

Shi Po let her gaze linger on Mrs. Kang, and let herself soften in sympathy. How horrible to love a man, to be his first wife, and yet have him move his Chinese mistress into your household. Better to hate your husband than live daily in such shame, to moment by moment pray that your man would cast you some small scrap of attention. A hideous fate, and one that was all too common in China. So Shi Po sought to share a moment of understanding with the woman.

She was sent a look of such venom, Shi Po could only drop her gaze to the floor. Mrs. Kang wanted no sympathy. Certainly not from any Han woman wearing a mistress's gown. Mrs. Kang would give no aid. Shi Po would have to fend for herself. Or rather, she and Kui Yu would find a solution by themselves. Together.

The thought brought such warmth that Shi Po actually smiled, adjusting a cushion for her husband. And as a good wife should, she filled his plate and poured his tea, all the while searching for any taint of poison in the food.

"Greetings, greetings, Mr. Tan," General Kang boomed in false good cheer. "Are you feeling better?"

"Much better," Kui Yu answered. But he sent a silent question to Shi Po as she set his plate before him: *Is the food dangerous?*

She shook her head slightly. No, she didn't believe so; but then they both knew that she couldn't be sure. So Kui Yu did not eat, though he was probably starving now that his fever was gone. He did, however, take the tea she offered with a smile. Shi Po had seen

Mrs. Kang pour from that exact teapot and seen the General drink. It, at least, was safe.

"General Kang," Kui Yu began, then sipped his tea in acknowledgment of his host. Except the Manchus had wretched teas, and Shi Po watched him smother a grimace. He set the cup down. "Why have you brought us here? Why did you imprison us? What have we ever done that is a threat to China or yourself?"

General Kang blinked, obviously startled that Kui Yu would ignore formalities. They were supposed to have a quiet, genial chat while they ate, not a sudden confrontation. But Kui Yu had never been trained in such niceties, and generally disliked the time they took. It was something Shi Po adored about him. She found herself hiding her smile.

Which, apparently, bothered the General. Obviously, he had thought many days trapped together would set her and Kui Yu at each other's throats. It would for many couples. But they had survived.

"You are not eating," said the General with more false cheer. "And you are my guests. I could not have—"

"A guest is invited," Kui Yu shot back. "A guest has clothing and time and freedom. General Kang, I ask you again, what do you want?"

The General grimaced then pushed away from the table in disgust. He began to pace, his manner angry, his movements abrupt. It was all Mrs. Kang could do to duck out of his way when he passed.

"Eat!" the man snapped. "The food is not poisoned. And perhaps it will improve your frame of mind."

Kui Yu did not move, but Shi Po did. She believed the General, so she reached out and tasted everything on her husband's plate. Let the poison affect her. Kui Yu made to stop her, but he was too late; she had already begun, and he would not argue in front of their audience. She whispered, "I will be able to taste it better than you."

He understood and reluctantly nodded. After all, she was the one who worked daily with herbs and poisons, not him. Fortunately, as the General had said, there was nothing untoward in the food, and in the end, they both ate heartily. After so long in prison, the fare was fit for an Emperor—or two humans freshly returned from Heaven.

While they ate, the General spoke, appearing completely in earnest. It began as Shi Po expected. He was desperately sorry for arresting them. He was a distraught father in search of a missing son, and they had unfortunately been caught in the middle. "You housed him with a white woman. This I know." He shot them an angry glare. Then he took a deep breath and resumed his pacing. "He and this Ly-dee-ah." He spat on the floor. A servant rushed forward to wipe it up.

He swung around and glared hard at Shi Po. "He says they are Immortals now. And the Empress Dowager has sent them to Hong Kong."

Where? Shi Po blinked. Immortal? She actually mouthed the words, repeating to herself what General Kang had said: They are Immortals now.

Immortals, plural.

"No," she whispered. Her revulsion grew in strength until she screamed silently in her mind. Another white woman could not possibly be an Immortal! Not when Shi Po still had not passed the antechamber. It wasn't possible. And yet, Kang's fury was all too obvious.

The General pretended to be happy. "My son is to

begin a temple there. On an ugly rock of an island. A temple to your religion." His voice lost all warmth. And yet, for all that he stood glaring at her, his muscular body quivering with rage, Shi Po caught a sheen of tears in his eyes, and she heard the catch in his voice. He clearly loved his son.

Kui Yu reached under the table and enfolded her hand in his. Shi Po felt the callouses on his palm, the rough caress of his fingers over her clenched knuckles. And she felt his warmth flow into her. She was reassured by that.

And . . . *love*. Whether he said it or not, she felt love in his touch. She was able to breathe, to see past her failure, to find some place beyond the bitterness.

"That is excellent news, your honor," she said. "Two new Immortals. China is richly blessed." And part of her—the part that held on to her husband—meant what she said.

General Kang hovered over her, hands on his hips, his eyes boring into hers. She dipped her head as was appropriate for a female when confronted by a male, but he reached down and roughly jerked her face up.

Beside her, Kui Yu stiffened and half rose out of his seat. She flipped her hand over and quickly pushed him down. General Kang did not intend to harm her; he merely wished to read her expression. As she wished to read his.

She was not in any danger yet, so she kept Kui Yu still. In the periphery of her vision, Shi Po saw Mrs. Kang smirk. Apparently, the woman enjoyed seeing her husband threaten others.

Words came impulsively, without thought or common sense, but sometimes Heaven's messages were sent in just that way. "You are vulnerable through your wife," Shi Po said. "A woman who lives in loneliness and is served bitterness will find a way to fight back. You teach her treachery, General Kang. Do not be surprised when you feel the prick of her knife in your back."

He did not slap her. Shi Po tensed, expecting a blow, but it did not come. Instead, she felt the slow slide of the General's fingers from where they gripped her chin to her cheek, then they found and lingered on her mouth. Beside her, Kui Yu stiffened. He wanted to fight the General, despite the large army of servants just outside the door. So Shi Po tightened her fingers and prayed her husband would remain prudent.

The General spoke, his voice low and apparently pitched for seduction. Or a threat. With this man, she couldn't tell. "Interesting suggestion," he said. "It might even be worth investigating." His gaze dropped to where Shi Po's leg was exposed by the slit of her dress. In this way, he let her know exactly what he wanted to investigate.

Shi Po's stomach roiled at the thought.

Abruptly, he released her. He stepped back and folded his arms across his chest. "Tell me about your religion," he said. She blinked at the sudden change in topic.

He shifted his gaze to Kui Yu. "You wish to know why you are here? I want to know what exactly has seduced my son." He grimaced. "Other than the obvious."

There was a moment's silence before Kui Yu's laughter broke like a distant boom of thunder across the room. It was loud, rolled, and filled the air with a disconcerting good humor. Everyone—including Shi Po—stared at him. All wondered if his mind had broken.

"Love seduced your son, General Kang," Kui Yu said between bursts of laughter. "Love. Not some religion or nefarious plot. Only a deep and true love could take a son from his father, a man from an empire, or a monk from his temple. Love, General. And if you cannot see that he loves this Lydia, then you will not understand any religion of my wife's or even the—"

"She is a white devil!" General Kang exploded. Spittle flew from his lips.

Staring at the man, Shi Po felt the pressure of true despair. General Kang had no interest in learning anything about what she taught, or even comprehending the tiniest part of his son's actions. He wanted a scapegoat, and he'd found one in her.

She sighed and decided to trust her husband and the Goddess and bluntly confront the truth. "What do you wish from us, General Kang? Do you seek to expose me as depraved? How will that return your son to you? Do you want a weapon to wield against him? To force him to renounce his white love and return to your control? You raised a son in your image: strong and independent. Could anything swerve you from your choices? No. So you likely will not sway your son, but only entrench his bitterness against you." She lifted her chin. "I ask you again: What do you want?"

His eyes went dead; from the moment she mentioned his son, his gaze flattened to an expression of absolute disgust. She knew as she spoke that he would not be convinced, so she was surprised when he stepped back and pulled open the door. She did not catch what he said to the servants outside, but the response was immediate.

Movement sounded outside the door: the shuffle of

271

feet, the muted outcry of a child, and the harsh grating tones of an angry woman. Shi Po swallowed, and fear chilled her bones. She glanced at her husband and saw the same horror seep into his features for all that they both would wish to remain impassive. Then their worse fears were realized: soldiers escorted their two sons inside.

Shi Po exclaimed in horror and rushed forward as fast as she could, Kui Yu at her side. But they were stopped by the soldiers, who barred their way with swords. Those weapons were pointed not at their own throats, but at their children's.

"What is the meaning of this!" Kui Yu bellowed. "Why would you bring them here? They have done nothing! They know nothing!"

Shi Po found her eyes burning hot as she studied her children for injuries. She saw bruises and dirt, but nothing uncommon for boys. Nothing except the stark terror in their eyes.

"How do you fare, my children?" she asked, struggling to keep her voice even.

Her eldest son—Jiao Long—nodded in reassurance, even as he gripped his younger brother's hand. "We are hungry," he said, his chin lifted in a stubborn gesture reminiscent of his father.

"Well," boomed the General, "then by all means eat!" He gestured to the table, and the guards miraculously stepped back to allow the the boys an open path to breakfast. But it was a path that took the pair away from their parents and closer to the General.

The boys did not move. They looked to their father.

Kui Yu nodded, his voice gentle. "Go ahead. If you are hungry, eat. And know that your mother and I deeply regret what is happening. We will do everything we can to keep you safe."

"Of course you will," returned the General, his voice all good cheer. It had happened just like He Yun predicted. Kang meant to keep her sons until he had whatever he wanted. Even if what he wanted was impossible. Even if he wanted his own son, Zou Tun, returned to him.

"Will your son forgive you this?" she asked, her heart beating painfully in her throat. "Will Zou Tun forgive you for using innocents to trap him?"

The General sneered, actually sneered, as he looked on her sons. "There are no innocents in a family of depravity. The father traffics with white devils and the wife trains whores."

"What do you intend?" This came from Kui Yu, his voice a low threat that made the soldiers shift nervously. It also brought the General's focus completely—exclusively—to Kui Yu. Which gave Shi Po a chance to slip quietly to her children's sides. The soldiers could have stopped her, but she knew men never thought to watch a woman when there was a dangerous man in the room. Not that she could do anything but touch her boys. She reassured herself that Jiao Long was without injury, that Shen Zhan breathed without restriction. And then she enfolded them in her arms.

The General spoke, outlining his plans with a cold, empty heart. "I plan to go to the Emperor. I plan to tell him of your crime, to expose your lewd and bestial acts. You are part of the disease that infects China, a filth that must be destroyed."

"That's ridiculous," Kui Yu countered. "Shi Po is the granddaughter of the great Tseng family. Her brother daily visits the Forbidden City. I, myself, have—"

"The great Tseng name has lately been tarnished—

one brother killed as a revolutionary, the other opium-addicted and diseased." His eyes narrowed. "I am afraid he never received your request for aid."

Shi Po winced. So much for hope of rescue from her brother.

"The Emperor will listen," gloated Kang. "Especially as . . ." His voice trailed away and he nodded to a soldier.

Again the door opened, and this time a small woman with narrowed red eyes shuffled into the room. If she intended to walk confidently, she failed. For though her chin was lifted with a kind of pride, her shoulders were stooped and her tiny feet shuffled. She was obviously terribly afraid.

"Auntie Ting!" Shi Po exclaimed. She shouldn't have been surprised to see the woman here who was, after all, part of her family for better or worse. If General Kang were gathering up all the relatives, Auntie Ting would surely be one of them. But if that were the case, where were her parents? Or Kui Yu's cousin? Why—

"Tell me again, Madame Sung, about this family," the General ordered as he held up a scroll. "Tell me what is written here and what I will show to the Emperor."

Auntie Ting flinched and her chin dropped down on her chest. But to her credit, she looked defiant. "The boys did nothing," she whispered. "They know nothing." Then she looked up at the General for confirmation of what she'd just said.

The General nodded, and his smile warmed. "Of course, the boys are innocent. That is why the Emperor will graciously allow me to raise them as my own. After all, they are completely innocent of their parents' crimes."

Shi Po felt her knees go out. The thought of this cold, angry man raising her sons sapped all strength from her body. Shen Zhan caught her and helped her to a chair. She held him and reached out to draw Jiao Long to her, using both boys' small bodies to keep herself alert and focused. For them she would keep going. For them, she would find a way through—*any* way—if only it meant that her boys would never spend another moment under this man's influence.

General Kang continued, his every word inflicting pain. "Tell it all," he ordered. And so, in halting words, Auntie Ting spoke.

"I have no knowledge of Kui Yu's dealings with the ghost people," she said, her voice dark and full of bitterness. "But money falls like rain into his hand. It cannot be from legitimate commerce."

"You lie!" Kui Yu bellowed, and her aunt shrunk even more. Shi Po could almost pity her, caught between two such powerful men. Almost. But her aunt was clever, and had often found answers in adversity.

"I know nothing of his business dealings," she repeated, "but I know my own." She lifted her chin and shifted her gaze not to the General, but to Shi Po. "I know he came to my establishment. He consorted regularly with a ghost woman. He even bought her from me and set her up in a handsome palace."

If Auntie Ting were looking for justification for her actions in this revelation, she had grossly miscalculated. Shi Po knew about Lily, knew that the so-called palace was actually a white person's temple. And so there came no horror to her eyes, no sudden condemnation of her husband.

Though there might have been, had this knowledge been a surprise.

"My husband has acted honorably," Shi Po stated

loudly. "He saved a woman from a life of prostitution at your hands, Auntie, and set her up in a temple of her own religion. Do not project your perversions onto my husband. You are the one who bought and sold that poor woman. Kui Yu merely saved her." She shifted her gaze to the General. "If the Emperor looks for corruption, do you honestly believe he would take the word of a notorious Shanghai madam over a respected businessman?"

Her aunt turned on her. "And why am I a madam?" She shrieked. "Why am I forced into a life of daily degradation and pain? Why? Because of you, you filthy whore. You! You killed my husband with your unnatural lust. You harvest yang, heedless of the results."

"Enough!" roared Kui Yu. He pushed forward, despite the restraining soldiers, and faced the General with black fury in his eyes. "I will speak to you now. Alone," he demanded.

But Auntie Ting was not finished. Still cringing away from both Kui Yu and the General, she continued to screech, "Ask her! Ask her if she was a virgin when you married her! Ask her where her dowry money came from. Ask her!"

Shi Po didn't answer. She didn't even have the strength to look up anymore. She simply held her sons—one in each arm—and wet her gown with tears. She thought not of Kui Yu, who was demanding to speak with the General, or of her hate-filled aunt, or even her long-dead uncle with the gentle smile and his thin, weak dragon; she thought of her boys. What ill would befall them now when they knew the worst of their mother? How would that damage their minds and spirits, to know such ugliness?

She should have killed herself so many nights ago. Now she wished she had not waited for Kui Yu's return. If she had been strong, if she had been firm in her resolve at the very beginning, none of this would ever have happened. Her husband would be mourning, but he would still have his business, his home, and his friends. Her sons would grieve, but they would not be lost now to the captivity of a pitiless Manchu and poisoned by their mother's perfidy.

She should have done it. And this was the penalty for her indecision.

Into this whirlwind of noise and humiliation, Kui Yu, at last, was heard. "You will see me now!" he bellowed at the General.

Kang nodded and turned to leave. But before he did, he paused and addressed one of his soldiers.

"Give the witch to the men to use as they will."

Shi Po whimpered, believing he meant her. But then she heard her aunt shriek as the soldiers grabbed her arms. "We had an agreement," Auntie Ting wailed. "I signed your document. I did all that you asked!"

The General smiled with good cheer. "And as reward, you will live and ply your trade with my men."

"But they'll hurt me! I'll die!" she cried.

Kang merely shrugged. "Such is the end of all whores." And with that she was dragged away. Try as she might, Shi Po could find no sympathy in her heart for the woman.

She shifted her attention to the General and Kui Yu. The two men would talk and make an arrangement. Knowing her husband, Shi Po had confidence that the best solution would be found. Kui Yu was a capable negotiator. And while that was happening, Shi Po would correct her error of indecision. Suicide was the only redemption for a fallen woman, and the only hope that her taint would not filter down to her sons.

❧

September 28, 1880

Kui Yu—

My grandmother once said that men of poetry are ever a woman's downfall. Swear to me. Give me some token. Promise that if I were the lowliest worm, the most miserable creature, even a opium-addicted, nail-shack prostitute, that you would still wed me. Swear this to me, and it shall be as you ask.

If you do so swear, then bring your token to Lun Po's tutor, as we have done with our letters. I will retrieve it tomorrow. And the next time you see my brother, do whatever foolishness he asks.

In hope,
Shi Po

September 30, 1880

To my most precious Shi Po—

The ghost people have a saying: Store your treasure in Heaven, for where your treasure is, so will your heart be. And so I have done. This is all I have in the world. My heart, I ask nothing, but promise everything. It is, and will always be, as you ask.

With great love,
Kui Yu

PS—*Do not tell your family what you have, especially your brother. If you do not understand the contents, then take the paper to any white missionary. They will explain. But bring a strong guard with you when you do.*

(Attached, a small box of modest design. Inside are ten taels of Imperial jade. Beneath it, an envelope with a cheque drawn on the Shanghai Bank of England in the amount of £9,426.)

An old man and his son were very obstinate in disposition. No matter what they did, they never gave way to anybody. One day the son was returning home with meat purchased for dinner. But at the city gate, he met a rough fellow. Since the gate was so narrow, one had to go first, but neither would give way to the other. So they stood there face-to-face.

Wondering at the delay, the father went in search of his son, only to find him standing opposite the big fellow. He immediately understood what had happened and rushed forward to stand beside his son.

"Go and take the meat home," he said. "I will stand here face-to-face until you return."

Chapter Sixteen

A man's office showed much about who he was and how he thought. Kui Yu expected to be led there. Instead, the General sent everyone else from the dining room. That General Kang refused to show Kui Yu to his room of business told him that the man had many secrets, many layers, and that no one ever came close to the heart of them. Indeed, Kui Yu doubted if General Kang even knew himself what lay in the deepest well of his spirit.

He and Kui Yu waited as servants cleared the table. They sat in uncomfortable chairs sipping tepid tea while all was busy about them. It was unusual and rude, but General Kang would not show Kui Yu any more of his home—or his life—than was absolutely necessary. And Kui Yu had already seen enough of General Kang to understand what motivated him.

It wasn't greed. It wasn't even a lust for power, though Kui Yu was sure that figured into the man's thinking. No, what drove the General most was a need of victory. It didn't matter that he had little reason to keep either Shi Po, Kui Yu, or their children. After all, Zou Tun had been found. But the boy had apparently bested his father and created a life with a woman he loved. Which meant General Kang had lost twice—once to Shi Po because she'd successfully hidden his son, and again by the son who was now on some remote island under the express protection of the Empress Dowager.

In short, Kang's son was out of reach. Which left only Shi Po and her family for vengeance. *That* was the real reason they had been incarcerated, the true purpose behind their prolonged time as pretend guests. It was so that the General could ferret out their weaknesses, and reassure himself that he was still a man of power, still able to defeat his enemies however pitiful and weak.

It was Kui Yu's job today to give the General the victory, to show him that he and Shi Po were sufficiently cowed. That they were miserable, wretched worms at his feet. General Kang could now let them go with absolute certainty that they would never threaten his peace again. Congratulations, honor upon his house and upon his name—he had to say whatever it took for the man to declare himself victor and then look for other prey.

The last servant left. The soldiers withdrew, but Kui Yu knew they would still be close by. Even Mrs. Kang had taken her black, treacherous stares and departed. Which left Kui Yu and General Kang staring at one another over the wretched tea.

Kui Yu dipped his head, doing his best to look completely defeated. In a hushed voice he said, "What do you wish from me, your honor? Money for weapons? Fine silks for your women? Name it, and it shall be yours."

The General's eyes were narrowed, his expression pensive. "You did know, didn't you? Before the vows."

Kui Yu considered lying, but the General probably knew some of the truth. It had been quite a scandal at the time. So he shrugged and chose honesty. "Yes, I knew."

"But you married her anyway. Why?"

"You know the reasons. Her name. Her family connections. All have been helpful to me in business."

The General sipped his tea, not even bothering to look up. "For every lie you speak, I will order your sons whipped ten times."

Kui Yu didn't need to fake his cringe. He did, however, need to instill a whine into his voice. "But I did tell the truth! Her name. Her money—"

"She had no money!" the General bellowed. "Her family has been begging for scraps for decades!"

"She came to me with a great dowry," Kui Yu returned, the memory stark in his mind.

"From her whoring?"

Kui Yu nodded, though it wasn't anything close to the full truth.

"You were a wealthy man. A barbarian's first boy. You could have married anyone, and yet you chose a whore. Why?"

"I loved her." Also the truth, and yet not nearly the whole truth.

"You are not such a fool," the General spat.

Kui Yu allowed his weariness to show. "She was beautiful and rich. I loved her. I married her. Surely you have better things to do than banter old history with me. What do you want?"

The General's gaze hardened. "She was a tigress even then, wasn't she?"

Kui Yu frowned. "I don't think so."

"I think she was. She lived with her aunt. She murdered her uncle. I think the tigresses are witches. They bespell a man to do their bidding. Why else would a man marry a whore? Why else would your every business venture prosper? She is a witch."

Kui Yu rolled his eyes. "If that were true, then she would have already entranced you."

The General visibly swelled with arrogance. "Oh, I have felt her power—the lust that burns in a man's loins at the sight of a beautiful woman. But I am too old to be led by such petty tricks."

"There is no magic, General."

"Ten lashes for your sons! Guard!"

The door burst open the same moment Kui Yu jumped to his feet. "It is the truth!" he bellowed.

"Twenty!"

"No!"

The guard waited at the door while Kui Yu and the General stared at one another. Then Kang leaned forward, his eyes narrowing to pinpricks. "Why did you marry her then, if you were not bespelled?"

"Release my sons. Unharmed."

The General shifted in his chair, and his powerful form made the wood creak. "You will tell me everything about your wedding—to the smallest detail—of why you decided to marry a whore."

283

Kui Yu glared down at his captor. "You will not like the answers."

"You will not like hearing your sons scream as the lash bites into their backs."

"Free them."

"And you will tell me all?"

Kui Yu nodded. He would spill his life's history if it meant safety for his sons.

The General glanced at the soldier. "Keep the boys safe," he grunted.

The guard nodded and stepped back outside.

"I said, 'free them!' " Kui Yu snapped.

"We will see if you answer honestly."

Kui Yu folded his arms across his chest, his mind working furiously. But no perfect solution presented itself, and he had precious little maneuvering room. "I will answer honestly, but will you believe it?"

"I am a general in the Imperial army!" Kang snapped. "I will know if you lie to me."

Kui Yu doubted it, but there was no way to convince Kang of that. So he settled back into his chair.

"Why did you marry her?" Kang pressed.

Kui Yu shrugged. "She was the granddaughter of a Ming viceroy and a virgin." His expression hardened as he said those words. "Of this I am absolutely certain."

The General grimaced in disgust. "She whored for her aunt."

"She was the protected flower of an honorable family and destined for much greater things than a white man's first boy. But she married me with her father's blessing. With everyone's great joy." Kui Yu looked up at his host. "Do you know why?"

General Kang might know. It had been a huge scandal at the time, for all that Shi Po's family had tried to quiet the rumors. But Kui Yu could tell from Kang's determinedly flat expression that he didn't. His network of spies didn't extended into the Shanghai social hierarchy, and like everyone else Kang desperately wanted to know the secret.

"Because she *chose* me. Unlike all the other girls of her caste, she had the intelligence to see my worth and to fight to get what she wanted."

General Kang frowned. He obviously did not understand the connection between Shi Po's marriage wishes and her virginity. And who could have? Certainly Kui Yu hadn't so many years ago.

"General, she had no more power than any other girl. Her father determined her worth and her suitors. I wasn't even considered, but she chose me. And she set out to make herself of equal value to me."

Kui Yu watched the General carefully. He had the man's rapt attention.

"She went to her aunt who ran a brothel, and there she sold her virginity to the highest bidder."

General Kang's face reddened in anger—the typical male reaction to a woman who dared chart her own course. But Kui Yu continued, pitching his voice low so the man had to lean forward to hear.

"Her family was horrified, of course. All her other suitors disappeared, for she made sure they knew of her crime. Only I remained. Only I didn't care." He took another sip of bad tea. "And the money she made bought my first store, which is the basis of all my current wealth. It was the beginning that I needed." He took a deep breath, still humbled by his wife's action, still awed by the strength of her resolve to do such a thing just so she could have him.

· "In this way, she married with the blessings of friends and family, we maintained the connections to her great family name, and I had all the money we needed to build a business. There was no other way for all that happen without her sacrifice. She debased herself in the most humiliating of ways so that we could be together." He pinned the General with his gaze. "Would your wife do so much? Would she risk so much for your future?"

The General paled. Mrs. Kang would more likely spit in her husband's face should he make such a suggestion, and they both knew it.

"So you see," Kui Yu drawled, loving the feel of superiority to this cruel man, "I knew after the fact of my wife's actions. And since I learned, I have honored her for it."

It was no lie. When he learned what she had done, he'd been so appalled, he'd vomited. How could the flower of China destroy herself in this manner? Why? He knew the answer. She had told him as much. She had done it for him, and for their life together. And in that moment, he'd realized Shi Po was a woman of extraordinary strength. She was more than an innocent virgin or a simpering beauty. Her one act revealed a character intelligent enough to find a miracle where he had seen only impediments. And then she had implemented her plan with a focus absent in most *men* of her age and class. That she was a woman made it even more amazing.

So great was her strength that he'd sat in awe before her. He still did.

"She makes me stronger, General. Whenever I waver, whenever I stumble, I remember what she did and I strive to deserve her glorious sacrifice."

Kang's skin flushed a dark red and his eyes narrowed in disgust. "You have been bespelled."

Kui Yu felt his hands clench in fury. "I am in love! If that is magic, then so be it!" He spat the words out like bad meat, but in his heart, a new warmth was spreading. He did love his wife. He still loved Shi Po! And it had taken sparring words with this terrible man to see it. "We are common people, General. Of no interest to the great men of China. A man besotted with his wife is of no significance to you. Take my gold. Buy weapons or armor or whatever you will. We are not worthy of your time."

The General stared at him, his expression pensive. Then he began to nod. It was the tiniest dip of his chin, but it was enough for relief to flood into Kui Yu's heart. Until the General spoke.

"Do you think my son an idiot?"

"What?"

"Do you think him weak in mind or spirit?"

Kui Yu thought back to the troubled man who had graced his home for so short a time. "He is a Shaolin monk. Why would he be weak in any such manner?"

"Many called him brilliant. He is the hope of the Empire."

"Of course."

"Until he met your wife. Until she bespelled him as she has done you." The General leaned forward. "How long did this Ly-dee-ah study with her? How is the magic cast?"

Kui Yu barely restrained himself from rolling his eyes. "There was no training. She was sick and mute. Your son brought her to us!"

The General was silent long enough for Kui Yu to believe he might have gotten through to him. Then he spoke, his words slow and pensive. "She was hurt when my son brought her to you?"

"Yes. Her throat had been injured."

"So, my son found her. And then she trained with your wife?"

Kui Yu shrugged. "There was some tutelage. Exercises and the like. For strengthening the belly muscles."

The General shook his head. "No, not for the belly. There is magic in these women."

The only magic in them was their ability to love fully and with great passion. But the General clearly did not understand that. He was too busy creating elaborate fantasies to explain his son's defection.

Kang frowned at his dark tea. "Your wife convinces men to do as she bids."

"Nonsense."

"You wed her honorably though she was a whore."

"She was no whore!" Kui Yu said again, though he knew it was useless. The General had already decided. And he believed that sorcery was involved. Odd, that the man had not appeared especially superstitious before. But then, every Han Chinese believed in omens, goddesses and magicians. Why wouldn't a Manchurian believe in sorcerers? "General Kang, on my sons' lives, I swear to you: there is no special magic."

"So you would have me believe."

"It is the truth."

The man leaned back in his chair and belched loudly. Then he smiled at Kui Yu. "I will see this ability to control men. I will see your woman's power with my own eyes."

"But there is no power!" Kui Yu cried again.

"You are besotted and therefore would not know." He smiled genially down at his prisoner. "But my son would have seen it. He must have found this white woman and tricked Shi Po into revealing her secrets."

"That is absurd."

"And then he ran from you for fear of reprisal."

"He ran from *you*, General."

"And then my son went to show his power to the Emperor as any good son of China would do. But he was stopped by the Empress Dowager. In danger of his life."

Kui Yu leaned forward, desperate to find a way to reach the General. "But if he had this great power, wouldn't he have used it to escape?"

Kang smiled, and his entire face lightened with the change. "He did. How else could he have gotten an island to himself with the Dowager Empress's own men protecting him?"

"You are completely mad," Kui Yu said softly.

The General shook his head. "I will see this great power. I will see my son wield it."

"How would this power be demonstrated? How—"

"That is for my son to say." General Kang pushed to his feet. "I will go to Hong Kong, and you will come with me. We will see this power in action."

"Or?" Kui Yu prompted, his heart in his throat.

"Or?" Kang responded with a slight lilt to his voice. "Or I will know that my son has lost his mind to a white witch."

Kui Yu stared. "And if that is what you believe?"

"Then he will die. As will the witch." The General's eyes narrowed, and he glared at Kui Yu. "As will you and your witch wife."

"You would kill your own son?" Kui Yu asked.

Kang nodded. "The taint would be too deep. I would never know if he acted in honesty or if he still lingered under some spell." He straightened and adjusted his armor, heading for the door. "If he is not in control of this power, then he will die. As will you. And then I shall begin again with your sons. They appear to be bright, filial sons, and I am yet young enough to train them."

Kui Yu could barely breathe through the constriction in his throat. "But they are Han boys. You cannot believe that—"

"I can, and I do. They will follow my direction or die."

Kui Yu straightened to his full height in desperate challenge. "Must you think so much of killing? Your son, my wife—what devastation you surround yourself with! All to win?"

Kang reared back, his revulsion clear. "You think I play a game? You think I am casual about destroying my own flesh and blood?" He stepped forward, his wide girth equaling Kui Yu's height. "You are a Han fool to speak of family and blood as a game. I fight for all of China, for a defense against the white disease that has captured even my own heir!"

The General shook his head, sad. "If your arm is diseased, though it pains you to the depths of your soul, you must cut it off or die. In the same way, China cannot allow these foreign devils dominion." Then he turned his back on Kui Yu. "Whatever magic these women wield will be turned to the benefit of China, or they will die." His hand found the door as he spoke, his knuckles white with the force of his passion. "And all who have been touched by their evil will die as well. That is what happens in a war." He nodded, obviously satisfied with his decision. "We leave tomorrow morning."

Kui Yu rushed forward. "You cannot simply exchange my sons for yours. You cannot wield men or women like swords. You cannot—"

"You are right," the General interrupted, and his face tightened into a frown. "Your sons are equally tainted." He sighed. "Very well. I will find others. Yours will die with you."

And with that, he drew open the door. It was with some shock that he nearly stumbled over his wife. Mrs. Kang stood in the doorway, obviously listening, obviously horrified. She knew her husband was mad, and she knew his plans. But if Kui Yu had thought to find aid from her, he was doomed. At one growl from General Kang, the woman dropped her head, put her hands together in prayer and backed away, bowing with each step.

Kui Yu stood alone in the ashes of his disaster. How had he started with the idea of allowing Kang to feel victorious and ended with a challenge to prove a white woman's mystical power? How had he gone from "we are worms at your feet, please kick us aside," to "yes, I will prove this power or see my entire family slaughtered"?

What had happened? And how could the situation be salvaged?

He didn't know, and he sank to his knees in despair at all he had wrought. And into his darkness came a woman. Mrs. Kang dropped to her knees before him, offering him more of her Manchu tea.

"Why did you come here?" she rasped, pushing the teacup into his hands. "Better to have died in birth than to ever see this day."

Kui Yu cradled her teacup but did not drink. Instead, he wearily pushed to his feet. He needed to find his wife. He needed to talk to her.

Then he stopped, his body frozen. The magnitude of that ridiculous thought was shocking. He was searching out his wife's advice? When had her lost

291

and searching spirit begun to make sense to him, especially so much so that other women seemed like noise? He didn't know. But he suddenly realized he loved her. Not in the way of his youth. Not with sweetened idealism or the passion of his dragon. But in the simple fact that he understood her most of the time. And when he didn't, he still cherished her hopes, desires, and methods.

He shook his head. This all made no sense, but feelings were not the province of logic. Emotions lent themselves to poetry and song, and he had no time for that now. His sons' lives were at stake; he needed a solution. Which meant he needed to talk to his wife.

With a sympathetic smile, he returned the tea to Mrs. Kang and left. There were no soldiers to escort him back to his room, but servants were on hand to point the way. And eyes watched his every move.

At the bedroom, he felt a great relief in the simple act of closing the door. Until he noticed the room was empty. Where was his wife?

Shi Po had no idea what Kui Yu intended, but to demand to speak in private with their captor suggested a plan of sorts. Excellent. That gave her hope and the distraction she needed. She followed Jiao Long and Shen Zhan to their room, doing her best to ignore the soldiers surrounding them. She was given scant time to speak with the boys, only enough to reassure herself again that they were well, and to repeat to them that all would be fine. Then she told the boys to stay in their room. Try to rest, she suggested. Recite Confucian quotes back and forth. Whatever it took to amuse themselves, but they should not leave their room.

Then she was escorted out. None of the soldiers accompanied her further; they simply led her from the room and took positions on either side of the boys' doorway. In other words, it appeared she was allowed to do what she willed in Kang's home, but her sons would stay under guard. It was assumed that neither Shi Po nor Kui Yu would do anything to endanger their offspring.

Shi Po nodded to the guards, wearing the wretched expression any good mother would. It wasn't hard to don. Indeed, she did feel miserable. But she also felt the quiet peace of resolve. She had a plan, and she would see it executed with all possible dispatch. She went in search of Kang's Han mistress.

She found He Yun easily enough; all she had to do was follow the sound of sobbing. Mother and daughter were pretending to play with dolls, but in truth the daughter was crying and the mother was watching in silent misery. A single doll was extended in hope of diverting the girl, as if a porcelain toy could relieve the ache that traveled up her legs and penetrated deep into the girl's spirit. Sometimes Shi Po thought all Chinese girls became permanently damaged the moment a mother folded her toes tight to her sole. But then she remembered the truth, and knew that there were much more hurtful things than bound feet.

But not many.

"Mistress Wu He Yun," she said to the concubine, in all possible formality. "I have a great need to speak with someone. Could you assist me, please?"

"Of course," the woman answered, and relief showed on her face. "You wish to tell me your Tigress secrets?"

"I will teach you all of them," she promised. "But first . . ." She scanned the room. There had been no servants in this area of the compound before, but she couldn't be sure. "Are we alone?"

"Mrs. Kang does not send maids to assist me," He Yun replied.

No, Mrs. Kang wouldn't. "Perhaps we could go to the stillroom," Shi Po suggested. "I will show you more herbs for your daughter." And they could speak quietly as they went.

He Yun rose to her feet, swaying elegantly as she moved. Without even missing a stride, she swooped down and lifted up her child, who immediately burrowed her face in her mother's neck.

Shi Po was hit but a sudden wave of wistfulness. She remembered those days: the feel of a child's nose against your skin, little arms tight about your neck. It mattered not how old you were, some memories never faded, some feelings were never forgotten. She swallowed. She would do anything in her power to save her sons. Anything at all.

"What are your secrets?" He Yun asked, her voice eager as they walked.

Shi Po grabbed hold of her arm, halting their progress in an empty hallway. "Mrs. Kang teeters on the edge of a great chasm. It will not be safe for you here should she fall."

He Yun lowered her eyes, and her body became stone.

"You already knew this," Shi Po realized.

The mistress lifted her eyes, and terror shimmered in their dark depths. "What do you know? And how?"

Shi Po bit her lip. In truth, she knew absolutely

nothing except that no woman could live in a household like this without darkness tainting her spirit. But it served her purposes to have He Yun afraid, and so she created the lie. "I must know what the General plans," she said. "What will he do if I die."

He Yun shook her head. "No. Tell me first—"

"I can help you escape."

A moment passed before hope flared in the woman's eyes. But then it was quickly crushed beneath a hard glare. "What can I do with the General here and a young child in my arms?"

"You can go to Shanghai. To my friends there. They will help you."

He Yun curled her lip in a sneer. "Do you think I am stupid? If you could escape, you would already be gone."

Shi Po barely held her temper. There was so little time. "I cannot escape," she snapped. "They are watching me. All the attention is fixed on me and my family. But no one looks at you." She touched the woman's arm. "Do they expect you to flee? When was the last time you attempted to escape?"

He Yun's gaze dropped to her daughter. "Not since before I became pregnant. They know a woman with a mixed-race child would have nowhere to go." She lifted her chin, her face and attitude hardening further. "I am safer here. There is nothing out there—"

"You can go to Shanghai. To Little Pearl, at the Tan household. Tell her everything. She will help you and your child."

"Why?" He Yun demanded. "Why would she help me? Why would you?"

Because Shi Po needed the chaos generated by an escape, but she didn't say that. Instead, she gripped

He Yun's arm. "Tell me what the General will do if he finds me dead. Will he release my family?"

The woman's eyes grew large. "He believes us all whores, and so he forces us—"

"Yes, yes," Shi Po interrupted. "But what will he do if I prove myself honorable? If I kill myself rather than accept his attention? Will he release my family?"

He Yun shook her head. "I don't know. Maybe." She gripped Shi Po's arm. "But they are certainly dead if you stay here. He will use them to force you."

"But will he kill them?"

"Yes."

"You are certain? With no doubt? You are—"

"He has done it four times now. He holds out hope, but there is none. He pretends, but his interest is fixed upon you."

Shi Po bit her lip. "What if I gave in to him?"

He Yun shook her head. "I gave in to him. As did the two before me and the one here before you." She gripped her child tight to her chest. "He uses your husband and your children—"

"Then an honorable death is the only hope?"

He Yun nodded. "They are of no use to him without you."

So it was decided. Shi Po's course was set. She touched He Yun's elbow, and they began walking again; though by necessity, their steps were small and light. And silent. "Take what jewels you have and flee. Today, while the General is occupied with us, and while his wife is busy serving him."

"And you?" He Yun asked. Her voice was stronger with resolve, but her eyes remained wide and her hands clutched her child's clothing with white knuckles.

For one moment, Shi Po allowed her fears and grief to show. Then, horrified by her weakness, she stopped herself and carefully blanked her face. "My path is set," she said, and was pleased that her voice did not quaver.

He Yun stared for a long moment at Shi Po. "You will be honored as a faithful wife and an excellent mother," she said.

Shi Po paused. She knew it was true, could see the reverence in He Yun's attitude and stance. It suffused her entire body. Indeed, even the child Wen Ai quieted long enough to gaze at Shi Po with large, fathomless eyes. Shi Po would be revered. Assuming her sons escaped Kang's clutches, they would be free of any poisonous gossip attached to her. After all, suicide was the great Chinese redeemer. It was the only way, at this point, to save her sons.

And yet . . . Shi Po slowed her steps until she stopped completely. And yet . . .

"There is poison in the stillroom," He Yun said.

Shi Po nodded. She had seen it.

"Or there is rope. In the garden shed."

Again, Shi Po nodded.

He Yun touched fingers to the back of Shi Po's hand. "Be strong. Honor must be earned." Then she pulled back as she resettled her arms around her child. "I will carry the tale of your glory to your friend."

Shi Po nodded. Her thoughts whirled, taking up less and less space in her spirit. It was as though she were shrinking into herself, and yet all parts of her were still there, whole, but kicked into a great frenzy. Would she not soon explode?

To distract herself, she quickly told He Yun what

was necessary to find Little Pearl in Shanghai; whom she could trust, where she could stay in secret. All these things she said, only to be startled when she finished, for there was no more to say and only one thing left to be done.

"Be strong, big sister," He Yun said, using a familiar term to show friendship. And solidarity. They shared strength and belief in a glorious end.

Rather than confess her waffling thoughts, Shi Po quickly turned He Yun around. "I know where the stillroom is. I know the poison. I am content. Now you must go." When the mistress hesitated, Shi Po pushed her. "Go!" she ordered. Then, on impulse, she added one last instruction: "Unbind her feet. She will need to run!" Then she watched mother and child scurry away.

Then they were gone, hopefully to be safe. But now came Shi Po's part, to her only means of ensuring her sons' lives.

And she couldn't do it. She couldn't force herself to gather the poison, to mix it into a drink and end her life. She just couldn't, because she didn't want to die. And what a strange thought that was.

She had been all too ready to embrace an end a few weeks ago. She'd been intent upon immortality, no matter what the cost. Now that she had an even more compelling reason to act, she'd abruptly discovered that she didn't want to die.

She tried to force herself to go to the stillroom to gather the poison, to have it on hand just in case. Perhaps she would change her mind. Perhaps she would realize that there was no more hope, that Kui Yu's plan had failed. That the only prayer for their release would be in her death. Then she would take the poison.

But she still couldn't make her feet move.

How long had she lived with the dream of suicide? How many stories had she been taught of the glory and honor to be found in such a death? She had been fed them with her first bowl of rice. She had been taught this end as an excellent option from the cradle. And yet, suddenly, she realized she did not believe in the happiness of such a possibility. She wanted to live more than she wanted any honor of dying. She wanted to stay with her husband, to love her children, even to struggle daily for a way to survive, so long as they were all together.

And so, as long as she had breath and will and strength, she would work toward what she wanted: a life with Kui Yu.

She still loved him, she realized. Even if he had given up such foolish and un-Chinese notions. And even if it meant sacrificing the honor of her children, that she could never speak with the Goddess Kwan Yin again, or that she would live a wretched life as Kang's tormented victim, she wanted to live. For and with Kui Yu.

No, she would not die. She would not allow herself the possibility. She turned away from the stillroom and headed for her bedroom and her husband. She would wait there to hear the results of his plan. She would wait for him, and together they would find a way to survive.

Together, in love, and most of all, alive.

*A man bought a piece of paper on which some magic
symbols were written. The seller claimed they had the
power to keep mosquitoes away. When the man
discovered that it didn't work, he complained.*

*"You must have put it in the wrong place," said
the seller.*

"Where's the right place?" the man asked.

"Inside mosquito netting."

Chapter Seventeen

Shi Po hurried back to the room, opened the door,
and was suddenly engulfed. She didn't even tense.
She knew immediately the embrace was Kui Yu, and
she twisted in his arms so that she could hold him
with equal strength and equal desperation.

He buried his face in her hair. "Are you all right?"
he asked, his voice muffled.

"Yes, I'm fine. And the boys are, too. They're
guarded on the other side of the compound, but I
know where they are."

He nodded. "Good. Good." But there was hope-
lessness in his voice. So she pulled back far enough to
look into his eyes. What she saw there frightened her.

"You have given up," she said. She swallowed.
"You have given in to Kang."

His eyes sparked with anger. "Never! Never think
that. I would never . . ." His voice trailed away, as did
his fury. His expression was bleak.

"What happened?" Shi Po asked, and she braced
herself.

"We are to leave tomorrow. For Hong Kong."

She frowned. "Where is that?"

He shrugged. "An island near Canton. We go to see Zou Tun and the white woman, Lydia. That is where—"

"The temple," Shi Po realized. "Kang said they are building a temple there under the protection of the Empress Dowager."

Kui Yu nodded, walking over and half-collapsing onto the bed. "He thinks . . . He is mad. . . . He wants his son back. He wants to win over us—as well as to win over his son." He shook his head. "And he wants to win over the whites."

Shi Po rolled her eyes. "So does everyone. That does not make it happen."

"But . . . he now thinks Lydia is a weapon. That you . . . that you and she have a magical power to control men."

Shi Po could not understand. "There is magic, of a sort. That is the word we use, but not 'weapon'."

"I know, I know. But he does not. He sees everything as assets or liabilities in his war. Us, his son . . ." He gestured the futility of such thinking. "He is a general fighting an enemy he cannot defeat, whom he cannot even comprehend. And now he has lost his son."

Shi Po bit her lip as she understood what her husband was trying to communicate: that General King was helpless and dangerous. "He is looking for a solution, any solution—even it if is magical women," she realized. Then shock chilled her blood. "We are going to have to prove it. He will want to see this magic or . . ." Her voice stopped dead. They both knew what would happen if they failed.

"The boys, too," Kui Yu agreed.

301

Shi Po could barely breathe; her mind and spirit felt trapped, compressed into the smallest place—one that even now continued to shrink. "What do we do?" she whispered.

Her husband's voice caught as he pulled her into his arms. "I have an idea. But . . ." He took a deep breath. "But it is uncertain. Can you think of any others?"

She nearly laughed out loud. "Husband, *you* are the one who thinks up options."

He shook his head, defeated, but she felt him smile as he pressed a kiss to her forehead. "What of Kang's mistress? Does she offer any help"

"Gone. I sent her to Little Pearl. Her disappearance will distract the General. I thought it might help with your plans."

She felt his body tighten with frustration. "My plans have failed. Your brother and my messenger to the Emperor—they can't help us. I do not believe the messages got through. Kang must have intercepted them."

Shi Po sighed and nodded. "They were good ideas, but we cannot depend on them." She shifted. "Is there another way to attack General Kang? To convince him or hurt him?"

Kui Yu thought in silence, then shook his head. "I do not believe so. I know of no weakness. I have but my one idea."

She agreed. She could think of nothing, either. "What is your plan, Kui Yu?"

Her husband took a deep breath, using the motion to tug her closer against him. He tucked her head nearer his shoulder. "We need help for it," he finally said. "We cannot accomplish it on our own."

Shi Po nodded. "Of course. But who?"

"The goddess Kwan Yin."

Shi Po stilled, and the pressure on her chest increased. Her breath became shallow and her heartbeat sped up, but she somehow managed to speak, her voice barely loud enough to hear. "You wish to seek her? Now? Through . . . practice?"

"Do you know of a better way to speak directly with Kwan Yin?" he asked. "To *know* she hears us?"

Shi Po shook her head. "But we may not make it to Heaven. She may not choose to appear. She—"

"Such is always the case with prayer," he interrupted.

"But . . . *now?*"

"The boys are safe. We leave tomorrow for Hong Kong. What other time do we have?"

"But . . ." She could not phrase her objection. Instead, shifting to face her husband, she found her mind completely blank.

"No!" he ordered, and his hands tightened to prevent her from moving. "I do not want you to reflect back my thoughts. Do not be a mirror, Shi Po."

She blinked, startled that he understood what had been going on. Her actions had been unconscious.

"You are the Tigress, Shi Po. I am merely a novice in this. Do you think we can do it? Do you think—"

"I have just resolved not to die!" she cried. Then she gasped, startled and confused.

He was confused as well, obviously, because this time he let her pull away, even pushed her back so that he could look into her eyes. "I am most pleased to hear that," he said slowly. "That is excellent news. So . . . why are you distressed?"

She threw up her hands to cover her face. "Don't

ask me questions! I don't have any answers. I—" She swallowed. She didn't know what she thought. She didn't know anything anymore.

Then she felt his caress: both hands, large and gentle, moving up and down her arms. Her body relaxed. She uncurled a little and allowed him to pull her hands from her face.

He pressed his month to her nose—the closest he could come to her lips. "Do not think so hard, Shi Po. Only tell me what you are feeling."

She shook her head, and words flowed out of her as water through a crack in the ground. "I don't know. I just . . . decided I don't want to die." She lifted her gaze to meet his. "I want to be . . . with you."

This time, he had full access to her mouth. This time he could catch her lips with his, and she clung to him until he stopped kissing her. He pulled back again to look into her eyes. She knew he wanted to know more of her feelings, but she shook her head. She didn't understand and couldn't explain, not yet. But more importantly, she didn't want to remember—not who she was, or what she'd wanted to be. She only wanted him and their life together. It was freeing and terrifying at the same time. She kept her lips pressed firmly closed, and his expression became resigned. "You are right," he finally said. "This is not the time."

She nodded, grateful for the excuse.

"But we still need help for my plan," he said. "And we have only until morn—"

His words were cut off by her kiss. He wished to practice? He needed to speak with Kwan Yin? She would do it. She would do whatever he wished. She would help him succeed.

"No." He pushed away, his frustration clear. "Tigress Shi Po, be honest. Can this be done? Can we speak to Kwan Yin? Now? Like this? You seemed hesitant before."

"If I say no, what will we do?" She asked.

He sighed. "We will try to escape."

"With the boys?"

He nodded.

"But won't the General be expecting such a move?" Shi Po asked.

Again her husband nodded, and his expression was grim. "Yes. And killing us would be one victory he craves. In his mind, he would believe it proves that those of your religion are charlatans, and he would feel he had the evidence he needs to move against the white woman, Lydia."

"He wants to regain his son," she agreed. "We cannot allow that to happen. And we cannot risk our sons."

Kui Yu didn't answer, but she could see the agreement in his face.

Shi Po reached to unfasten the clasps of the gown. "We will go see Kwan Yin," she pronounced. "We will beg for her help."

Kui Yu's eyes darkened, fixed on the fabric of the gown that began to slip open over her breasts. "So, it can be done?"

Shi Po merely shrugged. "It can be attempted. I can promise no more than that. Except . . ." Her hands stilled, and she was surprised by her thought. Indeed, it was so unlike her, unlike what she'd been taught, she wondered if it had truly come from her own mind.

"Except?" he prompted.

She met his gaze and allowed her puzzlement to shine through. "Except a woman in love can do many things." She straightened. "I love you. And I love my sons. Perhaps I—"

"We," he interrupted. "We can do many things with love."

She looked at him, ecstatic, then knew he had not said what she wanted. He had said "with love" not "in love." And yet, perhaps she didn't need the words. Perhaps her love alone was enough.

"I heard you speaking with Ru Shan," he suddenly said. "When you wrote his name on the list of Immortals."

She nodded. Not only had she written his name, but his white woman's name as well: Joanna Crane. That had been the beginning of this whole crazy time.

"He said that it was love that took him to Heaven, that love launched them both to the Immortal realm."

Shi Po nodded. She'd been afraid to believe it was true, and still was. She was worried that he was about to explain her failure to gain immortality as a lack of love. But he surprised her.

"Zou Tun and Lydia," her husband continued, "they attained immortality together. A man would have to be greatly in love with a woman to defy his father and give up an Empire." His eyes narrowed. "He could have been Emperor, but he gave that up to be with her."

Shi Po looked at Kui Yu. "You think it is love that completes the process," she prompted. "You think—"

"I love you." Her husband rushed the words out as if he could not bear to have them on his tongue.

Shi Po closed her eyes, her spirit shrinking.

"Lies will not serve us now, Kui Yu. Partners require honesty."

He was silent for a long time, long enough for her to grow concerned. Long enough for her to finally lift her gaze back to him. Only then did he speak.

"It is no lie, Shi Po."

She didn't dare argue with him, especially as he pressed his finger to her lips. He held it there while his other hand unfastened the rest of her gown. She had loosened the part that curved over her breast. He continued to free the fabric at her waist, then down along her hip, until it slipped open completely. She had not been given underclothing, so she was naked beneath the silk. The sudden rush of air was chilling.

Until, of course, his lips began to kiss her neck, her collarbone, and then slipped lower between her breasts. Only then did her husband begin to speak, his tone nostalgic. "You are nothing that I expected when I married you," he said.

He pressed her backward onto bed, sliding one hand over her left breast while his lips teased the skin on the right.

"I craved beauty. I saw your pointed breasts and creamy complexion, and nightly I dreamed of holding you in this way."

His hand began to move. He lifted and molded her breast until he squeezed the nipple. Yin surged inside her, strong enough to make her legs tremble. Her breast swelled, and the yin power of it pressed against his hand, seeking to connect with his yang.

"How I longed to taste you." His head descended to her other breast, and his tongue circled her nipple. Then, while she held her breath, he began to suck, drawing the pebbled peak inside his mouth, toying and nibbling while her entire chest began to throb.

He pulled back, drawing her breast with him, stretching her in a way that lengthened the power cord between her belly and breast, womb and nipple. It stretched her, and her yin vibrated harder, higher, faster—until he released her flesh and spoke again.

"After we married, I discovered that you had a mind: a strange and alien thing that twisted ideas in the most bizarre fashion."

She opened her eyes, startled. "I am . . . alien?"

He grinned. "Alien-brilliant. Genius is strange, I have learned, and a woman's genius even more so."

He sat up straighter and set both hands on her breasts, shifting and manipulating her yin power. He even emphasized his words with occasional squeezes or pinches that sent white-hot flashes through her body.

"I could not believe a woman had such intelligence. And yet, you do. Such a mind you have, I have had to stretch and strain to match you."

He leaned down to press reverent kisses to her breasts.

"I am smarter when I am with you," he said. He looked up and met her stunned eyes. "Believe me, I was shocked as well. But remember how quickly after we wed I came to ask your advice, to introduce you to business partners and to benefit from your opinion."

"I thought you were showing me your accomplishments, proving to me that I had made a worthy selection in a husband," she said.

He grinned. "It was that, too. But always I watched your reaction, always I asked your opinion."

"You mean, I always told you what I thought, whether you asked it or not. And whether in words or not."

He grinned and nipped again at her breasts. First the left, then the right, then back to the oh-so-wonderful left. "That, too, is part of your brilliance. And mine."

Her breath was unsteady now, and her belly quivered with rising yin. Then Kui Yu let his hands slip down her sides. They flowed around Shi Po's breasts, tightened along her waist, then flared over her hips and stopped. He held her there, keeping her still though she wanted to press closer to him, to move in rhythmic waves against him.

"You were so small, so delicate. I thought you the image of femininity, of the exquisite and the unattainable perfection that is the ideal." He scoffed. "A poetic heart was ever my downfall."

Shi Po nodded. "My hips are too wide, my legs too thick. Even my feet are large and badly formed," she said.

He tilted his head, looking down at her, as if considering her words. He shifted his hands to span her waist, then moved lower to measure her hips. He even slid them down to gauge the thickness of her thighs. He shook his head. "Your body is slim and delicate and beautiful," he finally stated. "But it is the strength in you that is so appealing." He laughed. "After all, I am a large man. I would not want to break you with my passion."

His good humor infused and warmed her, and she laughed too, surprised she could do so while her legs were drenched with yin rain. She was startled that the laughter enhanced the yin tide rather than stifled it. "You could not break me, Kui Yu," she chided. "You have ever been gentle."

Amazingly enough, he continued to laugh. "Not always, my wife." Then he abruptly lifted her leg away and pushed his thumb deep inside her. His eyes drifted shut in appreciation. She gasped, arching at the invasion, but spreading wider to allow him to deepen his presence. And as she moved, she heard him growl low in his throat. "Yes," he murmured, as much to himself as to her. "Oh, how I have missed your strength."

She felt her giggles continue. "This is not strength, Kui Yu. This is . . ." What was this comfortableness, this wonder in each other's bodies? Love?

He opened his eyes, continuing to move his thumb inside her. It twisted while the rest of his hand flowed around her, caressing every part he could reach. "I am always stronger when I am with you," he said. "And not only this way. . . ." He bent his first finger and rubbed its knuckle up and down over her yin pearl. She gasped as the yin tide roared through her.

"No, this is only strength of body," he said. "But when we join this way, when we touch each other"—he shook his head, obviously frustrated with words—"I am stronger. I gain from you. Together, we are unbeatable."

She frowned and thought. Could their spirits truly strengthen each other in mind in body? Could that happen from such contact as they now shared? More importantly, was it enough to defeat Kang? Enough to save their children? She reached out, needing to touch Kui Yu. She found his thigh and the corded muscles there. Without thought, she moved her hand higher, searching for his dragon, wanting his yang power in her hand.

And yet, she still doubted. "Do you truly believe that? That we are unbeatable together?"

He stilled his thumb, and she released a soft whimper. "I . . . ," he began. Then he shook his head. "I *feel* it, Shi Po. Whether it is true or not, I feel it inside." He abruptly withdrew his hand from her body, and she sat upright with the sudden loss. "When we were apart, when you denied me this"—he sighed—"I was weak, aimless, and easily distracted. I looked for a substitute."

Her gaze dropped. She did not want to bring

310

thoughts of his white friend Lily into this moment. But he raised her chin with his finger so that she looked directly into his eyes.

"I was wrong. We need each other, Shi Po. And there is no substitute." His words became a vow: "*I will never look elsewhere again. I swear it.*"

And she believed him, for he had never lied to her. "Nor I," she whispered.

He lowered his head, kissing first her belly, then lower down, trailing over her hipbones into the hair that had regrown over her tigress tattoo. She tensed, fearing he would be revolted, but he didn't pause. Indeed, he tongued her. He teased and tasted every part of her as he slowly, inevitably made his way down the tigress's neck to Shi Po's yin pearl.

But he didn't complete his motion, did not kiss her where she most wanted. He lifted his head, waiting until she met his gaze. He spoke:

"When we married, I could not possibly believe that a woman would make me feel complete. I wanted one—*you*—but she was a family name, a beauty, and an idea. But all those things were merely in complement to me." He shook his head. "I was such a fool. To read all that poetry and not understand any of it! To think that a woman—a wife—could exist outside of who I am is foolishness. I love you, and finally that love fills me with power."

She nodded. How could she not? It was true from her side as well. Kui Yu was part of her, and together, they were so much more.

"I love you," she said.

"And I love you," he repeated. Then he used his hands to open her body even wider. She trembled at his adjustments. She strained toward him, hungering for more as the yin tide pounded through her body.

"Kui Yu," she begged. "Let us climb to Heaven. Now."

But he denied her. "You must do something else for me first."

She lifted up onto her elbows, trying to see him better. "What?"

"You must laugh, my wife."

She blinked. She could not possibly have heard him correctly.

"You must laugh for me as you did when our children were born. As you did in prison."

She gaped at him.

"When you laugh, your entire body is set free. Your spirit. You release your desperate pain, your cares, your—"

"Earthly ties?" she asked.

He grinned. "Yes, exactly. You become free, Shi Po. I think it is the only time you fully release your spirit."

She snorted at that. He had again descended into bad poetics, and yet the humor of his words and wishes shimmered inside her: she had no other word for it. The thought, the laughter, it all sparkled inside her like a tiny jewel transmuted from fear and pain and confusion.

How she could laugh now, she had no idea. The same way, perhaps, that they could be making love the night before their possible execution. Whatever the reason, she did laugh. And the wonder of it all expanded inside her until that glitter of amusement became a light and the light became pure joy.

She laughed. And as Shi Po's body shook with happiness, Kui Yu dipped his head. His tongue found her yin pearl, his thumbs thrust inside her, and her trembling increased the yin. The surging power welled inside her, twisting her body in the jumping dance of a mature Tigress. She cried out in joy, her breath no longer able to sustain her mirth. Her body was contracting, shifting, riding the Tigress, but she didn't attempt Heaven yet. She knew she could not do what she must, not alone. She needed a partner. She needed her husband.

He understood. She watched him strip off his clothing with efficient speed. His dragon was already fully extended, flushed a dark and hungry red. She gripped his hips with her feet, and opened herself to him, and together they positioned him at the entrance to her cinnabar cave. The Tigress was tiring, the yin tide ebbing, so it was easier for him to settle upon her hips. But still he would not enter her.

"Kui Yu!" she gasped.

"Laugh," he answered.

"I cannot!" she gasped. She had no breath for more.

But he looked into her eyes and spoke. "I love you, and you love me," he said.

"Yes." Then it came again: The shimmer. The light. The joy. And she laughed. His dragon pushed a small way into her cave. She arched, wanting more, but he grabbed hold of her hips and kept her still.

"Again," he whispered.

"You are a foolish man," she chided.

He slipped his thumb down the Tigress's belly and rubbed her yin pearl. Her gasp ended on a giggle. And he pressed himself a little farther in. Again, he caressed her pearl, grinning as she cried out. He deepened his thrust when she turned her exclamation into a laugh.

"I love that sound," he murmured.

Then he was fully inside her, and she threw back her head. The yin tide exploded around Shi Po again, but this time she was not alone. This time he was with her as he pulled back and thrust in. He reached forward and took hold of her breasts. His movements were clumsy, but effective nonetheless.

He squeezed once, twice, and the yin circle began. It flowed from her breasts into his hands, into him. And with every thrust of his hips, every push of his dragon, he increased the flow, making the circle stronger. Wilder.

He was working hard, his breath coming in heavy pants. She helped as best she could. She gripped him with her legs, pulling him inside her again and again and again.

"Laugh!" he ordered.

She did, almost howling with delight.

"Again!"

She did. The sound filled the room, and the larger yang circle began. It made no sense to Shi Po, and yet she felt it. With every giggle, with every gasping sound of joy and light and love, the yang poured into her. Her breath drew it in. Her laughter encouraged it, and Kui Yu completed the journey.

His yang rushed down to meet her yin. Her yin rushed up to meet his yang. Two circles, two spirits, two chances at immortality.

Two spirits, two bodies.

One spirit, one body.

Heaven?

*Once a man was punished and paraded through the
streets for stealing. A friend saw him and asked what
happened.*

*"Bad luck!" the man replied. "I saw a rope on the
ground and thought to take it home."*

*"But why did they punish you so severely for such
a small thing?" his friend asked.*

*"Because I didn't see there was a cow at the other
end of the rope."*

Chapter Eighteen

Shi Po recognized where she'd landed; indeed, she'd
visited this room many times—first in reality, then in
her nightmares. But never had she expected to find
this instead of the Chamber of a Thousand Swinging
Lanterns.

Nonetheless, here she was, back in her aunt's
house, shocked by the sight of her fifteen-year-old
self lying on her bed. She'd spent a great deal of time
doing that: staring at the ceiling in a house that was
always cold, doing nothing, thinking nothing, being . . . nothing.

"Where are we?" came a voice from beside her: Kui
Yu.

Shi Po jumped, startled to find her husband inside
her nightmare. She had always been alone here. Except for her uncle. But he was different.

What did she say to Kui Yu, who looked about her
dark little room with eyes that missed nothing? And
how did she explain what she'd thought was an

amazing luxury back then: a chamber to herself. And her only task was to help Auntie Ting care for her dying uncle.

"What's this?" Kui Yu asked. He crouched down and extended a hand to a discarded scroll, half unrolled on the floor. He tried to pick it up, but his hand went through it. This was a Heavenly representation, or a bad dream, but either way they were not actually here and so he could not actually touch anything. Thus, in the end, he simply read what was already revealed.

Shi Po felt the cold weight of shame press down on her.

"So, this is when you started," her husband said.

She nodded. Her aunt had given her the Tigress scroll, which detailed exactly how to fellate a man's dragon to gather his yang. There had been no other instruction. She'd simply gotten pictures without context, practice without understanding. She hadn't learned the full truth for years. Not until Kui Yu's building collapsed and she'd had to find money some way. So she had gone back to her aunt, who had hired her to instruct her newest girls in the Tigress secrets. She had not whored, though all accused her of it. She had not been able to stomach the thought.

Thus, she had taught the new girls. She had given them a skill, and meaning to what they were forced to do. And she'd told her husband that Auntie Ting had loaned them the money out of kindness.

In truth it had been a kindness, because as an instructor Shi Po had searched far and wide to find more Tigress texts. She'd discovered that there was a thousand times more to being a Tigress than simple yang harvest. And she'd also learned she had a talent for teaching.

She'd already known she had skill in the practice.

"Where is this place?" Kui Yu asked, looking about the dilapidated house, at the room that had once been sumptuous but was now wretched.

"My aunt and uncle's old home. When he was still alive."

"The uncle that gambled everything away?"

Shi Po nodded, though honesty forced her to defend her uncle in some small measure. "Not everything. His illness took much as well."

"And you were brought in to care for him."

Shi Po nodded, validating the lie. But they were in an ethereal place, not on Earth, and it was not so easy to lie here. So, even as she nodded, her thoughts echoed in the room, were transmitted to her husband.

I was brought in to kill my uncle.

Kui Yu started, and his eyes grew wide with shock. "It is true then? You killed him?"

She nodded, but once again the lie was exposed. But . . . she hadn't even thought it was a lie. *My aunt could not do it alone. She needed my help.*

Kui Yu returned to her side and touched her arm. That filled her with warmth. "Did you know what you were doing?" He grimaced as he gestured to the scroll. "Beyond the obvious, of course."

Yes, she had daily fellated her uncle. Sometimes twice. But she had thought . . .

"My aunt told me it was a gift to my uncle, and his to me. I did not know yang loss could kill. I only knew that I felt stronger afterward, and . . ." She almost laughed at her naïveté. "And that he was happy."

Kui Yu stepped closer to her. "Your aunt brought you here to . . . to suck the life out of your uncle?"

Shi Po felt her shame like a great pressure in her mind. But she had to answer. This was Heaven and Kui Yu could hear her thoughts.

"Auntie Ting married a wastrel. He was from a good family and had a sweet temper, but had no head for business. And he loved gambling. Had he lived, they would have starved."

"Why didn't she just stab him them? Why involve a young girl in such a sick scheme?"

"Because she had no wish for prison. No one knew what we did. No one even guessed. Most thought it was lucky fortune. All knew what kind of man he was."

"So she forced you to see him? She made you do that?" He gestured angrily at the scroll on fellatio.

"It worked. It took no more than a few months. And no one knew any different."

"The bitch!" Kui Yu spat.

As if on cue, the dream bedroom door burst open and Auntie Ting pushed her head in. She was younger, but her hair was already gray. It wasn't until later, with renewed wealth, that she'd dyed it a midnight black.

"He is ready," ordered her aunt.

The image of the fifteen-year-old Shi Po straightened with a sigh, adjusted her clothing and hair, and filed out the door. The real Shi Po closed her eyes, ashamed at her youthful obedience. How pliant she had been, how stupid. Even Kui Yu stared in open shock, voicing the question she'd constantly asked herself.

"Didn't you object? You were a gently reared girl. You couldn't possibly have thought this was acceptable!"

Shi Po shrugged, but her thoughts again projected

clearly into the room. *I knew it was wrong. I cried. I even fought the first few times. But . . .* How to explain? She didn't even understand it herself.

"You were a child," Kui Yu said. "To whom would you complain? Your parents had given you to your aunt. And your father . . ."

"Would have thrown me out of both houses if he knew."

Kui Yu went on, "Better to keep it silent. Better to do as she asked."

Shi Po nodded, swallowing the lie. But she should have fought more. She should have thought harder, found a different answer; there were always alternatives for a resourceful person. But she had been young and stupid. She had simply accepted what she was told and prayed to Kwan Yin for an answer, for the goddess to swoop down and save her.

"I got what I wanted," she said to no one in particular, ignoring the twinge of pain in her heart. "I just didn't realize that the Goddess works in her own ways."

Kui Yu studied her, and his eyes narrowed. "Why are we here, Shi Po?" he asked.

She shook her head, not knowing the answer. Unless . . . "You want the same magical answer as I did, Kui Yu. You want Kwan Yin to save us, but she doesn't work that way."

He frowned, his attention drawn to where her younger self walked down the hallway. "What happened? Where are you going?"

Did he really want to know? Did he really need to see this?

Apparently he did, because no sooner had his question been asked than the answer appeared. The images shifted, and there was the young Shi Po walking into her uncle's bedroom. And Kui Yu watched in interest, gazing about the room.

The last of her uncle's wealth had been lavished here. His bed was thick, the rugs plush. Even the chair he sat in was large and elegantly carved, in the way of an Emperor's throne. And yet, her uncle seemed dwarfed by the seat, small and tiny in a silken shroud that he called his "smoking jacket" in the manner of the white barbarians.

Shi Po felt her stomach heave. How could she not know? How could she not see what she was doing to this kind-hearted man?

She glanced at her husband, who tilted his head to inspect her uncle. Though he was dying, her uncle still smiled warmly at the young Shi Po, and extended a small and withered hand to caress her hair.

"It is time for my medicine already?" he asked. Then he laughed at his own joke, the humor ending in a coughing wheeze. And she—stupid child that she was—hadn't even understood: What she'd done wasn't medicine; what she'd done was murder.

There she was, nodding her head like an imbecile. "Yes, uncle. The doctor said twice a day at least." But then the dream Shi Po frowned, showing that some part of her had wondered, that somewhere inside had been a spark of intelligence. "But are you sure it helps? Are you sure it makes you—"

"Absolutely," he said. "It is the most wonderful medicine ever." Then he waved her over and patted his lap in invitation. "But we needn't start immediately. Come, come, tell me what you did today."

So the young Shi Po went to him. She sat on his lap while he fondled her breasts and kissed her neck. She spoke of silly things: of shopping and the garden, of making tea and learning spices.

He had been the only one to listen to her, the only one who encouraged her interest in herbs. How she had blossomed under his rapt attention. How animated she became when she spoke. She didn't even mind when he touched her body, because he told her it helped him prepare for his medicine.

"Stop!" the older Shi Po ordered as she always did at this point. "Stop it now!" But it never ended. Instead, both uncle and youth stared at her, their dream mouths open in a kind of horror. But the horror was not enough to stop his hands.

She knew what came next. Hadn't she dreamed it often enough? Hadn't she lived through the nightmare time and time again? Why did she have to do it again now? With Kui Yu watching?

It continued as it always did. Without any volition on her part, she stepped forward. The younger Shi Po slipped off her uncle's lap, smiled sweetly and vapidly at her older self, then calmly walked out of the room. Beside her, Kui Yu frowned and tried to step in front of her.

"What are you doing?" he asked.

She felt her chest compress into a tight ball. She barely had enough breath to answer. "What I must. What I *did*," she answered.

And so it always was in her dream. Her younger self was saved, while the older one knelt before her uncle and gently separated his robe. Her uncle's dragon stood up as much as it ever did. And shouldn't that have told her younger self something? Shouldn't she have seen the clues, instead of just using the extra Tigress techniques for sluggish dragons?

But she'd thought it was medicine. She was told that her uncle had too much yang, which had to be purged daily. So she'd believed it was a service, a task as necessary as bathing the infirm or leeching a poison.

Shi Po bent herself to her task. With hand and tongue, she was an expert. That her husband watched was an added horror, but also a great relief. Finally he would know why she'd fought him so hard, why she had stopped drawing out his yang after their second son was born.

Though it took forever, eventually her uncle neared his release. His dragon was stiff and red, his breath a rapid pant. Shi Po closed her eyes. She envisioned the yang energy that built in the dragon's belly, and readied herself to draw it out, to accept what was to come.

She hadn't understood it then, but now she knew that his fondling had brought her yin tide to a heightened level. That the smaller circle was already established—it came so easily to the young. And that once his yang explosion came, that would be enough.

Nearly there. A moment more.

She prepared to receive her uncle's gift, to draw off what she'd been told was excess yang. And when it came . . .

Around her, the room disappeared. Her uncle's dilapidated house faded, and out stepped the young Shi Po into the Chamber of a Thousand Swinging Lanterns.

Young Shi Po walked in awe, breathed the Heavenly air, and laughed in delight. Such joy was in her heart as she danced and twirled in time with the Heavenly music. She knew nothing of where she was, of course. Only that there was a rich reward for those with enough yin and yang in combination.

It was Kwan Yin who explained it to her. As Kui Yu watched, the Goddess joined the ecstatic dream Shi

Po and told her they stood in the antechamber to Heaven. That there was so much more available if she wanted. If she was strong enough.

"I am!" the little one cried. "I will do anything to stay here!"

The young one hadn't seen the sadness etched on the Goddess's face. She was too busy laughing in delight, bubbling with the excitement that was Heaven. But the older Shi Po understood. She was the one who remained behind with her uncle.

He had toppled over as the last of his yang left him. There must have been some sign that he had died, some stiffening or jerking of his body. But if there was, Shi Po had confused it with the necessary muscle contractions of yang expulsion. She had not known what was happening, had not realized that he was dead, tipped forward to pin her beneath him, crouched between his legs and pressed against the hard wooden chair.

Behind her, Shi Po heard Kui Yu curse, but there was little he could do, and little time for him to do it. She knew from long repetition that the younger Shi Po would soon return. That there would be eons for the child to sit there, trapped and dazed from her Heavenly journey. Long moments of struggle would occur as she came back to herself only to think that her uncle was sleeping. That he might possibly . . . But he couldn't have . . . But he was so still and cold.

Eventually, she would call out. In time, she would gather her courage enough to yell for her aunt. And then another eternity would pass before the woman came to laugh and giggle in relief: Her torment was over; her wastrel husband was dead.

All the while, Auntie Ting would tug and push on her husband. But she was a small woman with little physical strength, and it would take her a long time to free the young Shi Po.

"Come out of there," Kui Yu ordered from beside her. Shi Po opened her eyes, her view obscured by her uncle's thin legs. But even at her canted angle, she could still see her husband where he stood beside them in the dream, ineffectively tugging at first her uncle, then at her. But he had insubstantial hands and they slipped through everything.

"Come out!" he said, a touch of desperation in his voice.

"No," Shi Po answered softly. "Let the young one stay in Heaven as long as possible. Let her dance a little longer." There would be plenty of time for understanding later.

"She's not real, Shi Po. Come out."

"No. I always stay here as long as I can. For her."

"Shi Po!" He appeared beside her. How he came to be directly before her eyes, she didn't understand, but he was there, and horror darkened his eyes.

So she shut her own; she didn't want to see. "You should go on," she said. "Talk to Kwan Yin. I will be fine here."

"Shi Po . . ." His voice was strangled. Softer, gentler, he added, "I'm not leaving you." She felt him touch her face. How he managed it when she was still trapped, she didn't know. But he stroked her cheek, and the warmth of his flesh spread through her. It provided a tiny circle of heat where the rest of her was cold and numb from compression.

"I understand now," he said. She couldn't see his face; her eyes were still closed, but she heard the compassion in his voice. "I understand now why death and Heaven are so intertwined in your mind."

She frowned, wondering what he meant.

"But it is not always true," he continued. "You can reach Heaven without death. That is what the Tigresses teach, isn't it?"

She didn't answer. She knew the teachings. Indeed, she had banners to that effect, poetry memorized to remind her students of just that truth. And yet . . .

"You never believed it, did you? Because of this. You knew that Heaven existed because you felt it, because you went there." In the background, she could still hear her younger self laughing, the sound full of innocent joy.

"But for you," her husband continued, "it always meant death."

"Great achievement requires great sacrifice," she said.

"Very true," Kui Yu responded. "But that does not mean it requires death."

She didn't answer. How could she, when she wasn't sure? Ever since her uncle's death, she had believed immortality required death. She had simply been fortunate enough to be available when her uncle passed on; otherwise, she never would have experienced Heaven. And even then she'd only seen the antechamber and not the true Immortal realm.

That was why she taught but did not practice any longer. It was why she went to the antechamber but not inside. And she had been content with that. Until Ru Shan and his white woman gained the Heavenly portals without dying. And now Zou Tun and his woman as well. How could they do such a thing without a death? It wasn't possible. And yet, they claimed to have succeeded.

"Step out, Shi Po," said her husband. "We do not need to die to speak to Kwan Yin."

She didn't believe him. Perhaps her mind did, but

in her heart, she didn't think it was possible. So she remained exactly where she was: compressed, trapped, barely able to breathe.

She felt Kui Yu's hand slide away. It had been a single press of warmth against her cheek, but now he moved. His hands separated, and she felt him on either side of her neck, then her shoulders. And still he continued touching her, moving down her arms to finally grab hold of her hands.

"Come to me, my wife," he ordered gently. "You can move a little. Believe that you can step out from under this atrocity."

She shook her head. "But then the young one will have to take my place."

"No," he answered firmly. "No one will be there. No one needs be there at all anymore."

When he said it, she could believe. And yet, she still hesitated.

"You said I give you other options," he pressed. "Believe in this one. Make the choice to believe."

And because he was holding her, because she loved him enough to want to please him, she did as he asked: She chose to believe. "No one," she whispered, willing it to be true. "No one need be here, pinned beneath a dead man."

"You will step away and be free."

She prayed it was true. She chose to believe it was true.

"Open your eyes."

She did. And saw swinging lanterns. She was still crouched down, but everything of Earth had faded. Her uncle and his home were gone. Kui Yu tugged on her arms, urging her to stand.

She did, though it felt difficult on numb legs. "I cannot feel anything," she said. Except, she could.

She could feel his hands around hers, his warmth expanding through her. Because she wanted it, and so she willed it to be.

She straightened to her full height. She couldn't do it by herself. He had to help her. He took hold of her elbows and lifted. It didn't work at first. Not until she looked into his eyes. Not until she chose to believe he could make it possible. Only then did she straighten. Only then did she know how good it felt to stand tall. Even better, in the distance, she could see her younger self still dancing. She could feel the excitement that filled the girl as it expanded to her.

She began to laugh.

It was a strange thing to laugh just then, but such was her liberation that she could not stop herself. Indeed, it felt as if she had been stuck beneath her uncle her entire life. Until now. Until her husband gave her another option.

"I love you," she said, though the words were inadequate to the feelings flowing through her.

"And I you," he answered as he drew her into his arms.

He held her, and she him. Together in love and most awesome joy. And then, they turned to watch the younger Shi Po dance. Except, she wasn't there anymore. In her place stood Kwan Yin, whose celestial eyes were filled with happiness, whose sweet face was joyous as she gestured behind her.

The gates of Heaven were open. What had been black space with swinging lights now became an open doorway into light, and from which emanated the sweetest music, felt more than heard, known more than experienced.

"Welcome," said Kwan Yin. "We are most pleased that you could come."

Kui Yu started forward immediately, but he stopped when he found himself alone. Shi Po couldn't force herself to move, though she had worked so hard for this very moment. She held back, and so restrained Kui Yu, and the Goddess as well.

"If we go through there, if we walk into Heaven . . ."

"Yes?" asked Kwan Yin.

"Will we die?"

"Do you wish to die?"

Shi Po shook her head, her denial immediate. "No, I don't. Not yet." She looked at her husband. "I want to live with Kui Yu."

"Then so it will be."

And so it was. She knew it then. The moment she allowed herself to believe it was true, she stepped onward. The gates of Heaven rushed forward and engulfed her in such wonder as she had not thought possible. She was in Heaven. She was an Immortal. As was Kui Yu.

"We did it!" she breathed, looking at her beloved. "We did it together."

He grinned, but his expression faded as he looked about them. He didn't seem frightened, just confused. His brows drew together. Shi Po turned as well, to absorb the glory that was Heaven: wonder, awe, peace, and most especially love. All were in abundance. Surrounding them, suffusing them. As it suffused everyone around.

People were everywhere, dozens of people. Her grandparents, long gone of a fever. Her younger sister, who had died at the same time. Her neighbors, who had been so kind. Her other neighbors, who had not been so kind. Even her uncle. All stood around her, all smiling and waving before wandering off on their business.

Shi Po stared. "They are all Immortals?" she breathed.

Kwan Yin answered, "All come here once they die on Earth, but then separate to their own tasks, their own work. They simply gathered here to greet you."

"But . . . but . . . ," she stammered. How could those people be here? They weren't trained as Tigresses or Dragons. They were just people who had died.

"We come and go," whispered Kui Yu beside her.

"But they—"

"They are here," answered Kwan Yin. Then she turned to him. "They came to greet you so you will know and not fear."

He shifted his gaze from his parents to the Goddess. "Know what?" he asked.

"This is where all come before they move on." Kwan Yin looked at Shi Po. "Tigress or dragon, emperor or peasant, all come here. To Heaven."

"And then move on," repeated Shi Po, her mind racing with the implications. "Then . . . all are Immortal."

The Goddess nodded. "Though few visit while still living."

"Then I was right! Death would have taken me here, to Heaven."

The Goddess smiled. "Of course. But you have studied hard. You can and should return to your bodies. *Now.*"

And with the word, Shi Po began to fall. Beside her, she heard Kui Yu gasp in surprise as he too began his descent. Unlike her, he fought it. He called out, he reached for the Goddess.

"No!" he cried. "We need your help. We are in danger. Our sons will be killed. Goddess, please!"

But their descent did not slow. If anything, Kui Yu's panic only increased it. Still, the Goddess remained close enough to smile and speak to them. "That is why they came to greet you," she reminded him. "So you understand."

"But you must save us!"

She was fading, but the Goddess's words came to them clearly. "Save you from what? Heaven awaits. What is there to fear?"

Then it was over. Their descent became a plummet until they reached their bodies. Then, like stones tossed off a path, they dropped into their flesh with jarring impact. Shi Po woke with a groan. Kui Yu woke with a curse. Even before Shi Po found the strength to do more than breathe, Kui Yu pushed himself upright, and his voice grew strong as he threw off the vestiges of Heaven.

"We must go back! She must understand!"

"She did understand," Shi Po answered. "I told you, Heaven responds according to its own rules. It is not for us to question." Though she did have many questions. As did Kui Yu.

"But she has to help us. She has to—"

"She doesn't have to do anything," Shi Po snapped, her irritation at the situation spilling over to her husband. "I tried to explain that to you before."

"But she has to help us. Our sons—" He cut off his words, and she too blinked away tears.

"Heaven awaits them," she murmured. "We must find our own way or find peace in that." Then she lost her battle against tears. They flowed freely as she shook in silent misery. They were all going to die.

"We must go back," Kui Yu repeated. "She must help us."

Shi Po shook her head. They could not attempt it

again. Not so soon after ascending. Neither of them had the energy. Both yin and yang were depleted. She could feel the hollowness of her exhausted body. Kui Yu must feel the same. Indeed, one look at his ashen face told her it was true.

He knew they couldn't return. He knew they were doomed.

"How soon?" he demanded as he grabbed her cold hands. He drew them tight to his chest. "When can we try again?"

She knew what he was thinking. They were to travel to Hong Kong to demonstrate their power. There were a few days yet. Perhaps they could manage again. Perhaps, if they said the right things . . .

"We could try," she began. From what she'd read, usually it took many months, sometimes years, before another successful trip could be made to Heaven. But she and Kui Yu had ascended three times now, and in a short period of time. Perhaps . . .

She shook her head. "Do not expect the Goddess's answer to be different. If we are destined to die, then—" She cut herself off.

But Kui Yu was adamant. "She didn't understand. She has to save our sons. She has to stop Kang."

Shi Po curled into herself. She drew up her knees to support her bowed head. Kui Yu was a man, and therefore had not been taught submission to Heaven's will. Even when given a clear answer from a Goddess, he still struggled to achieve the ends he wanted.

"Goddesses do not respond to our will, Kui Yu," she murmured helplessly. Was it weakness to accept what Heaven ordained?

"She just didn't understand. She just . . ." His voice trailed away. She could not see his face, for hers was buried in her arms, her tears sliding down her skin and onto the bedding. And as the silence stretched, she knew he began to understand. The Goddess had refused to intervene. There would be no divine rescue.

She felt his hand on her back, and his warmth slipped around her. Without thought, she leaned into his body, needing his strength to support herself.

Many times she had returned from the Heavenly antechamber to descend into tears. The loss of joy was extreme, the heaviness of Earth exhausting to the heart and body; tears were a natural result of such strain. Never had she thought to cry after becoming an Immortal, though. She had thought . . . She had assumed that such a being was beyond pain, had grown past Earthly cares.

How wrong she'd been.

She felt a wetness upon her forehead, a steady fall of tears from her husband's eyes. His, too, were silent. Like with her, the experience, the frustration, the overflow of emotions were too much for him to contain. They had to be expressed somehow. In anger. In laughter. In tears. And yet, it shook Shi Po to the core to know her strong husband wept.

She uncoiled enough to wrap her arms around him, to support him. And together, they straightened their bodies, lay back down in bed with their hearts and flesh intertwined.

"She has to help us. She has to understand," Kui Yu murmured into her hair. But there was no more anger in his tone, only a steely determination.

He was clearly working on a plan. He was thinking and struggling and still trying to bend all to his will. He did not understand. And yet, Shi Po cherished him all the more for his fight. She envied him his strength, and would do all she could to support him in his struggle. Because she loved him, and because she loved her children. Because she loved, she would defy Fate.

They did not sleep that night. They remained wrapped in each other's arms. And together, they found the strength to go on.

*A soldier on night patrol met a man on the street past
curfew. The man explained he was a student
returning from a late class. The soldier said, "If
you're a student, let me quiz you."*

*The student waited for a question, but no matter
how much the soldier racked his brains, he couldn't
think of any.*

*"What luck," the man cried with schoolboy joy.
"No examination tonight!"*

Chapter Nineteen

The morning dawned cold and clear. Shi Po and Kui
Yu were given warm clothes, but no weapons, were
allowed to see their children but not speak to them.
Then soldiers led them to horses, that they were not
allowed to mount. Instead, everyone stood in the
shivering dawn air and waited.

Shi Po huddled close to her beast for warmth, while
her ears strained to hear the soldiers' gossip. Apparently General Kang was in a furious mood. Sometime
the day before, his Han mistress had disappeared
with his bastard daughter. Kang had not only been
denied an evening of physical release but now he had
to leave on a long trip to Hong Kong where his passions would likely build to an even more difficult
level. The men in his personal guard were not looking forward to the next few weeks; their only hope,
they said, was in some miracle that might happen on
some desolate rock island. And with the practicality

of soldiers, they all sighed morosely. No one in China expected miracles.

Their only joy came in discussing the woman they had used the night before. Shi Po gathered from their crude comments that Auntie Ting had not survived the night. She tried to dredge up some feeling at the news—guilt, sadness, anything at all—but only emptiness echoed in her heart. Then she shifted her attention back to her own situation.

Shi Po moved away from her horse and the sour-smelling man who would be riding it with her on his lap. "I must speak with Mrs. Kang," she said firmly. She wasn't exactly sure what she intended; she only knew that the poisoned atmosphere of the Kang home had to change. The Kang family was too powerful to allow it to remain sick. After all, General Kang was China's great hope against white invasion. If he grew ill or unbalanced, who would protect China?

Perhaps she could explain this to Mrs. Kang. After all, there were ways to entice a wandering man back into one's arms, ways known to a Tigress. And Shi Po could write a letter to a Tigress in Peking introducing Mrs. Kang as a new student. Should she desire enlightenment.

Then, perhaps, the whole household would rebalance itself. Mrs. Kang would have her husband back, and General Kang would release his excess yang. If that happened, then there might be room for his gentler nature to shine through. Which would . . .

Be too late for herself or her children. She and Kui Yu would already be dead, but perhaps it would save someone else. Shi Po sighed. What else could she to do but stand in the cold, freezing her face and fingers? At least this way, she would get inside for a few moments.

Her guard allowed her to go. He had no fears she would escape, for they still had her sons. Meanwhile, when Kui Yu made to join her, his guard wasn't so forgiving. He was barred from her side, so she would have to act alone. But she didn't know what she going to do, anyway, besides step out of the wind.

There were guards huddled inside the second house gate. They gestured with their chins when she asked for Mrs. Kang, and so Shi Po walked slowly into the same room where they had breakfasted the day before. She pushed open the door, careful to move slowly, all the while scrambling for some delicate thing to say to Mrs. Kang. How did one broach the subject of wandering husbands with your captor's wife?

Fortunately, she was spared a decision, because the Kangs could not be interrupted just then. Mrs. Kang, dressed in regal silk, knelt before her husband, offering him tea.

Clearly, this was some ritual for them, otherwise why would Mrs. Kang be dressed so formally? She must have risen in the middle of the night to clothe herself so elaborately. Her gown was draped in intricate folds. She had wooden butterflies entwined in her hair, powder on her face, and a red rouge dot on her lower lip.

Unfortunately, the General did not seem very interested in his wife's elaborate costume. His attention was occupied with a scroll unrolled before him, and he was muttering angrily under his breath.

"The rebels go too far!" he exclaimed as he read further.

His wife waited patiently at his side, teacup in hand, a grimace of bitterness on her face.

Eventually, the General noticed. He looked up from his scroll to see his wife prostrate before him. At least he had the grace to blush, but beyond that he would not give. Without comment, he took hold of the cup and drained it. Then he pushed to his feet.

Only then did he see Shi Po. Only then did he curl his lip in disdain. "Sorceress," he sneered.

She stepped fully into the room and dropped her eyes in deference. "I seek only to speak with your wife, honorable sir. I would . . ." She hadn't quite figured out exactly what she planned, but it didn't matter.

The General's eyes grew glassy, and he gasped like a fish newly spilled from the nets. There was no stopping what came next, though it happened in a slow scene that would forever be etched on Shi Po's mind: The General raised his finger and pointed directly at her, but no sound came from his throat, no noise except from his slow tumble to the ground. And from the whisper of silk as Mrs. Kang crawled to kneel over her husband.

And still the General focused on Shi Po, believing her to be his murderer.

Then his wife whispered into his ear. "There will be no killing of sons today," she said. "Mine or anyone else's." She held his hand, and smiled sweetly at her husband who finally shifted his focus to her. Indeed, so fixed was his expression that he died with his eyes firmly trained on her smile.

Then came a signal, though Shi Po did not see it. Two servants stepped into the room—peasant women with thick arms and steady legs. They lifted the General between them and carried him out through the back door to the kitchen.

Mrs. Kang pushed to her feet and turned to coldly survey Shi Po. "Why should I spare you?"

She Po scrambled to order her wits. "We are all victims of your husband's madness," she offered lamely. "I have no wish to harm you and did nothing to create this havoc in your life." She paused to study Mrs. Kang, but the woman's face had hardened even further. Shi Po had to think of something fast. "I have taken care of He Yun for you. She will not trouble you further."

At last, a softening in the woman's face. "I shall make trade with you," she said. "My son for your sons."

Shi Po nodded though she was wary.

"Swear you will serve my son. Swear that you will protect him with your strange powers, that you will see to his future and assist him in all that he does."

Shi Po felt hope spark in her heart. Of course she would support Zou Tun. By all accounts, he was building a Tigress temple. "You will spare us? You will leave my entire family in peace?"

"Yes." Mrs. Kang extended a letter, folded small and written in a woman's elegant hand. "Give this to my son. Say nothing to the soldiers. They will take you to Zou Tun and turn you over to his care. Betray me or my son and there will be no place in China—"

"I will not betray you. My family and I will live with your son, assisting him in his holy work." In truth, it was exactly what she wanted to do.

Mrs. Kang waited a moment, obviously weighing her choices. In the end, she nodded then swept past Shi Po, through the main door and out into the hallway where the soldiers waited.

"The news from Peking is dire," she said to the gathered men. She spoke in a quiet, distressed voice, and appeared to be a tiny, cowed thing. "My husband orders you to Hong Kong to protect my son." She straightened and extended another letter to the captain of the guard. "These are your orders." She turned, her gaze landing hard and bitter on Shi Po. "Now, take these Han dogs out of my home."

"But—," began the captain.

Mrs. Kang whirled, her fury obvious in the tightness of her face. "Do not argue today, Captain," she hissed. "Too much is at stake."

He hesitated, and Shi Po held her breath in fear. If the man asked to speak with the General himself, if he had difficulty reading his supposed orders, if any of a million things made him question . . .

But he did not. He spun smartly on his heel and grabbed Shi Po's elbow, firmly escorting her away. Moments later, he and his men rode out of the courtyard with a thunder of hooves. Shi Po, Kui Yu, and their two sons went as well—bound as prisoners and treated like thieves, carried along on the tail of a headless monster.

Dead.

Shi Po repeated the written character twice on Kui Yu's arm that evening. The soldiers were being kind: they had let all four of the Tan family rest together. The boys were huddled close to their parents, tucked one on each side with Shi Po and Kui Yu in the center. All lay on two rough blankets near the horses, but as the children fell asleep they rolled a little ways away, curled into tight balls. That small separation gave Shi Po and Kui Yu a little room to move, but still no way to speak openly. Fortunately, they had their silent language on each other's bodies, and so Shi Po told her husband about General Kang.

Are you sure? came her husband's question.

Wife poisoned him. To save son, she answered.

Silence. She knew he was thinking, knew he was trying to fit this new information into a plan for their survival. He would come up with something, she was sure. But her thoughts were on something else, on Kwan Yin and her message to them.

Or rather, on her question to both of them. What would you give up to have what you most want?

I know, she wrote on Kui Yu's hand. He stilled, and she could see his frown even in the darkness.

"I know what I want, and what I would give up," she whispered.

He twisted slightly so he could see her face.

You, she wrote. *I want you. I'll give up everything but the children.*

Everything? he responded.

She leaned forward and nodded, pressing her lips to his. He needed to be able to do whatever he had to, and she didn't want him worried about her. They joined in a clinging kiss that opened her heart to him, and when they separated, she whispered into his ear: "I love you." Then she turned, her back spooned tightly against his rising dragon.

He whispered back, the heat of his breath as exciting as his words, "I want you. I love you, too. And I think I know what to do."

She stilled and waited for his explanation. He reached around and wrote the words on her quivering belly: *Can you give up everything? Money. Your school. My business.*

She nodded. She had already counted those things lost.

Will Zou Tun protect us? If we join him in his monastery?

She nodded again. There was a great deal of work involved in establishing a temple. All hands were welcome, and she had set him on his path.

"It is his monastery," Kui Yu said out loud. *You can't lead,* he wrote.

"He will let me teach," she answered. And in her heart, she knew that would be enough. There was much to do in a school; even more in a monastery. There would be plenty to occupy every one of them. Especially since . . .

Can you give up your business? she wrote on his hand.

He nodded and slipped his hand lower. He held her hips as his dragon burrowed toward her from behind. "I am becoming very religious," he murmured against her hair.

She shivered in delight at his intrusion, and arched her back enough to allow him to slip inside her. The action was accomplished with a minimum of movement, the smallest of thrusts, and yet she felt is if her world had righted. He was part of her. And she would never release him.

Still, she had to caution him; "The Goddess has been generous to us. Do not assume she will continue—"

"Hush," he whispered into her ear. "I know. I have you and the children. I need nothing else." Then he shifted his hands from her hips, caressing upward until he held her breasts in his hands underneath the blanket. With little movements he pinched and twisted her nipples, bringing her to a panting hunger.

Below, his dragon thrust deeply into her cave, its thickening girth already rubbing against the internal edge of her yin pearl. The tide rose quickly. His yang fire burned hot. This was not practice; it was pleasure. And yet even in this, Shi Po felt the whisper of the divine across her skin, the touch of perfect communion—spirit to spirit.

This was love. And for this, she would endure a thousand hardships, suffer a million pains. They would raise their sons in a monastery on a remote island called Hong Kong. There, they would create a temple with other Immortals. They would discuss and compare, learn and love, with the Empress Dowager's soldiers to protect them and the peace of a monastery in which to practice.

"A good life," she said out loud.

She felt her husband nod in agreement even as his dragon continued to thrust deeper and deeper within her.

"An excellent life," he concurred.

And then there were no more words, for the tide of yin engulfed Shi Po, matched only by the roar of yang. Their joined bodies, the completed circles—it was the magic of two souls in love.

When the silent tumult receded, Shi Po turned in her husband's arms and pressed a kiss to his lips.

"A very excellent life," they said at the very same moment. Then together, they descended into laughter.

Hungry Tigress

JADE LEE

Joanna Crane joined China's Boxer Rebellion because of the emptiness inside her. But when the rebels—anti-foreigner bandits with a taste for white flesh—turn out worse than their ruthless Qin enemies, her only hope is a Shaolin master with fists of steel and eyes like ice.

He has no wish to harm the meddling American, so, when she learns his secret, Joanna's captor determines to stash her at a Taoist temple. True, the sect is persecuted throughout the land, but he sees no harm in seeking divinity through love. What he does not see is that he and Joanna are already students, their hearts are on the path to Heaven, and salvation lies in a kiss, a touch, and sating the...*Hungry Tigress.*